Praise for Danny Simm
Three I

"[A]n irrestistible page-tur aw life in New York City's East Villa ull of the sex, sights, sounds, and so scene in the 1980s."

—Fab 5 Freddy

"*Three Days as the Crow Flies* is a wild Fellini-esque ride. . . . It stands as a testament to what happens to us—as individuals and as a society—when we force art into the restrictive paradigm that commodification requires. Still, it also testifies to whom and what we can become when we recognize and embrace the value art should hold in our lives, in our souls. And for saying this with such clarity and nuance, I am eternally grateful to Danny Simmons."

—Asha Bandele, author of *The Prisoner's Wife*

"[*Three Days as the Crow Flies*] is off the hook! I felt like I was right there in the middle of the story. In fact, I was right there. . . . Despite all the laughs and fun . . . the book makes important comments on racism, drug addiction, the art world and society at large. [Danny's] nailed it."

—Russell Simmons

"Danny Simmons has portrayed in visceral detail the dark, often gothic journey of a young man trying to find his way through the conflicted art world of the 1980s. His poetic voice is palpable and echoes the prophetic rhythms of an era haunted and entrapped by its own hype. One constantly wonders whether Crow will conjure the moral and mental muscle crucial to determining the meaning of his own reality through the intrigue of Simmons's dual narrative . . . looks like the beginning of a trilogy."

—Leslie King-Hammond, Ph.D., Dean of Graduate Studies,
Maryland Institute College of Art

"Danny Simmons is a remarkable storyteller. His writing evokes the memory of the marginalized art world of the East Village, one of mystery, sex, defiance, lost love, and deceit."

—Deborah Willis, author of *The Black Female Body: A Photographic History*

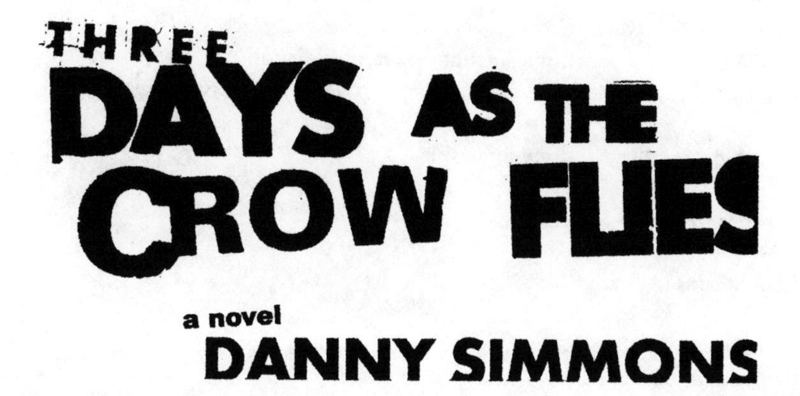

Washington Square Press
New York London Toronto Sydney

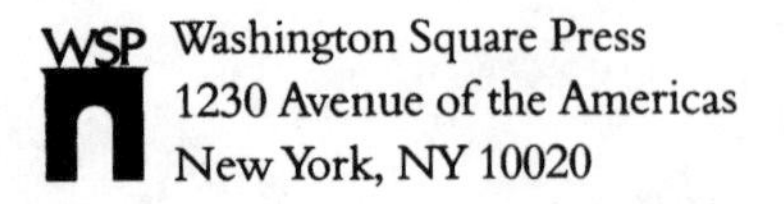

This book is a work of fiction. Names, characters, places and incidents are products of the author's imagination or are used fictitiously. Any resemblance to actual events or locales or persons living or dead is entirely coincidental.

Artwork by Danny Simmons

Photographs by Mark Blackshear

For information address Atria Books, 1230 Avenue of the Americas, New York, NY 10020

ISBN: 0-7434-6640-3
0-7434-6641-1 (Pbk)

First Washington Square Press trade paperback edition June 2004

10 9 8 7 6 5 4 3 2 1

Designed by Melissa Isriprashad

Manufactured in the United States of America

For information regarding special discounts for bulk purchases, please contact Simon & Schuster Special Sales at 1-800-456-6798 or business@simonandschuster.com

Dedicated to all the cokeheads
who made it through the fun and fabulous eighties
to be delivered into the arms of recovery

Acknowledgments

Thinking about whom to thank always leads first to my dad, Danny Sr. He's been my inspiration for writing and for just living a stand-up life. I thank my mother, Evelyn (deceased), for being my biggest fan and jump-starting my career as an artist. Thank you, Russell and Joey for being little brothers I could "look up to" and for always being in my corner. My stepmother, Shirley, has been a source of light during some dark times. My son, Jamel: the brightest one to come down the Simmons pike yet.

Then there's John McGregor, my pain-in-the-ass agent who believed in the book and me. He never once doubted its value or my ability as a writer.

A few people looked at the book during the editing process (Sharon Fitzgerald and Carol Taylor), but it was M. Raven Rowe who sat with me through long hours and temper tantrums to help beat some additional life into this story. After three drafts and countless rewrites, we came up with the version that Simon & Schuster picked up.

One editor, whose name I won't mention, told me he loved the book but didn't know how to categorize it. It's a great story, but it's "outside the box." My editor at Atria, Malaika Adero, is nothing short of amazing. Malaika thinks outside the box and so a perfect match was made between her and my book. Thank you to Demond Jarrett for navigating *Crow* through channels and to Judith Curr, the publisher, for her support.

Venus Dennison was the first person to read this book and encourage me to go back in and do some more work. The director of my art gallery, Seni Asfaw, held it down so I could get to writin'. Thank you to all my good friends who've encouraged and nurtured me throughout the years: My ex-wife, Joan Walrond, who has somehow managed to remain my best friend; Eric Edwards, my main running buddy; John Johnson, whose diabetes has just stolen his eyesight so he won't be able to read the finished version (before it's converted to braille); my partners Joe Beckles, Tom Richardson, and Walter Stevens, who passed away before this could be published. And lastly, thank you to the personalities who did walk-ons in the novel. They made the eighties the vibrant decade that it was. Crow thanks you for flying with him for those three defining days. We both hope you enjoy the trip.

Peace & Art
Danny Simmons

"I saw the best minds of my generation
destroyed by madness starving hysterical naked,
dragging themselves through the Negro streets
looking for an angry fix."

—Allen Ginsberg

THREE
DAYS AS THE
CROW FLIES

1

Crow

CROW WRAPPED A TOWEL around his waist and headed out of the tiny bathroom he shared with two other rooming-house tenants. Padding barefoot down the length of the long, narrow hall to the single room he occupied, he left wet footprints on the worn linoleum.

He opened his door and shook his head as he surveyed the remains of his worldly possessions. Aside from the cutoff straws littering the table and nightstand, a ragged poster of Bob Marley, his clothes, and a few dozen dog-eared comic books stacked on the floor, the television was his only possession. He sat on the edge of the narrow mattress, leaned forward, and turned on the TV.

Angry, restless, and discontent, Crow switched from one channel to another, then finally turned the set off altogether. *Damn, I need me some cocaine, shit,* he thought as he reached for a pair of jeans he had draped carefully over the back of a nearby metal folding chair. He sighed and mumbled out loud, "Where in the hell am I going to get some money from?" He thought about it a minute.

"Danny!" He'd paid his friend Danny back the hundred dollars he owed him last week and figured it was time to borrow it back. He finished dressing, grabbed his last twenty-three dollars and change off the dresser, and headed out.

Stopping at the bottom of the stairs, he inspected himself in the mirror there. Even when fiendin', Crow knew he looked good. At slightly over six feet tall, Crow Shade was wiry and well built. He had a head of short, curly black hair framing his thin, dark reddish-brown face. Even with a full beard he rarely did anything to, he always looked well groomed. He had clear, dark eyes that were almost constantly in motion—darting about, surveying the territory, clockin' the scene. By the sight of him, you would never guess that he was seriously using. Damned near every day, though, for the last six months, he had been drinking, smoking weed, sniffing coke, trying to figure out how to get more, and doing little else.

Most of the time, he was deceptively conservative in the way he dressed. College boy, Ivy League style almost. And today would be no different, except for one thing. He wore his black jeans, tan desert boots, a dark charcoal-gray crewneck with a white Brooks Brothers button-down oxford underneath, and a worn black leather jacket—a holdover from his gangster days.

His addiction had started almost the moment he'd returned to Brooklyn from Lincoln, Pennsylvania. He had been the oldest senior at Lincoln University—the first college established expressly for the cultivation and training of "colored boys" in the United States, but what had it been training them to do? A graduate from there would surely be acclaimed "a credit to his race," or so Crow'd been told. But insofar as he had spent his seven undergraduate years partying and selling weed, Crow left school in the trunk of a ragged 1974 Chevy Camaro in order to avoid arrest.

That was ancient history. Now, he wanted a beer, badly. He knew he couldn't stop at the corner bodega because he owed the coke-dealing proprietor, Flaco, fifty balls for the blow he'd copped on credit two nights before. He figured he'd hold out until he reached the deli on the corner of Danny's block, where he could get a tall can of ale on credit.

He barely noticed the people sitting on their stoops, children playing, and other life happening on the way to Danny's Bed-Stuy brownstone. He stopped at the store and got a sixteen-ounce can of ale. After popping the tab, he plunked in a straw and took a long sip. Refreshed, he rehearsed his pitch. "Yo, Danny, you know that *hunnid* I repaid you last week? Guess what? I need it back . . ." He paused a moment to think and refuel himself with more ale. "I'll tell him I'm behind in my rent. He'll go for that. He ain't gonna wanna see a brother *out-of-doors*."

As he got to the door of Danny's building, the second-floor tenant was leaving the house. He'd met her several times before, in the early morning when she was coming home from work and he was sitting on the steps talking to Danny. Today, she smiled, said hello, and held the door open for him. As they passed each other, Crow thought, *Fine motherfucker too; too bad she got kids and a nigger.* He thanked her and stepped inside.

He knocked twice on Danny's door. There was no answer, so he tried the knob. The door was unlocked, he let himself in. Crow knew that Danny was home because he could hear the mellow strains of some jazz virtuoso wafting from the studio in the back of the apartment.

Danny was doing all right for an artist, selling paintings and collecting rent. His parlor-floor apartment was airy and bright, with lots of bay windows. It resembled a small museum. Every surface was covered by some kind of traditional African or contemporary art. The deeply stained wood floors were polished to a high gloss. There were African hand-carved wooden tables and benches, leather couches made in South America, and several large steel sculptures that reminded Crow of cars mangled in horrible collisions that no one could have survived.

Walking farther into the apartment, he thought for a second about going into the studio. But when he saw several small painted canvases propped against a wall, he reasoned that he could probably get more than a hundred for a few of these pictures, and Danny probably wouldn't even miss them for a while. Without the slightest hesitation, Crow snatched up the three paintings.

He then noticed a folder filled with about two hundred typewritten pages, on a table nearby. *This must be the book he's been working on. Might as well take some reading material along with me. I can always bring it back later.* He grabbed the manuscript, tucking it and the paintings all under one arm as he ducked quietly back out the door he'd found unlocked.

Crow held down a momentary swell of conscience as he headed down the front steps. Stealing from a friend as good as Danny was triflin', and he knew it, but that wasn't going to stop him. He rationalized, *I'll hit Danny off with half the loot after I down this shit and get me a decent hit.* Clutching the paintings and the folder tighter, he hightailed it to the A train.

Crow hated riding the subway. He had wearied long ago of the sorry souls with whom he was forced to share his ride. It seemed to Crow—too smart for his own good sometimes—that at least half of 'em couldn't even count to ten, much less know what was *really* going on.

They always pretend they ain't looking. That fat cracker's either lookin' at me or that Spanish bitch's ass. Fuck him. Fuck him! And that pasty-lookin' old bitch next to him. Not a dime between 'em, I'll bet. Like they got any business thinkin' about what I'm *doin'* . . .

Crow was tweaking. The lack of cocaine had him edgy. He liked to think of it as hyperawareness instead of paranoia. But he'd been known to quote that old adage in jest, "Just because I'm paranoid don't mean they ain't out to get me."

In the tunnels between stations, you can see yourself in the darkened train windows and get lost in your own reflection or secretly ogle other passengers. There's usually a trace of fear in the older faces, while alienation or rebellion rages in the eyes of kids cutting school. On the stooped shoulders of others, you can almost measure the weight of long, empty years, as their bearers hurry home to dispassionate sex and fitful sleep. Predators pace from window to window, avoiding eye contact, perusing reflections, sizing up civilians, looking for the next victim. Like cats, they pace window to window grinning callously—they can tell who rides alone.

I wish this damn train would hurry the fuck up. These motherfuckers get on my nerves.

Crow decided to take a good look at the Latina he'd noticed when he first got on the train. He thought she looked completely exhausted now, but she must have once been very beautiful. She was trying to hold it together while being pulled in different directions by four squalling *niños,* none of whom looked anything alike.

Damn, that bitch do *got a sweet ass. Fuck her. Probably don't speak no English, ain't got no job, and stuck with a man who* kicks *that ass.*

Crow noticed the fat Cauc who'd been staring at the Latina. He was probably hurrying home to a couple brewskies and the last few innings of American's favorite pastime on TV. Now he sat with a scowl on his face, trying to ignore her, her ass, and her kids.

As the train pulled into the West Fourth Street station, Crow gathered the canvases and the manuscript and stepped out of the car and onto the platform jammed with people. The thoughts that had occupied him during the ride were as gone as last night's cocaine. He was scheming to get back to the neighborhood before the Dominicanos closed up the bodega for the night. Crow moved through the crowd and up the stairs, oblivious to the bodies bumping and jostling him. He was intent on escaping that black hole and filling his lungs with what passes in the city for fresh air.

Spell to Remove Unwanted Affection (2000)

2

The City

Crow pulled the paintings and folder closer to his chest. Even city air smelled fresh after the stench of the underground. The breeze held the crisp chill of autumn. He rounded a corner and almost collided with a corporate blue-suited threesome, whose smiles quickly soured at the sight of him. Moving in unison, they pivoted left, seemingly revolted by even the possibility of contact with a man of Crow's ilk. Crow shook his head and muttered, "Well, fuck you too, motherfuckers," as he continued to make his way toward the liquor store. Reaching it, he pressed his shoulder against the glass door and stepped inside.

Cat bells jingling in the doorjamb announced Crow's entrance to the man behind the counter. The clerk and the store's inventory were separated from potential customers by bulletproof glass. The procedure was to tell the clerk your selection and pay for it, and he would deliver your purchase and change on a Plexiglas lazy Susan.

But Crow noticed that a group of young white businessmen had been allowed behind the partition to make their own selections. They were huddled in the wine section, discussing vintages and prices while they searched the shelves for their choices. The clerk had stood up when Crow came in and now asked in an annoyed tone, "Can I help you?"

Crow refused to answer before he had leaned the paintings against the counter in front of him. He stood in front of the perforations in the Plexiglas, so that he could be heard. Smirking bitterly, he asked the counterman, "Does that mean that I don't get to come back there with the rest of your clientele?"

The clerk stared at Crow blankly and didn't respond. Crow read a sign that was handwritten in thick black marker and taped to the door of an old Philco refrigerator so customers could see it: "We do not sell pints of wine."

Crow sucked his teeth, with a little less of a smirk this time, and asked, "Is that company policy or personal bias?"

The clerk igged the comment and asked again, "Can I help you?"

"Yes, I'd like some help, man. Let me have a half-pint of Remy Martin," Crow answered with a heavy sigh.

Without expression, the clerk turned, reached over to the row of half-pints, retrieved a bottle, and placed it on the counter.

"That'll be five dollars and sixty-two cents," said the clerk.

Crow sighed again and shook his head. "Wrong Remy. That's the V.S. I want the V.S.O.P. The one in the frosted green bottle."

The clerk looked directly at Crow for the first time and then in exasperation turned back to the shelf and snatched up the other bottle. Dropping the V.S.O.P. into a bag, he sneered. "I'll tell you a little secret, buddy. There ain't no real difference between this Remy and the other one . . . 'cept the price."

Expressionless, Crow reached into his pocket. "How much for this one?"

Without looking at the price, the clerk answered, "Eight forty-six."

Crow pulled out the few bills he had in his pocket and handed him the twenty. Another customer came in and brushed against Crow's back. Involuntarily, he shuddered and wanted to ask, "Why you playin' me so close?" But instead, in a moment of unconscious protectiveness, Crow shifted the manuscript to his other hand as he waited for his change.

The guy standing behind him cleared his throat and said, "That's a really nice painting you've got there. You the artist?"

Crow turned around and looked at him as though the man's face had just flashed a green light that said *Victim!*

"What did you say, man?"

The customer was tall and slim and wore a black overcoat that was opened to reveal a white shirt with blue pinstripes and a yellow foulard tie. Crow had dated a yuppie white chick during a quick stint in D.C. a few years back. She bought him foulard ties. He dumped dozens of them in the trash when he left.

"I was wondering if you were the artist," the customer repeated.

Looking at the fancy, high-gloss, hand-tooled leather portfolio the man clutched beneath one arm, Crow smiled and said, "Yeah, I'm the artist." His lie was smooth, and he finished it with a broad, toothy smile. "I was just taking them to a place where I might be having a show. Are you a patron?" Crow had heard Danny use that word to describe people who buy expensive art. The game was on. "If you're interested, I'll make you a deal. We can cut out the middleman."

As Foulard Tie bent down to study the canvas with mock expertise, the clerk returned with Crow's change and jammed the bottle of Remy Martin V.S.O.P. into the lazy Susan and spun it around at Crow. Foulard Tie straightened up and replied, "At the moment, I'm not investing in art."

Crow's face sank. He grabbed up his change, stuffed the bottle into his jacket pocket, and shifted his attention to the store's other customers—the ones behind the glass. The wine-buying clientele had reached a consensus and were attempting to engage the clerk in an intense debate about the paucity of their selection.

Still annoyed at Crow's presence, he shot back at the wine connoisseurs, "I don't buy the stock, I just sell it."

Snickering at that exchange, Crow called out, "Any of you guys got a black marker?"

When nobody responded, Foulard Tie said, "As a matter of fact, I always keep a few in my bag." He fumbled through his portfolio and pulled out two markers. "Red or black?" he asked.

"I asked for black," Crow replied sharply, trying not to snap—he needed the marker.

Accepting the marker from Foulard Tie's hand and sidestepping quickly to the left, Crow picked up a painting and leaned it up against the glass at eye level. After signing it, he did the same with the other two and then returned the marker. "Can't sell the paintings without my signature," he said. "Doubles their value. Are you sure you're not interested?"

Foulard Tie looked at the signature: "Crow Shade, 1985." He looked from the painting to Crow. "Well, I guess it fits," he said. "Anyway, thanks for the offer. Maybe some other time."

"Yeah, maybe." Crow sneered back. Turning, he grabbed the paintings and headed toward the door. He glanced back one last time at the sign on the refrigerator, the one that read, "We do not sell pints of wine."

Outside, the wind smacked the side of Crow's face and almost snatched the paintings out of his hands. Pausing in a doorway, he rested the paintings against his leg and pulled the Remy from his pocket. He twisted the bottle cap open and gulped down a mouthful. It made him shudder. He capped the bottle, returned it to his pocket, buttoned his jacket, and clutched the paintings closer to his body. Warmed by the cognac, he headed down Waverly Place toward the East Side.

Walking along the south side of Waverly Place is different from walking on its north side. The south side has more street lamps. Older people walk there to avoid the darkness on the other side. Crow crossed Sixth Avenue against the light, dodging a car that seemed to speed up when the driver saw him approaching the curb. A cadre of suspicious-looking young men hurried past him as he walked, their hands stuffed deep in their pockets, their heads down. A small gray-haired woman, her left hand clutching the pages of a rumpled newspaper, waited patiently at the curb for her old dog to relieve himself.

The traffic sign blinked "Don't Walk" when Crow reached MacDougal and Waverly. Even though the street was clear of cars, Crow lingered at the corner watching as an assortment of characters skulked into the park to cop illicit substances. When the traffic sign finally blinked "Walk," Crow ignored it. He propped the paintings against his leg and pulled out the Remy again. Before taking a sip, he peered into the park at the people and muttered to himself, "Same sucker-ass shit. None of these lames would last about two seconds in my part of Brooklyn."

He gulped down more cognac, picked up the paintings, and stepped off the curb just as the light turned red. A car sped past. Getting nowhere near him, the driver was annoyed anyway and honked the horn long past necessary. When Crow reached the other side of the street, he heard the pusher's mantra: "Got that good Ses, blacktop jumbo dime crack, P-Funk."

One kid, white, maybe fourteen or fifteen years old, jumped off the fence and walked toward Crow. As he got closer, Crow could see a gaping space where two front teeth should have been. "Yo, brother-man," the kid said, not able to hit the *th* in *brother.* "I got them serious dimes a crack."

Crow just looked at him.

"Word, dis shit is *serious,*" the kid continued.

Crow looked at him for a few seconds more and said, "Yo, duke, I don't be smoking that shit. Got any powder?"

The kid's gestures got animated. He stretched out his hands and jerked his head to the side, then slid up closer to Crow. In hushed tones, he said, "Yo, I can get you all the powder you want. What you need?"

Crow looked at him sullenly and said, "Fuck it. I don't want nuthin'. Ain't no decent blow around here anyway. I don't wanna end up with a bagful of cut." He turned to leave the park.

"Nah, homes, it ain't like that," the kid persisted. "My man's got rocks, if that's what you looking for."

At that, Crow spun back around. "I ain't spending no serious dollars," he said.

The kid was a good hustler, and he wanted to make this sale. "I can get you dimes on up. Whatever you want," he said. "Just chill here a second. I'll be right back."

He turned quickly and disappeared deeper into the park. Crow sighed, leaned against the fence, pulled out his cognac, and took another sip. As he tried to put away the bottle, the canvases fell from underneath his arm and onto the ground. Picking them up, he looked closely at one of the paintings for the first time.

The canvas was layered with thick, textured paint. Crow closed his eyes and ran a finger over the brush strokes. The strokes became lines, and the lines connected to form the contour of two lovers embracing. Their arms and legs were so intertwined that it was impossible to tell where one body ended and the other began. The background was a gradation of dark and light shades painted in swirls, each color blending into the others. As he ran his finger over the woman's breast, he opened his eyes and studied the colors. Various shades of red, yellow, and brown played against one another, melding to form the lovers' bodies, which were nestled between the sky and the earth. Shades of blue had been used for the sky. Browns and greens had been used for the earth.

Propping the paintings against the fence, Crow smiled. *Damn, Danny's shit is pretty good,* he thought. *He paints about black people. But he's painting some dream black people—dancin', makin' love 'n' shit . . .* His thought was interrupted when the kid returned.

"Yo, boss, I told you I'd be right back," the kid said, smiling. There was a man standing behind him. He must have been at least six-foot-four with long, thick-locked hair, which he had piled up on top of his head and held in place with three wooden chopsticks. He had a bushy beard and wore dark glasses even though it was already reaching sundown. Thick Locks was good-looking but terribly thin, *magga* even. His clothes hung loosely from his bones. Crow liked him immediately.

"I don't smoke no crack, my man, but I could go for some regular coke," he said.

Thick Locks threw his head back and smiled, showing three gold-framed teeth. He took a deep pull on a huge spliff and said, "Me 'ear you, me bruddah. Me na smoke dat poison neider, mon. Sit wid me 'ere on de bench."

As Thick Locks headed for the bench, Crow picked up the paintings, thanked the kid, and followed. A white couple who had been sitting on the bench smoking reefer got up and left as Thick Locks and Crow sat down. Crow's eyes followed behind them as he muttered, "Punks."

Thick Locks smiled and said, "Speak troot, bruddah. When big man dem speak, pickney dem should leave de rooooom. 'Ere, take a likka toke a de ganja from back 'ome. Me faddah pluck it and sen' it to I from der."

He passed the spliff, and Crow took a long drag. The harsh smoke hit his throat, and he started coughing.

"Yes, bruddah," Thick Locks said, "de herb is strong wid spirits of de living."

When Crow finally stopped coughing, he passed the spliff back and asked, "Is the blow *that* good?"

Thick Locks stood, reached into a leather pouch at his side, and pulled out a plastic baggie.

"*Yo,* my brother!" Crow almost shouted, looking at the baggie. "You carry all that shit around with you?"

Thick Locks laughed and said, "Like I and you, these be of de eart, dees tings born to I. Jah protects I, and when Jah na lookin' me way, den de Smitt an' Wesson look over I." He lifted his jacket and displayed a dull, black nine-millimeter pistol. When he saw that the gun made Crow nervous, he said, "What you really want, me bruddah?"

Crow was embarrassed. "I told the kid it was no big thing, I only needed a dime."

"No problem, me bruddah," Thick Locks replied. "Hand me a bill."

Crow dug in his pocket, fished out a crisp one-dollar bill—change from the Remy—and passed it to Thick Locks. He creased the bill, stuck his hand in the bag, pulled out a medium-size rock of cocaine worth considerably more than ten dollars, and placed it in the center of the dollar. "This be peace, me bruddah," he said, passing the bill back to Crow. Palming the bill, Crow flashed a wicked smile and quickly slipped Thick Locks the ten dollars. Thick Locks rose from the bench and put the money in his pocket. "Walk with Jah, me bruddah," he said. "May we paths cross down de road." Then he disappeared in the direction of the fountain at the center of the park.

Crow sat still for a few seconds before looking over his shoulder. He glanced down at the bill and shook his head. *Rasta brotherman must be from the neighborhood,* he thought. *This is at least a fifty.* He put his tongue to the rock to taste it. The cocaine froze his tongue immediately. "Shit, this must be my lucky day," he exclaimed, almost squealing with delight, while digging through his pocket for a coin.

He found a quarter, folded the bill, and used the coin to crush the rock. He retrieved a ragged cut-down straw from his wallet and quickly inhaled four hefty snorts. Self-conscious, he looked over his shoulder again and tried to breathe normally to slow his racing heartbeat. Just that quickly, he was high, and higher than he had been in a good little while. He sat on the bench a moment longer and tried to regain his equilibrium. Picking up the manuscript beside him, he opened it to the first page. *All these pages,* he thought. *A brother just can't have that much to say.* Then he began to read:

> I am not the black man who sits at this desk, alone at late hours. I am that black man with only six bullets for his gun. The black man who has found the leisure to write this book is only an author's dream. But wait. Let me tell you a story . . .

Crow closed the folder. He dug into his pocket, reopened the bill, took another blast of cocaine, and quickly put the blow back in his pocket. *This is too heavy for me,* he thought about what he'd just read. *A brother talking deep shit like that should be living in the village, not in* the neighborhood. *This shit is too personal.*

He roused himself and stood up. His legs felt a bit shaky, but he knew that it was time to go. As he headed out of the park, a kid with hair arranged in orange spikes zoomed by on his skateboard. Chasing behind him was a little girl with green stripes in her blond hair. "David!" she shouted after him. "Mommy says you've got to come home and do your homework."

Her brother sailed toward the fountain, ignoring her, the latest hip-hop music blaring through his headphones. Crow dodged them and walked swiftly through the arch, exiting the park. Back on

Waverly Place, slowing his pace, he gazed through the fence and noticed that the east end of the park was deserted. To his left, on University Place, he could see couples clinging to each other, heading north and south. The flow of people caused him to stop and catch his breath for a moment. Leaning against the fence, he watched the parade of people for a second, then reopened the folder, his eyes instantly finding the line at which he had stopped reading before.

> . . . A story about every nigger living at every turn just beyond your corner. This nigger was born simultaneously in every inner city and in every rural town. He came from his mother, dry without tears and wearing sneakers. They nursed him on cold milk from the corner store. On the first day of his ninth month, he developed long scars on his back and thighs. His parents and their friends became afraid and first tried to remove his sneakers. Failing at this they shunned him and would not let him play with the puppy or his cousins when they came to visit. He learned not to care.
>
> When he turned three, he would leave the house alone and wander to the bus station. He used money stolen from his father's pants pocket to buy dark bars of chocolate and would sit and watch the buses leave. As each bus left, he cried. Hours later he would wander back home and crawl into bed and hold his stomach, sick from too much dark chocolate.

Crow looked up just in time to see an ebb in the flow of people. He shut the folder, grabbed the paintings, and hurried across University Place. On the other side of the street, hordes of students were headed to their night classes at NYU. Crow felt a brief moment of remorse that with only a semester to go, he had blown off the opportunity to get his degree. His eyes fell on the manuscript, and his thoughts shifted. *Yeah, what was left to learn? How to write some bullshit like this?*

Crow looked back at the students carrying their books, chattering excitedly, their faces smug and expectant. He curled his lip and reached for the bottle of Remy in his pocket.

A Meeting at the Crossroads (2001)

3

Bones

WHEN HE GOT TO ASTOR PLACE, Crow headed directly for the black cube sculpture on the square. God only knows where it came from, but it had been there for years. One day, Crow found out by watching some neighborhood kids that if pushed hard enough, the cube would rotate on its axis. He never forgot that. Looking around his old haunts, he also remembered hanging out at a club down a dark stairway called the Dome. It was just up the block and was always filled with couples dancing to Latin music, but wasn't a Latin club. Only niggas hung out there. The fellas wore these wide-legged, bell-bottomed pants called elephant bells and long, pointy-toed shoes. The women wore miniskirts and thigh-high vinyl boots. *Back in the day, niggas knew how to party,* he thought. *And if you couldn't Latin, you couldn't hang.*

Returning to the present, Crow looked around. Astor Place was busy with theatergoers, white kids selling reefer, and suburban bridge-and-tunnel types exploring the dangers of the Lower East Side, and the like. Smiling to himself, he thought, *If there's a sucker born every minute, most of 'em* must *end up here. On any crowded street, day or night, there's gotta be at least one hungry predator.* Crow was here and ready to feed. But the last thing he wanted to do was stand around with the lames trying to sell shit.

When he looked at the cube again, there had gathered a few musicians pulling instruments out of cases. *If these people were down for music,* he rationalized, *they probably liked art too.* He crossed the street and headed for the cube, paintings under one arm, manuscript under the other.

A skinny kid with holes in the knees of his jeans was attempting to tune a violin. Crow stopped directly in front of him, casting his shadow over the polished wood of the instrument. The kid jerked his head up, his posture stiffening.

"Hey, man," Crow began matter-of-factly, "I hope you won't mind if I set my paintings up over here." As Crow walked around him, the last vestiges of sunlight glinted across the violin's strings. Hearing no response, Crow started propping up canvases against the cube.

"It's a free country," the kid finally decided to answer.

Arranging each painting for maximum effect, Crow set the painting in the center on top of the manuscript and responded without looking up. *"Really.* Now, how did I *know* you'd see it that way? It's people like you that make this motherfucking country what it is today."

Crow looked at the trio, thinking that they weren't much to look at, and hoped they could play better than they looked. The cellist was a pale, pasty-faced, womanish creature, with long limp hair a color that brought to mind dishwater. "She" had been positioning a straw basket lined with white lace in front of where they were setting up. The third member was this tall, strange-looking guy with long legs. He might have been skinny too, if it hadn't been for his fat potbelly.

Each member of the group had a different approach to warming up. While the woman-creature plucked the strings of her cello and the skinny kid ran the bow back and forth across his violin strings, the other member of the trio kept spitting into his hand and rubbing it along the length of his bass strings and then on the side of his jacket. *Yuck, what the fuck does* that *do?* Crow wondered, a little disgusted. After what seemed like a really long time, and a whole lot of weird-ass behavior later, they started to play.

Damn, Crow thought, almost out loud. *This shit ain't fit for* radio. Lyrics from a rock-and-roll cut he used to dig ran through his head: "I shoulda learnt ta play that gui-tar, I shoulda learnt ta play them drums . . ." He laughed softly to himself as he called up his favorite line, "The little faggot in d'mink coat . . ." and then, without realizing it, he sang out loud, "The little faggot's a millionaire!" The woman-thing heard him and frowned as she lost her timing. *Didn't take much to throw you off, did it?* Crow thought.

Crow smiled and mouthed an apology to her—although he didn't know why. *They* should have been apologizing to *him,* he figured, and anyone else who could hear them. "Sorry, must've lost my head," and then, under his breath, for sure this time, he mumbled, "And wished like hell I'd lose my hearing." She looked annoyed, but then her eyes lingered for a moment and drifted down to his tightish jeans straining taut against equally taut thighs, as he squatted slightly to rearrange the paintings. Assuaged now, and a little aroused, she was able to fit herself back into whatever it was they'd been playing.

Crow turned to see that a couple in their early thirties had stopped a few feet away. The woman, although a little older, looked almost exactly like the girl in the trio—same hair and everything. The man with her was smoking the short end of a joint, with glazed eyes and burned fingers. He was wearing one of those Irish tweed jackets with brown suede patches on the elbows. They both wore faded jeans and brown loafers. Crow began shifting the paintings to get their attention, but they didn't even glance his way.

He called out to them, "Some really nice art for sale over here." The man looked over and said something to the woman. She looked at the paintings and then at Crow, her head doing something like nodding to the music. Flicking the roach of the joint into the street and rubbing his cheek, the man started walking over, eyes on the paintings.

"You look like you might like the one with the lovers," Crow said, bending over to pick up the canvas closest to him. It was the image of two figures that Crow had examined earlier. In that instant, Crow knew how to play this sucker.

"I call this one 'The Embrace.' " Crow heard the words flow like honey from his *own* lips. "Can you see how it's all about how we become one with that other person in our lives?" He looked at the painting again and added, "What's happening in the background shows how the world becomes darker or lighter with our perceptions and experiences. I used red in their bodies to indicate the lovers' passion. Here, dude," Crow said, trying to sound like a white boy. "Hold it up to the light, and take a good look."

Patched Elbows took the painting from Crow's hands and stared at it for a few seconds, then looked back at Crow. "I've never seen figures quite like these," he said. "But they're almost a cross between Matisse and Miró." Crow thought, *Mah-who and Me-what? He must be talking about some white guys.* Patched Elbows the pothead continued, "I like your style. This is good, man, really good."

He turned and called over his shoulder to the woman, "Hey, Jesse, come here for a second." The woman shook her stringy hair and walked over. "Jesse, look at this painting. I think it's really a fine piece," he said to her. "Can't you see it hanging over the bed?"

Before looking at the painting, she looked at Crow. He could tell that it was going to be a no sale. She no more than glanced at the painting, then said, "Dick, if we're going to buy art, then we should buy it as an investment. You just can't go buying something because you *like* it." She took a better look at the painting, then again at Crow. "You're right," she said. "It's a nice enough painting, but buying art on the street can't be smart. You were just saying how we should be careful to purchase items that will increase in value and that we should spend our money carefully."

Crow started to say something, but Dick cut him short. "But, sugar, we don't know if this is a good investment or not." He turned to Crow and asked, "Where have you exhibited?"

Crow's mind raced to think of the name of *any place.* When he could think of nothing even remotely artistic-sounding, he said,

"Hey, listen, I'm not asking that much for it. I'm really just trying to pay my rent. You know, starving artist and all that."

Dick—he really did look like a Dick too—handed Crow the canvas. Looking at the ground, he said, "You know how it is. She's right, we really do have to be careful how we spend." He looked back up at Crow and said, "But hey, man, I'm serious, I really think this is some good stuff, really fine work. I wish things weren't so tight. I'd like to have one of your pieces."

As they walked away, Crow yelled after them, "Hey, it's yours for thirty balls—I mean bucks!"

He heard Jesse say, "You see, if it was worth anything, he wouldn't sell it so cheap."

A few people had gathered around while Crow was making his pitch, although they pretended they weren't looking at the paintings. Crow motioned them closer. "Don't be shy, come on over. A little look-see can't hurt." One or two came to get a closer look, but that was all. Just then, Crow noticed that the trio had finished playing their first piece of whatever it was they called what they did with those instruments. The fact that they had gotten money for it absolutely blew his mind. "Shit! Da things dat pass for *culture* dees days! If dat's what dey call music, it's no wonder dey don't know good art when they sees it," he muttered to himself, exaggerated down-home-like.

Crow sat on the ground and for the first time took a good, long look at all the paintings he'd swiped from his boy, his home slice, his *ace boon coon.*

The three were of slightly varied sizes. One was of a curvaceous brown woman, standing in tall grass. She wore an orange robe with a hood that covered most of her face but revealed a long, sculptured neck, determined chin, and a set of the most luscious and beautiful full lips Crow had ever seen. The sky behind her was a deep purple, almost black. There were deep grooves running through the paint, making it appear that the sky was cracked and jagged. In the right corner, there was a splash of pale yellow paint that suggested a moon. The wind pressed the robe tightly against the woman's body. He liked it.

The other painting was of a woman's left profile, in which only one of her almond-shaped eyes could be seen. Its iris was golden. She had deep reddish-brown skin, like Crow's, and crimson lips. Her thick hair was braided and cascaded down her shoulder in the colors of flames. Across her forehead, along her cheek, and down her neck were golden marks with a raised texture that looked like African scarification or Indian war paint. Crow didn't know what they were, but he knew he liked *her.* The right side of the work was also raised with thick textured paint, but it was black, over which, painted in white, were these words:

Each day you rise and set my Raven free
Black against gray dawn
The briar cage forgotten
Clouds swollen with rain and
dreams . . .
your tender comforts
Evening to hurry home.

Crow stared hard at the face and read the words several times. Then he looked up at a streetlight and shook his head, thinking that Danny must have had a lot of time on his hands.

The people with the instruments started playing with them again. Crow stood up and said to no one in particular, "Feels like I've been standing here all night." He reached into his jacket, pulled out the Remy, and took a long swallow. Then he figured, since the musicians weren't paying him no mind and there weren't any people standing around, he might as well pull out the blow. Turning to face the cube, he took a few quick hits. When Crow turned back around, he found himself face to face with yet another thin man. This one had long, straight brown hair pulled back into a ponytail. Although this guy wore dark glasses, Crow could tell he was staring. The guy just stood there smiling. From his right ear dangled a long, pointy earring, made from some kind of bone. Crow was startled but regained his cool quickly.

"You like what you see?" Crow asked.

The guy kept smiling and replied, "Looks like good shit." Crow wasn't exactly sure what he meant.

"Think you might like to buy one?" Crow asked, pointing to the canvases.

The guy pulled a cigarette from his jacket pocket as he looked over the paintings. "You got a match?" Crow fumbled around and handed the guy a plastic lighter. The guy lit his cigarette and said, "My name's Bones, Bones Young." Then Bones put the lighter in his pocket.

"You got some interesting work here. I know art, so take that as a compliment." Crow got a little excited. *I might be able to hustle a* yard *outta this lame,* he thought. Bones ended Crow's fantasizing. "I don't buy art, though, I sell it. You interested in selling these?"

Crow looked at him hard. "What do you think? I came all the way out here to jerk off?"

Bones took a long drag from the cigarette, looked at Crow, and said, "Looks to me like you getting high and definitely not making no dollars." Crow looked at Bones's fingers as he brought the cigarette down from his mouth; he had rings on each one.

"Got another smoke?" Crow asked, not really interested.

"Nah, just bummed this one up the block. Want a drag?"

He passed the cigarette to Crow, who took a couple of pulls and handed it back, saying, "Yeah, so what we gonna do? Look at each other and talk shit all night?"

Bones grinned and said, "I hope not. I'm out here to pull some duckets. Looks to me like you got the product. You ready to make the money?"

Crow pulled out the Remy, took another swallow, passed it to Bones, and said, "I'm down, let's get busy."

Bones took the bottle and finished it in a gulp and said, "Let's do it. Hey, by the way, man, what's your name?"

"Crow, Crow Shade." Bones picked up one of the canvases and stuck it under his arm. Crow grabbed the other two and the manuscript. Turning toward St. Mark's Place, they headed east.

Spell to Look into the Next World (2001)

4

Candy's Store

"YO, DOC, SLOW THE FUCK UP," Crow yelled, stepping onto Third Avenue. Bones stood waiting for him on the corner. Crow stepped onto the sidewalk.

Smiling, Bones said, "*Now* we're in the *neighborhood.* Ain't nothing *really* happening as far west as you was, 'less you from Jersey and tryin' to sightsee." Bones sounded kinda hip, like the Lower East Side hood rat that he was. He took off his shades and stuffed them into the same pocket he'd gotten the cigarette from. "Let's grab a few brews for the walk."

"I was drinking Remy V.S.O.P., and where the fuck are we going anyways?" Crow demanded, a little annoyed.

"Just be cool," Bones responded, trying not to sound nervous. "We'll get there. Ain't no liquor stores around here. The closest one is on Avenue B. Let's ease on over there."

As they approached the corner of Second Street and Second Avenue, Crow spotted a dirty old man wearing a huge straw hat, dressed in women's clothes, with a long rubber snake draped over his shoulders. He was pushing a shopping cart full of bottles and heading right for them, a little too fast, Crow thought. And sure enough, even though Crow stepped aside to avoid the inevitable collision, the old drag queen slammed squarely into Crow's side with a bang.

"Yo! Watch what the fuck you doing, man!" Crow shrieked. "*That* shit hurt like a muthafuckah! I oughta smack the shit outta you . . ." The old man yanked the cart back with a start. Then, really quickly and with an amazing agility, he snatched several bottles from the cart and arranged them in rows like bowling pins, in front of Crow's feet. When he finished, he curtsied and apologized, first in French and then in Spanish. Crow glared at the bottles, then at Bones, then back down at the bottles. The old man in a dress grabbed the rubber snake by the head and pulled it from his shoulders. He then stuffed it into a large jar in the cart, tipped his sombrero, and rolled quickly across the street and out of sight.

Before crossing the street, Bones looked over at Crow, trying his damnedest to choke back a laugh. He shrugged his shoulders and said, "Welcome to the Lower East Side."

When Crow looked up and in the direction Bones had begun to walk, he saw a familiar sign in the window that read, "Open All Night."

As they entered the store, Bones nodded to the man behind the counter and headed toward a row of tall stainless-steel coolers in the back. "What you drinkin', Crow?"

Crow shouted back, "I'll take a sixteen-ounce ale, since we can't get no Remy here."

Crow and the Korean man behind the counter leered at each other. Crow knew from experience that if he followed Bones into the back, he'd have a couple of the owners' relatives following behind him. He didn't want the hassle, he just wanted the beer.

With a Bud in one hand and a Ballantine ale in the other, Bones returned triumphantly to the counter, the look on his face indicating a job well done. As he placed the tall cans on the counter, the store owner smiled, revealing tiny yellow-stained teeth. Returning his smile, Bones said, "Separate bags, a pack of Marlboro 100s, and a pack of Newports for the brotha."

"And put a straw in the bag with the ale," said Crow, adding a finish to Bones's thought.

As Crow reached for the bag, several pages of the manuscript, which he'd almost forgotten about, fell out of the folder under his arm and onto the counter. Crow had been too preoccupied with getting some loot and copping drugs to think of finding a bag to carry those damned papers in. Bones picked them up. As he was handing them back to Crow, he noticed a turned-down corner. He quickly started to skim the page:

> He would wait silently in his small room until all the noises of the house were gone. Then he would wait longer. He hid under the blanket and ran his nails across his closed eyes and over his lips. Maybe an hour after his father forced his mother to bed, when their room and all the house were silent, he would crack his door and call the puppy.
>
> "Mr. Dedalus, Sir Simon," he whispered. Without fail the puppy would rise from his box in the kitchen and climb the stairs. "Come, Sir Simon," he called, his words a whisper, barely loud enough for the air to carry.

"Say, man, give me that back. You take a lot for granted," Crow snapped.

Bones apologized. "You're right. I'm sorry. But it's good."

Crow snatched the pages from Bones. "Yeah, whatever. I don't even know you. Just let's do this and be done. That's all." Bones watched Crow stuff the pages back into the folder.

The streets were always more comfortable than the inside of any place for Crow. After readjusting the paintings and the folder for a better grip, he popped open his ale and stuck the straw in. Looking down the block and realizing where he was, he said to Bones, "Man, you know, maybe ten, fifteen years ago, I used to come down here to party. Just across the street, there was a spot called the Dome."

Bones rested the one painting he'd been carrying, the one Crow had named "The Embrace," against his leg and banged his pack of cigarettes against the back of his hand.

"Yeah, I remember. I grew up on this block. And the Electric Circus was upstairs. I lived a few doors down."

"Yeah, yeah!" Crow signified excitedly. "I was trying to remember the name of that spot, the Electric Circus. That was years ago."

Bones brought the subject of the manuscript back up. "Look, man, I'm serious, I'm sorry about reading your stuff."

Crow looked at him blankly. "Ain't no thing, baby, I'm just not ready for people to read it yet." He took another sip of ale before he continued, "C'mon, let's roll. Standing here ain't making me no money."

Crow was looking around the old neighborhood while trying to keep up with Bones. St. Mark's Place had changed. Except for the bums, everybody looked as if they were from out of town. And there were too many new restaurants on the block.

"Yo, Bones. Slow up, man, ain't no wings on my feet."

Bones stopped, turned around, and looked across the street. Gesturing toward a three-story tenement that looked as if it should have been torn down years ago, Bones squealed, "Check it out, Crow. My family used to own that brownstone over there, and we always ate in the healthy-food spot downstairs." Just then, Crow had to jump out of the way of a bald-headed couple of who-knows-what gender, wearing black leather and walking a particularly unsavory-looking rottweiler that they had dressed just like them. He landed next to Bones, who was still reminiscing and staring up at the restaurant sign. It had been turned into a Middle Eastern fast-food place. "Damn, every other decent spot around here ta eat's been turned into some kinda greasy-ass falafel or fast-food joint," Bones complained. " 'Tsa fuckin' shame. People got no respect for tradition!"

"Yeah, so what? My daddy's a highly decorated dead black cop. I don't get all misty every time I see a pig ride by. Just slow the fuck up. I ain't come down here to run no hunnid-yard dash. I look like Carl Lewis to you?"

Bones just stood and stared at the restaurant, lost in his thoughts. "You know, my father killed himself," he finally said. "Story was, in the summer of 'seventy-two, he took ten tabs of acid and sat on these here steps and drank a fuckin' gallon of yellow paint. Me and Moms was spending the summer with a bunch of their tripped-out back-to-the-land, motherfuckin' hippie commune friends in Vermont when we got a letter from him. All he had written were the words, 'They stopped the Sunshine'—whatever the hell that was supposed to mean. This broad who drove a psychedelic hack around the neighborhood, everybody called her Taxi Lady, saved this ring for me."

He brought the ring up to his face: a crudely honed hunk of silver with an omega, the symbol of resistance, etched roughly into its flattened top. He remembered his father had taken him to a Rolling Stones concert in 1970. Jagger had worn a skintight T-shirt with the omega embossed on the front. After that, his father put it on everything instead of the peace sign.

"Taxi Lady said she took it off his hand before the coroner took him away. Moms and me didn't come back to New York until the winter of 'seventy-three. I guess I was ten or eleven by then. She'd kept the ring in a shoebox for me all that time. A couple of months later, Taxi Lady OD'd. After that, my mother and me moved out to Long Island. Man, when Taxi Lady died was the only time I ever saw my mother cry. We used to live upstairs. You can even see my old bedroom window from here."

Crow just stood there sipping his beer. Bones could see he was uncomfortable. Crow didn't want to reminisce about anybody's dead father or cab driver. He had business, and he wanted to go about it. He needed to get back to Brooklyn. He let the straw slip from his lips and back into the can.

"Bones, this is New York. We all got a story, man. Life is hard, and then you die, and in between is pain. My boy's sister's married to some I-talian motherfucker who's always running around on her. My little brother might be smoking crack, and I bet at least one of those lames in that restaurant's got a credit card that don't work."

Bones turned his head slowly toward Crow, sucked his teeth, and said, "Yeah, you right. I still got the ring, though. It's the only fucking thing I got to remember him by. It's got a damned omega resistance symbol on it. Imagine that. The idiot, he should've *resisted* the urge to kill his damned self!"

Crow, startled by Bones's flare-up, said, "Little hostile, huh."

"More than a *little* hostile, man," Bones bit back.

As they continued walking, Bones started to come out of his reminiscence-induced funk—exacerbated by Crow's insensitivity—and started talking again. "Back when my father was alive, St. Mark's was the hub of the world, man. People would come from all over trying to start revolutions and build gardens out of parking lots. We went to school in the park and had different teachers every day."

Crow laughed. Giving in to Bones's insistence to reminisce, he chimed in, "When I was a kid, we cut school and chilled on the playground. Sometimes we ran around the projects chasing girls. But life keeps changing. Not too long ago, I had a whole different lifestyle." Snapping himself back to the present, Crow continued, talking more to himself than to Bones. "But shit changes. Today is today, and I figure it's best to just keep moving."

"I suppose living in the moment is the only true path to serenity."

Crow shook his head, looked Bones in the face, narrowed his eyes, and said, "Bones, this ain't about philosophy, it's about coming off. But just to move this along, consider this: If we believe most European philosophers, *there is no God.* So there can be no divine judgment and, therefore, no ultimate rules. There are man-made rules that are supposedly derived from something called the general consensus. These deny various avenues of self-fulfillment and expression. No matter how hard we try to change things, it just results in the rules changing, which does nothing. Remember, these people believe that rules are simply factors that restrict self-expression. To be free is supposed to be about exercising your 'right' to be an *individual* and express yourself however you choose and do whatever you want. No matter whether we ever understand how wants and desires are actually generated in the individual. I learned all that shit in Philosophy 101. Got an A in that shit. And imagine learning about all them white philosophical men talking shit in a *black* college! No matter where you go, all school is, is read, repeat, read, repeat. Most of what we got fucking running around in our heads is some ol' bullshit. Well, anyways, you and me, as individuals, got us some individual fulfilling to do in *this* moment, so let's live for that." They both took a big gulp of beer and started across Second Avenue.

The block between Second and First Avenues was poorly lit. Crow needed some blow, so when he spotted a row of darkened buildings, he crossed the street and walked toward them while pulling the bill with the coke in it out of his pocket.

"Want a hit? I've got enough left for you to get a good little blast."

While scanning the block for po-*lice,* Bones said, "Thought you'd never ask." They eased into the shadows of a nearby doorway. They both leaned the paintings they were carrying against the door façade, and Crow wedged the manuscript more tightly under his arm before taking a few quick snorts.

"Here, man," Crow said, jutting the bill at Bones. After two quick snorts, Bones ran his fingers across the paper and rubbed them over his gums before passing the bill back to Crow.

Feeling lifted, Bones smiled. "Bet, let's boogie." With a renewed spring in their step, they headed over to Avenue A, then turned down Sixth Street.

◈ ◈ ◈

On the south side of Tompkins Square Park, between A and B, there was a little liquor store that didn't look like much from the outside. Inside, a young woman, who looked to be about eighteen years old, stood behind the counter. Her long, tightly curled, ebony hair, which fell past her shoulders and stopped at the waist just above her backside, framed a beautifully angular face with expressively full yet delicate features. She had big, almond-shaped eyes so dark they could remind somebody of little pools of midnight sky; long, straight eyelashes that made her look kind of sleepy in a sexy, inviting way; chiseled cheekbones; and a soft, pouty mouth, all of which was set off by skin the color of orange honey. And at about five-foot-seven, she was just *baaaaaaad*. Well behind her, at a rickety card table, four old Boriqueno muchachos drank rum, smoked cigars, cursed, and laughed loudly while arguing over dominos.

As Bones walked to the counter, she greeted him. "Hey, Marvin, where you been, man?" She said, "You got a three-week-old tab," adding a sarcastic "Papi," at the end.

"Don't worry, sweetheart, we gonna be all right tonight. Check out these paintings." Passing her the one he had been carrying, Bones pointed to Crow and went on. "Candace Maria, allow me to introduce you. This is my man, Crow Shade. He's the artist. Pretty damned good, ain't he?"

Barely looking at the painting, Candace Maria laughed softly and jutted her right hand at Crow. When he didn't move, she said, "I don't bite . . . unless you *ask* me to. My name is Candy. Only *mi tío* Manny back there and *Marvin* here call me Candace Maria."

"Nice name," Crow muttered.

"When I was a little girl, Tío Manny told me and my brothers about Puerto Rico's African heritage. We all have names like mine. He says I was named after a very powerful dynasty of Nubian queens that defeated Greek and Roman invaders and the Christians' mother of Jesus, the savior, so I have a lot to live up to." Crow's ears perked up. She had looks, brains, and fire. He was always intrigued by people who knew a little something out of the ordinary, beyond the obvious, even if he didn't act like it. He accepted the hand, which felt like velvet to him. She smiled and said, "Nice to meet you, Crow. I like that name. I don't even care if that's your real name or not. *Crow* just suits you, with your smooth dark skin and dressed in black like that." He actually blushed. He felt himself liking her. Strange feeling.

"Yo, man, show Candy the other paintings. I think she'll like your work, and she knows a lot of the art people down here. She might could hook us up with a buyer."

Releasing Candy's hand, Crow passed Bones the paintings. "Here, *Marvin,* you take 'em, but I don't see how some *teenager* is gonna be able to do anything for us."

"I haven't seen my teens in a while, *morenito,"* Candy said sweetly, "so if that's your preference, you're shit outta luck. But I'm flattered."

Bones passed Candy the other two paintings. "See what I mean?" he said. Spreading the canvases out on the counter, Candy looked them over.

"Yes, I do," she said. "They're not flat like most of the work I'm seeing lately." Running her long red fingernails over the textured side of the one with the poem, she said, "I really like this one. The words are meaningful and inspired. I can feel them." She looked at Bones and then at Crow and said, "You can really write. The paintings are beautiful, but adding the words really makes this work something special."

Crow stepped up to the counter and quickly read the poem again. He felt her staring at him, but he avoided her eyes.

"Thanks. The words come and go. The painting comes and goes, too. Ain't none of it no real big deal. Like anything else, just something to do." Just then, one of the old men farted. Crow winced, caught himself, and tried to act as if he didn't hear it. Not knowing what to say, he did the only thing to do in a situation like this—or any situation in which there is a *fine* woman. He started looking her over, checking her out.

Candy wore a baggy, threadbare, faded, plaid flannel shirt. Three buttons were open from the neck down. Crow's eyes instinctively drifted to where he thought her nipples should be, and he was not disappointed to find them erect and making impressions in the thinning cloth. He then looked for but was unable to find cleavage because her breasts, although full, were set slightly apart on her chest. She watched as his eyes traveled down her body to a curvaceous set of hips and thighs over which she wore well-worn jeans, faded and torn at mid-thigh on the right leg. She tensed, realizing how tightly they were pressed against her otherwise bare crotch. Candy hadn't worn underwear since she *looked* as if she was fourteen but rarely thought about it. Now she did. While she had been obviously attracted to Crow on sight and was aware that it was she who had started the flirting, she did not appreciate the kind of attention her body was receiving from him. It made her feel as though he wasn't actually looking at *her* but at a collection of cushy parts with a pussy.

From behind Candace Maria, Tío Manny yelled out, "Man! You rotten inside!"

The one who must've dealt it responded, "The farts ain't smelt that bad 'til I just won."

Crow laughed, and Manny said, "Damn, Bones, open the door, make yourself useful. And what d'hell you been *eatin',* Tito?"

"Just your damned arroz con pollo, *pendejo!* You can't cook!"

Candy stopped rubbing the textured canvas so she could turn her head and said, "Tío Manny, we got customers in the store. Where's your manners?" Crow looked over at Bones as he headed toward the door. Before he opened it, Manny snapped, "Customers *carajo,* it's only beggin', Bones. He come to pay his damned tab?"

One of the other muchachos playing dominos shouted, *"Ron!"* and continued to curse in Spanish. Candy grabbed a pint bottle of Bacardi from under the counter and took it over to their table.

Shaking her head, she went back to the counter, where she continued to run her fingers over the texture of the canvas.

Bones held the door open for about three seconds before returning to where he'd been standing. Candy said, "It got cold in here," and reached under the counter, pulling out a sweater. Crow sucked his teeth. She shot him a look that said she didn't like what he was doing and he offered a smile, which she did not return.

A little embarrassed, Crow sputtered, "So you like the paintings, huh?" She put the sweater on but didn't button it. Crow kept looking at her breasts. She saw where he was looking and started to button the sweater.

Bones, who was completely unaware of what was going on between them, in a voice that was a little too loud, said, "I don't know what you're talking about, it ain't cold in here."

They both looked at him, then at each other, and laughed. She stopped buttoning the sweater and said, "You might be right, *Marvin*. She relaxed a little and refocused her attention on the paintings.

"These are really good, Crow. Are you showing anywhere?"

"Showing wha . . . ? Oh . . ." Crow caught himself. She must be talking about an *art show,* he thought, then spoke again. "Not right now," he lied. "I'm in between gigs."

She looked at him and raised an eyebrow. "Where are you from?"

"Brooklyn."

Just then, Candy noticed the folder under Crow's arm. "What's that?" she asked, pointing.

Crow followed her finger and looked down at his armpit. "It's a book I been working on. What *is* this, twenty questions?"

"I'm just curious. Besides, I can't represent someone I know nothing about." She turned and looked at Bones. "Where you taking the paintings?" she asked.

"Geoff's got an opening tonight, some freak-ass shit," Bones answered. "A bunch of photos of naked transvestites with their little fuckin' pedigree dogs in abandoned buildings and auto-body shops. The show's probably damn near over by now. I figure we go lean

Crow's shit against some Volvos and BMWs and wait till the chumps come out. We might not sell nothin', but it'll damn sure get Geoff's attention. Once we done that, it'll be easy. I think Crow's shit is hot. He ain't no Basquiat, but compared to what Geoff's *been* showing . . ."

Candy took off the sweater but buttoned the third button of her shirt. "Yeah, Bones, that's true, but no offense, Crow, people just ain't into too many blacks theses days. They already got Basquiat, Outtara, and Victor Matthews. So unless you doin' some *graffiti* or somethin', I don't know if the market down here can take another brother."

Bones shrugged his shoulders and looked at Crow. "Maybe we can play him off as a foreigner. Can you do any accents?" Bones asked, half serious. Crow cut his eyes at him, stomped over to the counter, slammed the manuscript down, and started to pick up the paintings.

Candy grabbed his hand and said, "Hold up, Bones was only bullshittin'. Good work is good work, no matter who does it—at least that's how it *should* be." Crow jerked away from her and grabbed one of the canvases.

"Fuck this. What the hell I need y'all for. The girl's right about one thing, though, good shit is good shit, and *this* shit is good. I can stand on any corner and down all three a dees in fit-teen, twenny minutes. *These* motherfuckers never gave a shit about a nigga before, but I still be clockin' dollars. I could even go back to Brooklyn and sell my shit." He picked up the rest of the paintings and started for the door.

Bones yelled after him, "Sure, you're right! That's why you was standing out in front that cube and ain't sell nothin'."

Crow stopped dead in his tracks, sighed, and said, "All right, so what we gon' do?"

"Besides, you couldn't leave without this," Candy said, holding up the manuscript.

"Candy, give me a pint of Remy and mark it down," Bones said real quick, hoping the lure of Crow's brand of choice would placate him long enough to get him to go along with the program. Bones hadn't fallen into this much promise in a *coon's* age, and he wasn't wasn't about to let Crow fuck it up for him.

"V.S.O.P., not that cheap shit, either," Crow added. Bones's play had worked . . . so far.

She turned around and reached up to grab a bottle off the shelf. Her tight-ass jeans showed no panty line. Stretching, one round cheek rose higher than the other, her shirt rising to show a hint of orange-honey flesh. The pants pulled tightly where her thighs grew thick and clung to the curve of her backside. When she turned back around, she placed the folder back on the counter and placed the Remy on top of it. She had to bend while doing this, and Crow's eyes focused once again on one of her breasts—one-track mind that he had. He thought that if she hadn't fastened that damn button, he might have caught sight of a nipple.

This time Bones was aware of what was going on. Bones and Candy had known each other since they were children. First grade. When they were about fifteen, they were on their way to a party and stopped in the park to smoke a joint. He'd kissed her and sneaked his hand under her blouse. She'd let him rub her breasts, but when he tried to undo the buttons, she stopped him. It never went any further, never happened again, and they never talked about it. Now, years later, he thought about her breasts and was jealous and still angry enough about what had *not* happened to care that Crow was thinking about them too.

"Yo, Crow," Bones snapped, surprising even himself. "Grab the Remy, and let's get the fuck on up."

Crow looked at him out of the corner of his eye and took a second to decide what to do about Bones's tone. Crow decided to let him slide on this one because now his attention was trained on Candy and the liquor.

"And go where? She *said* niggers don't sell no art down here. I might as well go back to the cube."

Before Bones could say anything, Candy asked again, this time expecting a better answer than before, "Crow, did you write that too?" Pointing at the folder.

Before Crow could respond, Bones blurted out, "Yeah, he wrote that too." She pushed the bottle of Remy aside and picked up the manuscript. "Can I take a look?" Crow paused, but then decided, "Why the fuck not?"

Candy opened the folder to the page where the corner had been turned down. She called Crow over and asked him why the page was marked. Crow replied, "I was reading it over; that's where I stopped." He stood there looking at the page, trying to read along with her. When she got to the part about the puppy, she looked up and asked him did he understand Joyce. Crow said, "Huh, what do you mean?"

She meant James Joyce, one of the greatest writers in English literature, or so they say.

"Well, you called the puppy Dedalus. Is there any particular reason?"

"Just a name, sugar, the same as mine." She continued to read out loud:

> Instead of rushing into the room, Sir Simon always stopped at the door and would roll on his back and whimper. The boy would duck under the covers and tie his sneakers and then crawl from the bed to rub the puppy's stomach until he fell silent. Together they would lie on the floor and sleep. His arm stretched across Sir Simon.
>
> One of the neighbors had a large tree in the yard. Birds came there from places that the boy could only imagine. Each dawn one began a song the others would follow. He would wake hearing them and cry because his voice could not sing. Then Sir Simon would again whimper and roll on his back. Sir Simon Dedalus left him each morning moving silently down the hall. The boy never knew that before Sir Simon struggled down the stairs he would pee at the entrance of the master

bedroom. After Sir Simon left he would crawl back to bed and hide under the covers. Untying his sneakers in that dark, dry womb. He never knew why his father kicked and cursed Mr. Dedalus each morning.

Without fail, every morning his mother would yank the blanket from him and force him to listen to different passages from the Old Testament. This jealous God so full of wrath didn't cause him to fear as much as his father's voice that sang from the bathroom.

One Sunday morning Sir Simon was missing, and when he went from the house to carry trash he found Sir Simon Dedalus lying broken among mounds of coffee grounds and eggshells. His side was caved in, and blood ran out of his ears and mouth. When he put his fingers to it, it was hard and dry. He did not cry.

He sat far from the house until noon. As the bells from the church began to ring, he ran to the house and first set fire to the couch and then to his father's bed and also the drapes that hung in the parlor.

All that afternoon he sat in the neighbor's tree where the birds would sing and found the song in his voice as he watched the fire. His voice became loud and strong. It didn't matter, and he wasn't aware he sang a broken song.

Candy looked up from the page and passed Crow the Remy. She looked at Bones, who had been pacing but stopped just as their eyes met.

"You ready to go?" she asked him.

Crow was still looking at the page. He took a long swallow of the liquor, closed the folder, capped the bottle, and shoved it into his pocket.

"You could have at least waited until we got out of *mi tío's* store before you did that," Candy scolded in a whisper. Her eyes looked wet.

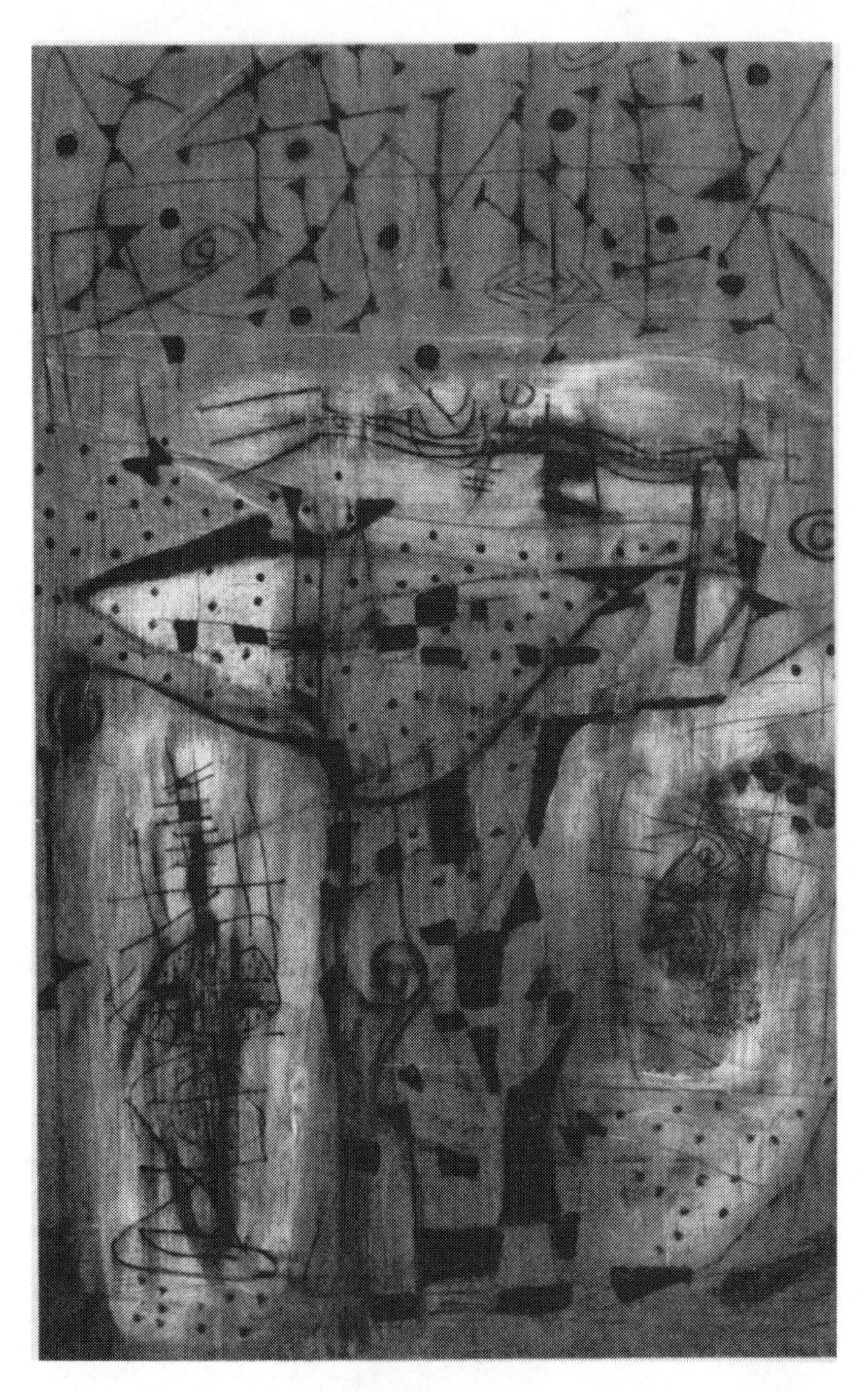

Hard Target (2000)

5

Let's Get On with This Shit

Tío Manny pitched a bitch when Candace Maria asked him if he would watch the store.

"It's *your* store," she reminded him. "And when was the last time you paid me, anyways?"

"I don't ask you to pay no rent, and you eat up everything that ain't nailed down," Tío Manny snapped, half joking. "And I don't know where she puts it!" Candace started to say something back, but Manny beat her to it. "I might be able to afford to pay you something if you didn't give all my top-shelf liquor to these bum friends of yours." He looked over at Bones and Crow.

"I don't know why you looking at me. I ain't in this shit. I don't owe *you* a dime." Crow scowled.

Tío Manny pointed at Bones and shot back, "If you with *that* damn bum, you gotta owe somebody sump'n. Birds of a feather, you know . . ." Manny's use of irony was lost on no one.

Bones spun around and slammed his fist against his heart. "Don Manuel!" he exclaimed, feigning a real bad and completely unidentifiable accent. "After all these years and all that our families have meant to each other. You wound me." Staggering dramatically toward Manny with his fist still pressed to his chest, Bones continued, "I am a man of honor from an honorable family, and I always pay my tab."

Manny looked up from the table slowly, his hands continuing to shuffle the dominos. "Heh heh! When? You a bad actor and a worse liar. When was the last time I seen any *dinero* with your fingerprints on it? As far as I'm concerned, no matter how long I know you, anyone who don't pay his bill is a damn bum. Your father always paid cash and was one of the best bid whist players I ever met. The man never cut his hair or used a razor, but he always paid cash. Goddamn *loco gringo* if I ever saw one. Kept damn good reefers too. Only hippie I ever liked. You'd do good to be more like him. Damn deadbeat." Bones's face got red.

"Chill out, Bones. Don't nobody fill they daddy's shoes," Crow said, looking at Manny. "Ask Manny here if he's the man his papa was. I don't know that anyone's supposed to be."

The third dominos player, Fernando was his name, who up till now had been silent, said something in Spanish even Candy didn't catch, then said in English, "The kid's right, my papa used to . . ." But Tito cut him short.

"Su papa, mi papa, Manny's *papa*—they all dead! All of them lying there in their graves. What the hell do they care about this damn world or what they did here?" Manny threw his tiles back onto the table with a crack. "Fernando, you old shit, don't you talk about *mi padre, amigo o no amigo!"* The three men started talking at the same time, their voices getting louder and louder.

"Don't you talk about *mi padre. A pendejo* like you would not have been fit to shine his *zapatos.* That man was a saint!"

"I wasn't talking about your father, that old . . ."

"Vete pal carajo!"

"We supposed to be playing dominos or what?"

"I'm telling you, don't you dare speak in disrespect *de mi papa. Mi padre* raised *nueve niños . . .*"

"Oh yeah? Well, there was twelve in my house, including Cousin Teresa, who was a little *loca.* She's a nun now . . ."

"She wasn't *that* damn crazy."

"Coño, where's the damn rum?"

"Teresa used to go off for days. Nobody ever knew where she went."

"I did."

"Your father got arrested for stealing chickens!"

"If we ain't gonna play no more, then I'm goin' home!"

"Mentiroso!"

"What do you mean, you knew where Teresa was going?"

Candace Maria came rushing from the back room, a flushing noise trailing that was almost drowned out by the loud voices. Crow was still standing in the same spot with the paintings and folder tucked under his arm. Bones had taken a seat on the counter. The first thing she said was, "Bones, get your narrow, hairy ass off my counter." She looked at Crow, whose face revealed nothing except for slightly amused eyes.

She stopped and threw her jacket onto the counter. "Would you three just stop it? Why you always have to fight like children? It's like a nursery school in here."

Tito and Fernando stopped talking immediately. Tío Manny, however, continued but lowered his voice. "He was innocent. Them chickens was in our yard and . . ."

"The birds were Roberto's fighting cocks, Tío Manny," Candy added passively. "Granddad stole them. Grandma musta said that a million times. Why don't you just finish playing your game? You should close the store soon, anyway."

Tío Manny made a sign of the cross in the air and then something else Crow'd never seen before and said, "Mama, bless her soul, she was a saint, but she didn't know her ass from a hole in the ground. Papa got a bum rap, I tell you. Thirty days in a work camp, and him with all us kids, the goats, and two cows to care for! *Vaya chica,* have fun!"

Turning back to Tito, Fernando, and his dominos, Manny said, "Damn kids these days, no sense of *responsabilidad o familia.* It's a wonder they learn anything. *Mira corazón,* before you go, bring over a half-pint of the rum Tito likes. Here, take this one back," he said, handing her the Bacardi. "And make sure you mark it on his tab. He's a bum, too." Tito objected—loudly.

Crow said to Bones, "I don't care where the fuck you go, all families act the same."

Leaning against the counter, his arms folded and head hung down, Bones answered without looking up, "Fuck families."

On the way out of the store, Candace Maria kissed Tío Manny on his forehead and put the rum Tito liked on the table. Manny said, "If you see Santo, you stay away from that . . . he's smoking that shit again, and the cop's looking for him for God knows what now, *carajo.*"

As they walked out, Candy headed down Sixth Street ahead of Crow and Bones. Crow noticed that the tail of her shirt hung lower than the faded green suede baseball jacket she wore, both of which were too short to completely cover her ass. He couldn't take his eyes off it. By the time they caught up to her, Crow was so mesmerized by its swingy rhythm he didn't know what to say next. But "Yo, I ain't carrying all this shit by myself," is what came out. Candy stopped suddenly, and Crow almost tripped over himself to keep from slamming into her. Crow, not being an inept motherfucker, was cool; he caught himself. In all the years since it had started working, his dick had never gotten so hard so fast—not even the first time he knew he was gettin' some, and especially not since he'd been doing so much coke.

"Then give me the big one," she said. Crow snickered under his breath almost loud enough for her to hear—he hoped.

"I'd love to, *mami chulo.*"

"Qué?!" she shrieked, half smirking, as she whipped around on Crow.

Straightening out his face real quick, he started to hand her the *painting* she'd asked for, when, in one swift motion, Bones stepped around Crow and then between him and Candy and grabbed it.

"I'll carry that shit, man," he said with a snarl.

"What the hell are you doing, *Marvin,* man?" Candy demanded, annoyed as hell. It finally hit Crow what the hell was going on. First looking at Candy, then at Bones, he smiled, dropped his head, and ran his whole hand down the length of his face with a dragging motion, from forehead to beard—a nervous, repetitive gesture developed when he had used heroin for a while, years ago.

"You got it, baby," Crow said, still smiling.

But it wasn't nothin' funny to Candy. Bones was cock blocking, and she was not amused. She'd told him about this shit before. "We *amigos,* Marvin, I just don't like you like that." She remembered the look on his face that Sunday morning on their way home from a party. They must have been fifteen or sixteen. She knew he always expected to be *the one,* her first. She half expected it too. Not because of any actual desire for him but more out of familiarity and, you know, the thing you just do because everybody expects it. After all, for what seemed like forever, they had been the only thing in each other's life. And he *was* the first guy she ever let put his hands in her shirt, that night in the park years ago.

Still smiling but not looking in her eyes, Crow said, "The man wants to be a gentleman. Why deny him? I'm still carrying the book anyway."

"Marvin, gimme that one. Crow, you just carry the book. We don't got time for the bullshit. Geoff ain't gonna stay open all night."

Crow pulled the Remy from his jacket pocket and said, "G-*off* can wait a minute," and opened the bottle.

Candy said, "Give me a swallow of that. I've been in the damn store all night sober as a nun." Crow took a swallow and passed the bottle.

"Do you blow—*cocaine,* I mean?" he asked her.

Bones, missing that, extended his free hand, answering for her, "The pope still Catholic?"

Candy, saying nothing, took a swig of the Remy. It made her shudder as it went down. Looking at Bones's outstretched hand, she passed it to him and said, "I see you still got that rare disease, *grabbititis,* the ol' hasty hand."

Digging in his pocket, Crow found what was left of the blow. Feeling cocky, he said, "Let's kill this. It's pretty good, probably make your nipples even harder." Bones banged the bottle against his front teeth. Candy, deciding to ig Crow's sexual innuendos completely, still said nothing. Crow passed the bottle cap to Marvin, saying, "You might as well carry that too."

They crossed the street and sat on a bench close to the edge of the park. Bones muttered something under his breath that no one heard. Crow opened the bill and saw that there wasn't that much left. He took a few small blows and handed it to Candy, saying, "Kill it." Bones mumbled something again.

She looked in the bill, then looked at Crow and said, "Ain't no hell of a lot here." He stuck out his hand and wiggled his fingers. "Won't none be lost if you don't want it. Wasn't expectin' no party. Give the motherfucker back." She ran the bill under her nose and inhaled deeply. She did that one more time and licked the bill.

"No need to get hostile, *brother.*" She gave the empty bill back to Crow.

"In her last life she used to be a Hoover upright," Bones commented snidely. Frustrated, he drank some more Remy.

Candy got up and grabbed two paintings. She inhaled deeply. "Quick but nice. We better get over to the gallery before it closes." Bones grabbed the other painting, and Crow grabbed the Remy from Bones's pocket.

"Yo, baby, you want another swig before we step off?" Crow asked. She shook her head.

Before they could leave, a big fat kid about six feet four with a fluorescent green Mohawk hustled over.

"Yo, Bones, we gotta talk." The kid had to weigh close to three hundred pounds.

"Not now, Terminal, I'm busy. I'll be at the club later."

He watched them leave the park, but before they were out of the range of his voice, he said, "I ain't shitting around, Bones. You would *want* to have my money."

Halfway down the block, Bones said to Crow, "Damn groupies. Always followin' me around."

Crow said, "Groupie, huh? Well, how much you owe that *groupie?*"

Bones looked at Crow and snickered while saying, "Who gives a fuck?"

Without missing a beat, Crow quickly turned his attention back to Candy. "What else you do besides work in the store?"

Feeling scampish, she answered, "I don't know, sometimes I lie naked in my bed and pretend I own a jet that I put on autopilot and then let it fly over the Black Sea until it runs out of gas. I would sit in a red velvet chair wearing black fishnet stockings and black suede spike heels with J. R. R. Tolkien's hobbits sitting at my feet licking my calves. Then, when the fuel runs out, we would leap without parachutes into the night. Only after we jumped would I let them lick between my legs. Can you imagine, I do all of that in a bed above a liquor store?"

"That shit's wild," Crow said. "Do you ever fall into the water, I mean, out of the bed?"

"Crow, *mi hijo,* when I start to fall out, not only are hobbits sucking my pussy, but wizards, elves, and the fair fantasy queens with sparkling blue eyes and golden hair suck and fuck me all the way down. They all work my finger's fantasy. And when I come, the Black Sea swallows me whole. My door has double locks. When I'm not doing that, I think I'm a writer or a dancer. That's what the hell else I do. And if my mother hadn't sent me to Catholic school for twelve years, I could have gotten rich selling pussy. But the hobbits get it free."

Bones said, "All that shit you talk, you should add politician to the list."

"You're better suited for that job, Bones. The only talent needed to be one is an ability to be full of shit and lie with a straight face. I was talking to Crow, anyway. You better think of what you're gonna do about Terminal Ill."

They continued walking and turned right on Avenue B going downtown. They were walking three abreast, so when Crow slipped his arm around Candy's waist, Bones didn't see it. Crow felt Candy stiffen, then yield to his touch, her silence sounding like acquiescence to him.

Along the way, they each downed more Remy and remained silent. Crow wanted to but didn't rub her ass. He decided just to enjoy the moment for what it was. Just nice.

At the corner of Third and B, they ran into a girl dressed in a rubber scuba-diving suit. Half of her head was shaved to the scalp, the other was bleached as white as black hair can get. She wore thick black glasses that had cracked lenses. Painted on her suit was an arrow pointing to her crotch. Written above the arrow were the words "Tainted Twat." Crow let go of Candy before Bones could see.

"Are you guys goin' to Geoff's?" she asked.

"Yeah," Candy answered.

"I'm terribly tired. See you at the club later?" She didn't wait for a reply. As she walked away, Crow saw painted on her ass, "Caution, ran out of toilet paper." Crow's face twisted as if he could actually smell it.

Candy looked at Crow and chuckled, saying, "She was probably part of the exhibit."

The gallery had once been a bodega. It still had the traditional bodega yellow and red awning with the yellow lights. Although the windows had been painted black, in the middle of one, a lighted sign still hung advertising malt liquor.

Rushing to get into a waiting line, a thin woman carrying a heavy fur coat and wearing a black lace teddy and black sequined stockings tripped and stumbled against a bald, pudgy man with a tan. He was wearing a white tux and patent-leather shoes. Nestled in his arms was a brown animal that looked like a large squirrel. Another couple dressed in black leather got on a motorcycle. She was driving, and he had a hard time getting into the sidecar. He held a plastic cup in his right hand.

Other people who didn't attract as much attention got into cars or walked up and down the block. A Chinese man stood at the curb peeing on the tire of a Porsche. A black woman with huge breasts was screaming at him to hurry up.

Crow hadn't realized, but he had stopped walking, awed by the spectacle. Candy kissed him on the cheek, telling him that it wasn't as bad as it looked.

"Nah, it's worse," Bones added dryly. The yellow and red sign read "Cold Beer, Heros, Cold Cuts and Cigarettes." A section had been covered in black paint, and lettered in pink Day-Glo were the words "Virgins—$1.99 a dozen." Crow heard the woman with the tits say to the Chinese man, "Would you stop pissing and save some till we get home?"

A man in a flowing blond wig and painted red lips stood at the front door shaking hands as the people left. When he saw Candy, he ran over and kissed her full on the lips. Then he saw Bones and said, "Oh, I see you're still associating with the underclasses."

"Nice to see you, too, Geoff."

He looked at Crow and said to Candy, "Well, dear, I guess you've grown tired of finger-fucking yourself while flying over the Sargasso. A Nubian buck, I love it."

"Fuck you, homo;" Crow spat.

"Oh my! An authentic primitive. Did you find him selling crack in Washington Square?"

Crow looked at Candy and said, "What the fuck is this? I'll lose my foot up this faggot's ass." He jerked loose from Candace and snatched the wig off Geoff's head. His not-too-long hair was strained into tiny plaits, held together at the ends by red rubber bands. Crow started laughing, as did Candy. Bones stammered and tried to apologize, but Geoff said, "Oh just shut the hell up." Several other people started laughing, not sure that it was appropriate.

Geoff snatched the wig from Crow's hand and ran. Crow said to no one in particular, "Shithead homo. This is a fucking freak show. Faggots, dumb bitches, motherfuckers walking around like confused, washed-up, has-been rock stars talking about somebody dey don't even know. This shit is sick, and those fucking Spanish niggas across the street look like they don't even notice this bullshit."

Candy cut Crow short. "Geoff's not gay," she said.

Crow said, "The Spanish boys I know out the way would have took that bitch's fur coat and stuck this whole motherfucker up."

Inside the gallery, Bones followed behind Geoff, trying to help him straighten out his wig. Geoff was frantically pacing back and forth, fixing his lipstick and tugging on the wig at the same time.

"Ruin my fucking show. Bring some pointy-head, bubble-lip spade down here, will you?"

The show's photographer was pouring wine from a gallon jug when Geoff banged into the table. The jug fell and broke, and the plastic glass fell from his hand. Wine splashed Geoff's stockings and heels. The photographer screamed, "Shit!" Then he found another glass and took a bottle of rosé off one of the shelves over where the table had been and filled it. Geoff was still fussing with the wig.

"Damn Lincoln and Martin Luther King. And fuck the Cosby show too," Geoff said in complete and utter disgust.

"Yo, man," Bones said to Geoff. "Just look at the paintings—the nigga is good."

The photographer looked up, saying, "Nigger, nigger, who you calling nigger, crackerboy? This is the eighties. There ain't no niggers no more."

Geoff stopped pacing. "Oh, I forgot! You're so right, Alton. It's just that we have to deal with so many uneducated negro bores. Do you remember that book that Violet wrote a few years ago, *Before Ellison,* about blacks and Asians being separate from art and history? I'm sorry, Marvin, but take him back to the ghetto, unless he can play the sax or dance."

"Geoff, you're starting to sound like a racist," Alton said, finishing his glass of wine. Bones walked over to the shelf and poured himself a drinking glass full of the rosè.

Outside, people were still hopping into cars, hailing cabs, walking east or west. Candy was trying to persuade Crow to go inside the gallery with her.

"Fuck that shit. I can't be bothered, and I am outta here. *He, she,* or whatever the fuck that was made sure of that. And I damn sure ain't no diplomat—kissing every white ass with two nickels. Crow reached for the painting Candy had tucked under her arm, and she grabbed his arm with her free hand and tried to pull him close. He didn't move.

"What do you do after the fire has gone out?" she asked. He looked at her and sucked his teeth.

"I ain't got the fucking time for riddles or bullshit questions. Let's just get the fuck out of here."

"Crow, I was talking about the little boy in the book. After you burn down the house, you've got to go somewhere. You lit the fire by fucking with Bones, and now you're here. Shit, being here's as good as being there. It's just how you play it. Don't tell me a fine, been-there-done-that brotha like yourself can't play this baby food situation." She laughed and yanked Crow's arm, throwing him off balance. Throwing her hands up in the air, she let him go flying. "Yo, doc, are we gonna get busy or what?" What and how she said it surprised Crow. He looked at her and started jerking his head from side to side in sharp downward motions. He threw up his free hand and ran his fingers under his nose.

"Yo, baby, you're right, I was illin'. Let's get busy, do work, and then break north." He stood, looking into her eyes, and when they didn't blink, he said, "I thought you were some kind of hippie, punk-rock chick or some shit like that, but I see you think you know what time it *really* is."

"Crow," she began, "by now, you should know that when the script changes, you got to get into the new characters."

Before their feet were firmly planted in the gallery, Geoff shouted, "Candace, kindly escort that barbaric gentleman right back outside."

"Just calm down, love of my life. Crow is neither a barbarian nor a gentleman. He is a talented *artiste,* and he has some stuff I know you can use. If you take a look, I promise not to tell everybody that you got a wife and three kids in Irvington and was still a social worker until last spring."

Crow started to wander through the gallery. He stopped and

read a sign under one exhibit: "Consumer items, Bodega, circa 1980s. Artist: Geoff Smithenhouser III." The piece consisted of four wooden shelves topped by a clock bearing a beer logo. The glass covering the clock had a long crack in it covered partially by masking tape. The clock's electrical wire hung down over the front shelves. In several places, the wire had been spliced and covered with Band-Aids of various colors. The top shelf was stacked with cans of various kinds of goya beans and Carnation condensed milk. The second shelf had a ten-pound bag of rice with a hole in its side. Some of the rice was scattered across the shelf. Crow tried to dust the rice off but found that each grain had been glued into place. On the right side of the shelf stood three boxes of Uncle Ben's rice. The third shelf was packed with cans of roach spray, roach motels, and mousetraps. One trap had a rubber rat caught in it, the corner of its mouth painted with lines of red paint that ran onto the shelf. The bottom shelf exhibited four boxes of dry breakfast cereal, a large can of Spam, a stack of sardines, a very large can of tuna, two cans of spaghetti and meatballs, and one can of La Choy chow mein. Under the shelves, a plastic garbage bag stood half filled with empty soda and beer cans. Taped to the left side of the exhibit were three one-dollar bills with expressions of good wishes written in marker.

Crow looked at the art for a while and decided that it was either a racist statement or unfinished renovation. He also decided that it would be better to stroke Geoff than further aggravate what had become an adversarial situation, one he had allowed two other strangers to land him in. He walked over to Geoff and said, "Now, that's clever. I mean, you have really captured the underclass urban experience—I'm blown away." Having said that, he executed a low and sweeping bow to Geoff.

Alton, busy pouring himself another glass of wine, paused long enough to say, "We have an aficionado among us. And your opinion of my contributions to this widely acclaimed exhibition?"

Bones had finally calmed himself down enough to be standing next to Alton at the folding table, which no one had bothered to pick up. Bones had leaned the painting he'd been carrying against the wall under the shelf where the rosé resided. Crow focused in on a stream of wine rolling slowly toward the painting. Crow dashed to grab the painting before it got wet and screamed at Bones, "What the fuck you think you doin'?! You need to be more careful. My paintings are *very* valuable. And you ain't got no money to pay for one if you ruin it."

Bones was oblivious to what had almost happened and stepped into the stream of wine, leaving wet half-footprints as he walked toward Crow with his face twisted. "What the hell are you talking about, Crow?"

Crow sucked his teeth and turned his head, dismissing Bones to look at a small photograph. It was of a man with a handlebar mustache, wearing a flowered sundress and army boots, trapped under the wheels of a junky old Chevy Impala. He was clutching a shaved miniature poodle sporting a pompadour. A naked girl with blond Shirley Temple curls sat behind the steering wheel of the car. She looked to be about five or six years old. The door of the car, which was rust-colored, hung ajar from its hinge. Each corner of the photograph was crossed by Scotch tape, which held it to the wall. A square yellow notepad, also held by tape, read, "Refuge of Divorce: Alton, 1984."

When Bones saw that Crow wasn't going to answer, he threw his arm over his shoulder. Bones yelled over to Alton, who had finally decided that someone should pick that table up, that everybody loved his piece. Without pause and using the same rush of air from his lungs, Bones asked Geoff how many pieces he had sold that night but didn't get a response because Candy had Geoff's attention.

She was busy showing him one of Crow's paintings. Alton shot several rapid and slurred words at Bones that sounded to Crow like "clumsy fool." He ended his speech with, "My work is done for the aesthetic value, you know, art for art's sake. Not for money."

Bones tried to pass his glass of rosé to Crow, but he refused it. "All I want is my damned Remy," he said.

Bones finished the rosé with one gulp. "Yeah," he said to Alton. "That shit is all well and good, but it don't pay none of Geoff's bills."

Crow was amused by their exchange but was really more interested in what the deal was between Candy and Geoff—he had his eye on her. Shaking Bones's arm from his shoulder, he got the Remy from his pocket, pulled the cap, and took a quick sip. He walked over to Candy and Geoff, who were now looking at and discussing one of the other paintings. Bones was still standing where Crow left him, his head twisting back and forth from Alton to the others.

Intuitively stopping short of intruding into their conversation, Crow gestured silently to get Candy's attention. He wanted to know if she wanted some of what he had—the Remy, that is. Geoff looked up.

"Am I invited to the party?" he asked.

"Sure, man, if you want to drink with a primitive, why the fuck not." Crow noticed that the man's voice had deepened considerably, and his movements seemed less effeminate. This made Geoff all the more bizarre-looking, considering the wig and makeup hadn't gone anywhere.

Bypassing Candy, Crow handed the bottle to Geoff. Before the bottle got to his mouth, Crow asked, "Yo, you ain't got no AIDS or no shit like that, do ya?" Then quickly added, "I'm just joking, man."

Geoff lowered the bottle and pulled a blue bandana from his back pocket and wiped his lipstick off. He took a swallow and said, "My wife sure hopes not."

By now, Bones had made it over to grabbing distance and extended his hand toward the bottle. Geoff passed it to Candy. She took it and walked over to the table that Alton had just finishing righting. Then she poured shots into four plastic cups, nearly emptying the bottle. "We might as well use cups since we got some. Despite popular opinion, I *am* a lady."

Bones took his glass and went back over to the table, picking up what was left of the Remy and the painting. Finding that he couldn't carry all three, he finished his wine and came back with the Remy bottle in one hand, the painting in the other. Alton remained at the table drinking wine, clearly drunk and still muttering. Excusing himself, Geoff went into a room at the back of the gallery.

"I think he likes your work," Candy whispered to Crow.

"Yeah, that's great. But what the hell does that mean?"

She threw up her hands B-boy style and said, "Yo, home slice, too early to tell."

Crow caught Bones turning the bottle up for the third time and snatched it from him. "I thought you was drinking wine, man. Leave a nigger a little of the only thing he's drinking."

Across the room, Alton fell out of his chair. His cup, freshly filled with wine, hit the floor with a splash. Crow looked around the room and said to no one in particular, "His photographs *are* interesting."

Geoff returned wearing a green Shetland pullover, black jeans, and white deck sneakers. He had washed his face, leaving a little eye shadow and liner over one eye. Busy taking rubber bands out of his hair, he missed seeing Alton take his nose dive onto the floor and didn't even notice him lying there, prone on the floor in the doorway. He almost tripped over him.

"All right, Alton, it's time to go," he said while bending over to pick him up off the floor. Alton began to protest, but Geoff eased him out the door amid a flurry of slurred curses.

Candy had to tell Bones to close his mouth. He was standing there looking at the real Geoff. He remembered seeing this person at the club but never put the two together. Geoff caught Bones's open mouth.

"What the fuck are you gawkin' at, son-of-a-hippie white trash?" Bones didn't reply but did shut his mouth. Geoff continued removing the rubber bands from his hair. When he finished, he placed four chairs around the table and wiped up the spilled wine with a few paper towels.

He pulled a black canister from his pocket and placed it on the center of the table. "Anybody care for a few lines?" he asked.

"I'd rather talk about the paintings," Crow said. Candy walked over to the table carrying two canvases. Bones followed behind Crow carrying the third. Before sitting down, Candy spread the paintings she had on the table and then took the one Bones carried over and propped it up in front of the table on an extra chair. Geoff had already opened the canister and taken a few blows. They passed it around, making various comments on the quality. Crow put what was left of the seemingly bottomless bottle of Remy on the table, and that passed from hand to hand too. Candy poured hers into the cup she still had.

Crow, after his second go-round with the blow and the bottle, actually peered into the bottle and muttered, "I gotta buy all my liquor from that store," and put the bottle back down on the table for another go-round. Then he said, "Yeah, all this shit is great. Less than half an hour ago, I was a nigger, and now I'm cool-as-a-motherfucker and a member of the joint chiefs of staff or some shit. But you still ain't said shit about the art."

Bones, who was waiting for Candy to pass the canister, said, *"Be chilly, Crow,"* kinda slurring the words all together, while extending his hand at her.

Geoff, who had just finished the last of the Remy, said, "Crow's right. I'm sure he can get drunk and sniff coke anywhere. He's here about his art."

He paused, holding the bottle over his open mouth, hoping for one last drop of cognac to trickle out. "I really like your stuff," he said. "But there ain't much we can do about it tonight. I think . . ." He stopped and looked at his watch. "It's ten after twelve. We should get high for a bit longer and then shoot over to the club. I'll tell people that I've found a new artist, introduce you around, and show this shit tomorrow night. If we play this right, we might be able to make you the new darkie in town. But you know, Crow, my man," Geoff said, "three paintings ain't no whole lotta stuff. We should have at least eight, ten pieces for a decent exhibit."

Crow shot back, "That's the fucking problem, man. I'm three months behind on my rent, and the landlord won't let me in until I bring him some dollars. I can't get to nothing else. That's why I'm down here in the first place. I'm trying to sell these so I can get into my apartment."

"Man, I sell art to make a commission," Geoff said. "I can't just buy them off you. If all you got is these, I'll just have to take some of those photos down and put these up, make it a group show."

"Yeah, man, I hear that." Crow shook his head.

Bones was quick to add, "Now that that's settled, let's get outta here and get high."

Geoff sang in a very bad falsetto, "I second that emotion," and reached past Bones to Candy and grabbed the blow out of her hand.

Now that her hand was free, she reached down and rubbed Crow's leg and whispered, "Don't worry, we got this."

The time was one-twenty in a very strange morning. Geoff closed the only half-empty black canister and threw the empty rosé bottle away. Crow agreed to leave the paintings in the gallery after Candy assured him that they were safe there. Geoff noticed the folder for the first time and asked about it.

"It's just some shit I'm writing."

Feigning shock, Geoff's voice went back up to drag octave when he said, "You paint *and* write? I might have to take back that 'primitive' comment. I guess *Jeffy* can be wrong sometimes."

Outside the gallery, Geoff pulled the gate down and snapped the lock into place. Before they headed further downtown and east, Candy decided to hug Crow and run her tongue along the side of his face. He didn't respond. Stepping back, her hands still around his waist, she couldn't read the look on his face. Was it worry? She pulled him close again and whispered, "Ain't no *thang* for a player, right?"

The coke made his throat dry and his stomach jumpy. He didn't bother to explain, he just pulled away, saying, "All this is just regular nine-to-five shit. I just ain't with all this overtime."

Sold Auction Lot 2001-1 Male Nigra (2000)

6

CHAOS

AS THEY WALKED, Geoff thought about ways to apologize to Crow for his racist comments earlier at the gallery. Finally, he just blurted out, "Look, Crow, I really didn't mean all those stupid-ass things I said before. It's just that down here, you get so into the role you're playing, you forget what's real and what's just for show."

The street they walked along was much darker than the one before it. The last one had intermittent bodegas, bars, and social clubs of a sort, which may have once been mom-and-pop-type stores that sold anything from religious artifacts or kosher foods to pet supplies. Now it was home to fly-by-night designer clothing boutiques. So many of the old buildings remained, majestic architecture intact, that even after the transition, the block had retained much of its original flavor. But this block didn't need to retain flavor. Littered mostly with rat-infested, damn near condemned tenements, its *flavor* had endured. Slivers of light squeezed from behind drawn shades, creating faint halos in apartment-window borders. But except for the streetlight at the corner of C and the spinning yellow light of the "All-Night" deli, the rest of the block was dark. Midway down the block, a group of all-night men stood on a stoop with their hands flailing about their heads, emphatically discoursing on the finer points of gentrification and the recent yuppie incursion. To an outsider, the voices would have sounded loud and angry.

Crow waited awhile before responding, thinking about the "dumb nigger" role he was playing himself. "Yeah, Geoff, it gets kinda complicated being all these people at the same time. Sometimes it gets so confusing I wonder if we ain't all real and all fake at the same fucking time. But I ain't never met a white man that didn't believe some of that shit on some level. It had to come out of your mouth from somewhere."

Candy looked at Geoff and said, "How much art does that cracker-homo shit sell, anyways?" Then she leaned in close to Crow's face and said, "I notice you slip back and forth too. Makes the trip all the more interesting when *you* do it, though."

Bones was conspicuously silent. He walked faster than the rest of them but slowed down every so often to let them catch up. "Is Bones always this hyper?" Crow asked Candy.

"Yeah, Bones is usually hyper, but it'll get worse as we go further east and the density of certain ethnic groups intensifies. I'm pretty sure he has no idea, though. I don't think he's a bigot, per se, and I know he doesn't think he is. The best way I can explain it is that his heart is big, but it pumps Kool-Aid. And I think he just can't escape his background. He's one of those kind of white boys who can only relate to people who act in a particular way. I don't think he could really even deal with *Italians.*"

"What the fuck you talking about? I thought he was from down here and ain't had two nickels to rub together. Who is he not to be able to *deal* with somebody?" Crow asked incredulously.

"Yeah, he's from down here—by way of *Westchester.*"

The thing that Bones had not explained to Crow during his daddy-suicide story is that he had come from one of those hippie families who, even when piss-poor, held elitist values and felt entitled, while considering themselves staunchly liberal. They had an upper-class mind-set, despite apparent economic circumstances, because hippism was an upper-class phenomenon about rich kids choosing to reject their inherited privilege. Most people knew who they were, though. Even the cops treated them in an upper-class way while arresting them.

Candy continued, "So Bones was a child of upper-class parents who rejected certain trappings of privilege but instilled in him all these upper-class, liberal, paternalistic values. He might have hung out with niggers and wanted to get it on with 'Spanish' chicks—even though I doubt he ever met anybody from *Spain*—but he knows who he is. *Poor* to people like Bones ain't got nothing to do with having money. They would all deny it, but poor or rich is all tied to their notion of social hierarchy. Even if he ain't had a dime in the last two weeks, he ain't *poor. Poor* people don't give a fuck about art shows; *poor* people don't get into those clubs; shit, poor people ain't even got the right to wear cheap old clothes. Poor motherfuckers wear cheap new clothes. Rich motherfuckers like *Marvin* wear cheap old clothes. Just another aspect of the game, because poor people ain't got *Marvin's* options. He wants to be in the game, but he don't want it to play him too close because it might rub off. He never talks about it, but Marvin has an out. Whenever it starts to get too scary, too dirty, or too real, he can leave this place and go back to the house his mother's family left her, which she will leave him. Nothing is what it seems, Crow; not Geoff, not Bones, not me. I've got a master's in art history and appraisal. That's why *mi tío* is so pissed at me half the time. Alls he wants is for me to get a good job and leave from around here before I end up like everybody else in our family: in jail, in rehab, or dead. You're probably not what you seem, either."

Crow was really starting to like Candy a lot. She was smarter than Crow usually appreciated in a woman he wanted to fuck, and she was starting to talk too much for his personal comfort level to be maintained. It was fine when she was talking about Bones really being from *Westchester* and herself. *Did she say she had a master's?* But when she turned her attention in the direction of Crow's game, he needed something to distract them both from what she was saying and what she was *seeing.*

He eased his hand off Candy's shoulder, past her jacket, into the opened top buttons of her shirt, and over her breast. He heard her gasp. His hand hardly lingered, but before he returned it to her shoulder, his thumb and forefinger found her nipple and pinched. She exhaled as his hand retreated, and then she quickly zipped her jacket to the top. He whispered a comment that covered size, firmness, and temperature. Without a word, she grabbed hold of Crow's shoulder with one hand and lifted her entire body up off the ground. With one easy, almost effortless motion, she landed the full force of her weight on Crow's left foot. Crow cried out, more out of shock than pain. Embarrassed, he quickly shut his mouth and endured the *pain* in silence.

Bones, half a block ahead, was startled by the scream and froze. Looking around nervously, he sputtered, "Wh-what the fuck happened?"

"Stubbed my toe, man, keep moving," Crow snapped, limping along and shaking his head. He couldn't believe she *did* that shit.

Crow could hear Geoff behind him, talking to himself and totally absorbed in his own trip. Oblivious to what was going on right in front of him, Geoff hadn't heard a thing. He was still rationalizing his actions. Eyes cast to the ground and muttering to no one in particular about how the single most important thing in this environment was image. He really hadn't meant the things he said earlier. Just as Crow stopped to go into the store with the spinning yellow lights, Geoff ended his digression with the fact that not only had he been a member of the SDS, but he'd kept in touch with Bobby Seale all these years, and some of his best friends were black.

Crow entered the store and saw that the man behind the counter was smoking a joint. A very large pistol hung on his hip from a holster that was dotted with silver studs and red crystals. It reminded Crow of a toy one he had when he was a kid. On his way to the cooler, he remembered a belt buckle that he used to wear back then as well. It had a derringer clipped onto it that fired a little plastic bullet when he expanded his stomach. At the bottom of the cooler he found the big forty-ounce bottle of Old Gold that he wanted.

This should hold us till we get there, he thought to himself.

Outside, Candy was telling Geoff that Crow didn't need any more explanations. Bones was rocking from foot to foot and wanted to know what Crow went into the store for. Candy, who was good at sucking her teeth, did it loudly enough for everyone to hear as Geoff continued to insist that sometimes he gets too far into the role. Bones and Geoff shut up abruptly when two men brushed past them to enter the store. Nobody noticed the unmarked gray Plymouth Fury when it parked across the street. When the store door closed behind the fat black man smoking the cigar and the middle-aged white dude wearing sneakers and a field jacket, Candy said, "I wish Crow would hurry the fuck up. That was Dave and his partner who just went in there. I hope it's not a bust."

Coming from the back to the counter, Crow still concentrated on kids' games. Done with cowboys, he had drifted into memories of playing Hot Peas and Butter on warm summer nights. Seeing the two cops at the counter didn't surprise him, but he was surprised to see that the joint just lay there burning in the ashtray as the white cop told the man behind the counter that he didn't need a bag for that half-pint of gin he'd asked for. He took the gin from the guntotin' clerk and put it in the top pocket of his field jacket.

The black cop turned and gave Crow a long look. The inspection started at the top of Crow's head and ended at the laces of his boots. Then the cop put his hand on his belt and said, "Brooklyn, huh?"

"You know it, boss. You look like Brooklyn too."

The cop pulled the cigar from his mouth. "Do or die, Bed-Stuy," he said.

Crow set the bottle on the counter with a thud and stuck out his hand as he said, "Home slice," but the cop ignored it and stuck the cigar back in his mouth.

"I'm workin'. I hope you ain't." The cop's words came out from behind a thick cloud of cigar smoke.

Crow dug into his pocket, pulling out a few bills to pay for the beer. Pushing them across the counter, he said, "Nah, brother, this one's entirely pleasure."

As the white cop made for the door, the man behind the counter stuck the joint back in his mouth and wrote something down on a small yellow pad. Before the door closed, the fat black cop said, "Careful with that pleasure. Neighborhood's crawlin' with AIDS."

Crow called out, "Good looking out." The car door slammed shut.

Crow came out of the store tilting the bottle to his head. Bones complained about the brand, and Candy dashed inside and quickly returned munching from a bag of barbecue pork rinds. Geoff simply asked Crow to pass him the bottle, which he did.

Across the street Crow saw the white cop turn his bottle up too. Do-or-Die Bed-Stuy was behind the wheel. He made a poor attempt at pulling out fast and burning rubber. It turned out flat. Then, as they zigzagged down the street, he beeped the horn three times, which made Crow smile.

Despite his complaints, Bones drank his fair share of the brew. Candy offered but wasn't disappointed that nobody wanted any of her pork rinds. As they walked away from the store, Crow tried to figure out whether or not he'd ever run into Officer Do-or-Die Bed-Stuy before. He was certain he'd never been busted by him. He'd only been snatched twice. Once in high school at a demonstration and then out of state when he was in college. Both times he was popped by a honky pig, as they were fondly called back then. Something about the cop was unsettlingly familiar. But he settled it by reckoning that the brother lived in the 'hood and he must have seen him in a laundromat or something.

When they turned toward Houston Street at Avenue D, they heard shouting from down the block, which sounded like the beginning of a fight. Candy ran the back of her hand across her lips and, while passing the 40 Dog to Crow, began translating. "One of them guys' wife just called him and his friends bums and threatened to take the kids and go back to San Juan if he didn't come upstairs. His boys told him to hurry up and finish his beer or he wouldn't get no pussy for a month. He said that was never going to happen because he wore the pants and that the only reason any of them would say something like that is because none of them was man enough to keep a wife as long as he had. Do you believe that shit? And Tío Manny wants to know when I'm gonna get married and have babies. Shit, I'd rather sew the damn pussy up."

Walking beside them now, Bones sarcastically commented that women of good breeding didn't speak in that manner. Candy responded in kind, saying, "Bones, you're so right. However, I may be exempted in view of possessing great beauty. As we all know, money and rare beauty transcend such restrictions."

Geoff added, "My dear, you forget to mention art," his voice now falsetto.

Crow picked up the end of the conversation and asked, "How do white boys like you who be fronting in dresses become culture? And a brother with a Ph.D. can't get no play 'less he playin' some Stepin Fetchit?" Putting the beer and the folder on the ground, he segued into an exaggerated B-boy stance. "And you!" he shot at Bones. "You slacker motherfucker, word!" They all stopped to watch Crow. "Trying to pass me off as culture is just part of yo' game. You don't have no knowledge of what me or this art be about, devil. Word is bond!"

Candy clapped. Geoff wanted to know if he really meant what he said. Crow told him that his eyeliner was smeared. Bones said, "Art is the universal expression. It's both game and culture."

"Yeah, Marv, it's some shit like that," Crow said, then he bowed. He grabbed the folder and the beer on his way up and continued down the block.

At the corner, Crow passed Bones the bottle and asked, "Where the hell is this at?"

Bones and Candy yelled in unison, "A few more blocks!"

Since Crow never addressed Geoff's question, Geoff became petulant. He paused to look into a car's side-view mirror to check his eyeliner, though. They crossed Houston Street.

"Even though you went through that elaborate apology," Crow said to Geoff, "they was just words, because you never really thought there was anything wrong with coming off on me like you did. And I'll bet I'm not the first, because you believe most of that shit you talk. If I hadn't called you on it, you would have seen no reason to apologize."

Geoff looked hurt. "I guess you're right, Crow," he said.

Not one to lose an opportunity, Candy added, "You know he's right."

On the other side of Houston was an open parking lot. Geoff suggested that since the club was only a block and a half away, they duck behind some cars and take a few blows before they went in. He didn't get any protests. Bones finished the beer, Candy the pork rinds, and then each took two healthy hits.

There were a few people standing outside the club. Where windows had been was now covered over by graffitied sheets of tin. Three young girls spotted Candy coming up the block and ran over, asking her to get them in. "I'll come back out and get you in later," she replied.

One of the girls pushed a bill into Candy's hand and asked, "Promise?"

Pushing the bill back into the girl's hand, Candy laughed. "Promise, cross my heart and hope to die," she said.

Bones rang the bell. A short, fat guy with round glasses opened the door. A red light burned overhead in the vestibule. The doorman wore an empty shoulder holster, but stuck in the waistband of his plaid polyester pants was an old military .45. He waved them in and said, "Welcome to Club Chaos. A little early for *you,* ain't it, Bones?" Then he scanned Bones and Geoff with a metal detector.

Crow was next, and the machine beeped when it detected the blade in his back pocket. Crow gave it to him, and he gave Crow a claim check. He took his time scanning Candy, rubbing the wand slowly up and down her thighs and over her breasts in circular motions. Candy told him to cut the shit. He asked how she would like having to do this shit from one to eleven in the morning. She said, "Fuck that, why don't you just go and buy some pussy?" He asked was she offering, but before she could reply, he pressed a buzzer and pushed the inner door open and waved them inside.

They had to step down to get to the first level. The floor had been dug out and was a good foot lower than the lobby. Not expecting that, Crow stumbled on his way inside. The floor was also covered by a thick layer of gravel, so when his foot hit, it slid out from under him. He struggled to regain his footing but still managed to maintain a modicum of cool. Crow realized as he walked farther into the club that the floor alternated between slight inclines and declines, which made walking tenuous. *Weird-ass design choice for a place with a bar in it,* he thought.

The ceiling must have been thirty or forty feet high. From it, nude or seminude men and women swung in nets that hung from chains. Scattered around the floor were huge steel oil drums. Some had chairs in front of them, others didn't. Along both walls there were black lacquer bars that ran the entire length of the club. High-backed stools were spaced intermittently along the bar on the left wall. Seated and standing at both bars were nude people of varying gender. Some were clearly either male or female. But there were other folks with breasts and penises, and some with vaginas and no tits. Some were dancing and some just lounging and sprawled on the bar.

The bartenders, all women, wore thin, super-tight, black latex body suits, which had holes cut out in front so that their breasts were exposed. They also wore matching latex, fingerless, elbow-length gloves and barbed leather dog collars. Crow grabbed Candy's arm and yanked her.

"Yo, baby, what kind of freak joint is this?" he asked.

Candy pulled away. "Crow, you're hurting me," she said. "Be cool, it's just something for the eyes. Just be cool."

"Yeah, okay, I'll try to play it your way. Just don't leave me nowheres alone, all right?" he said.

She moved closer to Crow and said suggestively, "Don't worry, I ain't going nowhere."

Bones and Geoff were already at the bar. Geoff ordered four Remys and called Crow and Candy over. "Tia," he yelled to the barmaid. "I want you to meet Crow Shade. He's this week's artist of the moment, and you're lucky enough to be one of the first to meet him."

Tia flashed her best barmaid smile and said, "Welcome to Chaos, Crow. I just love meeting new talent. You must be great if he's promoting your work." She grabbed a split of Moët from the box and handed it to Crow.

"This is on the house, love." Crow thanked her, not taking his eyes off her large pink nipples, both of which were pierced, with thick silver hoops dangling from them. Noticing his fascination, she lifted her breasts, shook them at Crow, and said, "Oh, you'll get used to these. Most nights just about everybody here sports a terrific set."

Crow looked around the club and saw breasts and other things of various sizes and shapes staring back at him. "I see what you mean," he said.

Bones said, "Shit, it's early, you ain't seen nothing yet."

As far as club time is measured, it was early—not quite two A.M. The club was pretty much empty, not counting the would-be actors employed by the club to be the naked people hanging from the ceiling and at the bars. Tia told Geoff that Maldonado had been in earlier and left a message for him with a small-time cocaine dealer called Front Street. Both Bones and Geoff nervously looked around the room. But Tia told them not to bother, Front Street and Club

Foot had both gone over to the projects about twenty minutes ago and probably wouldn't be back for a while. Bones asked Geoff in a low voice, "What does Maldonado want to talk to *you* about?"

Geoff muttered something, then just shook his head.

Crow was having problems getting the cork out of his split. "Give that to me," Candy said, reaching for the bottle. Wrapping her shirttail around the cork, she effortlessly twisted it back and forth a few times before it popped. Crow looked embarrassed that she opened the bottle with such ease. However, the real deal was that the bottle was open. When Candy motioned to pass it to him, Crow insisted that she have the first sip. She got a straw off the bar and stuck it down the bottle's neck. "All the girlies out the way drink cham-pag-ne with a straw," Candy said.

Bones turned around in time to see Geoff walk across the floor and sit down with a couple who occupied a dark corner table. Crow noticed this too. "What's up with that?" he asked. "Geoff ain't even touch his Remy."

"It must have something to do with that dude who's looking for him," Bones answered in a hushed voice.

Out of nowhere, Maldonado appeared behind Candy and was about to say something when she passed Crow the bottle. "Are you going to help me drink this? After all, you're the man of the hour," she said. Maldonado slipped back into the shadows unseen.

Contrary to how it may have looked to Bones and Crow, the conversation going on across the room was less than important. It consisted primarily of standard greetings and local news. The man at the table wore a black suit that matched his black-on-black 1980 Mercedes four-door sedan, parked a car's length away from the club's front door. The curling antenna on the car's trunk indicated that he possessed the kind of status meriting a phone in his car. Only Maldonado and possibly four or five other close associates knew that the phone company had cut his service two months ago. Four and a half weeks ago to the day, he had been fired as Maldonado's bodyguard and gofer. Geoff knew about the phone.

The conversation at the table drifted from the exhibit earlier to Black Suit's wife complaining about being tired of coming to Chaos. At least two nights a week, she told Geoff how most of the people who came here were sick and confused. Usually wives received undivided attention regardless of their conversation's merit, so Geoff had to sit and listen until she ran out of conversation or her husband told her to shut the fuck up.

The wife was fully aware that neither of them was really paying her the slightest bit of attention, but it amused her to see if they could respond to her at the proper intervals. Somewhere between telling Augusto that he should be looking for a regular job and that because he got fired, her trip to see her mother next month had to be canceled, Geoff thought he heard her say, "We should leave. Maldonado ain't here, and you know my sister's with the baby."

Augusto's eyes glazed over. "Fucking crackhead bitch," he said. "Last time she watched the kid, we came home to find the ho sucking some fat white guy's dick for five bucks. Damn baby was sleeping right next to her on the couch." He patted the small gun stuck in his waist. "If that bitch's got somebody in the house this time, I'm gonna blow both their fucking brains out." He looked at his wife and then at Geoff and said, "Yo, man, I'd better cut out and get home before this fucking crackhead sells my TV or something. Tell Maldonado when he gets back to give me a call at the house, all right?

Before Geoff could respond, the wife said, "Call you where? The phone was cut off yesterday, and the car phone ain't worked in weeks. And don't talk about my sister. She's going into detox."

Augusto said, "Shut up and get your goddamn coat." As his wife got up and walked away muttering obscenities, Augusto rose to follow her. "That bitch is going into detox like I'm gonna grow two more inches a dick," he said to Geoff as he was leaving.

Candy had gone to the bathroom, leaving Crow in Bones's care. He was well into telling Crow yet another club adventure. Each story had the same theme: mountains of drugs and sex with multiple women with Bones always playing the leading role. Crow knew he was putting plenty of yeast in the details, but considering what he'd seen so far, he was pretty sure Bones wasn't outright lying.

Bones was busy talking Crow into oblivion when Geoff reappeared at the bar. The DJ was mixing Run-DMC's "Peter Piper" and the Beastie Boys' "No Sleep 'Til Brooklyn." Bones hadn't heard Geoff return, and when he reached for his glass, Geoff's arm brushed Bones's side. The contact shut the conversation down, startling Bones, who spun around, causing Crow to look up also. "Oh, shit. It's only you, Geoff. So what's up with Augusto?" Bones stammered, trying to play off his fright. It was too late, though. It had now become clear to Crow that what Candy was telling him about Marvin was true.

"Well, who'd you think it was? Terminal Ill, maybe," Geoff chided, only half kidding.

From the speakers, Run-DMC's Run was rapping, "Peter Piper picked peppers, but Run rocks rhymes," and was cut by Ad-Rock of the Beastie Boys declaring, "Our manager's crazy, he always smokes dust, he's got his own room at the back of the bus." The DJ started scratching the record, finishing with the Beastie Boys screaming, "No Sleep 'Til Brooklyn!" Crow muttered under his breath, "No shit. Like some suburban white boy's gotta tell me that."

Bones, in typical liberal fashion, wanted to know what Crow thought of rap music. "Russell Rush could make money and rappers out of three bald-headed, stripe-ed-assed monkeys," Crow said, and laughed. "But seriously, anybody can throw a scratch and lift a sample. The rapper's worth depends on what they're talking about. It used to be that lyrics kept it real. These days, some of the shit is still real, but most of it is just for show. It's getting to be like everything else, about the dollars. It's a hard world for young boys. So if rap keeps them from acting crazy and killing each other over sneakers and leather jackets, while making it possible to feed their kids and buy houses for their mothers, then I'm down with it."

"Crow. *You* should be a preacher."

"Fuck you, *Marvie,*" Crow snapped. "Nothing means shit to you nohow." Bones wasn't ready for that kind of response. It was too serious and personal. He wanted to defend himself, but just then, Candy returned. She stood between them smiling, effectively ending the discussion.

Bones managed to spit out, "Ah, just fuck it."

She turned to face him. "Fuck what?" she asked.

Geoff laughed and said, "Fuck the pope. We were having a discussion concerning the continued usefulness of religion in the twentieth century. We were wondering if the pope was actually the devil's messenger."

Crow said, "Actually, what was more important was if a frog's ass was watertight."

"What the fuck are you talking about?" Candy asked.

Bones mimicked the way Candy sucked her teeth. "What it all boils down to was whether grits are groceries or not," he said.

"Oh, I get it now," Candy said, looking at the three of them. "If I hadn't intruded, by now there would be a heated debate on hearing trees that fell in the forest. Well, excuse the hell out of me."

Crow sucked the straw until it made the noises straws make when they've pulled the last drop from a glass. Then he slammed the bottle on the bar and ran the back of his hand across his mouth. Satisfied that he had accomplished the necessary level of exaggeration, he said, "My dear, you have taken us completely wrong. We should apologize to you."

"Affirmative!" Geoff added in equally dramatic fashion and continued, "Let's not forget the first paragraph of Chapter Two of Six-Toed Myron's Rules of Order. It clearly states that beautiful Puerto Rican women are not required to apologize in private clubs while standing within a twenty-foot proximity of the left-hand bar."

"How the hell could I have forgotten that?" Candy asked. "If you gentlemen would excuse me, I got someone I want Crow to meet." Then she hooked her arm through Crow's and told him to come the fuck on.

As Crow was being pulled away, he turned to Bones and Geoff

and said, "Whatever the fuck. It's got to be better than talking nonsense with the two of you."

As she pulled Crow away, Bones called out, "Good luck, Crow, you're going to need it."

Still pulling Crow toward the back of the club, Candy asked what all the bullshit was about. Crow yanked back, saying, "Stop pulling so hard, I'm coming. I like you, but you don't own me." She stopped and snatched her arm away. As she stepped back, he saw that he had upset her. He tried to say something, but she beat him to it.

"If you think that I think that, then you can go back over there. I don't need nobody fucking with my head."

Crow stepped close to her and hooked his arm back through hers, saying, "Damn, baby, don't start going off. I ain't mean nothing by it." When she didn't respond, he continued, "No shit. It wasn't nothing to that, really."

Looking at him for a second, she said, "It's all right. It's too early in the evening for us to start getting strange."

Still angling toward the back of the club, Crow saw that they were coming to a cluster of barrels on one of the elevated platforms. Hanging in a net above the barrels was a woman with one candle burning in each hand. She was letting hot wax drip on different parts of her body.

On a stool beneath the net, a woman sat with her forehead pressed flush on the barrel top. Her hair was extremely long and curly and flowed over the top and down the side of the barrel. Standing on the floor beside her was a crystal bucket holding a magnum of Perrier-Jouët champagne and a few crystal flutes. She didn't lift her head but, aware of their presence, said, "Come, sit with Melissa."

Spell to Unlock Closed Doors (2002)

7

Melissa

CROW AND CANDY silently sat on the stools at the barrels positioned on each side of Melissa, until Crow became impatient. "Yeah, I'm sitting with Melissa, so what happens next?" he asked.

Melissa abruptly raised her face from the barrel, startling Crow. Even in the dimly lit club, Crow was struck dumb by eyes impossibly green, like emeralds almost. He was instantly transfixed. He was completely immobilized, as if a light had been switched on inside him, albeit dimly. Next came an indescribable sensation followed by an overwhelming vision: an albino snow leopard. Its eyes were large, almond-shaped, and also a mesmerizing green that hypnotized its prey. Crow felt as if he were being lured into something to be avoided at all costs and yet unavoidable. He was released from the vision as suddenly as he had been riveted by it and continued looking at Melissa.

In the club's bluish light, her pale yellow skin looked almost translucent. Her jet-black eyebrows arched high. Instead of her mouth ending in points at the corners, her lips kept going into a full, large, pouty, pink oval. As she sat erect in her seat, her black and silver hair draped over her shoulders and midway down her back. Some sections were matted like locks, others were braided, and the rest fell freely. She wore a black sweater that, although loose, did little to conceal her rather generous figure. Before she spoke again, she leaned over and kissed Candy lightly on the lips. She then set three glass flutes on top of the barrel and filled them with champagne.

"Candy tells me that you have brought some life into this graveyard. Take off your jacket and relax," Melissa said. "Have some of this wine." She spoke in a throaty whisper, so Crow had to concentrate to hear her over the music.

Crow slipped off his jacket and hung it over the back of the stool. He had no real idea of what had just gone down, but he knew that this *Melissa* had shaken him to the very core. He was very uncomfortable and *very* self-conscious. He decided to decline the champagne. "Nah, that's okay," he said.

Melissa gestured to the folder that Crow laid on the barrel top. "Candy told me a little of the story you have there."

Crow turned to Candy and snapped, "When did you do that?"

Before Candy could respond, Melissa interrupted. "That's not important. The story sounds interesting, and I'd like to read it, but right now, I'd rather you improvise. Can you make something up just for me?" She lifted a flute to her lips with one hand and used the other to move a curtain of hair out of her face. Crow noticed that on each of three fingers of both hands, she wore some type of large ring. On both arms, she wore cuffs and bangles stacked elbow to wrist.

Crow was unsure how he was going to play this and stalled. "What, are you crazy?" he snarled.

Melissa, not going for it, said, "Yes. If that's possible."

Candy jumped in. "Crow, it doesn't have to be anything elaborate, just a couple of lines. What you've written already is so beautiful, a few lines should be a piece of cake. And Melissa loves performance."

"Just who the hell is *she* that I gotta do anything, much less improvise and perform? I ain't got nothing to say at the moment," Crow said.

Melissa chuckled long and throaty. "That's almost refreshing. A poet with nothing to say. I'm surprised you're that in tune with a world most people perceive to have no purpose but pretend otherwise. Every writer I've ever had either tried to force a design on a void or buried themselves under mountains of pens trying to describe the indescribable. Your approach is unique. You actually have nothing to say about something. Now, that is an accomplishment that should be left to stand as the ultimate end of insight. The stack of paper in front of you throws that bullshit out the window. So you might as well get busy and kick a little verse, brother. Although it might be foolish to offer, let's see what you can come up with. Use me as your subject. No pen or brush has come close to doing me justice in years. It would please me to see you try."

"Nice speech," Crow said. "All right, give me the damn champagne." She passed Crow one of the flutes. He took a long swallow and looked into Melissa's eyes again. They brought the snow cat back to mind. Crow had no idea what to say. Instinctively, he stopped trying, and the words began to flow:

From the mouth of my den I watch
spinning crystals fall and mix with this
endless blanket of white. Lazy, I lick my
paws and adjust my back. Some time ago my
restless spawns went for hunt and now
will not return. I do not miss them nor
should I.

Never can I sleep at
night. My wide and
terrible Emerald eyes.
Something moves not
far away.

Crow paused, gulped champagne, and continued, saying:

When I rise and stretch for hunt I'm
born, each turn and step is slow and
steady sex and I begin the climax picking
up speed. Seen too late I complete the
orgasm my body's weight forcing the prey
down, buried in wet snow. My Hungers done
and caught again without proper Change
for the cigarette machine.

Candy shook her head sharply. "Oh, shit," she said, and laughed, looking over at Melissa. Crow finished his glass and slid it in front of the bottle for a refill.

Melissa looked playfully at Candy and said, "You lied, baby. He's not a poet. He's a wolf in a stolen sheep's coat. A vision with a sweet mouth."

"Wasn't that what you wanted?" Crow asked.

Her emerald eyes narrowed, and she told Crow, "It was all that and more."

"Great, does that mean I'm a member now?" He stood up and pushed the chair away. "If you get me a cane, Candy, and a straw hat, I could do a little soft shoe," he said. His arms extended in a flourish, Crow affected an exaggerated finale.

Melissa smiled again. "No, but some of this might do," she said, as she pulled a big baggie from her purse filled with cocaine.

The shiny rocks in the bag reflected the available light and caught Crow's eye. While rubbing his hands together and licking his lips, he said, "Damn, now that's a *big* finish."

"Not hardly. Wrong bag," Melissa said, and pulled out another. This one was filled with fat brown mushrooms caps. "Deep inquiries and keen insights require something more subtle."

Candy's eyes lit up when she saw the mushrooms. She took the bag out of Melissa's hand and held it close to her face. "Shit, they're fresh too, full tips and wet, just beautiful . . ." she said.

Crow cut her short with, "I ain't tripped in years, and I sure ain't about to start doing that shit again, especially not with some shit I ain't never did before." But that didn't affect Candy's interest.

"Who got them for you?" she asked Melissa.

"You know I have my sources, baby," she cooed as she went back into her seemingly bottomless bag, pulling out a pack of tarot cards.

"Crow, have you had your cards read before?" she asked, spreading the cards across the top of the barrel.

"Yes, I have, but I am not hardly interested in your freak-sex-club interpretation of my future or anything else."

Melissa looked at him intently and asked, "Why, are you afraid of the truth?"

Without missing a beat, Crow responded, "No, I'm just not into card tricks, and I don't know you. And you can keep the mushrooms too." Then Crow asked for and was handed the baggie of blow. After taking a few healthy hits, he pushed himself back from the barrel and grabbed his jacket. When he got up, he whispered in Candace's ear, "Fuck the mushrooms. Get the blow for later." Shrugging into his jacket, he said to Melissa, "Nice meeting you, peace, groovy, way out, and all that, but I don't see how sitting here with you is making me any money. Let me know if you want to buy a painting. Until then, I'm wasting my time." As he walked away, he half turned back. "Candace, I'm going back over there," he said, gesturing across the dance floor toward the bar, and kept walking.

Crow stepped off the platform and began navigating the floor's rises and falls back to the bar. The blow was smoking, so when he reached the edge of the bar, he held on to the red Lucite rail, chuckled, and clenched his jaw. Soon he realized he was grinding his teeth. Once steadied and no longer concerned with the floor's rising and dipping hills and dales or sliding in the gravel, he once again found the whole situation absurd. His mind then switching to introspection, he thought, *Damn, I sold her that poem. Just put some words in order and made her night. That shit was easy.*

He looked down the length of the bar for Bones and Geoff. There was another guy standing and talking with them. It looked as if Bones was gesturing to Crow, urging him to come over. At the same time, Tia had placed a glass on the bar in front of Bones, who then laid a few dollars down. As she bent to scoop them up, he reached over and pinched one of her pink nipples. As Crow approached where Bones was standing, he clearly heard Tia spit at Bones. "Fuckin' asshole!" she yelled.

Bones chuckled, turning toward Crow with the glass extended. "For me, man?" Crow asked. "How thoughtful. Must have been Geoff's idea—or poisoned or some shit."

Bones quickly pulled the drink back, without spilling any. "Is my credibility that low with you, that you give some shit like that to me?"

"Damn, Marvin," Crow snapped back. "Everything ain't always that serious, homes." And then, hissing with exasperation, Crow said, "Motherfuckers down here need to learn to chill a little." He reached over and took the drink off the bar.

"That woman Candy dragged me over to meet is certifiable." Crow was on to the next thought. "She acts like she's from another planet," Crow said halfheartedly, without looking over at Bones.

"Melissa?" Bones asked, relieved that Crow had shrugged him off. "Nah, she's all right," he said. "But if you'd been doing half the shit she's been doin', as long as she been doin' it, you'd be a little eccentric or something too."

Crow turned to look at Bones and got a clear shot of Melissa on the platform, slightly above the dance floor. She was sitting with her face pressed against Candy's. He stared at her for a few seconds. "What are you talking about? She don't even look thirty-five," he said in disbelief.

"Nope. We were all at her fifty-fifth birthday party two weeks ago."

"Damn." Crow cut Bones off. "She is one fine, old-enough-to-be-my-mama motherfucker, ain't she, though?"

"You ain't never lied," Bones testified in response.

Crow, Candy, and Melissa were still sitting with their heads together. In the glow of the candle, Melissa's face had appeared unlined. Crow stood there, holding his drink and shaking his head. Bones seemingly reappeared out of nowhere.

"Crow, I want you to meet my man." Geoff came over with this white guy wearing a suit. He pushed his open hand past Bones. Crow clasped and pumped it sharply.

"Crow, this is my main man, Lead Base Paint. Lead Base, Crow," Geoff continued.

Crow greeted him. "Yo, Lead, what it look like?"

"Same ole shit. The whole fucking thing is on its way to hell in a handbasket," Lead Base replied.

"Sounds like something I thought earlier," Crow quipped.

Bones laughed and said, "Yo, Crow, check the glass. Remy Royal, top of the line."

Crow lifted his drink to his nose and sniffed it. "Excellent, a might fruity, but still a great *vintage*. Not unlike a good bottle of 'seventy-two. A good year for Thunderbird as well, I believe. It had a brownish hue *that* year," he said.

Lead Base slapped Geoff on the shoulder. "A rare find, my man: art, talent, *and* culture! And here I am wasting time scouring the *art schools* for such a package."

Crow turned to Bones and asked, "Can't any of these motherfuckers play it straight for once?" Ironic, when you consider that he'd started it with his Remy wine-tasting act.

Bones seemed to be thinking the question over, so Geoff answered it. "Take all this shit seriously, and you'll be crazy as Melissa over there."

"Ah, Melissa's all right," popped Bones.

"She's real bugged out," Crow added. "And fine as a motherfucker. Other than that, I don't know *what* to make of *her.*"

"What is she, like, sixty?" Geoff asked. "How many real, damn-near-sixty-year-old titties look and act like *those?*"

Crow looked again, this time concentrating his attention on Melissa's breasts. "Damn," Crow said out loud. When he turned back, Lead Base Paint was standing in front of him.

Unlike the others he'd met this night, this guy in the suit looked pretty close to regular—that is, if you didn't focus on the thick black eyeliner and the long, twisted copper wires that hung from the five or six holes in his left ear.

"You think I look pretty normal, huh?" Lead Base asked. "You'd look normal too, if you had to work for a rental-car joint to pay bills. Shit, you look pretty normal yourself, except that being a spade puts you in a whole 'nother category."

"Spade! Did you say *spade? Spade?!*" Crow couldn't believe he'd heard right. "What the fuck you mean, *spade?!*"

Lead Base Paint backed up off Crow a little and sputtered, "Hey, *brother,* don't get so uptight. It's just an expression, you know, like . . . 'my nigger.' Hey, when I was a teenager, I wanted to be a coon myself. They got all the basketball and track scholarships and all the cheerleaders. And, you know what they say, a man ain't a man till he's had some *black* pussy. It was a compliment."

Crow's head was spinning. He was about to be madder at a cracker than he'd been in a long time. "Yeah, well, Pussy Base, is it? I'm about to put my foot up your wanna-be-a-coon ass." Crow slammed his glass down on the bar, splashing a little on his hand, and started moving for Lead Base, who had the nerve to scoot behind Bones and Geoff, yelling, "Whoa! Geoff, hold your *boy* off."

"Oh, I got your *boy,* motherfucker," Crow stormed.

Bones grabbed Crow's arm but released it just as quickly when he caught the look in Crow's eyes. Geoff stood fast between Crow and Lead Base Paint, who had started to back away into the crowd, saying, "Look, Geoff, I guess it would be better if I talk to you another time."

Over Geoff's shoulder, Crow yelled into Lead's face, "Another time had better be another day, because this fucking place is too small for you to enjoy the rest of the night, *cracker.*"

Once Lead was gone, Crow had turned back to the bar.

"Crow. Lead Base ain't no racist," Bones said, trying to calm Crow down. "He's got a baby with a Korean chick."

Crow snatched his glass off the bar and took a long swallow. "You expect me to believe that *this* motherfucker right here fuckin' some Chink bitch means he ain't a racist? Like the white man hasn't gone all over the world forcing himself on the women of all the people he conquered. Next you'll be telling me that Thomas Jefferson wasn't a slave owner because he made that Hemmings woman have five of his half-breed bastards. Sure, Lead Base Paint ain't no damn racist. None of you is. You just don't know what to fuckin' say, is all. *Fuck* him, and fuck *you.*"

He swallowed down the rest of his drink and slammed the glass back down on the bar again, this time shattering it. He pulled his hand away without a scratch. "Where the fuck is the bathroom?" Crow demanded from Bones, who was visibly shaken—more by what Crow had said than by how angry he was. He pointed in stunned silence to a dark space beneath the balcony on the other side of the still-pretty-empty dance floor. Without another word, Crow stomped off in that direction.

Behind the stairs leading up to the balcony, there was an open fire door that led into a red-lighted corridor. At the end of this passageway were two unmarked doors. Not caring if he chose the right one, Crow pushed hard on the first door he came to, slamming it against the inside wall and stepping in. He looked up to find himself inside a gray cement room with a wall of sinks, another of urinals, and four stalls, all stainless steel. He relieved himself in one of the urinals. Feeling a little less angry after his piss, he went over to the sink, rinsed his hands, and decided to splash some water on his face.

He stood staring at his reflection in the mirror above the sink and tried to remember why he was here in the first place. He asked himself why he couldn't just leave these motherfuckers right here. He remembered the paintings and the hustle and Candy. But things were getting more complicated by the minute. And what the hell was that shit with Melissa about—a snow leopard?

He looked down at his watch. It was early Saturday morning. Just yesterday afternoon he'd been sitting on his bed with nothing to his name. Today, that name was on people's lips—that and, apparently, some racial slur ready to jump off at him. He wondered when he was going to wake up from this dream and what price he was going to have to pay for dreaming it. He leaned forward and gripped the edges of the sink as his head began to swim. He was out of his element, he thought. He didn't know how this game was supposed to be played or even if he could keep making it up as he went along. Wishing he had another drink or some blow, he stared at his face in the mirror again. His usually glowing, dark-red skin was dry, taut, and ashy. His big brown eyes were glazed and fire-engine red. He splashed his face again, then asked his reflection, "Damn, what have you gotten yourself into this time?" He shrugged his shoulders, and his reflection answered, "Too far out to swim back now. Might as well keep on stroking." He shook his head and stumbled toward the door. "Damn, I'm higher than a motherfucker," he rasped.

Crow walked back through the fire door and met a writhing wall of scantily clad bodies, throbbing to a heavy bass line. The club had become packed with people—dancing, drinking, laughing, making out in corners, or just standing around pulsing in their own worlds. "Damn, how long was I in there?" he asked himself.

The balcony, completely empty when he'd gone in, was hopping. From where he was standing, Crow could see that all the tables and couches on it were strewn with seminaked and otherwise leather-clad body parts. The rubber-body-suited waitresses were running up and down the stairs with trays of drinks and ice buckets with bottles in them. He almost had to fistfight his way through the crowd. He was pressed with every step.

Standing at the foot of the stairs that led up the balcony, a brother, also dressed in the staff black rubber and sporting a gold wedge of hair running down the center of his otherwise smooth, bald head, directed the staircase traffic. Crow shook his head and thought, *If that nigger was related, I'd have to kick ass daily.*

The chick talking to the blond Mohawk had on a platinum Afro wig, a silver lamé jumpsuit, and the highest platform heels Crow had ever seen. *How the fuck is she walking?* he wondered.

In the middle of the dance floor, a group of short, heavily muscled white boys disjointedly "danced," shrieked, and kissed all over each other. They were naked, except for things that looked to Crow like eye patches . . . and *fig leaves?* That did it. Crow knew now that he was definitely out of his element. He felt totally out of place, and he'd had enough of this freak-show—hustle or no hustle.

When he finally made it back to the bar, Lead Base Paint was nowhere to be found. "Better not be. Fucking cracker," Crow snarled under his breath.

After having himself a good eye roll and teeth suck, he noticed that Tia had cleaned the glass off the bar. Even with fixing drinks and moving up and down the bar, Tia had managed to catch most of what had gone down. She attempted to get Crow's attention by making kissing-sucking noises at him. "Crow, baby, let me put something in another glass for you."

"Nah, that's all right, love, you don't have to do that," Crow said, trying not to take out what happened on her. Ignoring his objection, she poured Crow half a tumbler of Remy V.S.O.P. "They keep their eye on the Royal and Cordon Bleu, but this oughta hold you."

Hesitating only a moment, Crow half smiled at her and reached for the glass. "I don't like that fruity shit, anyway. This is my drink." He took a sip. "Here, take this," he said, sliding two crumpled dollars across the bar at her.

"What did I just say? You hear bad or something? Look, don't take this the wrong way, but I don't like or dislike any one type no more or less than I do another motherfucker I run into. But that don't mean I don't notice that it's hard enough just being black down here, that to have to pay these prices for drinks is just adding insult to injury." Crow understood that this was Tia's way of saying that she had not condoned Lead Base's bullshit. "By the way, you left your jacket over there," she said, gesturing toward the end of the bar. "Give it to me, and I'll put it and your folder under the bar for you. They're safe with me."

Tia slid the folder off the bar, and when Crow returned with the jacket, she hid them somewhere down and out of sight. He was starting to feel better. Tia's conversation had helped calm his nerves—and the V.S.O.P wasn't bad, either. He reasoned that Tia was probably being so nice because she wanted to screw him. Slipping on the gravel underfoot again, he moved to the edge of the bar and held on to the red Lucite rail. He looked to see if he could still make out what Candy and Melissa were doing on Melissa's platform from across the dance floor and slightly above the crowd.

8

The Game

Over at the barrel, Melissa had her cards spread out in front of Candace Maria, who was busy pulling a pebble of coke out of the baggie. Finding one she wanted, she smashed it between two tarot cards, reducing it to a fine powder. Then, with the edge of one card, she gathered it into a tiny mountain and used its corner to bring a portion of it up to a flaring nostril. After inhaling deeply, she wiped her nose with the back of her hand, dipped the card back into the mountain, and offered Melissa a hit. "Not right now." Melissa waved the coke away, shaking her head.

Turning her interest to Crow, Melissa said, "I triggered something in him. He's waking up now."

"Just like with me?" Candy asked.

"Not quite," Melissa replied. "Unlike you, he is *totally* unaware. He just thinks he's high . . . or *clever.* But it amazes me that he saw her, though, and that she was so gentle with him. He must have some shit with him."

"Yeah, he's got some shit, all right, but what?" Candy asked before taking another hit. Feeling the coke drain down the back of her throat, numbing her vocal cords. She knew it would be difficult to continue shouting over the music, so she decided just to sit there and sniff quietly.

"Let's see what the cards have to say," said Melissa, looking up just in time to see Candace with one of the cards still up her nose. Snatching it out of her hand, Melissa rolled her eyes at Candy and mumbled, "So disrespectful."

Melissa pulled the first card. "It's the Fool. Figures." The next card was the Hangman. Melissa looked up at the idiot hanging from the ceiling in the net above her. "That's about right." Then she turned over a third card. "This one's for Crow." It was the Hermit.

Candace Maria asked, "What's the Hermit mean? Crow seems like someone best left alone," she said, only half joking.

"Oh, I see, first disrespectful, now you play stupid," Melissa countered. "This is the card of attainment. What it means is that the divine mysteries reveal themselves only to those who are prepared. It means his journey is beginning."

Just then, back at the bar, Geoff leaned forward, rustled through his pockets, and took off into the crowd.

"Where the hell is he off to?" Crow asked Bones.

"That might have been his beeper going off, probably his wife looking for him again."

Crow wanted to know if she knew that Geoff ran around in dresses most of the time. "How the hell would I know?" Bones yelled over the music. "*I* thought he always rocked a dress. Shocked the shit out of me when I found out he was supposed to be straight, with a wife and kids and shit. Who would have figured? I'll tell you something, man, I'm getting tired of the hype and bull-shit and all this everybody faking shit all the time." Bones paused to wash down two pills with a screwdriver. "Maybe my father had the right idea, ya know? I mean, what the fuck is this about, anyway? I mean, look around you. What the fuck is all this about?"

Bones was sounding as if he was about to go all back into it—the daddy-suicide philosophizing and reminiscing he'd been doing when he and Crow had passed through Bones's old neighborhood.

Between still being a little ticked at the whole Free Base incident—or whatever the fuck his name was—fantasizing about what he could do with all that *Candy,* and just being hit by the second wave of all the shit he'd been doing that night, Crow was certainly in no mood for Bones's recollections. Unwilling to suffer another bout of nostalgia, he cut Bones off.

"Listen, Marvin, it's just about doing the best a lame can with the hand he's holding. All we got is the game; might as well play it to the bitter bust. Not to say shit about your old man, but the game ain't over till you get up from the table—and he just got up too soon. I know motherfuckers who thought they'd lost everything and took the whole pot in the end. You never know how it'll play out till it's over." Crow figured that he'd said enough, but before he could stop himself, he'd put a hand on Bones's shoulder and added, "It's a tough world out here. You've got to use whatever you've got to claim a piece of it for yourself." Crow had surprised himself with his own words and wondered if he was going to take his own advice. He slammed back the rest of his Remy and asked Bones, "What the hell kind of pills did you just take?"

"Excedrins, man. I keep a headache," Bones answered. Then Crow wanted to know if Bones was worried about that kid they ran into at the park. "Who, Terminal Ill? Nah, he ain't no problem. Everybody wants something. That don't mean they can get it." Then he turned to Crow and forced a smile. "I'm just as hard up as you. You know, scamming to keep it going. He ought to know by now he ain't getting paid."

Crow was thinking that Bones was basically all right, just a pain in the ass. But Crow still couldn't figure why he kept fronting as if he didn't have anything. He finally decided that Bones was probably just trying to be hard, to blend in. He was just a kid who hated having to depend on his mother's money but who knew that he wouldn't last a minute in the real world without it. Bones took a long swallow of another drink Crow had not seen him order and turned away.

Staring at the side of Bones's head there, Crow thought about going back over to sit with Candace Maria and Melissa, but they were no longer seated at the barrels. He scanned the club and found them on the dance floor together.

In the background, the DJ starting mixing wicked cuts of Jimi Hendrix, the Doors, and the Temptations. The lyrics of "Dolly Dagger" and "People Are Strange" were scratched back and forth on the turntable and then ended with "Ball of Confusion":

"Dolly Dagger, her love's so heavy, gonna make you stagger . . ."

"When you're strange, faces come out of the rain . . ."

"People moving out, people moving in. Why? Because of the color of their skin. Run, run, run, but you sure can't hide . . ."

And then more Doors, "The end of laughter and soft lights . . ." more Temptations, "Hippies moving to the hills . . ." and back to the Doors, "Father . . . I want to kill you; Mother I want to . . ." and then more Jimi, "She drinks her blood from a jagged edge . . ." Then the Temps finished off with "Runaway child, runnin' wild . . . better go back home where you belong . . ."

Crow turned to Bones and asked if he thought there was a message in the music.

"I wish this fucking headache would go away, I know that," Bones said.

Just then, Geoff reappeared at the bar, looking a little exasperated. "What's up?" Bones asked him.

Geoff replied, "Same old shit. My wife told me if I wasn't home in an hour, she was filing for divorce in the morning—only this time, I think she's serious."

"Well, I guess you better get to getting your ass on home, then," Crow said.

"Can't, Crow. Ain't nothing for me in Jersey. Whenever I'm there, I'm just faking it."

Crow thought, *A dress ain't faking it?*

"I'd rather be down here where we all know it's a game, so that makes it real," Geoff continued.

It struck Crow that the problem with this whole scene, Geoff and all these motherfuckers, was that everybody poured thick layers of philosophy into their emptiness but never succeeded in feeding their hunger. And Geoff was *still* talking. "One morning I came home about six or seven and forgot to take off my eye shadow. That hag wanted to know if I'd turned homo."

Bones muttered under his breath, "Seems like a reasonable question to me."

Geoff either didn't hear Bones or paid him no attention, because he kept on. "Asked me that bullshit in front of my children," he said. "Now all the damn kids wanna know is if Daddy's a fuckin' bone smuggler. Daddy's just tired of the bullshit." His pager went off again, vibrating against his hip. Extremely annoyed, he darted off again.

All around the club, folks tossed down booze, passed around joints, folded dollar bills, tin foil packages, plastic bags, and any other drug-related thing you could imagine. Crow couldn't help wondering how these motherfuckers remained upright, let alone negotiated the gravel to dance. Meanwhile, Melissa and Candace Maria had returned to the barrels and seemed to be involved in an intense discussion. Crow wondered if they were talking about him. He was tired and was real tired of this. He had just made up his mind to walk across the floor when he felt something slam past his arm. Geoff had squeezed next to him at the bar, looking agitated and preoccupied. Crow offered him a drink. Geoff ordered rye.

"Now, that's a real white-boy drink." Crow chuckled.

Geoff ran a hand through his hair, moving it back and away off his face. He looked droopy and as if he'd aged ten years since he'd gone to answer his page.

"Damn! What's wrong?" Crow asked.

"Not now, man," Geoff snapped. "I ain't in the mood."

"What the hell happened?" Bones asked.

"That page was from Maldonado," Geoff answered, his voice cracking. "I don't know how he got my pager number. But that doesn't matter, he has it now."

"Just who the fuck is Maldonado, anyway?" Crow wanted to know.

"Real estate developer, loan shark, landlord, Mafia muscle, you name it," Geoff answered nervously, gulping air.

"Well, what he want with you?" Crow asked.

Geoff slammed his elbows on the bar and smacked his face in his hands. "I used to be an investment banker a lifetime ago. I made a lot of money. But more important, I used to get hot investment tips. I found that a great way to double my earnings was to—how can I put this—*share investment information.* That's how I met Augusto. I made a huge amount of money with and for him on one real estate development tip. With my share, I bought up a bunch of property in the East Village, real cheap, out from under another bidder. It was Maldonado. He's been pissed ever since."

"If this happened so long ago, what's the big deal now?" Crow asked.

"I haven't had much luck with the artists I'm representing because the art scene has been a little dry lately. So I'm shopping around some of those properties for partners so that I can continue carrying my galleries. When Maldonado heard I was looking for buyers, he decided that if I'm selling, it's going to be to him or no one at all. So he's been scaring off all interested parties. On the phone just now, he threatened me. He said that if I didn't sell to him, I was going to have an accident. Then he'd pick up the property cheap." Geoff, nervous as hell, turned back to the bar and waved Tia over, ordered a double, and kept talking. "Do you know that prick was here in the club, standing right here behind us? He even told me what I was wearing and who I was with. He just wanted me to know that he could reach out and touch me anytime. He's one scary motherfucker. Maybe I should just give him what he wants." As soon as the rye hit the bar, it was down his throat.

Crow shook his head and looked at Geoff and Bones. He thought it was funny that it didn't matter how much money you had, it didn't solve your problems.

Bones was trying to talk to Geoff, who was trying not to listen. Crow was tired of yelling over the music. His head was throbbing from all the coke and alcohol, and it had just occurred to him that he hadn't eaten anything all day. It was definitely time to leave.

Crow turned to Geoff and said, "Look, don't sweat it. Like you said, the show'll be a sellout. Just chill and lay low until then. I'm about to break out. Where do you want to meet up later?"

Geoff pulled a card out of his wallet and handed it to Crow. "Come to the gallery about eight o'clock tonight. Here's the address. My pager number is there as well. Don't let me down, okay? I'll see you later."

"Yeah, don't worry, I'll be there. Besides, you've got my shit already."

"By the way, you'll need to bring a few more paintings. We got wall space to cover."

Crow's heart skipped a beat. He'd forgotten his earlier lie about being locked out. His mind raced to come up with an answer. Involuntarily he stammered, "Yeah, I'll see what I can do." He hadn't painted more than a wall white before.

Just as Crow and Geoff were about to shake hands, a man dressed in leather, looking like one of the goddamned Village People, came over and asked Crow if he wanted to dance. Crow said, "Fuck this shit! It's time to go *now!* Tia, give me my shit!"

"Honey, it's still early. Why leave so soon? Give it another hour."

Crow said, "Listen. Just give me my shit, so I can get the hell out of here, okay? I'm tired of fuckin' around with this freak show."

"Sure, Crow, anything you say." She passed him the jacket and the book. Before Bones or Geoff could say anything, Crow had downed the last of his drink and snatched up his things and was headed toward Candace and Melissa. This time, his feet followed the floor's contours with ease, and the gravel gave him no trouble.

Melissa was putting the cards away when Crow got there. She said, "Seems like you're ready to move on."

"Read that in the cards, did you?" Crow smacked facetiously, with a "You motherfucker, you," mumbled behind it.

"I could have, but it's more gratifying to read it in your eyes, nigga," she purred with a seductive sarcasm. "But it's the jacket and the book that did it for me."

"I'm ready too," Candy said. "Melissa, walking our way?"

"Which way is that?" Crow asked.

Candace nonchalantly answered, "Over to my house."

Crow's heart skipped a second beat. "Damn, was that some kind of invitation?"

Candace cracked a little smirk. "Let's just break out," she said, to avoid answering directly.

When Melissa rose to drape the shawl over her shoulders, she stood close to an unnerving six feet tall. Crow noticed, though, that a good five to six inches of it was attached to the black patent-leather ankle boots she was playing. Form-fitting dark denim jeans covered with multicolored suede patches closely hugged her more than ample ass.

"Ain't nothing happening here, anyway," Melissa said, jumping down off the platform before turning to retrieve her bag o' tricks from the barrel top. "Is everybody ready?" she asked, as Crow started back across the floor. Keeping his balance had become a chore again.

Some woman at the far end of the bar gave Melissa another bottle of champagne before they left. Geoff told Crow to be at the gallery a little early. "We need time to set up," he said.

Candace Maria and Melissa must have planted at least a dozen kisses on various cheeks before they finally got to the door. Bones seemed as if he wanted to join them but just told Crow to be sure to get to the gallery on time.

Through the doors and outside, there were still dozens of people milling around hoping to get in. Candy negotiated with the doorman on behalf of the girls she'd seen on the way in. Crow looked at his watch: a quarter to four. Leaning on an old Chevy, Lead Base Paint pointed Crow out to Terminal Ill. They started to get up, but Ill saw Melissa come out from behind Candace Maria. Crow thought he heard him say something about "that old witch" with a little edge, like a hint of fear or something. As the trio passed, Crow winked at the two white boys.

Waiting for the light to change at the corner, Crow saw Lead Base Paint and Terminal Ill pushing their way through the crowd trying to get back into the club. Crow chuckled softly to himself. "I wonder what's to become of *Marvin?*"

Dr. Gris-Gris' Book of Potent Spells & Portents (2001)

9

TRIPPIN'

ON HOUSTON STREET, cars were either easing into tight spaces or already double-parked. Gang kids, New Jersey kids, and suburban kids rushed passed Crow, Candace Maria, and Melissa. Mixed in with them were the ultra-urbane fashion and art crowd, discussing the latest of fleeting trends. Every so often, a homeless person would emerge from the shadows to offer a witty quip or beg outright for even the smallest denomination of spare change from passersby. A middle-aged white woman with sparkling blue eyes and long, dirty fingernails, wearing a filthy but obviously once elegant ensemble, sat with her back against a wall rummaging through plastic bags. Melissa walked over to her and handed her a bill. After a short exchange of words, Melissa bent over, and they kissed.

As the trio continued up Houston, Crow asked Melissa, "Do you know her?" a little disgusted by the kiss.

Melissa ignored the implication and answered, "I know them all, Crow. Seeing Mary always reminds me of a poem I have at home. It was written by a young black poet, very much like you. Do you want to hear it?"

"Why not?" Crow said. "You listened to mine."

Melissa thought for a few seconds. "This might not be exactly how it was worded, but he called it 'Ragtime.' " Melissa stopped under a streetlight, closed her eyes, and started to recite:

Tonight the Urban homeless huddle,
wrapped close in the Sunday Supplement.
Winter has forced lovers from the park, hopes
abandoned for thirsty love in idle cars.
Alone she struggles with the pain of
lucidity, envious of October birds left
for Southern shores. With cracked and
swollen fingers her many bags are stuffed
with rags and broken toys.
The city pushes broken and confused infants
from her infected womb. Free, they flee from
off-Broadway plays, angry with false commitment.
Unable to speak spit flies from Park view high rises, sending the homeless Scurrying fearful of rain. The Church no longer offers Asylum as soothing cups of wine.

With winter comes the tears and lonely Death.
Bodies scattered on random streets,
fingers clutching steel grates.

Come Spring faint voices will be raised in praising
empty words read over shallow graves.

The rumble of the traffic and the din of the passing crowds broke the silence, and Crow spoke first. "Damn, he kicked some real shit there."

"It sounds like he lived it. Sounds like a lot of pain to be in," Candy offered.

"He told me it was just simple observation; he saw it, so he wrote it. Did it in a hurry with my eyeliner on a brown paper bag. I put it in a frame and hung it up on a wall in my bedroom so I can read it whenever I need to. Keeps me centered and makes the room seem larger somehow."

"Yeah, but no room is as large as being out-of-doors," Crow said, recalling several lines from a novel he'd read his freshman year in college, Toni Morrison's *The Bluest Eye:* "If you are put out, you go somewhere else; if you are outdoors, there is no place to go."

He knew about what that was like, having nowhere to go. After Crow finished his reflection, he saw that Melissa, who had stopped walking and was facing them, had become distant.

"Sometimes I think poverty and homelessness should not be subject to philosophical scrutiny. I never hear starving people discussing its existential realities. Mostly they talk about which restaurants discard the best scraps, or they just worry about staying warm and safe."

Melissa stopped talking suddenly and wrapped the shawl she was wearing more tightly around her shoulders. She said she had something to do and kissed Candy on the cheek. She'd call later, she said, and walked away. As Melissa started up the block, Crow watched her wide hips sway. Before she had gotten too far away, she turned around and called back, "Pleasure meeting you, Crow. Good luck tomorrow. If I don't see you sooner, I'll see you later, at the show."

The last thing Crow saw was the wiggle of her left hip round a corner before the night swallowed her up in a shadow.

"Damn," Crow blurted out. "That was abrupt."

"Yeah," Candy said. "Melissa's like that sometimes." They continued up Houston Street.

"You know, Crow, it's strange. Melissa rarely goes out during the day anymore. I was surprised that she said she'd be at the show."

"Yeah, that's great," Crow interrupted sharply. "Anyway, did she leave you with any blow?"

"Is that all you can think about? You really don't realize how important it is that she's coming, do you?"

"Actually, I'd rather think about you right now," Crow said, pulling Candace to him with his free hand—the folder in the other—and kissing her deeply. She was tasty, like licorice, brandy, and blow. At first, she resisted a little, but only briefly, before opening her mouth and wrapping her arms around his neck. However, the kiss lasted only a little longer, leaving Candy disappointed that she'd given herself over to it, only to have it taken away. Crow had ended the kiss because a group of kids started cheering and clapping.

"This is kind of public," he said, "and I guess I'd better be looking for a subway, anyway."

"What the hell do you want a subway for? I thought you'd be staying at my place tonight." Not wanting to seem too eager, she threw in, "I mean, it's too late for you to go all the way back to Brooklyn—oh, and how do you expect to get into your apartment, anyway?" His alleged predicament occurred to her in mid-sentence.

"You've got a good point there, baby," Crow replied quickly, remembering his lie. "I guess you could pull out a cot or something," he suggested facetiously.

"Cot, my ass," Candy whispered in a growl, her teeth clenched.

"What?" Crow wondered if he'd heard right.

"Oh, ah," Candy stuttered, pretending to catch herself. Countering his thinly veiled insinuation, she purred, "There's just my little bed, so I guess we'll just have to make do." Adding a hint of suggestiveness, the corners of her mouth turned up into a sly smile. She said, "But only if you promise to behave."

"Of course I promise!" replied Crow, working hard not to stammer. "But if you think it's a promise I can keep, you're as naive as you are beautiful . . . or as *I am* horny." He pretended to whisper that last part under his breath.

"I'll take my chances," Candy said, throwing her hair over her shoulder. She pretended not to hear what Crow had pretended he hadn't wanted her to hear. Smirking to themselves, they crossed Houston going west.

Although Crow's jacket hung below his waist, Candace noticed that one side was sticking out farther than the other. She decided to have a little fun and asked, "Does your jacket always do that?"

"Nah, it's just a strange fucking jacket," he replied smoothly, as he sought to adjust his obvious erection. "Yeah, this whole thing's strange, you pretty motherfucker, you fine motherfucker, you."

She was flattered. But as much as she enjoyed Crow's attention, she was wondering if Uncle Manny was still awake and figuring out how she could sneak Crow up to her room. The thought would persist.

Candy misjudged the height of the next curb, stumbled as she stepped up onto the sidewalk, and fell against Crow. He took the opportunity to grab her around the waist. Leaving his hand resting there, even after she'd been steadied, they continued up the block.

"Every little thing she does is magic . . ." Crow heard Sting's voice singing in his head.

"Crow," Candy said, interrupting the song. "When we get back to the crib, will you read me some more of your story?"

"Sure, baby, whatever you want, but only if you promise not to put that damn plane of yours on autopilot and give the fucking elves the night off!"

"Ha! You got yourself a deal!"

Just then, a gray Plymouth Fury, its red lights flashing, sped past them going west into the Lower East Side. The driver slowed the car some and yelled out, "Bed-Stuy!" Mission bound, he lost only minor momentum rounding the corner and accelerating again. Crow looked over just in time to see that it was the detective from the candy store. Crow screamed with an enthusiasm that surprised him, "Home slice!" with a rush of recognition that increased his passion. He squeezed Candy.

Crow caught himself and said, "There goes that cop again, and it's starting to bug me."

"What is?" Candy asked, excited too, but not really interested.

"I think he lives in the 'hood, but I can't figure out how I know him . . ." Crow stopped speaking and paused as two black-and-whites flew past with their lights flashing and sirens blasting. Then another unmarked police car careened around the corner and raced past them carrying two white detectives.

Crow stopped suddenly and turned to Candy. "How much coke you carryin'?"

She chuckled, saying, "You worried about the cops? Well, don't . . . they ain't invited."

"I'm serious, Candy," Crow snapped, a little annoyed at her flippancy. "I can't afford to get busted again for nothin', let alone with what I seen in Melissa's bag. Now, how much of it did you take?"

The severity of Crow's response had reminded Candy that he was out of his element and probably just needed a straight answer to feel comfortable. He'd already told her that *pig* was not exactly his favorite choice of meat—not to mention against somebody's religion. She also knew all too well that black men in America had every reason to feel however they felt about cops and the *in*justice system they served.

"Just a couple of grams. Don't worry. It's cool." She tried to sound soothing. "They ain't thinking about us. They're probably chasing some drunk white boys from Long Island, trashing cars on Eighth Street. This happens around here all the time."

Crow responded, "Just a couple of grams, huh?"

They picked up their pace just the same, ready to get off the street—and into each other's arms. Candy's thoughts went back to Uncle Manny, and for two full blocks they were silent.

Finally, they passed the candy store where he'd run into the detective earlier. It looked as if the counterman was still smoking reefer. At three forty-five in the morning, the block was deserted.

"I hope Tío Manny's asleep!" Candy blurted out.

Crow glanced at his watch. "Shit, it's almost four in the morning."

"That don't mean shit. He goes to sleep when he gets tired of drinking rum and playing dominos, and that might be never. Ain't no tellin'. Sometimes games drag on till the next day." She was more tense about the possibility of Manny being up than she'd realized.

They walked the last block in silence. As they got closer to the liquor store, Candy looked ahead. She didn't see any lights coming from any floor of her building. They got right in front and saw no signs of life in any of the windows on the ground floor. She felt better but not home free. They still had to get upstairs.

She turned and gave Crow a quick wet kiss before putting the key into the lock. She told Crow to wait while she went inside to check things out. Crow nodded, thinking that the last thing he needed was some old drunk Puerto Rican waving a machete around and trying to cut him too short to shit. He didn't get to dwell on the horrors of this possibility too long, because Candy opened the door and beckoned him inside. Crow moved quickly and quietly up the stairs to her room. After opening the door gingerly, Candace Maria and Crow tiptoed inside.

Taking Crow by the arm, she led him to her bed without turning on a light and whispered that he should sit. Then she disappeared back into the dark hallway. Crow lowered himself cautiously, not knowing how far down he had to go before reaching the bed. He eased off his jacket and sat listening for footsteps. As his eyes adjusted to the dark, he was able to make out traces of the things near him. It wasn't long before she slipped back into the room and he heard the click of a lock and a match being struck. She lit a candle. She slid a jazz tape into a portable cassette player, keeping the volume low. She told Crow to relax and then held up two bottles, sherry in one hand and the champagne she brought from the club in the other. She asked Crow which one he preferred.

"Don't you hippie types ever stop?" Crow asked.

"Me? I thought you said you wanted some more blow?"

"Now, coke, that's another thing altogether," he said excitedly. "Coke keeps you up. All this alcohol is starting to break me down."

"It just mellows the effect of the coke for me. Last thing you want is *me* all jittery and nervous," she said.

"Good point."

Still holding both bottles in front of her, she said, "My arms are getting tired. So you want a drink or what?"

Crow smiled. "Sure, why not? I think I'd like something a little sweet." He eyed the sherry and Candace at the same time.

Stepping over to a dresser against a wall, she moved two Flintstones jelly jar glasses to the edge and filled them both to the top with the amber liquid. She passed one of them to him before setting the bottle on the floor. She slipped off her jacket and flung it onto a chair in one fluid motion and sat down on the bed next to Crow.

"I'll be damned, I gots Dino!" Crow said, holding the sherry at arm's length. He took a sip and began to look around. Unable to see clearly by candlelight, he thought the walls were painted in different colors like pink, yellow, and black. It was hard to tell, because the walls and the ceiling were covered with what appeared to be randomly placed paintings, posters, collages, newspaper clippings, photos, beads, clay figures of various sizes, and other objects that hung or protruded. The longer Crow stared, the more he began to see that the different-colored beads were affixed to the wall in a pattern, like a single thread, which connected all the themes. In one corner stood a multicolored rocking horse, painted with what looked to Crow like religious symbols and various kinds of paper clippings pasted on it. A sign hung down from the ceiling above it that read, "A Horse of a Different Color."

The back of the bedroom door was painted in three levels: the first level depicted a man and a woman making love in a pool of shallow, emerald-green water; the second level was black with luminous white crosses of various sizes; the third level was a brilliant orange sunset over a shaded mountain range. Crow couldn't figure out the connection among the three disparate scenes. He just sat there and enjoyed it, though, deciding not to ask what it meant.

Lost in his thoughts, he was snapped back into the moment when Candy moved off the bed and over to her jacket. She pulled a piece of paper from her pocket and flopped back onto the bed against Crow, jostling him.

"What you got there?" he asked.

"I hope we got it right. I wrote it down. Melissa didn't want to forget it. We both got a copy."

"What is it?" Crow asked, only a little curious. His mind was on getting Candy out of those clothes and licking cocaine off her naked body.

She passed him the paper. "It's your poem. It was so beautiful we didn't want to forget it."

Crow was shocked. "Y'all wrote it down? For what?"

"Because . . . because it was so beautiful," Candy replied softly. "Did we get it right?"

Crow took the paper and glanced at it before he said, "How the fuck would I know?" Squinting in the candlelight, he had to read the words three times before he could accept that he'd actually said them. What he'd run down merely as bullshit, hustle, seemed a lot more serious, as if he was trying to say something he'd never thought about. He handed it back to Candace Maria and tried to sound nonchalant. "Seems about right." He really had no clue.

She handed him a pen. "Okay, then, sign it, and let's go to bed."

Crow leaned over the nightstand and signed his name and the date. Candy held it up to the candle and inspected it. She then got up again and reached over to the dresser. Crow could not see that it was painted black with pink dripping dots, which glowed in the dark. She opened a drawer, pulled out a bottle of glue, poured some on the horse's saddle, and stuck the poem to it.

After putting the glue away, she lifted her shirt over her head and stuffed it into another drawer. Crow saw that she had a small peace sign tattooed on her right shoulder blade: She went to the closet and pulled out a short, red silk kimono that had a dragon embroidered in gold thread on the back. She slipped her arms into the sleeves, and Crow was pleased that she'd neglected to tie the belt. He began to fantasize again about the size and shape of her breasts. He wondered if her nipples were stiff. Just thinking about them gave him a warm, animated feeling between his legs. He saw her pull two small plastic bags from her pants pocket and put them on the dresser. Then she unzipped her jeans and snatched them down over thick butter thighs and inched them over her slender ankles before stepping out of them and kicking them out from under her feet. Not one action had the slightest hint of sexual suggestion. She was home and comfortable. Crow was neither, but when she bent over to pick her jeans up, he was pleasantly surprised to see that she wasn't wearing panties, which made his crotch even more lively. As she stood erect again, his eyes were drawn to how the silk clung to her narrow waist and wide, full, yet firm hips. Her ass was round, and his dick was hard again.

She opened one of the baggies and pulled a mirror out of the second drawer along with a black box. Crow heard the unmistakable sound of a razor blade tapping on glass. A few lines went off in his head like a Roman candle:

Drugs, sex and alcohol
What's the call
Belly-up to the bar boys
Drugs, sex and alcohol.

Crow took a deep swallow of his sherry and muttered to himself, "Damn, this poetry shit is starting to come at me from nowheres."

Without turning around, Candy asked him to bring her the other glass. He stood up and crossed the small room with the sherry in his hand. Sidling up next to her, he strained to catch a glance inside the robe. Candy turned her head and noticed his stare. "What you look for to see?" she asked Crow playfully in an exaggerated

Puerto Rican Spanish accent. Then she asked him to pour a little sherry into her mouth.

A little flustered at the sight of her relaxed and open mouth, Crow inadvertently poured too much and overflowed its capacity. Candy did nothing to stop it, and the sherry ran in thin streams out the sides of her mouth, over her chin, down her neck, and into the lush valley between her breasts. Candy finally closed her mouth, rolled her eyes shut, and lifted her head. She swallowed and leaned in and ran her sweet, wet tongue over Crow's lips and around his chin, returning the *flavor.*

"Thanks," she said, without looking at Crow. Returning to her business, she said, "I'll be done in a sec. Put Pebbles here down on the dresser."

He lingered close to her for a hot second to watch her breasts bounce in the open vee of the kimono as she chopped the cocaine. Before he moved back toward the bed, he let his hand trace the contours of her sumptuous rump, which jiggled in little bounces as she worked. Crow sat down and figured it was a good idea to take off his boots while watching it. His dick was so hard that when he bent over to do that, it didn't give way. He snapped back up in pain. "Uh!" It took him a minute, but he figured a way around his erection and was able to unlace his boots and kick them off.

When Candy had finished her task, she turned around, and Crow saw that her breasts, although still partially covered by the silk of the kimono, were round and heavy. Her nipples were very large and very dark—just as he'd suspected. Holding the mirror with the coke on it in one hand and her drink and a plastic baggie in the other, she sat down next to him and held up the baggie. "Look at the two big mushrooms we got," she announced.

"Baby, I thought I told you. You can do as much of whatever you want, as you want, but I ain't eating none of that shit. Just hand me the blow," Crow smacked, getting a little impatient.

Shaking the bag, Candy said, "Don't be afraid. These won't hurt you, Crow. They might even help if you let them. This trip might be new for you, but it's an ancient journey. This is the best food for the thought of warriors—*and it don't hurt the sex none, either.* Cocaine leaves you empty because it's shallow fun leading to no ultimate meaning. It ain't far to go, just a little farther inside. Trust me."

Crow didn't normally trust anybody, but nothing about the last twelve hours had been normal. He looked at her, carefully taking her in as she sat with her robe falling open, and decided to go with it, because what the fuck? He thought if it would help him get the pussy, he was with it. But remembering a bad trip he had taken a few years ago, he needed to play off his fear about taking another hallucinogen.

"OK, OK. I guess it ain't right to go to a party and not dance."

They each ate one. Crow didn't like the dry, bitter taste of the mushroom, so he tried to cover it up with the dry, bitter, *but familiar* taste of cocaine. When that didn't work, he decided to give the coke a hand with a gulp of sherry.

"Read to me now, OK?" Candy said, lying back on the bed beside him and wrapping herself in her robe. Crow looked at the folder on the bed and thought for a moment about telling her the truth. But he liked her thinking he was special, that he had talent. He reached for the folder instead. Candy smiled and rubbed his leg, "What happened after the fire?"

Crow leafed through, watching the words run across the pages in neat rows. He started to feel hot and uncomfortable. His lies were starting to close in on him, but this was no time to bitch up. He shook his head, got it together, and started reading:

My father ran from the burning house, the flames leaping from his hair. My mother covered his head with a blanket and they rolled in the tall grass. Then I lost interest and stopped singing. I moved and the birds flew in many directions. They were silent. I jumped from the tree; it was the highest branch I ever leapt from. I must have been ten when I hit the ground. At least ten years old because I had grown so much taller. I twisted my ankle, so I sat for a while rubbing it, then I looked toward the house and it was gone. My sneakers still fit and I wasn't worried, but it was evening and I had again missed supper. I was hungry and my foot hurt. On the ground beside me I found a pair of dark glasses. The man I'd seen in the bus station wore glasses like these and so I put them on. Behind the dark glass evening became night. And although my foot hurt I hurried away, afraid to look back, never wanting to see my front porch again.

Not far away a blacktop road had a yellow line down the center. Behind me I heard the crickets calling to each other. I walked faster and shoved my hands in my pockets. There was money in one. I pulled it out but didn't count it and put it back.

I walked that road for some time. On the other side there were times that I saw other people moving along its edge headed the other way. The first few times this happened I removed the glasses to make sure, but nobody was ever there. After a while it no longer made any difference to me so I kept the glasses on. And since they didn't speak neither did I."

Crow stopped and drank from his glass. Then he took a deep breath and turned the page.

By the time I saw the lights ahead I was taller and a few years older. My foot stopped hurting but I was still hungry, hungrier than before. A woman surprised me by crossing the road and stepping in front of me. I stopped.

"Going into town?" she asked.

"I guess so."

"Nice place if you go in for that sort of thing. I just left here but I think I'll go back. I've heard it's pretty much the same back there," she said, pointing in the other direction.

"I'm being rude. My name is Pandora. My mother told me my father named me that because he really didn't want me. What's yours?"

"What do you think it is?"

She removed her dark glasses and looked at him. "Hmm, probably something plain like Mike or Pete, maybe even John."

He couldn't remember being called anything in particular, so he invented a name that fit how he felt.

"Wrong, my name is Exemption, but everybody calls me Exempt."

She said, "Ooh, that sounds so dreamy, sort of philosophical."

He pulled up his glasses, and she was gone. Then she was back when he lowered them. "Figures," he said. "It's not dreamy, just a deduction, if I remember correctly."

Crow stopped reading. "That's enough, Candace, I'm tired of this shit," he told her. Disappointed, she sucked her teeth and leaned against him.

"All right, but I want to hear more later, OK?"

"Yeah, more later, OK."

He bent the corner of the page and shut the folder. He sat there with it resting on his knees. His eyes were fixed on the folder, but his mind, which felt like a piece of slow-moving machinery, provided him with a series of nickelodeon pictures of past events. Images would stop and remain fixed on one picture, and then the machine would slowly start to roll again. The frozen frames depicted turning points in his life. Crow saw himself leaving school after he got busted; packing his things after he decided to move back to New York; his ex-girlfriend, Lisa, crying when he insisted that she get an abortion. He was looking at another freeze-frame of himself leaving Danny's apartment with the manuscript and the paintings, when the show stopped suddenly. Crow jerked his head up, and Candy was standing in front of him with the folder in her hand.

"I'll put this on the dresser for now," she said. She seemed to tower miles over him.

"Sure, yeah, cool . . . sure, that's cool," he stammered. As he watched her move the few steps to the dresser, it seemed he could feel her muscles stretching and contracting with each motion. "This shit feels like acid," he blurted out.

"Maybe at first, but it's really a whole different buzz. It's a high that happens inside you, not outside of you like acid and most other trips. You'll see."

Candace changed the tape. Mellow electronic music filled the room. "This is the latest recording by the group I'm in," she said.

There were sounds like a woman crying, thinly overlaid by marching feet and a noise like muffled gunshots, randomly fired. There was also a continuous undertone of rushing water. The sounds mixed into a cacophonous symphony and moved fluidly just beneath his skin, leaving Crow relaxed.

Candace leaned against the wall alluringly, watching the music and the mushroom wash over him. Crow sat fixed. He had not moved since he'd stopped reading. His consciousness took in the entire room at once. He was as cognizant of his surroundings as he was of Candace Maria. Everything held the same beautiful weight: the feel of the rough sheets on the bed, the sound of the music, the smell of the scented candle, and the color of the kimono against Candy's beautiful honey skin. When she moved, the vision shattered and turned into a series of snapshots, then the total picture.

She rummaged through the closet and found a green terry-cloth robe, which she flung toward Crow. As it sailed across the room, it transformed from a bunched mass of cloth into a thing that grew outstretched wings. Landing on his head, it turned back into a robe that kept flapping.

"You'll probably be more comfortable in that." Her voice bounced off the walls and ceiling, coming at him from all directions.

He struggled to get the flapping robe off his head, and he said,

"You're probably right," while frantically tugging at it. The robe finally gave in and slid down his face into his lap in a crumpled mass. Suddenly feeling funny about taking off his clothes in front of Candy, Crow just sat there holding it and saying to himself, "*Now* what should I do?"

Candace Maria returned to leaning against the wall. She dreamily listened to the music while absently fondling her right nipple with her left hand.

Crow, fighting his indecision, hadn't meant to but said out loud, "Fuck it," yanked his sweater and shirt over his head, and flung them into the corner. It was quickly followed by the rest of his clothes, leaving him bare-assed as a newborn babe, except for his socks. He went back to wrestling with the robe. "Why don't you tell this damn thing to leave me alone!"

Candy laughed and said, "The robe obviously has a mind of its own, but you think you might need some help with those socks?"

Once again, the robe relinquished its fierce independence, acquiesced, and allowed Crow his way with it. Emerging triumphant, he sat on the edge of the bed in white sweat socks with red and blue stripes and a green terry robe. Candace Maria came and sat next to him. "Need help with the socks?" she asked again.

Crow looked down at his feet and said, "Damn, I knew I forgot something."

Candace realized after a few seconds that Crow was unable to figure out how to get his socks off and said, "Oh, forget it, I'll do it."

"You know, this shit feels pretty good. It's hard to describe. Sorta mushy, like it's all blending together," he said, finally being able to get a full view of her tits, dangling as she bent over to remove his socks for him. Pausing in order to fully appreciate what hung there before him, he got beside himself. "When you're finished with that," he directed, "get me some more wine."

Candace laughed and asked, "Just who in the hell do you think you're talking to in that tone of voice, motherfuckah?" snapping his ass back to reality.

As she got up and passed him the bottle, she huffed, "Pour it your damn self, *pendejo.*" She also got the blow and took a few hits. "Want some of this too?" she asked.

"Maybe in a little while, but not right now," he answered.

They sat quietly for a while lost in the music. Every so often they'd find themselves looking at each other. The effects of the mushroom began to close in on Crow. He became uncomfortable with the silence and the inaction between them. Here he was, sitting with this *fine* woman, in dope-fiend paradise, and he couldn't figure out how to touch her, much less address the burning pussy issue. All he could manage to spit out was, "I like the music. What do you play?"

Without turning her head, she told him that she was the woman crying.

"Candace, why would you cry like that?"

Without a second to think, she answered, "I cry because they all compete to steal my joy. I cry because they make our tongues too thick to speak and plug our ears with lies. I cry because I do not kill. But mostly my tears are for hungry children who don't steal because of the religion they are given by the people stealing all their food and so they die. My emotions are the instrument I play best, my tears my sweetest music."

Candy slid across the bed and laid her head against his chest. When she looked up at him, tears were running slowly down her cheeks. To Crow, her tears appeared like thin lines of hot Day-Glo colors, luminescent green, pink, and gold. They were the most beautiful things he'd ever seen. He pulled her closer and began retracing the course of her tears with his tongue, from her chin to the corner of a big brown eye. Her tears tasted as good as they looked: lime, strawberry, and banana. He moved his face away from hers and tilted her face up to look into her eyes again, tears welled at their edges. He pulled back and asked her what was wrong. And as the drops began to flow past her lids, she said, "I wouldn't be crying if I thought you could cry at all. You're like a fragmented, disconnected puzzle. Not everything fits with you. And I don't think you know how to be whole. I feel like you're acting all of the time, pretending to be whatever is needed in order to play some game. I know it's all a game, anyway, but you, your greatest game is with yourself. Anyone who evades himself the way you do could not possibly ever reach anyone else."

Crow released her while she was still talking. Her words stung and drowned out the music. He leaned back on his elbows and listened without breathing. When she finished, he could hear the marching and crying coming from the speakers again. First up his left side and then down his right, the music hit him in repeating dull blows, pounding against his flesh. Her words stood in his mind in a bold-type truth that he could not deny, but he fought reading them anyway.

Crow became uncomfortable. His cover had been blown. Candace had touched a tender spot, and he winced. He lashed out. "Stop looking at me! What gives you the right to . . . ?" But she cut him off by falling next to him on the bed and pulling one of his arms over her.

Hoping to calm him, she spoke gently. "Knowing I can care about you gives me the right. Knowing that we're all going to die makes it urgent, and being high made it easier. Don't tell me I hurt your feelings. You can't be all that tender. I know you've heard worse, and it ain't nothin' you don't already know."

With her that close, both literally and figuratively, the room felt smaller and the air heavy. At first he just squirmed. But then, restless, with nowhere to go, he sprang up and seemed to continue upward for hundreds of feet. Looking down at her, he bellowed, "You don't know me! What makes you think you know me? You don't know me and nothing about me, nothing about me at all. Ain't even know a Crow motherfucker existed a few hours ago!"

"Shhh! Keep your voice down. Did I say anything that wasn't true? Ain't that you?"

Looking down at her, he said, "You ain't God!"

"You don't know that, and you saying that don't change nothing—unless there's something you want to tell me. Is there something you want to tell me, Crow?"

She rolled onto her back, head against the headboard, looking up at him, her robe exposing the tawny expanse from her collarbone down to the space between her breasts. Waiting for an answer, her stiff nipples strained against the silk.

Crow, seeing her nipples there jutting toward him, responded all right, by parting the silk and handling her breasts, leaning over to take one of the dark, succulent cherry buds, at last fully exposed, into his mouth. Candy's eyes fluttered shut, and she arched her back to meet his lips, breathing in deeply. Blazing colors rushed up her thighs into her moist temple and then across her stomach and exploded out her nipples. She slowly exhaled, her body trembling and her face flushed. Sex is always more pleasurable than thinking, and why were they there, he asked himself, to philosophize or to fuck? He needed to take his time with this. Pulling his face away from her reluctantly, Crow sat down with the colors draining like cocaine down the back of his throat.

Candace Maria drew the red silk back over herself, opened and then closed her eyes again, and began rocking from side to side. When she exhaled again, the tears showered out of her eyes, and pitiful sobbing broke from her throat. This was not the response he had expected. She was tripping. Looking down at her, Crow felt her pain reach inside and take hold of him. He felt as though she had jabbed him with a hypodermic and was slowly emptying herself into his veins. The unexpected rush caused him to grab her and hold on tight. Trying to reach her, he whispered, "*Candy,* baby, *Candy,* baby," but could not hear the sound of his own voice or feel her in his arms. *Damn, this mushroom shit is no joke,* he thought, without trying to speak again.

He became aware, just then, that the marching in the music had stopped, and Candy's crying synchronized with that emanating from the speaker. The swish of rushing water ceased, and he was left alone with the tears and sobs. Lowering himself down upon her, he placed his cheek against her face and whispered softly into her hair:

> *So now I dance our tears and beat back the hands of your pain from my throat. I'm left frantic and nervous in this tight box of fears from which there's no exit. You line its walls with mirrored glass that my pounding fists can't shatter. Denied the sanctuary of closed eyes or sleep's comfort. Even now I strain to reach out and find only my mocking ghost. In every mirror I see my face stained with tears and blood in my palms.*

Candace stopped rocking. She opened her eyes and looked up at him, only to see that he had not been crying at all. Crow's face was bone dry. Disappointed, she said with a sigh, "Crow, you lie beautifully."

"Not a lie, Candace, just the most I can reach. Can you accept that?"

She sat up and hugged him. "Of course I can." She sniffled, fighting back more tears. "You care, Crow, you care. That's all that matters to me for now," she whispered with a soft smile. For a long moment, they just sat, holding each other, which calmed her.

Letting go of him, she realized that the tape had run out and got up to turn it over. By the time she got back to the bed, the mushrooms had rearranged her mood; she had become lighter.

"What are you ready for?" she cheerily asked, offering him both the wine and the blow.

He sat there looking at her, her hair trailing across her shoulder, her body bronze and creamy in the candlelight, and thought, *I'm more ready for you than anything,* but he decided to have all three.

He reached up and opened her robe again, exposing the front of her body, and ran his fingers over her stomach, then between her thighs. He dipped his index finger into the sherry, coated it with coke, and smeared her nipples with the mixture. Candace placed the bottle and the mirror on the nightstand next to the bed and pulled up the thick curtain of curls her hair made as she lay across the bed. Crow pressed his face into her breasts and began licking and sucking them, drawing them deeply into his mouth, the cocaine numbing his tongue. He could feel her shudder even through his tongue's numbness. Crow moved toward the exposed skin on her side and slid his tongue across her breasts, over her ribs, then her hips, and down past her waist. Candace found her way into his robe and to his manhood, hard and throbbing.

Crow reached over to the mirror on the nightstand and rolled his finger around until he found a small pebble Candace's chopping had missed. Between his thumb and forefinger, he held it over the space between her breasts where her cleavage had been and crushed it, leaving a thin trail of cocaine crumbs from her breastbone to her velvety mound. Hovering over her, he slowly inhaled the line and then went back over it with his tongue. Candy giggled softly below him, as she pushed his head away and tried to slip out from under him. Crow persisted and gently eased her thighs apart.

He gazed down at the extended, dusky petals of her orchidlike pussy and became dizzy at the sight of its beauty and its perfume. With that, Crow dove in, tongue extended, and slowly flicked from side to side, her wetness invading his mouth and assaulting him with taste and texture. First like a thick honey and then like a burnt-wood cognac, bitter yet compelling at the same time. He let his tongue take on its own life, his mind drifting to some fantastic place that couldn't possibly exist, but they knew him there. And he felt welcome. Candy's moan brought him back home, his face buried deeply between her legs, his tongue snaking its way down her rabbit hole, hungry. Candy lay back, her face covered by the pillow to muffle her cries of pained ecstasy—they didn't need Tío Manny bursting in now, catching her bare ass up and rutting.

Crow pulled his face away and wiped the sticky wetness from

his beard and lips with the back of his hand. He looked up at her and smiled, but before he returned to the matter laid before him, he eased his way up her body and very lightly licked her chin. Candy's other lips, parted and he inserted his tongue into her waiting mouth. Crow knew she could taste herself on his lips, and, if possible, her pussy got even wetter and juicer. He explored the inside of her mouth and tongue with the same relish with which he had explored her vagina. Satisfied with his plunderment of yet another orifice, he slid back down, leaving a wet tongue trail as a memory of his passing through. Returning happily to his point of origin, he dove back into her quivering red snapper, his hands reaching up to pinch the promising buds topping her tits. Crow was in a psychedelic heaven. Candy kicked her legs higher and let loose a scream into the pillow that shook the bed. She came and went to mushroom heaven right along with him.

Candy's legs crumpled onto the bed. On the tape's flip side, there was only the sound of a voice and a harp doing something that sounded more akin to poetry than song. An occasional note from the flute cut through the lyrics as Candace lay panting on the bed. As her convulsions subsided, she stopped biting the pillow and dragged Crow up her body to lie next to her. They lay silently as she stroked up and down the length of his throbbing cock. Then, all of a sudden, Crow lifted himself and his erection over her. She reached up and grabbed it. He leaned over to explore her wetness, his fingers pulling and prodding, deeper and longer, his mouth on her neck, his tongue tracing the map to all her hot spots and hidden treasures.

As if by magic, *or mushroom,* a foil-wrapped condom appeared in her other hand. She tore it open with her teeth and positioned the rubber between her lips. Crow kneeled above her with his eyes closed, watching the colors kaleidoscoping beneath his eyelids, and shuddered each time her slippery hand slid over the head of his johnson. When he felt her sit up, his eyes opened in time to see her bringing her face toward his eager pole, mouth open. He grinned, but only until he felt the latex unfurling along his shaft. He began to protest, but Candy shushed him, and he acquiesced, giving in to her skilled application.

Just when he thought he would implode, she pulled away, turned over, and lifted herself to meet him. He took off his robe, positioned himself behind her, and grabbed two handfuls of that *sumptuous* ass. Gently parting her lips with the tip of his dancing dick, he salsa'd in, sinking deeply, surrendering to the warmth of her body.

She pulled him in like a Venus's-flytrap, holding him prisoner in the velvet folds of its petals. They went at each other as if this might be the first and only time they would have. The mushrooms turned every moment into a lifetime, and each time he attempted to pull away, she let him get just so far before vacuuming him down deeper, holding him hostage in the newness and the beauty of the moment. By the time they erupted and rolled carefully over on the narrow bed, they were breathless, sweating . . . but ready for more.

Just then Candy heard the notes of a flute floating up from the street through the open window. Crow had heard it first but paid it no attention. Candace jumped up and ran to the window, bare bottom bouncing and yelled, "Oh, shit! It's Melissa . . ."

Spell to Increase Virility (2001)

10

Casa Josefa and Melissa's Crib

Candy's voice snapped Crow out of it. "Shit, it's Melissa!" Candy exclaimed again. "What time is it?" The question made him focus, but he couldn't find his voice. He thought he might've left it inside Candy somewhere. He sat on the edge of the bed with a throbbing-hard erection, half dressed in shorts and socks, trying to figure out what the hell had happened. Crow looked around the room, just barely illuminated by dawn's light, and shook his head. "Crow! What time is it?" Candace asked again, a little irritated.

"Just a minute!" Crow rose on stiff and shaky legs and staggered over to the dresser to look at his watch. He shook it and answered, "This motherfucker stopped at twenty to six. I don't know what the fuck time it is."

When Crow looked over, Candy was bent over, still looking out the window, her round, flannel-pajama-covered butt staring Crow in the face. "When did you put *those* things on?" he asked, having expected to see her in the red silk kimono.

"What you say?"

"When did you put those flannel things on? Where's the red thing?"

"What red thing?" She stood and faced him. "I came back from the bathroom with these on. Don't you remember? You said flannel was as sexy as Grandma, Sunday mornin', and home cooking and made your dick soft."

With the kind of hard-on he had pressed against the dresser just then, he couldn't believe his dick had ever been soft around her.

"I could have sworn . . ." Crow began. "Didn't we . . ." He cut himself off and looked around for any sign of the condom, the foil wrapper, anything. Not a trace. Candy stood there, fully dressed and staring at him blankly. Not a trace of that thing girls get in their faces "the morning after."

"Melissa's outside, Crow. I think we better get dressed and go meet her."

Candace pulled her pajama bottoms up higher and dashed out of the room. Crow threw down a gulp of sherry, trying to level off, and said, "Fuckin' mushrooms. I really do hate trippin'." He continued to mutter unintelligibly as he realized that his eyes were following a translucent golden blob of light darting about the room. A few minutes later, Candy came back with a damp wash cloth.

"Hurry up and wash off, Crow. Besides Bones and Geoff waitin', there's some other folks want to meet you over at Josie's."

Crow thought she'd lost her mind. "Can't that wait?" he asked plaintively.

"Apparently not. Because Melissa doesn't think so," she told him as she opened the closet door and stepped in.

"And I know you're not trying to act like you forgot why you're here in the first place," she said.

"OK, OK, I know why I'm here, and God forbid I should disappoint Mistress Melissa," Crow grumbled before heaving himself out of a tangle of his own arms and legs. A little out of breath, he asked, "But damn, don't you people ever stop? And how do *you* know what Melissa's thinking?"

"I talked to her when I went downstairs just now," she responded, becoming irritated again.

Crow mumbled something under his breath that sounded like "Cranky-ass bitch." He took another slug of the sherry, gathered up his clothes, and started out in search of the bathroom, but stopped just outside Candy's bedroom door and asked, "Where's your uncle at?"

"Don't worry about him. He sleeps till noon on Saturdays."

When Crow returned from the bathroom washed-up and dressed, he found Candy waiting at the top of the stairs looking fly for a girl who had been up all night. She was dressed in tight brown leather straight-legs, scuffed tan suede workboots, a white T-shirt, and the same plaid flannel shirt from the night before. They sneaked quietly down the stairs and past the bedroom of the still sleeping Tío Manny and were out on the street in a few minutes.

Crow hit the street carrying the sherry bottle in one hand and the manuscript tightly clutched in the other. Melissa stood across the street leaning on the fence, still blowing the flute when they came out. It was the melody Crow'd heard on the tape earlier. When Crow looked up, he saw the rising sun smoke and burn like a rubber tire in the sky. "Fuckin' mushrooms," he grumbled once again. Coronas of color haloed the streetlights overhead. Crow couldn't tell if they were still lit or not. Down the block, lights were flicking on and off behind apartment windows like little bomb blasts. *Oh, shit,* he thought. *This shit is ill.*

When Melissa saw them coming out of the building, she began crossing the street to meet them. Several of Candy's neighbors, some with heads down and hands stuffed in their pockets, others pushing shopping carts or dragging complaining children behind them, greeted her in hurried "Good mornings" and checked out her companions. When Candace turned the key in the lock of the liquor store door, the sound of the bolt moving into place echoed loudly, and Crow's wine- and mushroom-soaked head flashed back to the clank of a cell door slamming behind him. A hard shiver hit and ran through his body, striking him to the quick with its terrible sound of finality.

Candace Maria and Melissa hugged, and Crow, struggling to get it together, mumbled a feeble "Hello." He was having a hard time getting through the flashback.

They started back toward the East Side. He was still tripping, and each step Crow took felt as if he were bouncing along a rubber road. The things that caught his attention appeared to blend together and somehow had lost their autonomy. Crow had to work hard to keep up as Candace and Melissa, walking slightly ahead, hurried along talking intently. Although their words sounded just beyond his earshot for the most part, Crow could make out enough of what they were saying to know that they were discussing him. But he wasn't all that interested in hearing their entire conversation, and his mind began to wander.

Crow was beginning to experience the first throbs of a headache and the slight pangs of hunger. He tried to remember when he'd eaten last. Friday seemed so long ago. He could barely remember sneaking out of Danny's apartment with jones-induced visions of a quick scam. He thought about the poems he'd said for Candace and Melissa earlier. Here he was, never having been good with words before outside of scams and hustles, and didn't give two shits about a poem. But now, after meeting fine, brown Candy, off the top of his head he'd run off verse after verse, three times in one night. And focusing on the pussy and tripping hadn't given him time to think about it since. Now, walking silently through the gray streets of the early morning, feeling alone, he tried again, but the words wouldn't come. He couldn't recall a single verse. He tried to blame his newly found eloquence on the mushrooms, but that wouldn't explain the first poem. Bothered, he tried to string a new one together, but the words just wouldn't connect. He wondered where they'd come from last night and if he'd ever be able to do it again. After several more attempts that didn't get past the first few lines, he gave up. He walked silently, still just beyond earshot of the conversation taking place a few paces ahead.

When they stopped for a light on Avenue C, a familiar gray sedan rolled up beside them. It was the detective. He still had that cigar clamped in his jaw. It finally dawned on Crow that this guy reminded him of the fat cop Godfrey Cambridge played in *Cotton Comes to Harlem:* Grave Digger Jones.

The cop rolled down the window and yelled out, "I see you made it till morning, Brooklyn!"

Crow glared at him through bleary eyes and slurred back, "Yeah, blood, I've been keeping good comp'ny, man."

"I can see that," the cop answered, eyeing Crow's companions. "How goes it, Miss Melissa?"

" 'Bout same as always, Big Dave. How's by you, baby?"

"Usual. Punk kids from the Island and Jersey trashing cars on Eighth Street. Grabbed a couple of shithead crack dealers too," he said. He snatched the cigar out of his mouth, hacked a couple times, spit something brown out onto the sidewalk in front of them, and stuck it back in.

Melissa looked on the ground and grimaced, then looked into Dave's face. "That's real nasty, Dave. If you want to get better, why don't you stop smoking? Them things gonna kill you."

"Yeah," he said. "If running around the Alphabet don't. We all going one way or the other, anyway."

Candy chimed in, "As the song goes, 'No one gets out of here alive,' do they?"

Dave's partner yelled from the other side of the car, "No shit about that!"

"Be cool, Brooklyn. See you around, Miss M, Candy," Dave said, and the gray Fury moved slowly uptown.

"Where the hell do I know him from?" Crow thought again.

Candy turned to Melissa and screeched, "Is it just the mushrooms, or does Dave's partner really look like a big, pink hog?"

After Melissa stopped laughing, she turned to Crow and said, "Dave seems to have taken a liking to you. He don't usually have that much to say to people."

"He seems to think that he knows me from somewhere, but he's just another pig to me," Crow said, shrugging, but not completely convinced either about not knowing Dave or Dave being just another pig.

Melissa began her response slowly, trying to maintain her cool about it. "There's cops, and then there's *cops,* just like there are other kinds of people. Dave's not like—"

Crow interrupted, trying to laugh off the tension he picked up in her voice. "Sure, he ain't. I believe you. None of 'em are. I've known you five minutes less than I've known *her,*" he said, gesturing at Candy, "so why shouldn't I take *your* word for it? Ever since I got down here with y'all, I've had to take people's word for some shit or another. Why should this be any different?"

Candy cut in. "Have any of us told you anything wrong since we hooked up?"

"How the hell would I know?" Crow asked with mock hysteria. "It's too early to tell."

"Crow, haven't you ever noticed that it's always too early to tell, until it's too late?" Candy asked. "You trust your instincts and take your chances. Ask yourself, why the hell should *we* trust *you?* We don't know you from a hole in the ground. You just some brother we never seen before, show up out the blue with paintings and a manuscript under his arm and a fucking attitude about it all. Yet here we all are."

Melissa, annoyed at having been interrupted in addition to Crow's generalization, almost completely ignored what Candy was saying and continued. "Dave's been working the streets down here since the sixties, and he's gotten rid of some real bad people and has never killed anybody doing it. You know any other cops like that? Most of 'em can't wait to get out on their beats and use their guns—

like they're compensating for something God didn't give 'em to use at home. Dave told me when we first met that he joined the force against the wishes of his revolutionary family so that he could make a difference from the inside. I know we hear that all the time, but he said that if he could keep one brother from being shot or beaten to death by another cop, then he had done what God had put him on earth to do—to save black lives. I've seen him face down other cops over a bad bust or 'excessive force,' and even got himself suspended a few times over shit like that. We still laugh about how he even got that promotion to detective instead of fired. The point is that if there was ever a cop that ain't 'just another *pig,*' it's Dave."

Something about the way Melissa spoke told Crow many things about her. The most important thing he'd learned about her, though, was that he couldn't talk to her the way he was used to talking to women, especially women he didn't know. He had the vague impression that something special was about to happen, and he didn't want to blow it by being a smart-ass about something he really didn't give a shit about.

"I didn't mean to insult your friend, Melissa," Crow offered gingerly, "but my experience with the law being what it's been, you might understand my distaste for anything in blue, even if it *is* promoted, unmarked, and black."

They jumped onto the curb to avoid being splashed by a sanitation truck barreling their way. When she was sure they were well out of its range, Melissa said, "I can see your point, Crow. If I were in your shoes and I didn't know Dave, I'm sure I'd have said something similar. Let's just drop it."

Crow held the bottle of sherry up to the light. It was more than three-quarters gone. He pulled the cork with his teeth, spat it out, and took a hit. Then he shook the bottle from side to side and asked, "Anyone?"

They both reached for the bottle at the same time. Crow laughed and said, "Ah, a case of that rare disease, grabbititis."

Both ladies laughed, and Melissa snatched the bottle and playfully said, "Age before beauty." She held the bottle and made her hand shake as if she were in desperate need of a drink.

"Been afflicted for years, doctors say it's terminal," she said, turning the bottle up to her face. She passed the bottle to Candace Maria, stopped in mid-stride, pulled the flute back up to her lips, and blew out a flurry of notes in a burst. As she fiddled with the scale, Crow asked if she ever played whole songs.

"All the time," she answered, and began to play one that Crow didn't recognize as they walked. The disjointed melody, high-pitched and warm, filled the street. People hustling along lifted their heads as they passed.

"Do it IAN, the shit's thicker than a brick!" Candy yelled. While the reference was lost on Crow, the music wasn't, and neither was Melissa's obvious talent.

"All this shit going on out here, and all I'm doing is stealing another motherfucker's art," he said to himself.

Melissa was still playing as Candace Maria threw the empty bottle into a trashcan. It hit the bottom with a thud and a crash. They turned right on Avenue B, then left onto Third Street. About a quarter of the way up the block, nestled between a Chinese restaurant and a tire shop, was a brick building with a lavender-painted door with two huge potted plants sitting outside. On the door was a small gold plaque with "Casa Josefa" inscribed on it. Below the plaque was a peephole. Melissa blew three sharp, high notes, and a bloodshot eye appeared in the hole. Then the door swung open.

A tall, thin, olive-complexioned Cubano with jet-black hair slicked back, a pencil-thin mustache, and a large diamond stud in his left ear opened the door. He wore a brand-new, shiny black silk suit and a tight black T-shirt. Melissa always *did* think he was fine but had sworn *never* to date another Cuban, ever. He kissed Melissa and Candy on both cheeks and called them both Mami. He eyed Crow suspiciously but then stepped aside to let them in without saying anything else.

This club was tiny in comparison to Chaos, and there were only ten or fifteen people in the whole place. Another good-looking, muscular Cuban in a black turtleneck was working a long, highly polished wooden bar that started just inside the door on the right and ran almost to the end of the room. A huge bouquet of orchids sat at either end of the bar. The exposed brick walls had several dim blue lights along the floor. There was a two-foot-high platform at the back of the room, where a man and a woman danced absently to La Lupe blasting from two small speakers over their heads. On the floor behind them, a shiny-bald black man sat playing the vibes in time with the music. Paintings and photos competed for space along the walls. Crow could smell the thick, cloyingly sweet stench of angel dust in the air. A desperately thin Asian girl, in full geisha body paint, sat in a stupor by the stage. She was hunched over with her elbows on the table and her chin resting on the heel of her hand. Her hair was ebony and lank. It accented the bluish whiteness of her painted shoulders. She stared off into space with glassy, red-rimmed eyes.

Bones and Geoff were sitting at a table near the stage, and there were four other people sitting at the table next to them, speaking softly and passing around a joint. Bones saw them, jumped up, and hurried over. Face all smiles, he ushered them over to the table. Candace Maria and Crow followed, but Melissa went over to the painted woman and sat beside her. Crow watched as Melissa gently stroked her forehead. When they got to the table, Geoff slapped Crow on the back as if he were a long-lost brother, called a waiter over, and ordered Remys for Candace and Crow. Crow saw that Geoff was drinking something bright green in a tall, thin glass, but he didn't know if it was really that color or just the mushrooms talking again. Candy, on whom the effects were rapidly waning, confirmed that the liquid was green.

The bar was out of Remy, so Geoff ordered Martell instead. Crow told the bartender he'd rather have sherry. Candy wanted sherry too. Crow's attention was on Melissa as she massaged the woman's temples. He thought he heard her singing softly to her.

Crow's attention was diverted when Bones's hand landed abruptly on his shoulder

"Hey, Bones, what it be like? I see the punker ain't do you no damage. How'd the night go?" Crow asked.

"I told you that shit wasn't about nothing, Crow. So many really fine ladies came in after you guys left. Man, I got a pocket full of new numbers. I invited a bunch of 'em to your show."

Candy leaned forward at the table and watched the dancers. They were bone-thin Asians, dressed in black tights and fuzzy orange house slippers. At different points they would dance out of their slippers and then scramble to put on another pair.

Bones noticed that Crow's eyes refocused on Melissa. He looked at Candy intently watching the dancers and slid his chair around Crow's to get closer to her. After a few seconds of fumbling to secure his space, he settled down and watched the performance without interest. Uncomfortable, Bones quickly finished his drink and lit a cigarette. Every motion he made seemed like a major task he had to complete. Candace Maria noticed his awkwardness and asked, "Why don't you just sit your ass still?"

"I guess I'm wired. You know how it gets after two days of this shit. I should go home and crash." But then he added, "I'll probably stick it out for a while, though."

"I know how you feel. Once you're on a roll, it's hard to slow down," Candy said.

"Yeah," he said. "Don't you ever feel like getting off the track and doing something else for a while?" he asked her.

"Don't we all, Bones? But really, what else is there to do?"

"I hear that, baby. What did you and Crow do last night?" Candy knew that this was what the whole conversation had been leading up to—Bones trying to get all in her business. She was surprised that it had taken him this long.

"Nothin' much," she said, smiling nonchalantly. "Went back to my house, dropped some mushrooms and shit, fucked, and listened to some music. Oh, yeah, Crow made me a poem and read some of his book to me. Then Melissa came to get us, and we came over here."

Bones's cigarette fell to the floor. He tried to play it off by putting it out with vigorous twists and turns of his heel to make it look intentional. But he couldn't mask the shock as his composure abandoned him, leaving him nervous and defensive. He grabbed his glass and damned it for being empty. Candy pretended that her attention had returned to the dancers, feeling a little diminished by her own assault.

After what felt like a long while, Bones had regained enough of his equanimity to mutter something about getting another drink, devoting his full attention to feigning a casual retreat. As she watched him slink over to the bar, looking all dejected, her ears filled with the sound of the vibes and dancing feet. She was still feeling that momentary twang of regret but then decided that it was his own fault for being so busy worrying about what she did with her pussy, anyway—even if she *hadn't* done anything with it . . . *yet.*

Crow stopped watching Melissa when the painted woman sat up. He began talking to two pasty-looking white guys Geoff had called over.

Keith and Kenny, Geoff told Crow, were rich, famous, and the hottest things on the SoHo art scene. Earlier, Geoff had told them about Crow's work and the show later that day. Now, they were taking turns explaining their artistic impetus and pointing to paintings of theirs that hung on the walls around them.

As they talked, Crow thought to himself that their stuff looked more like cartoons than serious artwork. *But who the fuck am I to criticize? At least they painted that stuff themselves.* Crow's "art" had been stolen from someone who had treated him as if he mattered. He knew he wasn't shit right now.

Crow was lying some more about how much he liked this or that painting when he felt a sudden, sharp, blinding pain and saw stars. Bones had elbowed Crow hard in the back of the head and was trying to play it off as if he didn't know what he had done.

Geoff and the artists jumped as Crow cried out and lurched forward. Crow turned to see Bones behind him, hovering and staring nonchalantly toward the bar. By now, the mushrooms had just about worn off, and the alcohol was taking over. Crow leaped from his chair, grabbed Bones by his lank hair, and spun him around, screaming, "What the fuck is wrong with you?"

Crow had backed Bones across the room and had him pinned against the bar so fast he didn't know what hit him. Crow in the meantime was only vaguely aware that the manuscript had fallen to the floor.

"What's wrong, man?" Bones stammered, nearly pissing his pants.

Crow, still clutching a handful of Bones's hair, yelled, "Fuckin' asshole, you *know* what the fuck you did! Don't nobody hits that hard by accident! What the fuck was that about?"

Candy rushed over and tried to pull Crow off Bones. After he saw that Crow hadn't turned on her, Geoff moved closer and tried to calm Crow down. But as swiftly as he'd grabbed Bones, Crow yanked his hands out of his hair and throttled him against the bar. Geoff backed up again.

Josefa ran over from the stage, yelling, "Ayeee! *Dios mio!* Whooo eez *trr*yeeeng to brek up my cloob? *Oye!* Wha' you theenk? Tables and chairs grow on treez?"

Candy was screaming from behind her, "What happened?"

"That motherfucker elbowed me in the back of my head for no fuckin' reason!" Crow shouted.

Geoff, attempting in his own chicken-shit way to defuse the situation, offered meekly from a safe distance, "Man, it had to be an accident. Why would Bones knock *you* in the head?"

Keith and Kenny were egging the whole thing on by shouting, "Fight! Fight! Fight!" from behind Candy.

Candy shot them an icy glare, and they settled down quickly.

"I hope he kicks Bones's ass!" Kenny giggled excitedly to Keith. "He never paid me for that painting he sold for me last year."

"No shit, huh?" Keith replied. "Well, I never liked Bones anyway, and now he won't even shake my hand since he found out I'm sick."

"That sucks," Kenny said with sympathy in his voice.

"You going to Crow's show?" Keith asked.

"Why the fuck not?" Kenny answered.

"Yeah, me too. I need to do as much as I can while I'm still able, you know. Besides, maybe Crow might be a big hit, and you know Geoff always throws such a smokin' party."

Back at the bar, Candy was shouting, "Accident, my ass! Bones, you know you did that shit on purpose, you mean, petty motherfucker! We both know why you did it. I should let Crow break your neck!"

Bones remained silent—gagging, really—his eyes welling up with tears. Melissa sauntered over, looking unconcerned. She grabbed Crow's hands and loosed his grip on Bones's throat. Crow let his hand slip away but remained firmly planted, huffing and puffing, in front of Bones, who squirmed and rubbed his neck.

Melissa gave Bones a few seconds to catch his breath and said, "Bones did it on purpose but didn't mean it, if that makes any sense, and he's sorry, right, Bones?" He didn't respond. She pushed Bones gently back out of Crow's face and said, "Why don't you go home and get some sleep? You're getting a little beside yourself, and you need to lie down. We all do. We'll see you later."

Bones turned quickly to leave. When he reached the door, he turned back and called, "I *am* sorry, Crow. I *didn't* mean it," and hurried out the door.

"Fuck you, Bones, man!" Crow yelled back. Glaring at Melissa, he asked, "What the hell was the point of coming here, anyways?"

Geoff, who had picked the manuscript up off of the floor and put it back into the folder before finally inching his way to the bar, answered. "I just wanted you to meet some other artists. Keith and Kenny will spread the word about the show, and with all this drama—you know, no publicity is bad publicity—I'm sure nobody will want to miss it now."

Crow slumped against the bar and wheezed. "More hype, huh?"

Feeling Crow's sudden exhaustion, Candy slipped her arm around his waist and asked Melissa if she was ready to go.

"Yeah, but let's have one last toast to Crow's impending success and Bones's narrow escape, before we split." Melissa fished out two yards from her bag o' tricks and said, "A magnum of Dom and ten glasses!"

Melissa, Crow, Candy, Keith, Kenny, the bartender, the fine doorman, Geoff, the painted woman, and a relieved Josefa raised their glasses.

They each downed the champagne in one gulp. The excitement over, the painted woman slunk back to her table by the stage and resumed her seated slump. Crow shook hands with Kenny, Keith, and finally Geoff, who then ambled back to their table to finish his breakfast. Josefa patted Melissa lovingly on the bottom, winked, and said, "Ayee seeee you laaaaater, honey," then turned to Crow and wished him good luck. "Maybee Aye see you at dee show later. *Vaya con Dios.*"

As the trio headed to the door, Josefa called behind Crow, "You no breakee that *blanquito's* neck. He already dead!"

"Like I give a fuck," Crow mumbled under his breath.

Past the doorman and outside, it was a sunny morning. Melissa, Crow, and Candace Maria stood for a second in front of the club they were leaving and watched. Stores were being opened, folks waited at bus stops, others hailed cabs. Everyday people doing everyday shit.

"It always amazes me, coming out of clubs in the morning, all fucked up. I mean, look. People are going to work and shit," Melissa said to no one in particular. "Anyway," she continued, looking at the others, "I know Crow's not going home to Brooklyn now, and you two already got past Uncle Manny once. I don't think you ought to be pressing your luck. So I guess everybody gets to come home with me."

"Tired as I am, anything sounds good," Crow said through a yawn.

"Thanks, Melissa," Candace said, searching her pockets for change. "I better call home, though. He worries if I ain't home when he gets up."

"Call from my place. Now, let's get a cab. I want to get home."

Getting a cab wasn't going to be a problem. Most of the A.M. drivers cruised the after-hours spots until noon. Two seconds after Melissa stuck her hand out, a black Lincoln pulled up, and the three of them piled into the backseat. Slamming the door behind them, Melissa said, "One twenty-one St. Mark's."

The driver turned around smiling and said in some kind of heavy accent, "As many times as I'm taking you there, I know where you're living by now."

Melissa flashed a smile but said nothing. They rode in silence a few blocks and pulled in front of a five-story redbrick townhouse. Instead of a front lawn, there was a huge sculpture of a white fish shooting water out of its mouth into an urn held by a naked woman crouching in a fountain. Melissa dug a ten-dollar bill out of her pocket, stuffed it into the slot in the partition, and said, "Thanks. Keep the change."

The driver turned around, accepted the money, winked, and said, "Many thanks." He slid the partition open quickly and passed her a card before she got out. "Don't forget. Whenever you need ride, call base asking for—"

"Car Fifty-four. Yes, I know, I know," Melissa interrupted, and finished his sentence. "As many times as you are taking me here, I know what car you are driving by now!" she said, imitating his accent with a smile.

Crow crawled out of the cab, stretched, and asked, "This your crib?" Melissa didn't respond. "What floor you live on?" Crow asked.

Candy, recognizing what Crow was really asking, replied, "Don't worry, she don't live at the top."

"I occupy the first three and rent out the other two," Melissa said.

"You own this place?" Crow asked. "I'm impressed." Crow was trying to figure out how she could do drugs as she did and still own property.

"Don't be, it's just a place to live," Melissa flatly responded.

Candy sucked her teeth. "This place is a little more than *just a place to live.*"

They climbed the steps to the front door. As Melissa stuck the key in the lock, the polished oak door swung open, and they entered on the parlor floor. Melissa flicked a light switch, and amber-colored light flooded the oak-walled vestibule. Crow stared at the huge yellow crystal chandelier that dangled overhead. Melissa took off her shoes and hung her jacket on a tall, shiny brass coat stand and asked that they do the same.

A fabulous Oriental rug ran the length of the hall that led to the dining room. Abstract paintings hung the length of the corridor, which made it look like a gallery. Candace pointed to them and said, "Melissa did these long before I met her."

The corridor ended in a huge dining room with polished parquet floors. In the center of the room sat an oversized oblong black marble table, surrounded by four intricately detailed, high-back wrought-iron chairs with red velvet seat cushions. Two elegant silver candelabra stood in the center of the table, each holding four tall, thin black candles. On each wall hung an abstract tapestry. Crow asked Candy, pointing to the hangings, "Melissa too?" and Candy nodded.

A spiral staircase climbed a far corner of the room. Melissa led them past it and into the eggshell-white kitchen. In the center of a rust-colored slate floor stood a stainless-steel stove next to a matching sink. Extending from one wall, a black marble counter, like a dining-room table, ran the length of the kitchen. To the rear stood stained-glass doors through which could be seen a backyard. It was small but filled with finely manicured trees and bushes, giving it a Japanese garden feel. There was even a small marijuana patch.

Melissa got champagne and orange juice out of the refrigerator. "Let's go upstairs and chill before we crash," she suggested.

Crow didn't respond. He was too busy being fascinated by the colorfully painted metal mobiles that hung at staggered lengths from the kitchen ceiling. *This shit would get on my nerves,* he thought, as he quietly followed behind Melissa and Candace.

They climbed the spiral staircase and ended up in a room where the floor was almost entirely covered by pillows of various sizes, shapes, and colors. It reminded him of Melissa's abstract tapestries. He wondered if the pillows had been numbered, so if one got out of place, she'd know where to put it back. Built into the walls were bookcases that had been stuffed to their limit. There were even more books stacked in rows on the floor in front of the shelves.

Crow flopped down onto the pillows and asked in a sarcastic tone, "You got a whole damn library in here?"

Melissa got three black flutes from a cabinet. "Yes, I do," she answered. "And you might find some interesting stuff in here." She popped open the champagne and filled the glasses with it, topping it off with some of the juice.

"Before I drink another thing," Crow said, grabbing his crotch, "I'd better go pee."

Candace pointed and said, "Through there, out the double doors, second door on your left."

Crow struggled to get up, his hands slipping from under him on a satin pillow. When his foot found something solid, he stood and wobbled through the maze out the door.

At the front of the next room, sunlight strained through four shuttered windows that looked out onto the street. As he entered the room, an inexplicable calmness washed over him. Then he noticed that African masks and sculptures, positioned all around, seemed to inspect him from every angle. The living room, in sharp contrast to the pillow room, was sparsely furnished, except for the statuary. A white leather couch and two matching chairs stood alone. Overhead, yet another crystal chandelier hung, refracting faint strains of sunlight, sending rainbows onto the faces of the masks and sculptures. On the mantel of a massive marble fireplace sat a number of smaller pieces. Some were pierced with nails, others encrusted with sacrificial offerings or bound with ropes and covered with cowrie shells. Without realizing it, Crow was smiling. He exited into the hallway and found the bathroom.

Crow hit the light switch. A sunken tub with shining gold fixtures, a shower, the ceiling and floor, as well as a vanity and chair and something that looked like a cross between a toilet and a sink, were all black marble. All four walls were mirrored. "Damn," he mumbled. "I am fucked up," he said, confronted by his red-glazed eyes glaring back at him everywhere he turned. He shrugged it off, found the marble toilet, lifted the black vinyl seat, and peed, hitting the rim. After rinsing his hands in the marble sink, he headed back for the girls, his head spinning.

Back in the pillow room, Candace and Melissa were pouring champagne out of the bottle into each other's mouth and laughing, taking tiny hits of blow in between. They didn't acknowledge Crow's return until he had resettled himself comfortably among the pillows. Candace passed Crow his glass. "Check this out," she said, as she passed him something else. It was a thin red book with frayed edges. "This is the first copy of Melissa's very first book of poetry." The title, *Mistaking My Reflection for Myself,* was printed in small black letters in the upper left corner.

"What don't you do, Melissa?" Crow asked incredulously.

"Oh, I guess whatever I haven't thought of yet." She paused for a second and added, "But I think that's pretty much the same for everybody. Can't do what you ain't thought of." She passed the blow to Crow, who took two hits.

Crow passed it to Candy and said, "No more coke right now. I'm too wasted to enjoy it anymore. And my nose is all fucked up."

Candy asked him, "You ready to crash?"

Crow nodded. "Yeah."

Melissa started to get up, but Candace stopped her. "Relax, we'll use the guest room."

Surprised at Candy's indirect invitation, Crow gulped down a mouthful of mimosa and said to Melissa, " 'Preciate you lettin' me stay."

Melissa said nothing and watched them disappear out of the room. She swallowed the rest of her drink, took two quick hits of cocaine, and closed the case. She stretched out on her back, unbuttoned and then wriggled out of her jeans, and threw them into a corner without sitting up. They were soon followed by her black cashmere crewneck and a big lacy bra. With only her panties left on, she yawned, rolled over, and pulled a pillow over her head.

Candy held Crow's hand as they walked down the hall. The walls around them were covered with words, top to bottom. He assumed it to be more of Melissa's work. The shiny black lettering had been done without concern for uniformity. Multicolored figures and symbols had been appointed to divide the rows, and a few of the letters were slightly larger and painted bright red for emphasis.

Crow had been getting high every day for the last ten or twelve years but was now reeling from the sheer volume of drugs and alcohol he'd consumed since he'd hooked up with these people. He looked at Candace, who seemed as straight as when he met her, and felt like a sucker. "Damn," he said to himself, almost in awe of her tolerance level.

He tried to focus on the words on the walls, but they blurred and ran together. Candace, already two or three feet ahead of Crow, turned the knob of the door in front of her. When it wouldn't open, she jiggled the gold skeleton key that protruded from the lock until it clicked. The entire hallway, the door Candace opened, and the three walls that lay beyond it were completely covered with words. Crow looked overhead and was relieved that the ceiling was bare. As Candace pulled him into the room, his vision suddenly cleared, and he caught a line that was painted in red on the closet door: "I only wish you would remove your shovel from my soul; our grave is now far too deep to fill or hide from my broken lovers." He wondered aloud, "What the fuck?"

Candace pushed the door closed behind them. Crow straightened his back, attempting to regain some semblance of lucidity, but his shoulders still sagged, and his eyes revealed fatigue. He knew he was through and said, "Fuck it, I can't hang with y'all. I'm fucked up. I'm going to sleep."

Candace grabbed the bottom of Crow's sweater and said, "Here, let me help you get your shit off."

Crow chuckled at the double entendre and raised his arms as she pulled his sweater off. He managed to unbutton his own pants and let them fall. And then, as if by magic, his shirt and socks were off too. Without a trace of modesty, Candace stripped herself bare and threw her clothes on top of Crow's. Seeing how she was buck naked and all, Crow followed suit and added his BVDs to the pile.

When Candace hugged him with a passion he was just too weak to return, Crow thought, *This is bullshit, I'm too high to fuck!*

Poor Crow. Here he was in a dope fiend's paradise, with this *fine* motherfucker, and he didn't even have the strength to hug her back, much less address the burning pussy issue. All he could manage was a thin, raspy "Damn, Candy. You is one fine motherfucker,"

Crow struggled to get his arms around her, and his hands slid down her smooth, honey-colored back and fell on top of her round, firm, *sumptuous* ass. He licked weakly along the side of her neck, then backed his head away and moved in to run his tongue over her lips. Her fat, stiff nipples pressed hard against his chest, and his soft dick hung against her belly. Crow, knowing he was too tired and high to get it up, said regretfully, "The spirit is willing, but the flesh just can't."

Candace, stroking his bearded, chocolate-brown face, looked deeply into his bright red eyes and said, "That's fine, baby. The pussy ain't goin' nowheres. When it's ready, I'll bet ten balls that you'll get tired of this before I get tired of that," she said, gently stroking his flaccid penis.

Slightly embarrassed by the limp dick situation, Crow hugged her halfheartedly again. "Bet. But it's my money, and I never lose shit," he said with false bravado.

After another kiss and a long hug, they flopped onto a futon mattress on the floor. Under an antique, hand-sewn quilt and wrapped between silk sheets, their heads melted into the fluffy goose-down pillows. Seconds before Crow drifted off to sleep, he draped his wiry leg over hers and stretched his arm across her shoulder, tangling his fingers in her hair, long, coarse, and curly.

Candace pulled her shapely hips closer to Crow, and he snuggled her. Her palm rested comfortably on his tight black ass.

No sooner had she settled than she thought, *Damn, I got to go to the bathroom.* She looked at Crow and was reluctant to disturb him. He had fallen into an incredibly deep sleep as soon as his head hit the pillow. He was snoring louder than anyone she had ever heard in her life. The noise filled the room. His breathing shot out in arrhythmic bursts, and it sounded to Candace as if he was choking to death. Not knowing what was going on with him and a little afraid, she shook, pushed, turned him over, and finally sat up and softly slapped him in the face. Crow snored on. She rolled slowly from the mattress and onto the floor, jumped up, and headed for the marble bathroom.

The vinyl padded toilet seat was cold. It made her hurry. When she was done, she moved over to the bidet, also black and marble, squatted, and turned the water on full blast. A strong, steady stream of warm, pulsating water flooded her in waves of rapture. She got so aroused that she came almost immediately. Candace turned the water off and dried herself, running the soft tissue back and forth over the lips of her vagina and across her clitoris. Her labia were spread, and her clit was swollen and unhooded. She sat for a few more seconds and used a finger on the tip of it. *Shit, I'm horny,* she thought as she stuffed two fingers into her pussy, finding it, of course, still wet and grasping.

Leaving the bathroom, Candy closed the door behind her and scanned the hallway walls for the segment of words that held her favorite passage. She found and read them again:

Pressed nude against the tree, I found more pleasure from the bark tearing at my flesh than you find in this poem. We fought for sex refusing to concede that experience has left us void. Stiff and dripping, still miles apart. In the open grave I rub myself in fevered attempt as six feet above he explodes and fills this empty space with wet soil and fallen autumn leaves, repeatedly burying me with my finger pressed to my flesh, again abandoned without confirmation.

Candace stopped reading and dashed down the steps to the pillow room to get herself some champagne. Melissa was snuggled between two large pillows, fast asleep. She was nude except for some old yellow panties. Her head was partially covered by a large, round pillow with a faux African print. Melissa was a mulatto with pale yellow, almost white skin. She had big, fat titties with deep rose-colored nipples and thick, supple thighs that ran into full hips and a narrow waist, with faint traces of stretch marks around it. Candace's eyes lingered over her body, remembering that a few years ago, she and Melissa, high and alone together, had attempted to make love. It turned out badly, though. That night, both the mescaline and the half-assed pussy eating left them let down. Most of the night, they just sat together, nude and playing music. The love they had developed for each other since then was about more than hot, sweating bodies, and what they felt was far more important than sex, so they never tried it again.

Candace smiled to herself and took in the full measure of Melissa's luscious body again and wanted to touch her. But she stepped carefully around her instead, filled a glass with champagne, and headed back out of the room. She stopped for a second and watched those big titties rise and fall a few more times, and her eyes lingered on the tufts of salt and pepper that poked out from beneath the edges of her frayed panties. Candy was glad that Melissa's face was covered—the last thing she wanted was for Melissa to wake up and find her standing over her and staring at her. Her parting glance took in the delicate lattice the stretch marks made and the waves of silver hair that cascaded over the pillows. She left the room feeling a tangle of desire, admiration, and envy. She couldn't *wait* to get back upstairs . . .

Climbing the steps, her butter thighs rubbed together. She felt the warm, wet and sticky juice from her pussy sliding down and between them. At the top of the stairs, she stopped and ran her hand between her legs and over her dripping lips and licked the warm wetness from them. Then she recited the last line of the piece she'd started earlier:

> *Covered completely by dark I see you so vividly now, your frantic rush to free me; but it's all too late for your empty attempts, lines of others are forming behind you.*

Leaning against one of the walls in front of the guest room, Candace stuck her finger into the champagne. She sucked it off and then pushed it in past the lips of her pussy and deep inside herself. The penetration caused a shudder, and she absently closed her eyes. After a second, she dipped her wet finger back into the champagne and then pulled it back into her mouth, savoring the bittersweet combination of champagne and pussy.

Inside the room, Crow was still sleeping, deeply and *very* loudly. She sat down in a white wicker chair opposite the futon to drink her champagne. After a few minutes of playing with her pussy and pinching her nipples, she rose and walked over to pull the quilt off of Crow's body. She took another sip of the champagne and put the glass down on the floor beside her and sat back down.

Sliding lower into the chair, she began slowing rubbing herself, eyes on Crow's ebony manhood, impressive even though soft, she thought, and slipped into a fantasy . . .

She was the pilot of a plane. Crow was the copilot and sat in a leather swivel chair behind her. He leaned back and placed his heels on the armrests on either side of her. She leaned over to lick his toes, and the plane fell into a dive. She jerked her head up, snatched the stick with both hands, and leveled it off. Then she kicked it into autopilot and continued tonguing Crow's toes. Her lingual acumen made him quiver.

She rose from the command seat and stripped herself of her uniform, except for her captain's hat and the high-heeled red patent-leather shoes and garter-suspended, black fishnet stockings. Her breasts were larger than life, and they bounced with jiggly abandon when she fell to her knees and sank deep into the white shag carpet in the cockpit. Candace began licking up Crow's calves, which he stopped before she got to his knees. She filled his empty glass with dark red wine, and he drank till he was satisfied.

She unbuttoned his shirt and sucked hungrily on his nipples. Crow's attempts to appear detached made her laugh. Then she removed his underwear, but he was soft, the bulbous head of his shiny black johnson lying on the cool black leather before her. In one motion, she pulled a long, thick cucumber from the chair's side compartment and slid it up into her cunt and ran her tongue over the chair's cold leather until her lips found his dick. She lifted him with her tongue and sucked his length into her mouth, nearly swallowing it. Crow moaned aloud, and when she released him, he was hard as a rock and glistening with her saliva. He tugged gently on her nipples, as he watched his once dead dick come to life under the guidance of her skilled attention.

She made soft cooing noises as she easily slid the cucumber back and forth, in and out of herself, her thumb flicking the tip of her extended clit. Crow stopped twisting her nipples, and she rolled back onto the floor and spread her legs wide. He snatched the cucumber away from her and plunged it into her himself, roughly, moving it faster, shoving it deeper. Then he slid out of the chair, face first, and pulled the cucumber out with his teeth, dropped it on the floor beside her, and began licking her pussy.

Candace came hard and cried out, which shook her from the fantasy. Her eyes focused on Crow, stretched out on the futon, she licked the come off her fingers, moved from the chair, and kneeled over him. She knew she couldn't wake him but began to suck his dick anyway. Crow moaned in his sleep and kept on snoring. She sucked him until he was hard—just like in the fantasy—and fingered herself until she just about came again. She lifted herself and squatted on the balls of her feet, hovering, pussy dripping, over Crow's hard dick. Guiding it in gently, she tried to be careful not to press her weight on his body. As ready as she'd ever been, she slid her soaking pussy up and down on his hard dick. Desperately trying not to shake him too much, she couldn't hit it as hard as she wanted. Candy carefully cupped Crow's balls in one hand and steadied herself on the futon with the other. Her cunt sucked his throbbing cock ravenously until she started to shake and came yet again, pumping her nectar down the thickness of his shaft. She then opened her pussy, released him, and moved her face down to lick her sticky juices from his still-stiff member.

Crow continued to moan and snore alternately as he had since she'd started. She slid back and away to return to the white wicker chair and watched his dick jerk, shake, and slowly relax while she finished the champagne. Before Crow rolled back onto his side, Candace got down next to him and pulled the quilt over them. His arm found her when she returned. She kissed him twice before she, too, fell into deep slumber. Crow's snoring was no longer invasive.

Spell to Keep the Others Out of Your Hut (2002)

11

Creative Juices

It was about ten a.m., and Bones was still sitting in the park drinking a warm bottle of German beer. An hour earlier, he had fallen asleep with it in his hand, and now he wondered if during that brief nod he'd missed Candy's return home.

He was sitting there in the park feeling sorry for himself, jealous about Crow and Candy, but told whomever he'd seen passing by about Crow's exhibit anyway. Finally finished with his beer and tired of waiting, he rose from the bench and started toward the West Side. Bones assured himself that she was upstairs asleep—*alone*—and he'd just missed her when he nodded off.

At the edge of the park, he ran into a short, thick Latina he knew and petted her dog. She looked Bones in his red eye and said, "Jeez, you need to get you some zzz's. You look like something my dog did."

Bones agreed but added, "Yeah, but I'm promoting this big show for Candy and this black dude named Crow. He's gonna be a big-time artist, and I found him." He rambled on as his eyes roamed lasciviously over her wide hips and thick thighs. Silently objecting to his *reckless eyeballing,* she walked away from him while he was still talking.

As he walked up Avenue A, an old-timer he knew gave him a high five. "Man, I wish I could still swing all night like you," the old man said. "Wearing a damn tie all day is killing me, ya know."

"I know what you mean, Earl. These fucking ties are killing me too," Bones replied, practically having to drag the words out of his own mouth. He walked past the old man a few steps and then doubled back to promote the show. "It should be still happening by the time you get home from work. And tell Eddy and Quick Cripple Carl about the thing too. Me and Geoff got a little something special planned," Bones slurred.

"You know I'll try and be there, but Nancy's into cooking dinner nowadays. I hate it when she gets into her wifey mode. Pra-bly see you later, though, man."

"Sure thing, Earl, no sweat. Hope you can make it."

Three encounters later, Bones made it home and lost very little time finding his way into bed. It took him some time to fall asleep, though. Thoughts of Candace Maria were floating through his mind. The last thing he thought before he dozed off was if the bitch ever *did* offer him the pussy, he probably wouldn't even want it. He sang out loud an old Stones lyric, "You can't always get what you want," and felt a little better about shit.

Geoff, Keith, and Kenny went over to Fat Amy's loft on West Broadway off Broome Street and snorted some heroin to relax. They met the midday nodding and sipping seltzer water with floating twists of lime. At noon, Geoff left, needing time to do his makeup and arrange the paintings. Plus, he had to phone his wife in an effort to stave off the ever-impending litigation.

❖ ❖ ❖

Melissa pulled herself from under the pillows a little after eleven-thirty. First, she went to the bathroom and washed the little makeup she wore off her face. She studied the thin black scar that ran across her cheek and thought that later she might paint small orange circles decorating the left side of it for the exhibit. She calculated the many years the mark had been there, once again reflecting on the camping trip tragedy in the summer of '67 that had left the wound.

Turning from the mirror and squatting on the john, she muttered, "Who would have ever thought that this thing would add so much character to this old face?"

Finished relieving herself, she set the dial to regulate the heat of the water in the shower. Shedding her panties she looked at the tear along the seam, shook her head, and thought, *What if I brought someone home wearing drawers like these?*

She sauntered over to the blue-tinted glass stall that housed her black marble shower and pushed a black enamel button. Warm water sprayed from five separate showerheads. Stepping inside, she let water wash over her for a few minutes before she began to lather her breasts with one of the expensive perfumed soaps. As she ran the scented, transparent bar over her nipples, they stiffened. Then she adjusted the showerhead that had been mounted at waist level at an angle, so that a steady stream of water pounded her crotch. She slowly ran the soap between her legs. She moved the head spraying behind her so the water hit the top of the crack of her ass, moving the dial so the water flowed in one thick stream. Bending over, Melissa spread the cheeks of her ass so the water hit her asshole.

After quite a few minutes, as exciting as the sensation always was to her, she hit the control button, shutting off the water before she got into anything heavy—she had something else in mind. Stepping from the shower, her feet sank into the thick carpet, and she patted lightly with a fluffy black towel. Stroking her vagina with the soft corner of the towel, Melissa was reminded that it had been more than six months since she'd done it—with someone besides *herself.* She'd wanted to join Candace and Crow in bed earlier, but he was too tired, and she was pretty sure for all his bravado and hustler bullshit, Crow was a little too square to appreciate a threesome without some manipulating.

As she brushed her teeth, her thoughts shifted to the exhibit. Three pieces were clearly not enough. While Melissa rubbed a clear, scented, slippery oil over her damp body, she decided to wake Crow and try to persuade him to do another piece or two.

She went downstairs and into the kitchen, where she poured several different protein powders into a blender and filled it with orange juice and champagne. The sun flooded the kitchen, shining through the glass doors. Its rays striking her body made tiny rainbows in the beads of oil all over her. The drink was thick and sweet. She poured a glass for Crow and headed upstairs. On her way up, she wondered if she should dress before waking him. She said aloud, "Fuck it, I'm comfortable." Also, she wanted to see if her being naked would shock the tough guy from Brooklyn.

Melissa opened the door to their room quietly. She was hit with a quick flash of envy, seeing Crow and Candy wrapped together, arms and legs. She studied them for a few seconds and wondered how Candace could sleep so soundly with the noises Crow made. Crow's snoring reminded her of the father of her first child—a girl they named Breeze. She remembered when the two of them spent time in the mountains with the Yaquis tripping on peyote. After about a week, an overvigilant sheriff and a posse of deputies trashed their campsite, beat them both unmercifully, and locked them up for two days on the dubious charge of being "commie pinko hippies." When they returned to New York, he joined a revolutionary group called the Weathermen and changed his name from Paul to Insurrection. She loved him. But when a bomb he was making exploded and destroyed the building they were working out of, he disappeared and hadn't been heard from since. No bodies were ever found. An image of the tightly curled blondish hair that hung down to his waist in a thick braid came to her, the tips of it dyed red.

Her thoughts returned to the present, and she bent over and shook Crow's shoulder. He muttered something but didn't wake. Melissa shook his shoulder harder. Rolling over toward her this time, Crow blurted out, "Huh, OK, OK," but his eyes remained shut. After a few seconds, he began to snore again. As she shook him for the third time, she called out his name. "Shit," Crow muttered as his eyes slowly opened. Lying on his back, he looked up at Melissa standing over the bed, her green eyes boring into his. It took Crow a few seconds to realize that she was stark naked. His eyes drifted from her eyes down past her breasts, over the narrow waist, lingered a moment on the wide, full hips, the salt-and-pepper patch of curls, and then continued down the thick thighs and shapely calves. Her standing over him naked confused him.

Melissa smiled and said, "I'm truly flattered. It's been quite some time since I've gotten a gaze like that. Unfortunately, I'm not here for that." She bent over, handing the glass to Crow. Her titties swung forward as she did.

"Here," she said. "Drink this and get up. We've got to talk." As he sat up to take the glass from her, she asked him to move carefully so he wouldn't wake Candy.

Sitting up in bed and looking down into the glass, Crow asked, "What the fuck is this?" trying to speak softly.

"Energy in a glass. Proteins, vitamins, and orange juice with a dash of champagne; all you need to get *this* day started." Crow drank it, easing out of bed slowly. Melissa was thrilled, watching as his eyes roamed over her body. She told him to follow her downstairs. He found his pants in the pile of his and Candy's clothes and threw them over his shoulder. Melissa was already on her way down the stairs before Crow could tell her that he had to stop in the bathroom. "Damn, this hippie-dippie lifestyle sure is a motherfucker," he said to himself.

When Crow got downstairs, he found Melissa sitting cross-legged in the pillow room. Crow had put his pants on in the bathroom. She was still naked. Crow sat on a large pillow directly in front of her. "What time is it?" he asked.

"Somewhere between noon and twelve-thirty, I guess," she answered as she fished the black canister from under a pillow. "Here, take a few good hits."

As he reached for the spoon and the container, Crow noticed that the way she sat caused the lips between her legs to part, exposing the tender flesh inside. She smiled when she saw his pants bulge.

"Should I put a robe on? If my being nude is distracting you, I'll slip something on."

He hit the coke before he answered, "Nah, it's fine by me. I'm just not all that used to sitting around and talking to naked ladies. Besides, although I could see you was fine wit' your clothes on, I just didn't imagine you could be *this* fine with 'em off. No offense, but I just didn't know a bitch your age could look *that* good naked." He heard himself call Melissa "bitch" and apologized, saying, "I ain't mean nothing by calling you a bitch. Just a bad habit I should break."

Melissa smiled. "Sounded like a compliment to me," she said.

Then she got up and walked down to the kitchen. Crow's eyes followed her jiggle until she was out of view. He took a few more blows and said to himself, "This shit gets crazier by the minute." Then it struck him that none of this was really all that crazy, and it only seemed strange to him because he had never been around people like them before. His eyes looked around the room, and for the first time he realized that *he* was the square here.

Melissa came back upstairs carrying two glasses and half a bottle of champagne. She sat, tucking her legs under herself. She filled both glasses and handed one to Crow.

"The reason I woke you this early is that I think you need to do some more painting for the show. Three pieces aren't enough. I've got a full studio in the basement that you can use. It's got everything—brushes, paints, canvases. Anything you might need, I've got."

Crow choked on the champagne. "Are you crazy? You expect me to do a painting now? Just whip something up right here, in the next few seconds? I'm an artist, not Houdini."

Melissa took the blow from him and took two quick hits. "I'm confident you can handle it," she said.

Crow panicked. "No way, sugar!" he exclaimed.

After another blow and a swallow of champagne, her eyes found and held his. "Maybe you're right, but at least try to come up with something." Then she said, "Please try."

That made his stomach quiver. All of a sudden, he was overwhelmed and felt compelled to do whatever she asked. He looked at Melissa, sucked his teeth, and said with resignation, "Just pass me the damn coke."

Melissa dashed upstairs, leaving Crow alone and wondering, *What the fuck am I going to do?* While he worried, Crow shoveled several heaping mounds of cocaine up his nose and then finished his champagne in a gulp. After filling the glass a second time, he drained the bottle.

He heard Melissa coming down the stairs. She appeared in a worn black flannel robe that fell to mid-thigh and fuzzy black house slippers. The robe hung open, its edges draped around the sides of her breasts. She flung a pair of brown leather slippers at Crow, saying, "The basement floor is cement and is always ice cold. Grab the blow and the glass." She continued as she wove her way through the piles of pillows, "There's an artist's smock in the studio." Melissa walked past him to the kitchen and returned with another bottle of champagne. Holding the bottle up, she said, "I guess we're about ready. Now, come on."

Crow followed her down the stairs through a narrow hallway to a door that led to the basement. Melissa slid a bolt lock back that secured the door. Sliding her hand over the wall, she found the light switch. At the bottom of the stairs, a light flickered a few times and then cast a dim glow. Holding on to a shaky wooden rail, she started down. Crow moved slowly behind her, suspicious of each creaking step. Melissa hit another switch when they reached the bottom. He was relieved that he had successfully navigated the steps, considering the condition he was in—partly because of the champagne and blow Melissa had just given him but mostly a holdover from all the doping and drinking they'd done the previous night. Crow looked around the basement. It was filled with old furniture and boxes. Several bikes stood in a rack. One was an antique type that had a huge front wheel and a small rear one; another was built for four. There were three locked brass-studded chests piled next to the bikes. Melissa walked through a doorway and urged Crow to come in.

She pushed open the heavy wooden door and turned on the lights. Crow stood behind her and looked over her shoulder into the room. Two rows of high-intensity track lights flashed on overhead. In the center of the floor was an easel next to a tall swivel stool. On the left side of the room stood a five-foot steel cabinet. On the opposite wall were several shelves filled with hundreds of tubes and jars of paint. Melissa stepped into the room and began pulling open the cabinet drawers. As the drawers opened, she described the contents of each.

"The large brushes are in this drawer, the medium-sized ones are here, and the really tiny ones are over here. These are the small canvases; here are the mid-sized ones. The unstretched canvases are in the bottom drawer here, but you ain't got the time to stretch any. You'll have to use the ones that are already done."

As Melissa bent down to open the lower drawers, the robe rose to the tip of her ass. On impulse, Crow slid behind her and cupped her cheeks. Melissa trembled and froze. Crow held her ass with one hand and moved the other around to her front, catching a stiff nipple between his fingers and squeezing her breast with the rest of his hand. She reached and grabbed his hand, pressing it closer, and moved her behind slowly from side to side. Suddenly, she pulled away. "Not now, Crow. You've got shit to do." But she stood facing him and then ran her hand over his burgeoning crotch. "Hmm, this feels good. What the hell difference would a few minutes make, anyway?"

Melissa slowly sank to her knees and yanked Crow's zipper down. She snaked her hand inside his fly and inched him out. "Mmmmyyyy, how nice," she purred before slipping her lips over the head and moving the length of him down into her throat. Crow shook, and his eyes rolled back in his head. He moaned, "God damn," as Melissa's tongue got busy. His hands groped at her until he found her nipples, pulling and pinching until she cried out in pain and pleasure. It didn't take long before she got his dick hot and humming. Crow involuntarily rotated his hips, sliding his engorged penis back, forth, and all around. Releasing her nipples, he hefted her full breast in his hands as he began to vibrate. Melissa felt him tense, and as he began to spasm, she sucked harder, and in one violent eruption, he sprayed his jism into her succulent kisser. As he issued, Crow moaned, "Oh, shit!" exclaiming it over and over again. Melissa gasped for air, cum hitting the roof of her mouth and shooting down her throat.

Drained, he went limp, and Melissa pulled away, letting his shrinking cock fall gently from her lips. She smiled up at him, swallowed, and devilishly licked her lips. Crow's hands fell languidly to his sides as he struggled to catch his breath.

"That was quick but nice. Care for some champagne?" she asked. Still too dazed to speak, Crow just nodded.

After a quick sip and a few more blows of coke, Melissa showed him the intercom system and said she was going upstairs. "Buzz me if you need anything," she said, sashaying out of the room and up the stairs. Melissa had left him the coke and the champagne, so he snorted some more.

Not quite fully recovered, Crow looked around absently. "Damn. What have I gotten myself into?" he mumbled to himself. "I ain't no damned *artist.* I ain't playing this right. How am I gonna pull this off?"

Just then, he spotted several large books piled on top of a cabinet in the corner. He walked over and picked one up in each hand and discovered that they were picture books about art.

"What have we here?" he asked himself out loud. "I might be able to pull something off after all."

He put one down and began to flip through the pages of the other. The title on the shiny red cover announced that its topic was something called surrealism. He didn't quite know what that was about and figured he didn't have the time to figure it out, so he didn't bother with the text other than the captions under the pictures.

He decided that Salvador Dali's work was too technical to imitate. When he got to paintings done by Joan Miró, he looked them over carefully. *Shit, this looks easy enough,* he thought.

Melissa had left him a medium-sized canvas on the easel. He went to the drawer that held the brushes and selected four or five of various sizes.

Crow knew from hanging out with Danny that oil paint took too long to dry, so he found several tubes of bright acrylic paint and laid them on the shelf of the easel.

Seated on the stool with the book spread out in front of him, Crow said to himself, "What the fuck," and opened a tube of blue paint. He squeezed a glob of it onto a wide, long-bristled brush and began his first attempt at being an artist.

Crow started slowly smearing a glob of blue across the top of the canvas. As his hand held the brush, his mind began to move beyond the act itself, becoming all hand and eye. Almost instinctively trancelike, he began covering the top of the canvas with disconnected yet harmonious strokes of blue. At first, to his eye, the slashes appeared random, but as his hand led him in, he understood that they formed a subtle but complex interconnection. Without a second thought, he flung the brush he'd been using into a nearby metal slop sink, snatched up the champagne, took a hearty gulp, grabbed the next brush with the other hand, and began filling the empty spaces on top with a deep, rich yellow. The room he was in began to fade from his consciousness, and all that was left was the need to create a compelling sky. He became that sky. And as his hand and brush found the empty spaces between the blue, he filled them not only with yellow but also with himself. Then, from somewhere else, the yellow was being mixed with red as the sky cried out in brilliant orange tones. Crow was no longer painting but had become a vessel that brought the canvas and life together. When the orange was starting to go on too thick, Crow remembered Danny thinning acrylics with water to create a more fluid consistency. Without a second thought, he filled a glass from the tap and dipped the brush in, wiping the excess on his pants. He turned and reached back toward the canvas, only to be swallowed by it. As he dabbed and stroked, Crow felt waves of electricity vibrate off the canvas, up the brush, down his arm, sending tiny hot tingles throughout his body. Almost imperceptibly to himself, Crow had moved into another realm. He started talking, giving himself instructions: "First, paint the rest of the spaces water blue, let the surface dry, and then streak the motherfucker with orange." He repeated the phrase several times, creating a mantralike rhythm to the work.

Finally feeling finished, he stepped back, exhausted. The room came back into focus. Breathing heavily, he again wiped the brush on his jeans, creating a blue, yellow, and orange pattern on the right leg. Without taking his eyes off the canvas, he walked over to the slop sink and dropped the second brush into it. Crow plopped onto the stool and looked from the picture to his pants. All of a sudden, he started feeling anxious and uncomfortable. The distinct notion that something or someone besides himself was involved in creating this work was painfully persistent. Crow knew that some strange shit *had to be* kicking off in order for him to fuck up a perfectly good pair of jeans by wiping indelible shit on them. Plus, he didn't even half remember doing this shit.

Afraid to think more about it, Crow reflexively reached for the cocaine. He rapidly sucked down several big blows before a familiar feeling washed over him. He was high again and immediately *felt* as if he was more in control. He leaned back and let the blow drain down and numb his throat, his thoughts drifting while he waited for the watery blue color to dry.

Man, he thought, *I done hooked up with not one but* two *fine-ass hoes.* He laughed and corrected himself. *Women.* Not to mention an endless supply of blow and booze. He leaned over to see how close the color was to dry without touching it and sat back up, talking out loud to himself. "I'm in nigga heaven." He laughed again. "Actually, nigga coke-fiend heaven!" It wasn't the first time he'd had that thought since this trip began and wouldn't be the last before it was over.

His thoughts shifted suddenly to the coming show, and anxiety washed over him in waves. "Maybe I'll wake up soon, and all this shit will have been a dream," he mumbled. But the image was quite real and staring him in the face. He knew, dream or not, he had plenty more painting in him. This time, he leaned forward, extended a cautious finger, and found that the canvas was almost dry in the section he'd done last. Another quick hit, and he picked up the brush. Once again, the room faded, and he stepped back into the painting. He began repeating the mantra again, "Streak the motherfucker with orange," as the brush did its own thing.

Just beyond earshot and down in the pit of his stomach, Crow began to feel drums and chanting. In a slow crescendo, the sounds filled the room, the painting, and, finally, Crow himself. His mind's eye flashed to an image of the completed canvas. His connection to the landscape in the painting was immediate and primal. Crow wasn't sure how he knew this place, but the attachment ran deep, very deep. Intuitively, he knew it to be of African origin and that the forces guiding him and forging through the thick veil of drugs and alcohol were also African. Although higher than he had ever been before, he knew it was the Spirit working through him to pull this image from his insides. As he moved around the canvas, he felt as though he were watching himself from outside and waiting. And as the images materialized, he watched himself being moved around the canvas, being led by the collective mind and force of the Spirit.

Standing several feet away from the canvas, he was pleased by what he saw. Another idea struck, and he rushed to the canvas to see if the section he'd painted with the thick orange was dry. Since he'd covered the thick blue with orange, he wanted to cover the thick orange with thin blue. But he was impatient and didn't want to wait for the orange to dry, so he took another brush and placed a thick, jagged square of red, about six inches down from the left corner and four inches from the border over the patches of blue and orange. He didn't wait until that dried, either, before he found a tube of black paint, which he opened and pointed at the square sun, squirting a thick circle of darkness into the middle of it. After wiping the red off the tip of the first tube on his other pants leg, he returned it to the shelf. Looking back at the canvas, Crow couldn't remember the last time he was this content. The situation would have called for more champagne before now, but just looking at what he had done seemed reward enough.

The brush in the basin didn't have enough blue left on it to cover the patches of thick orange, so he got another bowl and made another wash of paint. He was beginning to like the way the colors contrasted with his black jeans, so he cleaned the brush's end by making three blue diagonal stripes across his left thigh. The orange was dry enough to cover it in blue without mixing the colors. This time, he wanted the wash to run and quickly dabbed the brush, soaking wet, over the thick orange paint.

Finished with the sky, Crow sat on the stool with his arms folded, staring at the canvas. He stayed that way for a few minutes and then got up and turned the painting upside down. He went to the shelves and found three different shades of brown, got another wide bush from the drawer, and with the darkest brown paint repeated how he had started with the blue. The first row of brown was done with longer strokes than the second, which he painted in the next deepest brown shade. The third row was done with the lightest of the browns, these strokes briefer than the others. The open spaces between them were closer than the spaces he'd left between the rows of blue. Leaving about two inches between the top and the bottom, he filled them with two different shades of green and painted the strokes side by side, leaving no spaces between the alternating slashes of color. He painted the greens so they reached into the blues and oranges. He found a tube of rust-colored paint and thinned it slightly. The rust color connected all the spaces between the browns and served as a thin buffer between the browns and the greens. He turned the canvas upright and found he'd finished his first landscape. The work wasn't finished, because all that stood before him was a barren, abstract landscape.

Crow went and got a smaller brush and the black paint and painted a large black bird gliding upward. The bird's body was a graceful upward arc. The head was narrow, the beak long and curved. It flew into the sun with its proud wings thrown back. Below the bird, he added two lovers standing. Their legs from the knees down were hidden beneath the abstracted green foliage. The bodies were entwined, dissolving into each other. The bird and the lovers were variations on themes that appeared in the paintings he'd *appropriated* from Danny. But these images had been meaningful to him before he met the Brooklyn artist. He signed the painting "Shade."

Released from his "state of grace," Crow collapsed back onto the chair and reached for the blow. He brought a hit to his nose but then didn't sniff it. He let the powder fall to the floor and sat dazed, marveling at the scene set on the easel before him.

Melissa was upstairs on the pillows skimming the manuscript Crow had left behind. She started to read from the page Crow had folded down at its corner.

Candace Maria stirred from the soundest sleep she could remember since she'd started doing so much coke, turned over, and found the other side of the bed empty and the room silent. She went into the hall and knocked on the bathroom door. No one answered, so she headed downstairs. She found Melissa reading.

"What happened to Crow?" Candy asked.

"He's downstairs painting," Melissa told her.

"Oh, that's great!" Candy said. She noted that Melissa was naked on the pillows. She asked with tinge of jealousy, "Did you *fuck* him?"

"Almost," Melissa nonchalantly answered. "I wanted to, but him *doing* another *piece* was more important at the moment."

Candace wondered what she meant by "almost" but asked instead, "What do you think of the book?"

"I haven't gotten too into it, but it sounds interesting so far. I started to read here, where the page is folded down, just before you came in."

"That's where he stopped reading to me last night," Candy said with a hint of possessiveness in her voice. She lay down on the pillows next to Melissa. Both women, bare asses up, tits pressed into the soft pillows, squirmed around until they were comfortable. Candy finally relaxed, asked Melissa playfully and childlike, "Would you read some to me? I was really getting into the story when Crow was reading it, but we got distracted." Candy spoke out of the corner of her mouth, in a less than subtle attempt to reinforce in Melissa's mind whom he had come there with. "Read a little, OK?" she finished, trying to sound innocent of what she was actually saying and what she was actually doing.

"Of course baby, but first let me fix you a protein drink." Melissa got up, jiggling, and pulled a baggie full of cocaine and a spoon out of a drawer. She handed it to Candy, telling her that it would help her wake up, as she continued on to the kitchen.

Candy took a few hits as she listened to the faint hum of the blender. She wondered again what Melissa had meant when she said she *almost* fucked Crow. She spilled some coke on a purple velvet pillow and licked it up, freezing the tip of her tongue.

Crow sat transfixed, staring at the image before him, unaware of the passage of time. He hopped up and took the painting down.

He looked around the room, found a fresh canvas, and placed it on the easel. Its blankness was like a movie screen before the projector starts to roll. He stared until his eyes began to hurt. He stood up and began to pace back and forth. *What the fuck,* he thought. *How in the hell am I gonna come up with something else?* He leafed through the art books again and became even more frustrated. None of the pictures looked anything like what he'd paint if he *were* an artist. They looked too technical, too childlike, or just too *white*. He wondered what Danny would do. He remembered what Danny had said a few months back: "Sometimes, I don't create the work at all. I just grab a brush and let the ancestors guide me. I go to the canvas with a color in my mind, I pick up the brush, and the spirits do the rest."

At the time, Crow thought Danny was bullshitting him, but now, as he looked over at the finished work leaning against the wall, he knew he'd gotten help from somewhere. Crow looked to the ceiling and said, "The only ancestor I know of who might give a brotha like me some help is my daddy. Pops, if you is list'nin', I could sure use some assistance right about now—I *do* want to make you proud of me one day."

The room was silent. After a few seconds of just sitting, Crow sucked his teeth and mumbled, "So much for the spirits. Maybe the bottled kind can help a nigga out." He grabbed the champagne and drained the last of it. Looking back at the canvas, he sighed. "Welp, this ain't getting me nowheres," he said, and dipped the tip of the brush he'd chosen into one of the acrylics. "Fuck it," he spat, as he approached the canvas. As soon as the brush made contact with it, the tingle reappeared. He felt himself say, "Oh, shit. Something's happening," and laugh, but the voice was not his own. The sound seemed older than time and connected Crow through time to its source, at the beginning.

The canvas became the light at the end of a long tunnel, and as he moved through and toward it, the electrifying tingle became many hands touching him, each feeding him rich images emanating from the source of all time . . .

Small, dark brown men with wide, flaring nostrils releasing sculpture from tree trunks and stone blocks; blue-black women, ornately dressed and draped in gold, looms between their strong, firm thighs, weaving intricate raffia textile in Kuba villages deep in the bright green bush; Nilotic iron smelters and Ife bronze casters fashioning ancestral figures from memories they'd never had themselves. And there were thousands upon thousands of other fundi—artisans—crafting images from the beginning of time: a palace sareq in Nubia; the stelae of Meroe; tekhenwy throughout the Tawi; mortuary tombs at Saqqara; an incense burner in Qustul; a limestone "zodiac" in Het-Heru's temple at Dendera; and even the fantastic basalt heads at Tres Zapotes and the colossal black Buddhas with peppercorn hair that are still venerated in Asia. Then there were the carvers of ceremonial masks in Hausaland, Yorubaland, Swaziland, and of the Fon, Fang, and Dan; the medicinal power figures and totem along the Kongo and the Kanaga of the Dogon; the majestic architecture of Namoratunga, Great Zimbabwe, and, of course, Giza—all of which serve to re-create astronomical events. MDW NTR bas reliefs from Kush to Alexandria led Crow into the barkcloth paintings of the Mbuti, Deng, and Twa and the tile work of the Tuareg that is meant to express the importance of the human hand in the spiritual arts . . .

These places, peoples, and art flooded into Crow, and when he emerged from the tunnel the ancestors had taken him through, he found he had completed not one but two more "new" works. Spent and sobered, he slumped down to the floor. As the spirits departed, they left Crow rocking back and forth, weeping softly. "I didn't know, I *didn't* know."

After a few minutes, his head began to clear. This experience left him shaken to the core. He tried to rationalize what had taken place. He tried to blame the whole thing on the mushrooms, but he knew better. The experiences were too complete and too revealing for it to have been just some drug shit.

As the memory of what he had been through receded, the paintings remained. They were tightly constructed mosaics of what had been revealed to him, and they were breathtaking. This experience had brought Crow to something he had been consciously avoiding his entire life: a spiritual awakening. He was wide open now and couldn't figure out or avoid what was coming.

Melissa rejoined Candy with a tall goblet filled with orange liquid. "Let me guess: orange juice, vodka, and protein powders, right?" Candy asked.

"*Almost.* Champagne today, honey. Only the best this morning—I mean, afternoon," Melissa said. She handed Candy the glass and flopped down on the pillows. Then she grabbed the folder and scooted over next to Candace. She saw some powder on the pillows that Candy had missed and licked it up.

"Ready to listen?" Melissa asked, starting to read before she got an answer:

> "Going into town?" she asked. I told her I guess so. I tried to move on but she kept—

Candy cut her off. "I've heard that part already. Start right after he tells her his name." Melissa scanned the pages until she found the right one. She began again:

> Pandora laughed. "That's funny," she said.
>
> "I don't see where being the family deduction's so funny," he snapped at her.
>
> "Yeah, I guess you're right. I thought you were joking. Nobody gave a shit about me, neither, excepting Cousin Jordan. But then he raped me in the basement last year. I ain't cry,

though. I just wiped the blood off my legs when he was done and just kept walking. I was on my way back home when I ran into you."

"So why don't you go on home then?" he asked, starting to walk off.

"Because I really ain't wanna go home. I might not have even gotten there. I guess I'm just wandering. You don't really mind if I go back with you, do you?" she said, walking alongside him.

Picking up his pace, he said, "I guess it don't matter one way or the other."

"Ooh," she affected in a high pitch, "goody, and I won't even charge you the standard tour guide fee." They walked for a while in silence. Pandora noticed Exemption continually looking across the road. "What you looking at, sugar?" she asked him.

He lifted his glasses, and she and the other figures disappeared again. "I guess I ain't looking at nothing," he said to the vacant space where he last saw her. When he lowered the shades Pandora was walking several paces ahead of him. "I wasn't looking at nothing," he mumbled to himself as he stepped faster.

"I know what you mean, I really do," she said as he slowed to match her pace. Ahead the lights from the town were getting brighter. "Good thing we've got some dark glasses," she commented absently. "Sometimes the lights get so bright they can blind you." Exemption said nothing, so they struggled through the thick silence. Beads of sweat rolled from his armpits along his sides and formed on his upper lip. It seemed the lights sent waves of heat matching their brilliant glare.

Melissa paused for a second and said, "Ah, my dear, the high road to adventure. Seems like some roads I've been down before."

"Ain't we all," Candace added, reaching for the blow. She hit it once, her head snapping back from the hefty snort. "Damn, here, have a hit!"

Melissa shook her head. "Not right now, baby. Let me read some more of the story before we get dressed."

Candace got up to go to the kitchen. "Don't read no more till I get back," she called to Melissa, disappearing through the door.

Melissa wondered how Crow was doing downstairs. She listened to Candace Maria fumbling around in the kitchen. She took a sip from her drink, thought about what she believed to be Crow's story on her lap, and looked at the stacks of books all around her in the room. "I must have spent at least half my damn life reading," she said to herself. "Hurry up, Candy, it's getting late."

Candy bounced back upstairs holding a new glass, declaring that she'd made a Bloody Mary.

"How are you gonna drink this stuff now?" Melissa exclaimed. "Tomato juice and orange juice don't mix!"

Candy sat down and took a few swallows. Putting the glass aside, she lay diagonal to Melissa, resting the back of her head on the woman's full, pale rump. Then she squirmed onto her side, finally resting her cheek on Melissa's ass.

"OK, you can read some more, I'm comfortable now." Melissa wiggled her ass and asked Candace if she was sure."For now" was the reply she got.

For the last quarter-mile or so the road leading to the town was paved with thick cobblestones. On both sides of the street wooden posts with brass hitching rings stood spaced several feet apart. Exemption wanted to know if the posts were still used, but then a naked man on a motorcycle roared out of the darkness from the other side of the road, bumped across the cobbles in front of them, and disappeared into the wall of night at their left. The sound of the engine immediately swallowed as the rider rode into the wall of black, Exemption's question suddenly rendered pointless. "Same thing happened to me when I was on my way there," Pandora told him.

Exemption thought for a while before he said, "I bet most

people would think all this is real weird, but I don't. I didn't tell you that I was born wearing sneakers, or that I'm at least ten or twelve years older than I was a little while ago. As a matter of fact, these are the very sneakers I was born in. Shit, they still fit."

"Is that so?" Pandora said. "Well, I was born with hair on my thing, and by the time I was four I had bigger tits than my mama. On top of that, ever since I can remember, all my dolls were anatomically correct. But the shit don't stop there. Right during the middle of my fifth birthday party, I turned into an Oriental. Six months later, on my folks' seventh anniversary and in a doctor's office when the doctor was trying to figure out a reason why I wasn't pink with blond hair, I turned into an eight-year-old colored boy with red hair and green eyes. A day later I was back to my old self but a year older and couldn't get enough watermelon. For about the next two years or so, I'd change into something else. My daddy took me to all kinds of healers and conjure workers. I think I was an Eskimo one day when I ate some bad sardines. Everybody swore I was gonna die, and I almost died, but then I turned into what you see now, white with black hair and gray eyes. I still had big hooters, and after a month or so without switching to something else, Mama let me go back outside. You ain't the only one who's got stock in the weird market."

He wasn't sure if he believed her or not but said, "It's been rough, ain't it?"

"Tell me about it."

Ahead, there seemed to be a commotion at the gates to the city. From where they were, they were able to see a small crowd of people walking in a circle carrying signs. "What the hell is going on?" Exemption asked Pandora.

"Oh, that's nothing, it goes on all the time. They're just people who can't get into the place because they came with a purpose in mind. When the man at the gate asks you why you're there, just tell him you don't know, and he'll let you right in. I met a girl on my way here, and she told him she came to find herself, and he wouldn't let her in. I told him one place was as good as any other, and I got right in. When I left, she was still there carrying a sign that said, 'Don't enter . . . unfair to people with plans.' "

Exemption and Pandora were greeted with slurs and catcalls when they crossed the picket line. Once through the line and past the white and orange wooden horses that were built to look like horses with straw hanging where their tails should be, Pandora leaned across a saddle and waited until her friend marched by. "Candy, Candy," she called. The girl, who looked to be about sixteen, stepped out of line and walked over. Exemption looked at the sign that hung from her neck. It now read, "Boycott this city, it denies self-exploration."

"How's it going, Pandora?" the girl asked.

"About the same," Pandora told her. "Why don't you just walk away, wait for a few minutes, and come back? I bet you'll get in."

"I don't want to get in anymore. I came here to find myself, and now I'm doing something that I believe in. There's no reason anymore for me to come inside. We've got portable toilets and showers, and the local officials provide us with sleeping bags and three squares a day. Few people know it, but there's a whole different party happening on this side of the road. Listen, I'll see you later. I've got to put in the full eight on line. Five days a week for nine months to pass my probation period." With that, she got back into the circle and picked up the chant the group had started.

Pandora moved over to Exemption and shrugged her shoulders. "What can I say? I guess happiness is where you find it."

Melissa stopped reading at the end of the paragraph and said to Candace, "I see your name is in the story."

Candace Maria laughed and proclaimed, *"Yo soy Señorita Candace Maria,* not some *pendejo* named Candy, OK?"

Melissa laughed and said, "Well, I'll be a receptionist. Ms.

Candace Maria using her native tongue and showing that renowned Latin temper."

Candy rolled over onto her stomach and bit Melissa on the ass. Melissa cried out—more from shock than pain.

"I'll give you some *native tongue,*" Candy said before she spread Melissa's cheeks and darted her tongue into her pursed asshole. Melissa shook as the tip of Candace's tongue forced its way inside her. Her ass rose to meet the probing of Candace's wet tongue.

"Candy, Candy, Candy, baby. I wasn't ready for this." Candace ran her tongue along the crack of Melissa's ass, flicking its tip sharply when she reached the woman's hole. Then she sat up and left Melissa panting. Candace called her a horny *gringa* and drank some more of her Bloody Mary. Melissa asked her why she'd stopped. Candace reached for the coke, took a few blows, and told her to turn over. Candace sprinkled a few blows on the tip of her tongue and spread Melissa's legs wide. Candace moved to kneel between the open thighs, and as Melissa's eyes fluttered shut, Candace's head moved down to the open pussy, spread wide by Melissa's fingers. Candace's powdered tongue slid slowly over the pink protruding clit and then lapped the exposed slit. Melissa ground her pussy into Candace's face. It was hot, wet, and sticky, clinging to her lips, nose, and cheeks. Candace slid her hands under Melissa, cupping the cheeks of her ass, and sent her tongue deep into the pink opening. Melissa came, releasing her pussy to squeeze Candace's nipples. When Melissa's panting and heaving began to cease, Candace slipped away to take a sip from her glass.

After a few seconds, Melissa's eyes opened. Candace said, "So much for that native tongue. Now, read me some more."

"My pleasure," Melissa replied, still a little out of breath and only half talking about the reading. She turned back over and started to read. Candace laid her head back on Melissa's ass.

> The man in the tower looked down at Pandora and Exemption and said to Pandora, "You just left. I thought you were going home."

THREE DAYS AS THE CROW FLIES

Pandora called up to him, "Wasn't any reason to."

"You're right about that. Who's that you've brought with you?"

"He's a friend," she explained. "His name is Exemption. He didn't know where he was going when I ran into him."

"Oh, I see," the man called down, another one just like any other one. "What's your story?"

"Let me tell you my story," Melissa said. Candy sat up so that she could look into Melissa's eyes as she spoke.

"The reason I'm so light-skinned, or 'light, bright, and damned near white,' as they used to say," Melissa began, "started two generations ago. My grandmama, who folks called Auntie Marie, was a coal-black conjure woman who loved me. Beautiful and wild, she never went to church like the other girls in town. She spent time studying lessons her grandma the African had written down and passed on to her. Anyway, she developed a reputation for making the best juju potions and amulets in all of Louisiana. Auntie Marie wasn't more than sixteen years old—and *fine*—when the mean and spoiled son of the town's richest cracker, called Little Joe, and one of his buddies came calling to buy themselves a love potion to make their girlfriends have sex with them. Little Joe was the mayor's boy, twenty-one years old, and had a reputation as a ladies' man. Marie knew them crackers was gonna be big trouble the moment she saw them coming. She had 'the gift,' you know, and was never wrong. Joe and his buddy didn't wanna pay for her services, at least not with money. Joe figured the pleasure of him giving it to her would be payment enough. When she turned him down, Joe's buddy held Marie down while Joe raped her repeatedly. Laughing, Joe left saying she was lucky that's all that happened to her, and if she told anyone, they'd send the local Klan to 'burn her out and string her black ass up.' Marie didn't have any intentions of telling any earthly beings, but that night, she called on the ancestral spirits to set things right. The next afternoon, Joe stepped out of his house as usual and took him a stroll down Main Street. The only difference was that to everyone who saw him, Little Joe appeared to be the bluest black nigger that they had ever seen. And there he goes walking down the street just tipping his hat and waving and smiling at white folks. The white people were too shocked to react until this nigger, bold as brass, kissed the lily-white daughter of a prominent citizen on her hand in the middle of the town square. He even winked at her as he strode away. For that, he was beaten senseless by an irate gang of crackers, many of whom were his friends. They proceeded to initiate a burning and lynching right there on the spot despite Joe's protests and acclamations of who he was. He was hung and set on fire. Just as flames reached his head, through the crackle of the fire, Joe's visage returned to normal. Nobody could or wanted to explain what had happened. Later that night, Joe's accomplice was having a dinner of hot, spicy gumbo when he suddenly burst into flames. Nobody wanted to explain that, either. The two were laid to rest in unmarked graves and were never mentioned again in public. My mama was born as a result of that rape.

"Mama's story was different. She ain't have the power. You see, it sometimes skips a generation—especially when *rape* is involved. As long as anybody can remember, Mama wanted to be a singer, and when she heard that black folks like Josephine Baker were getting big play over in Europe, she set out for Paris."

Candy interrupted her. "Hold up. You mean to tell me your grandmother burnt up two white guys and lived to tell you about it?"

"First of all, my grandmama didn't burn up anybody. Them rednecks burnt up Little Joe, and I reckon it was that spicy gumbo that got to his partner. The spirits of our ancestors might have fanned the flames along, but it was only justice. Second, Grandmama didn't tell anybody what they did to her, and them white boys hadn't exactly advertised it, neither, so there was no reason to suspect Grandmama of anything. So, let me finish. Anyway, Mama got over there to Europe and found out that the only difference between there and here was that they let one or two niggers get up on a stage every now and again. This was right before World War Two, and times were getting hard. The popular story was that my mother, whose name was Jasmine, fell in love with and married my daddy, a Parisian club and brothel owner. I myself believe that a combination of desperation and ambition on my mother's part fueled that marriage. If that was the case, Mama never let on. My daddy was killed during the war, so I only have the vaguest memory of the man. The few pictures I've seen show him as tall and thin with hawkish good looks. I guess he had to be a little good-looking to be a pimp. Mama took over the business and made a shit load of money. When she realized I had some small talent for the old religion, she sent me back to be trained by her mama. Mama moved to Zanzibar in the early fifties and got involved in all kinds of shit. I used to go see her every year, and she always sent tons of cash to Grandmama and me. I haven't spoken to her in years. Last I heard, though, she was in deep hiding because of some political stuff. When Grandmama passed, I came up here and opened a beatnik bar. I manufactured Orange Sunshine Acid with Timothy Leary in the sixties and other shit that if I told you, I might have to kill you." Melissa laughed.

Candy sat with her mouth hanging open. "Damn," she said. "That's almost as freaky as Crow's story. Maybe one day I'll tell you about *mi abuela.* She knew a little bit of shit herself."

Before either Candy or Melissa could say any more, Crow's voice came over the intercom. "Melissa, I think I'm finished. You wanna come down and see?"

Candace jumped up and pushed the button. "Can I come too?" she asked.

"Is that you, Candy, baby? Both of y'all come on down."

"We'll be right there," Melissa called out, surprised at herself for being a little jealous that Crow had called Candy "baby."

Making their way across the basement to the studio, Candy was still plagued by the thought of what Melissa might have meant when she said she'd *almost* fucked Crow.

The studio door was halfway open. Crow sat on the stool with arms folded, looking at the paintings. He heard them when the door creaked open wider but didn't turn around to greet them. He pretended to be absorbed and unaware that they'd entered. It was only when Candy called his name that he swung around in the chair. Seeing the two naked women standing together shocked him so badly that he almost slipped off the stool.

Candace ran over to him, throwing her arms around his head, pressing his face into her breasts. When she bent down to kiss him, Crow caught the distinct smell of pussy on her face. He kissed her back and said, "Hmm, your face smells familiar. You been eatin' pussy?"

Candy's brown cheeks turned red. "I *guess* so," she answered with a small voice.

Crow looked at Melissa, who refused to divert her attention from the paintings. He looked back to Candace. "I'm down here working my ass off, and you two are upstairs sucking each other's brains out. I don't call that fair," he said.

"Maybe it ain't fair, but alls I managed to do was come. You've created something new for this world," Melissa said. "Which one do you think is more important? And don't act like you ain't get none, either."

Candy shot them both an icy glare that demanded answers, but they both ignored her. Crow got up and wrapped an arm around each of their waists and looked at the paintings with them. Candy stiffened in his arm and sucked her teeth.

"So what do you think?" he quickly asked.

Melissa said, "Beautiful," and Candy tried to relax and said that she liked them better than any of the other ones.

"I had to use acrylics instead of oils so that by the time we get ready to head out, they should be dry," Crow said, trying to impress them with his knowledge. "When do you think is a good time to get over to the store?" he asked.

"The gallery, honey. I don't think it's quite five o'clock yet, but we'd better start getting ready," Melissa said. Her eyes caught the streaks of paint on Crow's pants. She grabbed a brush and dipped it into the red paint and added a long, wavering stroke from his right pocket, across the fly, and ending on his upper right thigh. "What else should we add?" she asked, looking at Candy.

Candy, who had decided to let it go until she could get Crow alone, stood back and placed her index finger under her chin. "Hmm, let's see," she said, looking at his pants. "We don't want it to look too contrived. Just dip the brush in some of that bright green and put on a lopsided rectangle over that knee." She pointed at Crow's right leg.

Melissa dashed off the rectangle, which became a mixture of green and red at the end. "Looks good, looks good, but we should use colors that ain't in the painting," Candy said. "How about some random shots of that yellowish green under the left pocket and another green farther down the leg. Then call it a day. It ain't like he's been painting in those pants for years, know what I mean?"

As Melissa worked on his pants, Crow was shaking his head. "Everything's hype, huh? Even down to *how* to fuck up my brand-new black jeans," he said, reaching carefully over to the shelf for the blow.

Melissa was on one knee adding dashes of blue near the right cuff. "Spare us the sermon. This shit is baby food compared to the real hype out there." She bounced up and looked at the pants, then said to Candy, "I believe he's good to go now, you agree?"

"This man looks like an Express Mail package from frenzied creativity. Good enough to eat. Perfect, just perfect. A tad of paint on his boots, and art and artist are one."

"Yo! Listen. I ain't goin' to get my boots . . . we just gonna leave the damn boots alone. Enough is enough, and I ain't fucking up no *hunnid-dollah* shoes to impress nobody," Crow snapped sharply.

"Well, at least take the laces out, then," Melissa suggested.

"Who the fuck do I look like, Run DMC or some damned body? How the fuck am I gonna walk?"

They finally agreed that he would leave the laces untied, not wear the sweater, unbutton the button-down collar on the shirt, and leave the shirttails hanging. Finished with the details, Crow said, "Give the crowd as little Brooklyn negro as possible, huh? Too bad we ain't got no Dixie Peach and Nadinola to round this shit out."

Candy sucked her teeth again and exaggerated. "Whass up? Lost yo' player's heart so soon? I thought you was about getting busy. We just helping you do some work. Don't go and lose your focus on me, home slice."

Her words washed over him like cool water. *She's dead right,* he thought. *I'm standing here in front of two buck-naked, grown-ass* women, *acting like some kind a sucker.*

He looked at the paintings again and thought, *This shit I painted is* real, *not some bullshit game. These motherfuckers came out of* me; I *said that poetry. And I* did *steal them other paintings, though, but I'm too far into the movie to change my role now.*

"You right, baby. But once in a while, everybody gets weary of playing. You two been so nice to me, and I'm just a little tired of everything being nothing and something at the same time is all," Crow said after his reflection.

Melissa smiled and said, "It takes a lifetime of hard work to reconcile the world to its contradictions. Only saints and deep thinkers and another chosen few ever really come to terms with the paradoxes and dichotomies. Just feel good that you're beginning to work some of this stuff out. Do the best you can."

"Let's go upstairs now. We can talk this shit later," Crow said.

On the way up the stairs, Crow remembered the blow sitting on the shelf. He mentioned it to Melissa, who said they could get it later. Crow watched their asses bounce as Melissa led them up the stairs to the third floor. Reaching it, she gave Crow and Candace fresh towels. Candace went back downstairs to shower. Melissa went into the kitchen and grabbed a dishtowel out of one of the drawers by the sink. She wet it under the faucet and wiped herself down with it.

Melissa's bedroom was on the second floor, third door on the right. She used a key hidden on the ledge of another door to open it. She sank into thick black wool pile carpet. The walls were painted Day-Glo pink, with a large black circle in the center of each. She fell across a low, circular bed, banging her shin on the black lacquer frame. On the wall behind the bed was a gun rack, which held several different gauges of shotguns and automatic weapons. She looked at the pile of handwritten pages on the floor and remembered that nothing new had been added to the book she was writing in several weeks. She hadn't even been in this room except to get clothes or something out of the safe. She picked up page 637 and read the last few sentences:

> My heart pounded trying its best to burst from both breasts at once. My nipples were crimson. I struggled between hiding or running my finger over the sharp sliver of broken blue mirror. Dry blood was caked under my nails.

She threw the page down to the floor. *How can I justify this murder?* It was the question that had left her pen idle for weeks. She jumped up from the bed, pulled a black suede T-shirt from the dresser drawer and black leather pants from the closet, and laid them across the bed. Then she got a slip of paper with a series of numbers written on it from under the mattress and repeated the sequence that opened the safe.

The safe was built of a dense black steel. She pushed. Before she pulled the door open, she considered how much money she should have had left. The top shelf was stacked with bills according to denomination.

After yesterday's seven hundred, I should have about sixty-four grand left in here, she thought. Melissa opened the door and counted out ten one-hundred-dollar bills. Then she grabbed three fifty-dollar bills and a few twenties. *Just in case,* she thought.

The second shelf was lined with plastic vials, each one labeled to reflect which exceptional hallucinogen it contained. Lying on top of the drugs was a thin jewelry case. She pulled that out and selected a strand of pearls to wear. She closed the safe door with the push of a button.

The long strand of pearls with the emerald pendant contrasted with the black suede midriff top she'd selected to show off the sexy, delicate gold waist chain she always wore. Looking in the dresser mirror, she carefully drew a trail of teardrops with black eyeliner, which ran from the corners of her eyes and over her cheeks, ending at the chin. She tipped her eyelashes with bright blue watercolor paint, to dramatic effect. Silently, she damned her drawer full of tattered underpants and decided to wear none. Down on her hands and knees, she found a pair of silver-studded, black suede boots with kick-ass high heels and pointy toes under the bed. She gingerly tugged the boots past the tiny silver bells on the jingling anklet she was known for. She stood and inhaled deeply to fasten the top button on her skintight leather jeans. She fluffed her hair, and her next quick glance in the mirror made her smile. "Damned near fifty-six and still as bad as I wanna be," she said.

Melissa passed the room Crow and Candy had slept in and saw that the door was open. She peeked and saw Crow sitting on the bed putting his boots on. When Crow saw her, he stood up and spun around. "Presentable?" he asked. Candy had just made it back up to the second-floor landing wrapped in the towel in time to hear his question. She and Melissa both yelled, "Perfect!" at the same time. Everybody laughed.

"We're ready. You've got to move it, Candy," Melissa said, patting Candy's ass under the towel as she ran past. Crow strapped on his watch and flipped the collar of his shirt up. He and Melissa went downstairs as Candy quickly dressed.

When she finally joined them, Candy found Crow in the pillow room looking through Melissa's stacks of books. She could hear Melissa's voice coming from down the hall and walked past Crow to peek out the door.

Melissa was standing in the old-fashioned phone booth, leaning back against the open door. Candy heard her tell someone to make sure that they got here. She hung up and took another dime from the change dispenser on the wall next to the phone, slipped it into the slot, and began dialing.

After a few seconds, Melissa raised her voice, saying, "Just get out of bed! Get Checkers together and put on your good Republican cloth coat and come on over to Geoff's place about six-thirty. There's some new talent you have to see."

After a short pause to let the person on the other end respond, Melissa said tersely, "Of course! Have I ever been wrong before? Look, Fae, I've got to run. I'll see you over there." She fished out another dime.

Satisfied with her eavesdropping, Candace ducked back into the pillow room toward Crow. She stepped carefully around and through pillows, pausing every so often to plot out the next few steps through the maze.

Crow looked up from the book he was reading and watched her awkward advance. When she finally grabbed his arm to steady herself, he asked her if Melissa had written the book he was holding. He read the title, *My Life as an Icon Trapped in a Church's Stained-glass Window,* by "M."

"Yeah, I think so," Candace answered. "It's probably one of the early ones."

"Damn, this bitch is *bad,*" Crow said. "How the fuck does one person get so much talent? Listen to the first poem. It's called 'Early Mass.' "

A child threw a stone through my neighbor's crown of thorns
while his mother debated the price of green apples.

She didn't buy them and a week later they ruined the view by
covering us with wire mesh. Now turned to rust.

It's bitter irony that he can't lift that cross off his bent back while
one white opaque tear will rest forever on my cold glass cheek.

The congregation, clergy, and the fools, also each year's arrogant altar boys thinking . . .

This tear is for him. I'm not the virgin. In the next window, I want to tear free and run with men much younger than my gothic years. Do nasty things in parked cars. Hike this damn see-through blue robe high past my hips. Exposed as a harlot and excommunicated with glee.

But today it's enough that mass is soon over. If I could only ram his crown in the fat lady's throat from the third pew. She sings terribly off key. Much like me and this man forever broken by his burden.

"M" 1956

Crow closed the book and asked Candy what she thought of the poem.

"I like it, but it's really not one of my favorites. I like her more personal stuff. That one sounds like social commentary. But all her stuff is pretty good."

Crow reared back and looked at her with one eye. "You crazy. You can't get no more personal than that. What the hell is the social about? Isn't it people that make up the social? Doesn't each person have a *personal* experience of the social?"

Candy, startled by Crow's thoughtful interpretation, responded slowly, in a low voice. "Melissa was writing about ineffectiveness and alienation of society at large, using the woman in the glass to describe it. I don't know if this is *her* personal experience or not."

"Bullshit, and don't talk to me like I'm some kind of Philistine." Crow was having a flashback from one of the social philosophy classes he had taken in college. It felt kind of good. Once, in his sophomore year, he'd considered joining the debate team but decided that it was for chumps and that getting high felt better than winning a good argument by being better informed about something than an opponent. Seven years and many kilos later, he had almost forgotten how much he enjoyed this kind of thing. "Melissa was talking about the box she is in and how she is unable to do anything about it," he said.

Crow noticed Melissa was leaning in the doorway, enjoying the discourse and smiling.

"You're both right, and you're both wrong," she said. "I wrote that book sitting in the back of a church the last Sunday morning I ever went, high on mescaline tea and hash brownies. It's what I thought that the woman—who is *not* me, by the way—in the window might be thinking, something like that. Everything is personal *and* social, because it is *you* that is in the world. That was very astute of you, Crow, and right on the money. It is never an either/or proposition, and it can't be any other way. Anyway, I called a limo, and it'll be here in a few. Crow, you better go downstairs and get the paintings—and please be careful. Some of that paint looked awfully thick and may not be completely dry, acrylic or not."

He put the book down and playfully stuck his tongue out at Candace Maria and headed for the basement, taking the same path through the pillows that she had blazed earlier. Candy took a playful swing at Crow, too, as he stumbled past her, but she missed. When he was out of earshot, she asked Melissa if she'd really gotten a limo.

"Not quite a limo. I talked Burt into driving us over in his Maserati Quattroporte. It's jet black with black leather seats, a phone, and blacked-out windows. The car is tuff and beats a limo hands down."

In her best valley girl imitation, Candace affected a loud and enthusiastic, "No way, man! I've seen Burt's new ride! How'd you hook that up?"

"He owes me a favor—quite a few, in fact."

After the story Melissa had told her that day, including how she had come about her "gift" for the "old-time religion," Candace just said, "Oh," and left it at that.

A minute or so later, Crow came back into the room carrying the paintings and the blow he'd left downstairs. He passed the blow to Melissa, who said he should hang on to it. Crow took a few hits and put it in his pocket. He stood there holding one of the canvases up in front of him and mumbling to himself about how he was getting tired of all this constant drug shit.

Candace moved up behind him, slipping her arms around his waist. "You're not nervous, are you, baby?" He admitted he was but didn't have much else to say. He would not have known how to begin telling her about his out-of-body experience in the studio, and he sure couldn't tell her how surprised he was that it resulted in paintings And *three* paintings at that!

"What's wrong, Crow?" Melissa asked, "You keep shaking your head. Not satisfied with the work?"

"It's not that I'm not satisfied, but there are a few things I should have done a little differently," he replied, trying to sound as if he'd actually had some control over what was in those pictures.

"I know the feeling." Melissa said. "An artist can see something else to change, add, or take away every time he looks at his shit. It's part of what drives the artist to his or her medium in the first place, the longing to make the perfect statement. Like now, usually it's too late to change anything. It's the same as trying to change things gone past in your life."

The bell rang. "That's probably Burt," Melissa said. They filed into the corridor with the amber chandelier. Bones was standing there when Melissa opened the front door. Candace Maria sucked her teeth.

"I was pretty sure you'd left already, but since your house is on my way, I thought I'd give it a shot," Bones said. He saw Candy and pretended to be oblivious to how unwelcome by her he was.

Crow called out from behind her, "Close your mouth, Bones, and come inside. I want to show you something." Bones pushed the door open and slumped in behind Crow as he led the group back into the dining room and switched on the light. Crow looked down at the work with a slight smile playing across his lips. A few minutes went by before Candy asked Bones what he thought.

"When did you have time to do this?" Bones asked incredulously.

"He did them today, *pendejo,* when do you think?" Candy snapped before Crow had a chance to answer.

"You gotta be shitting me," Bones kind of muttered, stupefied by a combination of the incredible work staring him in the face and Candy's hostility toward him. After what he'd done at Josefa's, though, he knew he really couldn't blame her.

"Have you ever known me to bullshit, *Marvin?*" she responded in a slightly icy tone.

"Sometimes," he sheepishly responded.

"Well, this is not one of those times," Melissa added in a similarly icy tone.

Crow was enjoying how uncomfortable Marvin was feeling. He hadn't forgotten what Bones did at Josefa's, either. He repeated Candy's question. "So tell us, *Marvin,* what do you think?"

Bones studied the painting a little longer before he said, "It's good, Crow," and then he saw everyone was waiting for more, so he added, "It's damn good, Crow."

"Thanks, Marvin," Crow said. "That's all I needed."

The bell rang again. "That had better be Burt!" Melissa announced, her own growing impatience beginning to show itself.

Again, they filed to the door, and this time when she opened it, Melissa threw her arms around the neck of a tall, dark Middle Eastern man with thick, straight, jet-black, close-cut hair. Crow noticed that Burt wore a large solitaire diamond in a plain white-gold setting on his index finger and a heavy gold Rolex on his wrist, its black face studded with diamonds where most people had numbers. Burt whispered to Candace Maria, "Long time no see, Candy."

"You haven't been around much lately," Candace said in return.

"Been running," he told her as he moved farther in, extending his hand to Bones. "You must be the fresh meat."

Bones accepted the handshake but pointed to Crow. "Not me. Meet Crow. He's the man of the hour."

Burt stopped short and looked at Crow with disdain. "Him?" he asked in a disappointed voice, and then looked back over his shoulder toward Melissa.

Before Melissa could say anything, Crow was hissing in Burt's direction, "What the fuck is wrong with you?" Crow leaned the paintings against the wall and started toward him.

"Be cool, brother," Candace said as she grabbed Crow's arm. "He's out of your league. Just be cool."

"Move, Candy. I just want to meet the man up close," Crow snarled with a little nasty smirk.

Melissa shoved herself between Burt and Crow. "Let him go, Candace," she said, cool as a cucumber.

Candy let Crow go. He lurched forward again. Melissa blocked his path. "You know you shouldn't push past me, don't you, Crow?" she said as their eyes met. Crow stopped and asked Melissa to please move. She shook her head. "Crow, you're special, we all know it. You've got too much to do to die here tonight, and I'm serious. You don't want to get in Burt's face. Believe me."

"Who the fuck is he?" Crow asked with lessening conviction. He sensed that she wasn't lying, and when he looked past her, he saw the menacing smile on the dark man's pockmarked face. Melissa's words and whatever it was Crow saw in that face immobilized him, but he kept talking.

"Just what is this, some *more* racist shit? Who does he think *he* is? Better question, *what* does he think he is, and who in the hell do he think he better than? We all the same to *them,* Akhmed, or whatever the fuck your real name is!" Crow shouted down the hall at Burt.

The other man's smile broadened as he said, "Step forward and find out what my name is . . . *boy.*"

Crow remained calm this time and almost played past the remark.

But then he decided to go old school on him and said, "Your M-O-T-H-E-R," slowly, perfectly enunciating each letter while rolling his eyes.

Burt roared, "*That* dares to say this to me," and pulled a silver derringer from his pocket. Crow ducked when he saw the gun. Candy screamed, jumped in front of him, and yelled out, "Don't!" several times as Bones pressed himself against the wall.

Melissa turned and began a chant in a language Crow had never heard before. Burt knew very well that Melissa hailed from a long line of bayou conjure women, and he had seen what she could do for himself. Unwilling to take any chances, he dropped the gun and fell to his knees. Melissa walked over to him with her arm extended and hand open and softly said, "The keys and papers, please." Everyone was dumbfounded as they watched him scramble to get Melissa what she'd asked for. She passed the items to Bones and said dryly, "I hope you can drive."

Marvin stammered, "No problem, baby."

"Crow, get your paintings, and let's go," Melissa said. They all walked out past Burt, who was still on the floor with his head down in what appeared to be abject fear. As Melissa walked past him, she ordered him to get up. He did and followed her outside. Locking the doors, Melissa leered at Burt and spoke softly, "Don't you ever threaten anyone in my home. Now, just go somewhere and wait until I call you." Thanking her and pleading her forgiveness, he hurried away.

"What the hell was that all about?" Crow asked Melissa.

"Nothing, really. He disrespected my friends and my house, so I sent him away."

"Yeah, I see that, but what did you do to him?"

Melissa nonchalantly answered, "It's not what I did but what he knows I can do—he and I go back a long way. But we're late, and it's time to get moving."

"Oh, shit, what kind of ride is that? It's the bomb." Crow noticed the car.

"Don't tell me your Brooklyn ass ain't never seen a four-door Maserati before!" Bones replied.

"I can't lie, this is my first," Crow said, then he laughed. "And, Good Lord, be gentle with me."

Melissa showed Bones how to open the trunk, and Crow put the paintings in. One at a time, they climbed down into the car, and each ass molded snugly into the soft leather differently.

Bones called Geoff and said they were on their way to the gallery. When he put the phone down, he informed the party, "Geoff is frantic. His voice is an octave or two higher than his usual false falsetto, but I think he'll live."

"He don't really have much choice, now, do he?" Crow remarked.

The car responded to Bones's every wish. He glided around a corner doing seventy. Because of the evenness of the ride, Crow and Candy were unaware of the liberties Bones was taking. Only Melissa was aware that he was slightly out of control. She noticed how close he'd come to sideswiping a fireplug.

"Having a ball, huh, Marvin?" Melissa asked.

"This machine is incredible!" he yelled.

"Yeah, but before you kill us all in this incredible machine, slow down. Pull over to the liquor store in the middle of the block, and get us four splits of champagne. Get some straws too."

Bones exaggerated a feigned fear and started shaking. "*Yes,* my queen, your wish is my—"

"Forget the BS." Melissa cut him short. "You got enough to cover it?"

"Well . . ." He didn't get to finish that sentence, either. She floated a hundred over the seat into his lap.

"Keep the change," she snapped. "When you get your commission, I want it all back. Is that OK with you?"

Before Marvin screeched to a halt, he asked Melissa why they were all being so hard on him.

"Because you're too intelligent to act like a fucking asshole *all* the time. I expect more from you, and you should expect more of yourself."

Bones sulked as he got out of the car. "Asshole, huh? Wouldn't none of 'em be going to no art show if I ain't find Crow trying to hawk his fuckin' shit on the streets," he muttered to himself.

Crow, who could neither see his face nor hear him mumbling, called after him, "Yo, man, I'd rather have a tall can of ale with my straw."

"Yeah, man, whatever. I'm just the damn butler anyway," Bones shot back.

"I guess he's got an attitude," Candy said, and grinned.

Bones returned, passed the drinks, and slipped Melissa her change. "No telling how shit's gonna turn out," he said. Without looking at anyone in the car, he twisted his ass deep in the leather seat, started the car, and gunned it.

Melissa watched Bones as she popped the cork on her split, slipped the straw in, and took a sip. "Burt really does love this automobile, and I'd hate to see him any more angry than he was back at the house," she said, still watching him. He slowed down to forty.

Crow could see Geoff standing in the doorway as they pulled up to the gallery. People dressed as women flounced up, kissing everyone on both cheeks and screeching "Hello!" in shrill falsettos. Geoff was wearing a flowered housedress and bowed patent-leather pumps, his red wig falling in two long braids over his shoulders. On each cheek he'd painted rosy red circles and black freckles, trying to look like Raggedy Ann or some shit. Crow was fascinated.

Melissa looked at Geoff, smiled, and offered a vial of coke to Crow. He accepted it, took a hit, and put it in his pocket.

As Bones backed the Maserati down the sidewalk, people shrieked and jumped out of its way. He wondered how many of them recognized the car and thought he was Burt. Burt killed people for money. Bones knew it, and so did a lot of other people. He hit the brakes and shut the engine off, stopping five or six feet away from Geoff, who was the only one standing on the sidewalk at that point. He stood there defiant, with his hands on his hips.

Crow rolled his eyes, fished around in his pocket, and pulled out the vial of coke. "I really need another hit before I face *these* motherfuckers."

"Well, hurry up," Melissa barked. "We cannot diminish the impact of this grand arrival. We're here for Crow. Let's look like it. You too, Marvin." Melissa faced Crow and asked, "Are you ready?" He nodded with his finger up his nose.

Geoff made it around the car, saying something no one could hear, trying to peer into the back windows. Crow asked Bones to roll the window down.

"Evenin', Miss Geoff. You look *lovely* in that dress!" Crow exclaimed loudly, trying to get into the role.

"Nice of you to notice, Crow, baby!" Geoff shouted back, prancing around the car to the door and smoothing his dress. "And it's about time you all got here too!"

When he went to open the door for Crow, Bones sprang out of the front seat and ran over to Crow's door, snatching Geoff's hand away from the handle. Sweeping low as he opened the door, he said sarcastically to Geoff, "What the fuck you doing? Can't you see that I'm the official butler?"

Geoff fluttered his long blue eyelashes and said, "Oh, Marvie dear, I do think you mean *chauffeur,*" and patted him twice on the ass.

The people who had jumped out of the car's way were now starting to crowd around it. Bones and Geoff reached down to help him up out of the low car. Each held one of Crow's arms tightly as they lifted him out. And with that, Crow had arrived.

Spell to Call on the Ancestors for Help (2002)

12

The Show

Crow couldn't believe his eyes. It was only seven o'clock, and already the gallery was so full of people that they were spilling out onto the street. Town cars and taxis pulled up to the curb filled with even more people. Were they really all here to see *his* "work"?

When Crow figured out that Geoff was supposed to be dressed up as Raggedy Ann, he burst out laughing. Melissa looked from Crow to Geoff and back. "Well, all right, then, let's greet your adoring public, baby," she said with a snicker.

Bones rushed to open the door for Melissa. She brushed past him, though, ignoring the arm. Crow opened the door for Candy, who happily accepted his assistance. There was a brief hush as the four made their way up the stairs, most of the crowd stopping to stare. Melissa hooked on to Crow's other arm. The women triumphantly ushered him through the crowd. Geoff sashayed behind them, bouncing his red pigtails.

As they approached the door, Geoff whispered in Crow's ear,

"The culture vultures are circling, and you're the soup du jour!"

Bones walked up behind them with the new paintings. After kissing his cheeks, Geoff took one of the canvases from him and held it at arm's length.

"Simply magnificent!" he exclaimed. "What are these, Crow, *three* new paintings? I love this one! It's so expressive! Powerful! What do you call it?"

As he glanced over at the painting Geoff held, Crow's mind swam. He hadn't thought to title them. His experience had been so profound and overwhelming that he had been reluctant to focus on it. Now, as the memory of the moment returned, he could only think of it as "Seeing with New Eyes." "The others," he continued coolly, "are called 'Looking Back' and 'First Love.' " Crow was amazed at himself.

Melissa, intuitive to the point of clairvoyance sometimes, chuckled and whispered to Crow, "Damn, you're quick."

"Are the others this good?" Geoff continued to exude enthusiastically. "Where did they come from? Did you manage to get into your apartment today?"

Before Crow could get his next answer together, Melissa laughed and interjected, "No, Geoff. Our Crow here is prolific; he produced all of this since you saw him last. If this crowd is any indication, he's off to an auspicious beginning of a very long and productive career!"

Geoff shook his head in disbelief. He called over a tall, young white kid with a shaved head and a Fu Manchu mustache, dressed in a black and white jumpsuit. Tattooed on his forehead in bold letters were the words "Eat Me." Geoff asked him to find a prominent place for the paintings and to be very careful with them. He then ushered Crow and his entourage past the crowd.

Melissa had gotten the word out that something special was happening that night, and the beautiful people had shown up. Geoff was grinning from ear to ear, with dollar signs in his eyes.

There wasn't the slightest indication that Crow's works and Danny's were last-minute additions to an existing show.

Geoff and "Eat Me" had been busy. The gallery looked great, Crow thought. Even the severely worn, black linoleum tile floor of the former bodega had been polished to a high-gloss, slippery shine. But it was toward the back of the gallery that Geoff had really added a special touch. He had a long mahogany bar set up, attended by two of the barmaids from Club Chaos. Dressed in their leather cutout catsuits, they caused quite a stir among the drooling suburban types. Two other similarly dressed waitresses circled the gallery, offering drinks and hors d'oeuvres from hammered-silver trays.

Alton, the photographer in the exhibit, was standing just inside the doors with a glass of champagne in his hand when he saw the group walk in. He pushed through the people trying to get in ahead of them, greeted everyone, and shook Crow's hand, saying, "Those last paintings are beautiful, man. Congratulations." He signaled a waiter over and handed out glasses of champagne from a tray to everyone before raising a glass and toasting Crow.

"You've arrived, Crow. These people are your new public. The night belongs to you!" Alton said.

After everyone had slugged their champagne down, they began to work the room, which was getting more crowded by the second.

Before they'd gotten too far into the crowd, Melissa waved over a man who was leaning on a support beam staring at one of Crow's paintings. He came over, kissed her on both cheeks, and held her hands, warmly smiling into her eyes.

"Crow, this is David Salle," Melissa began, returning David's obvious affection but more coolly. "David, I'm thrilled to introduce you to Crow Shade, the artist whose work you were just looking at. You know everybody else."

David placed an arm around Crow's shoulder. "This work is causing quite a sensation. I love it. It's deep, and I'm mystified by the symbolism. Where've you shown, man?" David asked without pausing to hear Crow's reply. "Maybe you should talk to my agent.

Larry's great. I could take you to his gallery. In fact, he'll probably show up here tonight, and I'll introduce you."

"That's what makes this so priceless, David." Geoff jumped in. "This show, at *my* gallery, is his debut."

David turned back to Crow. "Sold anything yet, man? Talk to Larry. He's made me a fortune, a few times over."

"Crow's already got representation, David," Geoff interrupted again. "So, if Larry's interested in *buying* any of Crow's work, tell him to call me. Perhaps *you* should consider coming over to my representation as well. I'm sure I could do as well for you as I'm doing for Crow already."

David laughed. "I'll talk to Larry about it, Geoff."

David kissed Melissa on both cheeks again and turned to Crow. "Nice meeting you, man. If you want to get together, Melissa's got my number. I'll see you around." Then he walked off toward the bar.

Candy waited until David was out of earshot and said, "Nice try, Geoff. That would have been quite a coup. But why should David leave Larry's gallery for yours? You're barely keeping this place afloat."

"That would be the point, now, wouldn't it, Miss Smarty Pants? If David came over, I would be able to pay my fucking bills!"

Geoff leaned toward Crow and whispered in his ear, "David is a giant in the art world. He's been around a few years. He's really hot right now. You could become just as rich as he has. You're just as talented, maybe even more so. Stick with me, kid. Have I let you down yet?"

"The night's young," Crow smacked with a smile. But Crow was only half joking around. Crow knew that if he couldn't make Geoff any real money, He'd be out as fast as they'd met. Crow mused to himself in a low voice, "This shit is just like the drug game—crackers at the top making all the loot and niggers doing all the work and taking all the risk. At some point we gotta flip this script. There's gotta be some black dealers somewheres. Where the fuck does Danny sell his shit?"

Geoff spotted rap music mogul Russell Simmons sauntering in. Right behind him was his little brother Run, of Run DMC, who was sporting his signature black leather Adidas suit, velour fedora, and Adidas shell toes with no laces and a shit load of dookie gold chains. And behind them came King Ad-Rock of the Beastie Boys, who glided up on a skateboard, swigging on a forty-ounce bottle of Old English 800 Malt Liquor.

Geoff left Crow standing there. He tripped over himself rushing to shake Russell's hand.

"Mr. Simmons," Geoff stammered excitedly, extending his hand and deepening his voice. "It's such an honor to have you in my gallery."

Russell paused and looked Geoff up and down, trying to be cool about the fact that this freak with a man's voice and Raggedy Ann's head was actually talking to him. "Yeah, whatever . . . *man?*" he said. "Look, ah, I hear you're showing a brother—real rare down here—so I had to come through. Anyways, my older brother in Brooklyn paints. I'd like it if you could look at some of his shit sometime." Russell then took Geoff's outstretched hand and excused himself. He made his way through the crowd, slyly wiping his hand off on his jeans as he went.

Geoff kept watching as Russell disappeared from sight. Whatever he was thinking, he kept it to himself. Just then, he caught sight of Ad-Rock circumventing the ever-thickening crowd on his skateboard. He silently wished that somehow Lady Luck would stick her foot out and trip the idiot all over himself. That would certainly add to the mounting spectacle.

Geoff noticed that a small set had gathered at about mid-gallery and went back over to where Crow was standing. Geoff tapped Crow on the shoulder. "Let's see what the to-do is over there," he said.

Ad-Rock zoomed past on his skateboard, causing people to jump out of his way. He almost knocked Crow over as he went by. Steadying himself, Crow started to get pissed but remembered the setting he was in.

"Who the hell was that?" Crow asked, not recognizing the guy.

"He came in with Russell Simmons. He's one of the Beastie Boys. It's part of their persona to be fucking annoying," Geoff responded as they navigated their way through the crowd.

Crow had never made the connection that the "Russell" and "Joey" Danny spoke of so casually were Def Jam's cofounder Russell Simmons and Run of Run-DMC. Even now, staring them in the face, it eluded him. He could not fathom that someone he knew as well as he thought he knew Danny was related to anyone famous.

Finally reaching the gaggle, Geoff was stunned to see Andy Warhol holding court. "D-d-do you know who that *is?*" He turned to Crow and stammered.

Crow looked at the thin, pale, strangely dressed man with even stranger pointy white hair and shrugged his shoulders. "He looks like he got that AIDS shit."

"Be that as it may." Geoff chuckled. "That's *the* Andy Warhol. This is big, really big!" he shrieked. "Melissa must have called in a shit load of favors to get him here."

"I saw one of his movies once when I was in college. He's the guy who paints the soup cans, right?"

"Right," Geoff said, a little out of breath.

"Damn, he looks like a vampire or a succubus or something," Crow said.

"What the hell's a succubus, Crow?" Geoff asked.

Crow laughed and answered, "Something like you."

A thin brother about Crow's own age was standing next to Warhol. His glassy eyes were flickering at half mast, and he rubbed his nose methodically up and down with the palm of his hand. He wore a small, fitted black suit with tight, high-water pants and had short, wild, locked hair which stuck out at odd angles all over his head.

"Who's the dope-fiend brother with him?" Crow whispered to Geoff.

Geoff was not easily shocked, but to have first Russell Simmons and Run and now Andy Warhol and Jean-Michel Basquiat together in his gallery was a lot to absorb. Geoff answered with his mouth hanging open and as if he were speaking from far away.

"That's *the* Jean-Michel Basquiat, Crow. He's only the hottest artist in the entire world right now. This is *soooooo* big. Crow, you have no idea how big this could be for both of us," Geoff excitedly tittered.

Geoff and Crow pushed through a few more people and stood face to face with the reigning kings of the art world. Crow wasn't nearly as flustered as Geoff. Finally, Geoff said, "Mr. Warhol, Mr. Basquiat, I am *Gee*-off. Welcome to my gallery. This is Crow Shade, one of the exhibiting artists. We are *so* pleased to have you at his opening."

When Geoff began speaking to them, Basquiat had his back turned, whispering something to Ad-Rock, who had rolled up behind him. Warhol extended his hand to both Crow and Geoff but did not say anything, as if waiting for Geoff to say something of more importance.

As Basquiat turned to face them, scratching his cheek, Ad-Rock skated off, this time rolling over toes and knocking someone into a wall who screamed after him, "I don't give a fuck how many records you sold, you asshole!"

Basquiat said to Crow, "Yo, I hear you from Brooklyn. My family's from Haiti, but I grew up in Brooklyn. Nice to see another blood from the 'hood gettin' some play down here from these fake-ass liberals. Maybe you'll be next month's new, dark-skinned flavor. But between you and me," he continued, leaning in, eyes rolled closed, "I don't know if *this* art world is equipped to handle the two of us at the same time. Good luck, though, my brother."

He swayed back and forth a few times, turned to Warhol, and said, "Yo, Andy, me and Ad-Rock are gonna jet. I'll see you back at the Factory."

Warhol asked in a low, flat voice, "Jean-Michel, haven't you had enough?"

Basquiat shot back, "I ain't dead, am I?" Then he was gone.

Warhol appeared nervous now. He shook his head and said, "Nice to meet you both," and walked off into the crowd.

"Damn, what the fuck was that all about?" Crow asked Geoff.

Geoff shrugged without a word and followed behind Warhol into what had become a throng of patrons, groupies, and other people from the neighborhood. Crow was left standing by himself.

Crow stood there looking around the room in disbelief. There was a short, round man in a leather duster and a cowboy hat. He also had on fringed chaps that left his behind exposed. A bald couple came in, dressed alike in black from head to toe. Crow couldn't tell which was the man and which was the woman. He recognized Tia from Chaos standing across the room, statuesque and buxom in a black leather bustier with a plunging neckline. There was an Asian contingent in a corner. They chain-smoked and gestured with their cigarettes and cameras. Everyone around him was busy smiling and posturing. He felt so much like all the tapdancing niggers before him, he wondered when the little blond girl with the curls named after her was going to come up to him out of the crowd and take his hand.

Then Crow saw this fine, curvaceous chocolate sister. She had a short, tightly curled, bleached-white 'fro, with eyebrows and eyelashes to match. He reverted to his old player self. He grabbed her by the arm as she was about to pass him. She smiled suspiciously but stopped. He introduced himself as "the artist" and showed his landscape to her. While skillfully bullshitting a philosophy relating to the significance of the various sizes of the squares in his work, he secretly pondered the merits of asking if her pubes matched her head and face.

They were looking at the painting from across the room when Crow noticed that the woman who'd been put out of the gallery yesterday was trying to remove a can of tuna from Geoff's bodega exhibit. It looked as if she refused to accept that the tuna had been permanently affixed. Crow excused himself from the conversation and started across the floor toward the woman. When he was halfway there, she saw him coming and bolted. Crow hurried to the doorway and called out for her to come back inside. She stuck out her tongue, laughed, and tore up the ticket that had been stuck under one of the windshield wipers on the Maserati. Then she reached into her pocket, pulled out a handful of pennies, and threw them up into the air. By the time they hit the sidewalk, she'd already run halfway up the block. Crow shook his head as he watched her slow down to kick an empty beer can into the street.

Crow stood by the door looking around the room for Geoff, but he caught Candace sitting by herself instead, leaning back on the rear legs of a metal folding chair. She was staring into a half-empty plastic cup. Geoff saw Crow and waved, calling him over. Crow ambiguously gestured, then walked over to Candy. Her eyes rose to meet his.

His red-glazed eyes peering down at her, he smiled and said, "Hey, lady, you all alone at this thing too? I thought you were giving this party."

Candace rocked the chair down onto all fours, her eyes finding the center of the pool of white wine. "I'm OK," she said.

Crow pulled over a red plastic milk crate and sat down next to her. He waited awhile for her to continue, and when she didn't, he said, "Yeah, I can dig it. I'm starting to get tired of shit too . . ."

Candy interrupted, "It's not that. What Melissa did with Burt . . ." she began.

"Yeah, she might've saved my life. What the fuck is up with you? You afraid she gonna put a *spell* on you or something?"

Candace slid her chair back and yelled, "This ain't no damn joke, Crow!" A number of people turned to look at her and turned back away when she looked in their direction. She muttered, "Shit."

"Calm the fuck back down, please," Crow said.

Candace started to get up and walk away, but Crow asked her to please stay, and she sat back down. They sat quietly side by side. Crow leaned over and kissed her cheek and then the corner of her eye.

"Do you mind if I say something to you?" he asked. Candace nodded, her eyes again fixed on the cup of wine. "I guess that means it don't matter much if I talk or not. It's funny how people don't really see themselves. I mean, you fed me some shit that Indians used to see their ancestors with and expect me to be with it. Then you ask me to walk into this phony-ass shit and play it like it ain't no thing. You've been taking me through all kinds of wild shit and want me to play it out, but as soon as something don't fit your ideas of what shit should be like, you lose your cool. What the hell would you do if you had to come to Brooklyn? You fronting in dope cars with rich motherfuckers, while I got a store on my corner that only sells state lottery tickets and nickels of crack. Shit, even if Melissa shot fire out her ass, I'm still with the program. In the end, it's gonna benefit me and ultimately you too."

Candace gulped down the rest of her wine. "Nice speech, baby, but I'm not afraid of her or whatever she did to Burt. If she hadn't done whatever she did, he *might* have shot you. I haven't had a chance to tell you any of my stories yet. *Mi abuela* was a bad motherfucker—no disrespect—her damn self. Some of the stuff I seen in my life, here and in PR, *Dios mío,* would uncurl your hair. You met me at a time when I'm not really trying to think about anything, but the spirit realm and the things it takes to access it are not strange to me at all. At any time, my dear departed *abuelita* or *titi* Nilda might show me a little something. Earlier, I was much more upset about the gun than I was about what Melissa did. Some things just scare me, all right? I didn't know how much I was caring about you till I saw the gun and that look on Burt's face, is all."

Crow reached into his pocket and passed Candace Maria the

blow, trying to change the subject. "Meet me over there by Geoff when you're done, OK?"

A little disappointed with his response, or lack of one, Candace said, "Sure, Crow, I'll be over in a few seconds."

Bones intercepted Crow on his way across the floor and asked, "What's up with her?"

"Fuck if I know," Crow quipped, trying to minimize his own feelings. "Maybe it's that time of the month."

Bones looked back and saw Candy opening the bathroom door. "Maybe a blow or two will help," he said.

"What the fuck doesn't it help?" Crow asked in reply.

Still several feet away, Geoff's falsetto could be heard over the clatter of the other voices, and Bones went to go listen to what bullshit he was talking now.

Crow went looking for Brown, Blond, and Fine he'd been talking to because he wanted to get her number for later. He found himself stuck listening absentmindedly to a skinny man with orange hair who went on and on about a performance art piece he'd done last week. He looked around desperately, hoping someone would rescue him. The conversation had quickly degenerated into a monologue and reenactment of something that had to do with the insertion of a yam.

Bones rode in to Crow's rescue.

Excitedly, he began, "Yo, Crow, motherfuckers is coming in droves. You can't just stand in one place all night when your public awaits. Excuse us."

With a relief that Crow had never experienced outside a bathroom, he threw his arm around Bones's shoulder and thanked him. "Who the fuck are these motherfuckers, man? Where the fuck do you get 'em from, and how the hell can we get rid of them?"

"It don't really matter who they are; they buyin' your shit. But really, people like this will go someplace just because they think they should be there, and not for nothing, but we wouldn't have a scene without them. Think about it. It's almost as if being talented is besides the point. Not to take nothin' from the work, and you're obviously talented, but you're still lucky you hooked into the right clique," Bones said impassively.

Crow drew his arm from around Bones's shoulder. "Bones, you just stopped short of saying I owe all this to you."

"True enough," Bones said. "Picture me shirking the *burden* of my responsibility by refusing the pleasure of helping out my fellowman. That's not what I was trying to say. I was simply commenting on the game. You don't owe me spit you don't wanna owe me. Geoff pays me. Besides, you're talented, and what's real is real." He grabbed Crow's shoulder. "Yo, man, what I did to you last night was real, too—it was fucked up, but it was real."

Crow pushed Bones's hand away, stuck his finger in his face, and said, "Yeah, it was fucked up, and I should have punched you in your face behind it, but it showed you got feelings, even if you ain't got no sense. You could have been a little more up front with it, but if a motherfucker don't get mad about pussy, what the fuck else he's got to get mad about?"

"Money!" Bones blurted out.

"Yeah, that too," Crow concurred. Then he saw Melissa and another woman working their way through all the hairdos and cigarette smoke toward them. "Somebody said money can't buy you love, but it sure can buy everything else, can't it?" he shouted out just as the women reached them.

Melissa caught Crow's comment and said, "Money shouldn't be what's important; it should simply be a byproduct of doing what you're good at."

Crow and Bones laughed. Then Bones looked Melissa up and down. "Oh, yeah? Great pearls, mama," he said sarcastically.

Melissa bowed gracefully. "Touché, *son.*"

"Crow, I want you to meet Élan," she said. Crow smiled and nodded. Élan said something to Melissa in French. "She's very pleased to meet you and likes your work very much," Melissa translated. "In fact, she's interested in 'Wrap' and wants to make an offer on it."

Crow put his arm around Melissa's waist and pressed himself against her bottom. "Tell her she's got great tits, and I'd be happy to sell her the painting."

Melissa did not translate, but Élan's face turned beet red.

"I thought you said she didn't understand no English, Melissa!" Crow exclaimed, letting her go.

"I never said that," Melissa said with a smirk.

Bones whispered in Crow's ear, "Don't feel bad, man. That bitch has been here a fucking decade and still pretends she can't speak English."

"I don't feel bad, man, shit," Crow quipped, trying to shake off his embarrassment.

Melissa and Élan spoke for a few more seconds before Élan said that she'd pay two thousand dollars for the piece.

Crow was bowled over but maintained his composure. "Tell her I had hoped to get a bit more."

Melissa translated and then offered Élan's response. "She said she feels the price is fair because it's a relatively small work, and you're an unknown. She wants you to know that while she is purchasing it for purely aesthetic reasons, she believes you have great promise as an artist."

"I'll go with whatever Melissa thinks is fair," Crow said, addressing Élan. "But there are circles in which my art is well regarded, even if I am unknown down here." Crow spoke in defense of Danny's recognition as an artist—the least he could do considering she was buying one of Danny's paintings, after all.

Melissa informed Élan of Crow's acceptance, and she nodded with a smile before walking away with Melissa to sort out the details.

Crow waited until they were out of earshot and said to Bones, "I can't believe we just made two grand."

Bones slapped him five. "And it's gonna snowball from here! Let's get some champagne. This calls for a toast," he said.

Crow and Bones ran into Alton and Candy, who were drinking red wine at the bar. Élan and a bald-headed guy had just walked away. Alton said that the Frenchwoman and the guy with the bald head had just bought a photograph.

"I'm not quite sure which one he bought," Alton said, "but he paid an extra five hundred for the negative."

Crow whispered to Bones, "They're buying up everything."

Bones passed Crow a glass and whispered, "The fat bald dude with Élan is a mime in an off-Broadway show. They're a good combo. She's been here for more than ten years and won't speak English and he don't talk at all. He's French too, and they got more bank than a televangelist. The buzz for a while had been that some mime troupe had stashed millions from a 1970s French dope connection. Most of the big cash down here is old drug money."

Alton heard most of what was being said and piped up. "That's right, and Wall Street money and Washington, D.C., money too. Seventy percent of the rich people's money is dope money. We artists should emulate lawyers and charge them extra for their past indiscretions. Who knows, maybe a year or so from now, my photo might be used as part of a plea bargain."

Bones, Crow, and Candy left Alton mumbling into his drink about bad money buying good art. They went over to where a small group of people had gathered in front of one of Crow's paintings. Again, Geoff's falsetto pierced the crowd-generated din.

"What struck me immediately about this piece is Crow's searing use of tangible symbols to express the alienation of the woman in the painting. Here, the artist is describing—and quite clearly, I might add—man's singular condition in the world. When I first saw the piece, I was moved to tears."

Bones bent toward Crow and whispered, "I love his particular brand of bullshit. He's the master of pseudo-philosophical, analytic babble as art gallery sales pitch. Geoff and Melissa make a great team; she gets all the right people in the right place, and Geoff talks them into wanting things they don't need and buying things they don't want."

"No shit," Crow concurred. "I'll bet *that* motherfucker could kick it in pig latin if he had to."

"No doubt, no doubt." Bones chuckled. "I've heard Alton say that Geoff has sold ice sculptures in the Amazon and there are a couple Eskimos driving Porsches across the frozen tundra."

When they both laughed out loud, Geoff heard them and swung around, tossing his man-made tresses and slamming his right hand firmly down on his narrow, flat ass. His gestures were so comical that Crow almost choked on his laughter.

"Well, if it isn't the hottest new thing this town has seen, deciding to grace us with his presence. Crow!" Geoff squealed. "I was just talking about you!"

"I hope so. You need to earn your outrageous commission," Crow said, smiling broadly and playing the role to the hilt.

"And might I add," Geoff yelled, thrusting a hip in Bones's direction, "the man who can be said to have 'discovered' him, the always delicious Mr. Skin and Bones! A credit to his kind—whatever *kind* that may be!"

Bones sighed but said nothing.

"And you know Señorita Candace!" added Geoff.

Crow smiled and responded, looking at Geoff, "I feel so honored—just don't try to kiss me."

Extending his hand to a couple, Crow said in his best newly affected schmooze, "If we have to wait for Geoff here to introduce us, it might be all day."

The man looked familiar to Crow, wearing a brown tweed jacket with suede elbow patches. The man put a monocle up to his eye and gingerly took Crow's hand. As they shook, Crow realized this was the same asshole who had let his wife talk him out of buying the same painting he was standing in front of for thirty dollars at the cube on Astor Place.

The man spoke to Crow. "He said a lot of nice things about

you and your work. *Jefferson* and I go way back, so I don't pay much mind to what *Ge-off* here has to say. We lived two doors away from him and his family in Jersey until a couple of months ago. My wife and I have since moved into a little condo on the Upper East Side. My name's Dick, Dick Theman, and this is my wife, Ann." He reached over and guided Ms. Ann forward by her elbow.

Apparently, Dick Theman had not recognized Crow or the painting—the one his *wife* had rejected as a "bad investment." As Crow accepted and shook Ms. Ann's hand, he wondered if the wife who had questioned Dick's artistic acumen at the cube would have recognized it.

"I really appreciate your work," Ms. Ann said. "I know you must hear this sort of thing all the time," she continued, "but I'm honestly impressed. So is Dick. The poem in that one is really beautiful, but I simply must have the woman standing alone in the grass. It says scads to me."

Amused as hell, Crow thanked her again and slipped deeper into his role. "When I painted that one, I was going to put a child in the picture with her, but I thought people might miss the message of how isolated most of *you* feel, even in the company of your fellowmen, so I left her standing alone with the wind blowing the grass and the hood of her robe across her face. Like most people here, not only is she alone, but she's anonymous, even to herself."

Really enjoying this and looking to stir up some trouble for Dick as kind of a payback for dissing Danny's work, Crow stared deeply into Ms. Ann's eyes. Slowly, with a very dramatic tremble in his voice, he asked, "Do you two have any children?"

Before she could answer, Dick interjected quickly, "Ah, not yet!" Catching himself, he continued, "Ah, you know, right now we're concentrating on each other before we take such a big step."

Ms. Ann turned to Dick, who reddened when she asked him

pointedly, "Don't you think we should get married first?" He reddened more. "And actually, speaking of steps, Dick, don't you think you should get a *divorce* first? Jesse might not take too kindly to us having children while you're still married to *her*. And I'm still not sure about *you* moving into the condo until the divorce is final, you know. I don't care whose name is on the lease."

Crow wished he had someone to bow to. He could imagine an audience yelling for him to do an encore. Crow offered apologies to them for the can of worms he'd opened but could not be heard over Dick explaining to a stone-faced Ann that after six and a half years together, they couldn't be more married than they were.

"Not according to my parents!" Ms. Ann snapped, quite effectively ending the discussion. Without blinking, she turned back to Crow and placed her hand on his arm. "Crow, I love the piece. I want to offer fifteen hundred for it."

"That's a sweet offer, dear, but we just got another of three thousand a moment ago. I couldn't take anything less than that," Geoff interrupted. "The resale on this is going to shoot up the minute you buy it. Crow's work isn't only art, it's an *investment.*"

The irony of Geoff's choice of sales pitch here, considering what Jesse had said to Dick at the cube, was not lost on Crow, who could not have scripted it better.

"We're friends, of course," Geoff continued, "but I'm friends with everyone in the room! I'm firm on the price, and you'd better make a decision quickly, because I see Augusto and Cassandra heading this way, and you know how Cassandra is when she wants something—and how Augusto gets when he can't get it for her. You might end up paying double or altogether losing the piece—or an arm, or a leg!"

Crow knew from the club that Augusto was dead broke and unemployed. Seeing how Geoff would use any tactic to make the sale, Crow glanced at him and smirked.

Ms. Ann looked over as Cassandra and Augusto made their way

across the room, their bodyguard acting like a buffer against the crowd. Dick was busy looking at Crow, who moment by moment began to seem increasingly familiar to him.

Ms. Ann turned nervously to Geoff. Grabbing his hand and pumping it excitedly, she barked, "Deal, Geoff! We'll sign on the dotted line later! Um, I see someone I want to talk to, um, *over there,* uh, gotta go!"

Before Dick could figure out where he'd met Crow before, she said, "Now, don't let me hear that you've sold that painting out from under us—and don't mention who you sold it to!" She disappeared into the crowd, dragging a sputtering Dick behind her.

Meanwhile, still a little ways away, Augusto whispered to his bodyguard, "Listen, Arturo, just look tough and don't smile at nobody!"

Arturo was muscle-bound, six-foot-five, and, at two-ninety, more than stocky. He was blockheaded, clean-shaven, and dimwitted. He slowly replied, "Whatever you say, Tío Auggie."

"Shit! I thought I told you don't call me that when you're working!"

"Sorry Tí—I mean, *sir.* But is it working when I ain't gettin' paid?"

"*Cállate!* Just shut up! *Dios mío,* if you weren't my sister's kid . . . !"

Even without Arturo, the sight of Augusto—all rippling five-foot-eight of him, dressed to the nines in a shiny cranberry silk-look suit, black form-fitting nylon T, pointy silver-tipped faux-alligator boots, and hair blown straight and heavily moussed into spiked peaks, looking as if he were on his way to a cockfight—heading your way could make anybody, if not run screaming, at the very least do a sidestep. Augusto and Cassandra, following their bodyguard, moved through the gallery. It was an impressive spectacle to behold as the crowd, almost in unison and as though rehearsed, created a wave to rival the parting of the Red Sea.

Reaching the circle where Geoff and Crow were first, Cassandra squeezed in past two idle bystanders. She was stunning in a sleeveless white sequined Givenchy sheath, her throat adorned with a thick, diamond-encrusted platinum choker. She wore long white satin gloves that ended just below her elbow. Cassandra extended her gloved hand to Geoff, who accepted it, unsure whether to shake or kiss it. Considering the entrance they'd made, he decided to kiss it.

Cassandra shrieked with delight in her best Castilian-afflicted Spanglish, "*Ge*-off, *mi corathon!* I *thi*mply must have *doth o treth* of *ethte caballero'th arteth.* They're thimply *fabulotho!*"

It was all Candy—who knew that Cassandra was Puerto Rican—could do to keep from busting out laughing.

Over Cassandra's shoulder, Geoff could see Augusto gesturing frantically. It was easy enough to figure out what he was trying to say.

"Do *not* sell her anything!" came through loud and clear. Following a subtle nod of acknowledgment over Cassandra's head, Geoff could see the panic drain from Augusto's face. Augusto breathed a sigh of relief and stepped forward, now ready to participate in the charade.

As Augusto took his place beside Geoff, the bodyguard just stood there, already getting bored but trying to look alert. He knew all too well what it was like to make Tío Auggie mad, and had the damned scars to prove it.

"Geoff, my man, how the hell are you?" Augusto yelled. "How long's it been? Yesterday? Well, seems like ages," he croaked, seeming pleased with his own little joke. "Anything my lady wants," he added with a wink and a smile.

Cassandra turned to Geoff and arched an eyebrow. "Who was that *gringa fea* I just saw you talking to in front of this one lovely *cuadro?* Naughty, naughty, Geoff! You *know* you are supposed to give to *me* the private showings before any *otro* deals."

Geoff stepped in and took Cassandra's hand in his. "Now,

nay-na . . . you know nothing is a done deal at a show until the piece has been delivered. If you especially like something, I'll make sure you get it, honey. Now, give your Gee-Gee a kiss, and go and look around!"

As Cassandra and Augusto walked away, following behind the solid wall that was Arturo, Crow overheard Augusto chiding Cassandra in Spanglish, *muy malo.*

"*Carajo pendejo! Por qué* the fuck *tú siempre* have to fucking do dat fucking shit? You trying to *keel* me? *Tú sabes* we ain't got no fucking *dinero.* I'm about to hock that fucking necklace you wearin' t'pay the fucking rent. *Y tú* fucking *estás aquí,* fucking fronting all the fucking time. Getting me into fucking *deudas,* and me with no fucking way *hacer bien* on the fucking shit you fucking buying. *Coño,* man!"

Cassandra answered coolly, "*Miras, mi hijo* . . . fuck you, OK? You *no* fucking *hablas a mí* that fucking way in heah, OK? *Tenemos dinero hoy,* no fucking *tenemos dinero mañana* . . . *Coño,* man! *Tú* fucking *sabes,* OK? *Siempre el mismo!* And you'll be getting this choker *de mi madre muerta,* over *your own* fucking dead body, OK! *Déjame!*"

Crow stood there, amazed and amused listening to this exchange and, of course, only half understanding it. Turning to say something to Geoff, who was no longer standing there, he said to Bones instead, "This is a nuthouse, man. I don't know how you do this all the time. These people make me tired! I mean, broke-ass hustlers, French bitches spending drug money and refusing to speak English they understands just fine, hangin' with mimes who don't talk no shit at all, and all this other shit, damn! Don't nobody down here fucking play it straight? I mean, I know all about fronting, but damn! Most people even I know got some sort of gig."

Bones looked at Crow. "And what is it you do for a living, man?" He didn't wait for an answer. "Listen, I've spent most of my adult life trying to get away from my family's money. But still, I've never really figured out a way to live without it, fully knowing I've always got this safety net. Life's about choices. Even if you don't have a dime in your pocket, you have a choice—you're richer than a millionaire with nowhere to turn. Melissa's in her element here, but do you know that she hasn't been to any art-related functions in about a year? You have to be something special for her to be here. Sure, these people are phony and decadent, but they're not stupid. If they didn't think they could find a bargain on a good investment, they wouldn't be down here. So, don't be so hard on yourself. Look, I'm gonna get us a drink. Those waitresses are never around when you need them," and he took off for the bar.

Crow called to Bones's back as it receded into the crowd, "I thought art was supposed to be about more than money . . . you know, spiritual and all that?" Crow thought he heard Bones reply, through the din of the crowd, "Yeah, sho', you right."

There was only one person in the room Crow really wanted to meet: DJ Run. He spotted him standing off to the side, looking bored. He was trying to ignore some kid wearing tight black jeans, matching jeans jacket, red nylon T-shirt, backward red baseball cap, and blue suede Pumas, gesticulating wildly, working very hard to keep Run's attention.

Crow headed across the room toward them. Getting his nerve together by the time he reached Run, Crow stuck his hand out and said, "Yo, Run, what you doin' at my show, man?" After he said it, he thought it was a stupid question. Run looked relieved that the conversation he was trying not to have was being interrupted. He grabbed Crow's hand as if he were the Savior. He pumped it hard and started talking fast.

"Yo, I was hanging with my brother Russell, and we ended up here," he said. "I like what you do. Some of it reminds me of the shit my other brother paints—he's an artist too, but he ain't had no show down here yet, though. He mostly shows at the neighborhood black galleries in Brooklyn and other places. I heard Russell say something about putting up a show for him in the new offices. Anyway, it's good to meet a brother doing his thing. Call me Joe. I ain't performing, so I ain't Run right now. Your name is Crow, huh? What's your real name?"

Crow looked perplexed and asked, "What you mean?" Joe looked perplexed back. "Well, anyway," Crow said, "I ain't been paintin' long." Wasn't that the truth? "Everybody is making such a big deal about how blacks don't get shown. I guess me being here is a big deal, and I just lucked the fuck out, because this is my first show. It'll be cool if Russell gives your brother a show, though. I'd like to see his work."

The guy who'd been talking Run's ear off jumped into the conversation. "IwastellingRunherethatI'manartisttoo. Sort of like graffiti. Maybe you seen some of my stuff in the subways. By the way, my name is Daze. I'msupposedtohaveashownextmonthwith thisguyTonyShafazzioverinSoHo. MaybeyouandRussellcouldshow uptoo. I'lldropsomeinvitesoffwithGeoff."

The guy talked so fast that Crow and Run only caught a few words, and before Run could ask him to repeat his name, he'd darted off.

"What the hell was his name?" Crow asked Run.

"*Days* or some shit. I didn't catch that much of what he was saying," Run answered. "Listen, man, good luck. Looks like you might make some loot. Maybe I'll see you again. I'm gonna find Russell and head back to Hollis."

As Run walked away, Crow yelled, "Yo, thanks for coming." As the words left his lips, the reality of his duplicity really began closing in on him.

Crow found an empty space in a corner of the room and stood alone for several minutes, trying to figure out how he fit into the events unfolding around him. He thought about his own lies and double-dealing, wondering how he was going to face Danny. Sliding him a few dollars wouldn't hurt. This should be one of the coolest days in Crow's life, but something was wrong. A tear welled up and rolled from his eye. Catching it with the tip of his tongue, he tasted the salt. He wiped its trail with the palm of his hand and was glad when Bones came back with a glass of champagne. He wanted to get the taste of remorse out of his mouth.

Bones handed him one of the glasses, raised his in a silent toast, and said, "Crow, you're uncomfortable because you're not in control of this, and you don't know how it's going to turn out. But remember, all artists are victims of some kind. The dealers and the buyers control the art world, not the artists."

Crow didn't let on that Bones had totally missed the mark. Instead, he mustered some bravado and said, "You're right, man, I can step off right now and still be way ahead. I just made crazy dollars for something I was trying to sell yesterday for fifty. Whatever kicks off from here, I've won. And another thing: It's funny how you sometimes have to step out of your world and into someone else's to see yourself how other people see you. A couple days ago, I was hanging out on street corners waiting for something to happen, watching little old white ladies clutching their purses when they passed me. Today I'm making something happen with French bitches battin' their eyes at me, and frontin' in dope rides, sniffing an unlimited supply of coke. Yesterday, Ms. Ann, who just paid three Gs for my shit, would've crossed the street to avoid me. Today, I'm her hero. And they say *niggers* ain't shit? Hustle or no hustle, I ain't got *shit* on these motherfuckers! Bones, man, I feel like I'm ready to break out. I don't care if I'm the man of the hour, the week, or the year. I'm just as black as I was last week when I'm sure none of these people would have given me the time of day, and this is just too much bullshit for me."

"What? The game getting too thick for *you?* You think that to all of these people here you're just a nigger who can paint? How many artists of any kind paint and die without anybody seeing their work? If you want to look at this all negatively, that's fine. Do whatever you gotta do to make sense of it, but remember, talent and success don't always find each other." Bones stopped talking because he felt self-conscious for saying so much without having thrown in some bullshit. "I need some air and a brew," he said nervously, and darted off toward the door.

Candy squeezed past some people just then, wanting to be alone with Crow for a minute. She asked him if he wanted to get some air. On their way outside, they stopped several times to meet patrons and talk shit. Just as they made it to the door, Bones strode up and snatched it open, taking a green bottle of beer away from his lips.

"Yo, man, that crazy crack broad who was here earlier just got hit by a car. I saw the whole shit. I was coming out of the store at the corner, when I saw her chase an empty Quarter Pounder box she had kicked into the street. The fool got run over by an ambulance. The shit was surreal! She was just lying there bleeding, never made a sound or nothing, and two dudes in the ambulance jumped out wearing white gloves and suits and shoved her in the back real quick and kept going. They never even turned their siren and lights off."

Crow pushed past Bones and ran into the middle of the street and looked up the block. Cars were coming and going as usual. After a few seconds, he walked back to the sidewalk and stood silently with Candy and Bones. He asked Bones for a sip of his beer. Passing the bottle back, he asked, looking up and down the block, "You sure all that happened just now? Looks pretty calm out here to me."

"I swear on my dead daddy." Bones looked hurt.

"I guess they had to hurry. You know, I hear those ambulance MFs get paid by the pound," Crow responded.

Bones sipped the last of the beer and stood it on the center of the roof of the Maserati. He adjusted the bottle to make sure it was perfectly centered. "Ah, now this would be a perfect photo for Alton, if he could get a naked blond chick to sit behind the wheel," he said.

Candy and Crow didn't respond. "They pay for most people from around here by the ounce, man," Bones rambled.

Crow walked away. He spat on the ground and shouted at Bones,

"Fuck you, man! Fuck *all* this bull-ass shit." He yanked the door open. "Nothin' don't mean shit to you, do it?" he said, going inside.

As the door closed behind Crow, Bones turned to Candy. "What the hell did I say?" he asked.

"Let's just go on inside, OK?" Candace said.

Candy opened the door. Bones looked around the room for Crow.

"That 'crack broad,' as you called her, was a victim," Candy said to Bones. "I think what bothers Crow is that lots of us only see two choices. We end up being either the hunter or the hunted. For the most part, Crow thought of himself as the hunter. Maybe he's beginning to see both sides and realizing that there ain't no winners in the game. You gotta be ready for shit like that. It's a hard pill to swallow, finding out that you ain't nothing to these people but a commodity."

"Fuck that metaphysical bullshit, Candy. How many motherfuckers everywhere can paint and die without anybody seeing their shit? If you want to call it being a nigger, that's fine with me . . ."

"That's the whole fucking point, Bones. The whole fucking point. Who the hell was that woman that got run over? That's the point, Bones." She sucked her teeth and was finished with the conversation.

The guy with the Rolex and his lady brushed past with their painting in tow. Only a few feet away, Geoff was handing flyers to people who were leaving. Bones told Candace he'd be back in a few minutes and went to stand by the door to shake hands. Geoff smiled at a woman with huge breasts, thin legs, and a jet-black braid that fell from the center of her bald head to the middle of her back. A pearl and diamond brooch hung from the end of her braid. She patted him on the rump and said, "Please be a dear, and don't give me one of those dreadful throwaways."

Geoff feigned a deep frown and said to her, "Well, dear, just what do you expect me to do with them, if not have my best patrons herald them on to their fates?"

The woman twirled the braid in her hand and said, "I hear you've run out of bathroom tissue, but that's only hearsay." Then she kissed him on the cheek. "Great show. I just hope my lady likes this photo I bought." Candace watched in amazement at how adept the woman was at tossing the length of her hair over her shoulder and bouncing her tits at the same time.

Geoff swung his right arm in an arc over his head and batted his eyes. "Well, if she doesn't like it, it's her own fault. The bitch should have been here. Don't worry, honey, she'll love it. Now, take a few of these damn things, and go the hell on home," Geoff said, thrusting a few flyers into the neck of her blouse.

She called him a cat and left, the papers jutting from between her titties.

Turning to Candy, Geoff said, "I've got to get the fuck out of here. My father-in-law, who is also my wife's attorney, called and said if I don't get my ass home, Ronnie is moving back to Hartford with them tonight and filing for a divorce in the morning. Shit, I answered the damn phone sounding like Geoff and not *Jefferson,* and the bastard called me a 'cock-sucking faggot'! Shit, Candy, I mean, I ain't down here fucking around. I make a lot more money now than I did when I was doing the nine-to-five. Still, that ain't enough for 'em. I better take my act on the road. Can you help me get these freaks out of here?"

Candace laughed and said, "Go on and take care of your business in the back. I'll take care of things out here. But I got one question. Why don't you just give up your other life?"

"It's no worse than this—and none of it's real. I can't be home all the time, and I can't be here in drag every day, either. But it don't matter. I float between the worlds, what the fuck?"

Just as Geoff finished his sentence, Crow walked up, and then there was a commotion at the door. "Fab Five!" Melissa screamed out.

Crow turned to see a tall, dark-skinned, impeccably dressed brother gliding across the floor toward them. Freddy Braithwaite.

The former graffiti artist and downtown celebrity exuded coolness, surveying the scene from behind black-and-gold-trimmed Cazal shades. Walking toward them, Fab Five Freddy stopped several times on his way to give pounds and exchange kisses. Behind him, Crow recognized Keith Haring and Kenny Scharf from Josefa's.

"Who the fuck is that?" Crow wanted to know.

"That's Fab Five Freddy," Candy responded in a tone that left him feeling woefully ill informed. "Haven't you ever heard 'Rapture' by Blondie?"

Melissa trotted up to Freddy and gave him a hug that made Crow a little jealous. He'd heard the name before but couldn't remember where or why. Just then, the rap went off in his head: "Fab Five Freddy says everybody's fly, DJ's spinning, I said 'my, my', Flash is fast, Flash is cool . . ." Then he got it.

Keith and Kenny were standing behind Freddy, waiting to be greeted. As Crow shook Freddy's hand, the line from the song played several times over in his head: "Fab Five Freddy says everybody's fly . . . Fab Five Freddy says everybody's fly . . ."

After more handshakes and hugs, Braithwaite looked around the space. He turned to Crow and said, "Good show. I'm out. Later," and was *out.*

As the trio made their way to the door, Melissa had made her way over to Crow and sighed. She followed Freddy out the door with her eyes. "That's one smooth nee-gro," she said.

"Let me ditch this frock before we go. I can't go home with this thing on. I'll never hear the end of it," Geoff said, and excused himself.

"Crow," Melissa said. "You're going to have to decide what you're going to do with yourself. Geoff wants to represent you. I also think that you could have a successful career as a writer. The little I've read of your story is provocative."

Crow looked down at his watch, feeling uneasy about taking credit for Danny's book again, on top of having sold Danny's paintings as his own—and for so much money, too. He began to wonder how he was going to face Danny tomorrow. He could go no further than to say to Melissa, "Right now, I ain't too sure what I'm going to do about anything."

There was a pause in the conversation. Alton stumbled up, now happily drunk and pleased to inform them that he'd sold three more photos. He wasn't sure which ones had been bought or by whom, but they were sold. "After all," he said, "my duty is to create, as it's Geoff's to promote and sell the fruits of my labors. I'm sure you agree."

Crow congratulated him on the sales and said, "Yeah, I guess everybody has a mission." He thought and added, "Well, at least almost everybody."

As Crow finished the champagne in his glass, Melissa said, "Oh, by the way, Crow, Geoff sold the painting with the poem for four thousand dollars. I'm buying the one that looks like a landscape for three."

Crow's jaw dropped. "What? You don't have to do that, Melissa. Hell, I owe most of this to you. Keep your money. I want to give it to you. Consider it a thank-you. It's the least I can do."

"I want to pay for it, Crow. Consider it the first installment of my patronage. All artists need patrons. Even though I had money, I had a patron when I first started out. I consider it my duty to help someone else get started. It might as well be you."

"I'm not really sure what a patron does, but patron or no patron," Crow said, "I feel like I owe you something, not the other way around."

"But I insist, Crow . . ."

They went back and forth like this until Candy suggested that since Crow would obviously need the money for art supplies, Melissa could let him use her studio and keep it stocked with materials. "Besides," she threw in, "nothing has to be decided for sure tonight, now, does it?" They both agreed.

Geoff came back in men's clothes and announced, "Oh, I forgot to tell you guys, I also sold the new landscape for four grand."

Crow shook his head in disbelief before saying, "Too late, it's already been taken by the lady with green snow-leopard eyes, my *patron-ess,* is it?"

Melissa said, "Damn, that's the one I wanted! But take the money, Crow. You can always paint another one for me anytime."

Crow was surprised at himself for offering the piece to Melissa versus taking the money. *I'm drunk or some shit, or getting sentimental or something,* he thought to himself. *I barely know her!*

Geoff laughed and said, "Well, that was close." He pulled two envelopes from his pocket and handed one to Crow and the other to Alton.

"Here, Crow, this is minus my commission. Bones, I'll give you a hundred now and the rest after some checks clear."

"OK," Bones said.

Melissa pulled Élan's check out of her pocket and passed it to Geoff. "Here's the other one."

Geoff folded it and said, "Thanks," putting it away. "He can give me a check for your percentage, and I'll give you cash," Melissa said to Crow.

Crow bristled. "You ain't the only one with a checking account." Then he thought about it. "Well, at least I *had* a checking account. I ain't put nothing in it for so long, it might be dead by now."

Geoff leaned on the table and wrote another check to Melissa. "Well, Crow, what are you going to do with your new windfall?" Geoff asked. "You'll probably end up with close to six grand, after everybody gets their cut."

Crow just stood there shaking his head. He thought about Danny but said, "I don't really believe it, Geoff, and it probably won't hit me until I'm back in Brooklyn. Right now, it all seems like a dream to me." Thoughts of Danny persisted.

Crow's descent into guilt was interrupted by the realization that Geoff was no longer wearing a dress and makeup.

"Damn, doc, you sure look played like that," Crow said to Geoff.

"Yeah, I know I must. But that has far more to do with what I'm gonna have to face at home than what I'm wearing. I need a drink. Alton, please pour me some of that wine."

Alton poured the last of the bottle into the glass for him. Geoff thanked him.

He sipped some and said, "Listen, people, I've got to make a hasty exit. The party's over, at least for now, anyway."

"Let's get the fuck out of here," Candace said.

Geoff stood up and pushed the chair away. "Listen, why don't you guys come home with me? I really don't want to face this crap alone, and I damn sure can use a ride. The PATH train is a pain in the ass."

"Sorry, but I only want to go home and sleep until spring," Alton said.

"My permanent boundaries have become Delancey to Fourteenth Street," Melissa declared.

"I've never been to Middle America before," Candy said with a chuckle. "Let's go with Geoff. It'll be good to get out of the city and smell some raw sewage and toxic waste."

"Yeah, OK, I'll drive," Bones said. "We'll meet you later tonight, if that's all right, Melissa?"

"Fine with me, but you guys gotta drop me home first and promise to be careful with the car."

"Shit, no sweat, honey," Bones said.

Candace Maria started skipping toward the door, singing, "We're off to see the wizard . . ."

"Well, OK, I guess that's our cue. Let's break camp, troops," Crow said. He threw his hand over his head and said, "Forward, ho."

Candace stopped singing. "Who you calling a *ho?*" she asked.

When everybody was out of the gallery, Geoff turned off the lights and locked the door. Bones was already revving the engine when Geoff began pulling the steel gates down.

"Yo, you forgot to put the locks on the gate," Crow said, sliding into the car.

"I never got around to buying any," Geoff replied. "I'd probably lose the keys, anyway."

"Or your mind, wondering if somebody was cutting the locks off," Melissa said.

They waved goodbye to Alton, who was drinking from a half-full gallon of white. He wiped his mouth on his sleeve and waved back before he turned the bottle back up to his head. *It's always good to have a stash when the stash is gone,* Alton thought as he stumbled up the street.

Spell to Induce Euphoria (2002)

13

Running on Empty

Melissa woke up in the pillow room. She pulled a large green linen pillow from between her thighs. She'd only slept for a few hours, but then she hadn't slept for more than five at a time in years. She scratched her side where the thin links of the gold waist chain had bitten into her flesh and left a red imprint. Except for her jewelry and the makeup she hadn't washed off, Melissa was naked. Rolling between and over the pillows, she stretched her limbs to their limits in every direction. A small red velvet pillow with long gold fringe and "Greetings from Niagara Falls" embroidered on it slid off a black satin one and onto her face. She removed a few strands of fringe from her nose but left the pillow where it landed. Staring at the ceiling with her exposed left eye, she tried to wiggle her ears. *Shit, I'll probably go to my fucking grave without being able to wiggle my damn ears,* she thought. She flung the pillow across the room and lay there thinking of some other things she'd never been able to do. Like whistle with two fingers in her mouth. Blow tiny spit bubbles off the tip of her tongue. Cup her hands together and blow into them to make a sound. And while she had practiced yoga for years, she had never been able to stand on her head for more than five seconds.

Before she got up, she shook her legs in the air so that the tiny silver bells on the anklets she wore would ring. She was disappointed that she wasn't able to produce the riff of sound she wanted. "Shit, I guess we all have our shortcomings," she groused, rising to her feet.

Standing made her aware of the pressure building in her bladder, so she jiggled and climbed her way through the maze of pillows and dashed for the bathroom. Ever since she'd read somewhere how people closed the bathroom door even if nobody else was in the house, she made it a point to leave the door open. After she peed, she stood staring into the mirror at the teardrops she'd drawn on her face the night before. She wondered if she should wash them off because they were smeared or if they had become more interesting like that. She grabbed a washcloth and scrubbed her face.

Back down in the kitchen, Melissa decided that she would prefer a glass of champagne instead of a Bloody Mary. She took a bottle that had already been opened out of the refrigerator and put it down on the counter. The champagne produced a listless pop when she took the cork out. "Shit." Melissa sighed. She rummaged through cabinets stocked with bottles of vitamins and minerals. She selected about a dozen pills, placing them together on a paper towel. She emptied the remainder of the bottle into a large water glass and gulped down two handfuls of vitamins. She looked at the wall clock, thinking that the crew should have been back from Geoff's already. Grabbing the glass, she sauntered out of the kitchen. "I guess they'll be back when they get back," she murmured to herself, and turned off the light. Bells chiming with every step, she made her way back to the pillow room, putting disquieting thoughts of Bones driving Burt's car unattended out of her mind.

Melissa settled down into a comfortable position on the pillows and looked for where she'd left off in the story. She found the page and began to read:

"My story," Exemption said, "is as common as it is unique. It's because I'm fresh from the forge and I'm walking on the only road my feet have found that I find myself trying to explain the story of who I've been. The only man I've ever known is my father, and now my memory of him is dim, but I feel I am not like him. I am common because you are asking me the common question. I am unique in that I don't know the common answer. If there is a common answer. My story is that you are asking me a question, the question. Pandora, you, these people, and myself is the only answer I can think of. Shit, If you let me in I am right, If you don't I am right. Either way something is done and that makes it part of my story. All of this is but a part of a page in the story. I can't win or lose because it's all the same shit. Now, with that shit in mind, what the fuck are you gonna do?"

The man looked down at Exemption and Pandora, then scratched the side of his head, but before he was able to reply, Pandora began to applaud. She started calling for an encore. Exemption cracked his knuckles and pulled off his glasses. They all disappeared. Ahead of him, the black tar road ran on. He smiled and put the glasses back on. Pandora was wiping the palms of her hands down the sides of his pants, and the man above them was making noises attempting to clear his throat. He turned his head from the man to Pandora and asked, "Well, how the hell did I do?"

Pandora answered, "You were super."

The man above cleared his throat once more and said, "It stands to reason that someone who is on the way to no place should have nothing to say. But taking the time to say nothing is the same thing as taking the time to make the trip to nowhere.

Since it's all the same to you, I really can't say if you can come or go. Do whatever you decide if that means anything."

Exemption turned his head and looked into the void at the side of the road and said, "I guess that's cool. Hey, thanks for the advice."

The man reared his head back and shot a piercing stare at them from the corner of his right eye. His squinting eye held them for several seconds before he shifted his gaze to Pandora and said, "You know, you just can't keep coming in here and going out all the damn time. It would be better for you and everybody else in the long run if you decided what direction to take or at least apply for a temporary visa." Pandora asked absently if he was talking to her. He replied, "Well, shit, I'm not talking to the goddamn demonstrators."

To that she said, "Oh."

Tired of the exchange, Exemption grabbed her by the arm and pulled her through the parting gates.

The sound of the gates slamming shut echoed behind them. As they walked down the cobblestone road, Exemption noticed hundreds of tiny yellow eyes peering out from patches of thick grass that grew on both sides of the road. The sound of frenzied laughter was obscured by an orchestra of croaking frogs and clicking crickets. In the distance, the low moan of a train whistle complemented the harmony of sounds. A few feet ahead, a crackle broke from a large gray speaker that was hung on wires from a slender neck of a streetlight.

Coming to a halt, they stood silently under the speaker and waited. "Testing, testing. Hey, great, they finally got the damn thing working. Anyway, I was supposed to tell you guys that almost anything you do is all right in here but remember, don't get caught drinking diet cola or chewing sugar-free gum. Don't even bother to ask me why. I'm just a grade five doing a job but that's the skinny." The speaker crackled again a few times and went dead.

Exemption yelled up at the speaker, "But those were the first things I was gonna do."

Pandora gently rubbed his back and said, "Don't let it bug you out. We can find all kinds of other stuff to get into."

He looked at her and shook his head and asked with a whining voice, "Are you sure? Promise?" His cynicism was lost on Pandora, so finally he said, "You could have fooled me," after she assured him that there were a bunch of other things to do.

She patted him on the stomach and said, "You don't need those diet things, anyway."

He was going to keep messing with her, but he was hungry and his feet hurt, so he let the conversation drop. They continued their walk into town, traveling along the side of the road. Pandora walked with one leg on the road and kept the other tramping in the grass. She squealed with delight each time a frog hopped away from her foot. Every time one darted across the road and disappeared into the grasses on the other side, she said to Exemption, "I hope it's got relatives over there." After the third time she said that, he asked her how long she had been out here on her own. She told him longer than anybody else she knew and asked why did he want to know. "Just wondering, that's all," he told her, and thought, *I've been out here longer than anybody else I know, too. I wonder if anybody tells anybody anything that means anything.*

The boy jumped at the sudden sound of glass shattering and turned in time to see a pink toilet sail throughout the air from the upstairs window of one of the narrow houses that were set back far away from the road. Then several rolls of toilet paper were flung through the hole in the window. The rolls of paper unwound during their fall, and Pandora said to Exemption that the lengths of paper that were trailing behind looked like the tails of kites. Exemption wanted to know what a kite was but didn't ask. Inside the house, the upstairs light went off, and someone began to play a harp. After several chords, the harping was complemented by the low moans of a bass fiddle. The music ceased when a baby began to cry, and then they heard a woman scream for it to shut up. The woman demanded several times that the baby shut up. When it didn't, a few seconds later, the baby was thrown from the window, and then the music began again. Exemption started running through the grass toward where the baby hit the ground, but before he could get there, a small child wearing night clothes came running out the front door and snatched the baby and dashed with it into the forest of trees behind the house. Exemption turned and walked slowly back to Pandora. When he reached her, she told him not to worry because the witch woman of the woods would care for them.

He put his arm over her shoulder, and they continued the walk into town. His attention was divided between watching her turn her head every few seconds to look back toward the house and trying to decide if the noises he heard up ahead were the sounds from a party or a fight. A scream came from behind them, and the bass fiddle ceased to play. Pandora said, "Don't pay that any attention. I've heard that whenever I get here. It's the first night of the lunatic moon. Things always change for the better once you've had a stiff drink and a bowl of stew at the First Stop Tavern."

Exemption said, "Is that right?"

And the harpist began to play again. He thought the tune sounded like the "Battle Hymn of the Republic," but the shattering sound of glass left him wondering how the flow of notes had progressed. When Pandora didn't comment about the noises, he said, "Sounded like the kitchen sink to me."

"First Stop Tavern is the building up there on the left," she said, pointing to a cinder-block cube with a weathered green awning. "That section of road always bothers me. Somebody told me that the people in that house are part of a management-sponsored theater company whose subsidy depends on presenting a scary first impression of the town. I wouldn't bet on that, though. I've seen some of the people who come and go from that place, and I think that they're anti-establishment chemistry majors who take a lot of funny drugs."

Exemption asked her why she thought that, and she told him because all the men she'd seen around here had long beards. He vaguely remembered his father having a beard, but his was short and edged up. "Hmm. Anyway, how good is the stew over there?" he asked, starting across the road toward the First Stop Tavern. Pandora told him it was good, but he had to be careful not to eat a lot of it, because the cook, One Foot Jimmy Jackson, put something in it that made most people act kinda dumb. Exemption said, "I think I got it straight so far—gum, soda, too much stew, and an eye peeled for guys with hair hanging off their faces. But all in all, we can do what we like. Does that sound about right?"

Pandora yanked his arm off her shoulder and said, "Don't make fun of me. I'm just trying to tell you how to keep from getting in trouble. These ain't things I'm making up to vex you. The main reason I'm here is because I thought that maybe you were kinda nice. But since you thought up that pretty answer to get in here, you've been treating me like a damn fool. I think you should try and act a bit more like that fellow I hooked into more than nine months ago." He tried to say something to defend himself and ask about her conception of time, but Pandora was already waiting to stifle any explanation he could offer.

"Don't get into trying to make how you been acting toward me all right. Just 'cause you got them tricky words together to get in this here place don't mean you, me, or the guy back there really thinks that you think that ain't nothing any more something than anything else. I heard all the stuff you said, and I ain't hear you explain why if none of this really matters, then why did you start to walking anywhere, nowhere, or anyplace in the first place? If everything you said is true, I think instead of getting on up to walk and get older, you would have laid your ass on down and died."

Exemption shouted, "All right, all right, can I say one little thing? I mean, if you've finished with telling me how rude I've been acting, I just want to say, you're right and I'm wrong. No, that's not really it. I really should be acting better. My mama always told me to act polite. I ain't been doing that, but I wasn't trying to hurt you; you've got to believe that. My puppy and you are the only people that I remember ever tried to make it all right for me."

Pandora smiled and said, "Simon says to take two giant steps." Rubbing the sides of her thighs, she said, "Never a cheerleader, and I'm sure I would have flunked gym class if I went. I should have gone for six or seven baby steps."

Exemption smiled and said, "Giant steps must be better exercise. But if we hurry and take teensy-weensy steps, we'll get to get some of that stew before the place closes."

Pandora shuffled her feet forward with short, choppy exact motions. She turned her head and said, "Well, let's get going. Once you get the rhythm of these itsy-bitsy steps, it's a piece of cake." She thought a second and asked, "Am I supposed to take itsy-bitsy steps or teensy-weensy steps?"

Exemption quickly caught up to her and then cut his pace in an effort to walk alongside her. "I think the only one who knows the real difference is Simon, and ain't nobody seen Simon for years," Exemption answered.

Pandora refused to stop shuffling along regardless of Exemption's pleas. When he finally figured out that he had to say, "Simon Says walk with normal steps," they had reached the row of hitching posts provided for the convenience of the patrons. Exemption read the sloppy red-lettered words that covered the entire top of the gray cinder wall.

"The First Stop Tavern," he said, and added, "I guess this is the place."

Neither of them saw the man who sat with his back propped against the last post. Both of his hands were wrapped around the neck of a whiskey bottle. A long beard hung from his chin in braids. He startled them when he declared, "It's only the first stop if you is headed into town. If you be headed out, the wall over on that side says 'Last Stop.' " Then he laughed and went on to say, "It don't make me a bit of difference nohow since they ain't let me in the place in years." He was wearing a dusty, tattered black tuxedo.

Exemption turned to Pandora to say something, but she was busy watching the man wiggle and spread apart his long, thin toes. His feet were caked with thick mud except for the nails, which were painted glossy red. Exemption cleared his throat several times in the same manner as the man at the gate did to get his attention before saying, "I hope that you've alerted the proper people about this. You can't take this sort of thing sitting down, you know."

Pandora tugged at his arm and whispered, "I don't think it's a good idea for you to screw around with this dude. I know for a fact that he's way up the ladder with those chemist guys. They do strange stuff to people who get on their bad side." But the man hadn't heard anything they said and was busy trying to straighten out his cummerbund.

Exemption wiped his brow and said, "Another close brush with death luckily avoided." Pulling Pandora along, he said, "Let's just go get something to eat."

Melissa put the folder down and propped herself up on one elbow. She'd stopped reading because the last paragraph ended the typed section of the story. Beyond that, it was continued on two yellow legal pads. Flipping the pages of the pad, she noted how carefully the words had been written.

She ran a finger over the folder. The paradoxical logic and surrealistic tone of what she'd read seemed too metaphysical to jibe with what seemed to be Crow's usual pragmatic, self-centered thinking. But doubting Crow made her uncomfortable, and she wondered if that was because she had spent too much of her life with those way-too-laid-back East Village bohemian types to truly be able to appreciate Crow's frame of reference.

She thought about it and was pretty sure that her life had been too insulated and that it would probably do her some good to venture off her beaten path and make her way a little further "uptown," as it were.

She heard the phone ring on the way back to the kitchen. As she dashed for it, the glass slipped from her hand and bounced off her thigh, causing the drops of champagne remaining in the glass to run down her leg before the glass hit one of the pillows, without breaking. She picked up the receiver, panting while wiping the wet off her thigh. Before she could say anything, Burt began apologetically, "I hope I didn't disturb you."

Melissa, trying to catch her breath, was disappointed to hear Burt's voice. She didn't say anything.

A few seconds of silence passed before he asked, "Is it all right if I come and get the car now?"

"If I am not mistaken," she started, "I told you that *I* would call *you.*" Melissa spoke quietly but tersely.

Burt screamed into the phone, "You're letting those savages ride around in my car without you in it?"

Melissa asked calmly, "Whom do you think you are yelling at, Burt? We've already been through this." She hung up the phone. Looking over at the clock, she muttered, "They should have been back by now."

Driving way too fast, Bones made a turn that took them farther downtown. "Oh, hell no, Bones," Candy smacked. "Turn this thing around, and drive it directly to Melissa's." She said something in Spanish that no one understood. Whatever it was, it had curse words in it that everyone recognized.

Bones made an abrupt U-turn that started Candy to cussing in Spanish again. Then he turned the radio on, catching the end of Jim Morrison singing, "When the music is over." Geoff demanded that Bones not sing.

"Let him sing, man," Crow said, and laughed.

"How the hell can you say that after hearing him screw up the words to nearly every damn song that comes on the radio?" Geoff asked Crow. "And what note is that you keep hitting? I hope to hell it hits you back," he snapped at Bones.

"Shit, he's the only one who ain't been fuckin' depressing since we broke out of the gallery."

Bones sped up to beat a changing light and sang off-key along with the also off-key Jim Morrison. Bones warbled, "Cancel my subscription to the resurrection, send my credentials to the house of detention, I've got some friends inside . . ."

The light turned red before Bones reached the intersection, and he slammed on the brakes, causing the car to fishtail to a halt. He held up his head and said, "It's all in the wrist, my dear, all in the wrist," parodying W. C. Fields or somebody.

Geoff spun his head around and said to Crow and Candace, "I thought it was all in the hands."

"Can we just drop this bullshit?" Candace sucked her teeth and screamed.

"See, I said y'all were startin' to get cranky," Crow said.

She laid her head on his shoulder and said, "I'd be less cranky if . . ."

Crow wasn't sure what she meant, but he ran the back of his hand down the side of her face and said playfully, "I'm sorry, baby, Daddy didn't mean to neglect you."

Both Bones and Geoff snickered, which made Candace Maria pull away from Crow before his hand had found a comfortable place to hold on to her.

She leaned her head out the window and said, "I am being serious, Crow . . . but I guess everybody's on this late-night sitcom rerun thing."

Bones said, "I'm up for the Marx Brothers or W.C."

"Shut *up,* Bones! Damn! You just don't know *when* to give it a rest, do you? Everything don't require a punchline, man," Crow snapped. He'd finally had enough of Bones's antics.

Geoff said, "Let's just go to Melissa's. I think this car is getting a little too close."

Crow leaned over and slipped an arm around Candace's waist. She moved in slightly, so he was able to wrap her all the way around.

Before they got to Melissa's house, Geoff had to tell Bones twice to stop screaming out the window to people he knew. Crow was trying to tell Candy he hadn't intended to neglect her. "The night had been so crazy," he started to explain. "I thought that we would spend some quality time later." This seemed to relax her, and she slid closer to him.

After the third trip around Melissa's block looking for a parking space, Bones parked the car in front of a hydrant a few doors away from her house. He turned off the radio and said, "Well, it seems like everyone enjoyed our little excursion. Please exit slowly and carefully, and thank you for riding with Bones's Magical Mystery Tour."

Melissa, in anticipation of their arrival, had donned a pink terry-cloth robe, diamond earrings, black lipstick, and spiked heels. She met them at the door, smoking a long thin black cigar for effect.

"Well, I see you sure know how to spice shit up," Crow said when he saw her.

Melissa blew smoke rings and kisses. She was surprised to see Geoff again, though. He had said he was going home to his wife. She wondered what happened and figured she'd get the story later. His being there made everything seem to be an unbroken chain of events, and she hadn't really wanted this thing to end—not just yet, anyway.

"It's about time you guys got back," she said, leaning out of the doorway and stretching her body past Candy to look for the car.

Seeing it intact, she leaned back and gave Candace a smile. Candy did not return the smile.

"Whatever I might need to know about your trip will probably be better told inside," Melissa said, and stepped back from the door.

Bones stepped aside to let Geoff into the house before him. Bones was still acting the fool and ushered Geoff on with a low bow and a sweep of his hand. Crow and Melissa laughed. Candy kissed Melissa on the cheek as she passed. The kiss looked to Crow like all formality, no affection.

In the hallway, Candace stood still next to Geoff. Bones bowed up and down and asked, "Who's next?"

"Just go the fuck on," Crow said, and pushed Bones through the door.

Bones stumbled past Melissa and halted at rigid attention in front of Geoff and Candace. He gave Crow a brisk salute and said, "Reporting as ordered, sir."

Crow exhaled in exasperation and said, "Damn, what a fucking freak show."

When they got to the pillow room, Candace Maria flopped face first into a huge square pillow covered in African mud cloth and pulled a red silk one over her head. Geoff headed for the bathroom. Crow lay down next to Candace. Melissa sat down next to them and wrapped her arms around the tops of her knees, pulling them in so she was able to rest her head on them. Her robe slid open, and Crow rolled onto his side and ran his hand along her leg. He fell back and stared up at the ceiling. "We had to rescue Geoff from hostile aliens. Bones even brought one back to study more closely, but he dropped it off at a club that used to be a supermarket."

Melissa asked, "What really happened?"

Crow answered, "OK, we drove to Geoff's house, way the fuck out there in No-man's Land, and then things got crazy. He made us call him *Jeff*."

Candy interrupted before Crow could finish. Snatching the

pillow off her head, she shouted, "We went there, and damn near his wife's whole family was waiting. They looked at us funny, we looked at them like they were crazy, then Geoff asked his wife to split with us. She ain't say shit, so he left her all his dollars. We was trying to split and found Bones sitting in the backseat of the car with his arm stuffed up the twat of a neighbor's daughter. She was a dizzy little thing who thought that Bones and the rest of us were celebrities. She begged to come—even though she already had—so we brought her and dropped her across town. Now we're back."

Melissa let her knees go and leaned back, resting on her palms. "Damn, that's too much information. Maybe I ain't really needed to know all of that after all," she said.

"What the hell do you mean, *thought* we were celebrities?" Bones asked. "We *are* fucking celebrities. When was the last time you've been excluded from anything?"

"I'm usually excluded from this type a shit. I'm a brown-skinned nee-gro from Brooklyn, remember?" Crow asked.

Geoff stood in the doorway and said, "Bones's right, we are sorta important down here, and I guess that's one of the reasons I don't feel right in mundane New Jersey anymore, but sometimes I really get tired of looking in my mirror and not knowing which cartoon character I'm going to find looking back at me." Everybody turned around.

"So stop putting all that bullshit on your face. Your mug is ridiculous enough as it is," Candace said, then she buried her face back in the pillow and pulled the other one back over her head again. Nobody laughed.

Geoff pulled off his shoes and maneuvered through the pillows to sit down near Candace's feet. He'd sat facing Melissa and inadvertently caught a glimpse of her thighs. Embarrassed, he looked up to see if she'd seen him and met her emerald gaze. Melissa's face had a slight smile on it, and he wanted to apologize but couldn't find the words. Not knowing what else to do, he shifted his eyes to the bookcase and said to Candace Maria, "Maybe you're right, this drag queen act *is* getting kinda tired. But it does sell art."

Bones slid down the wall and squatted cross-legged on a black, shiny pillow, his back against the bookcase. He looked pensive for a second before he blurted out, "You know, Geoff, until last night I always thought you was a gay. I mean, I ain't got nothing against a homo, but I mean, either you gay or you ain't. I mean, why act like something you ain't? I guess you think it gets you more dinero or something, but I really don't think nobody in the art world gives a shit one way or another. You came off stupid to Crow because you felt you had to act like you thought a shithead, racist homo would act. I mean, I did some shit to fuck with Crow; he did some shit to fuck with me. But it was all real shit. You were acting. Imagine getting your ass kicked 'cause you did some dumb shit you ain't really mean? I've been acting crazy all night 'cause it was fun, and I mean to have fun until my life is over. My fucking father killed himself 'cause he couldn't see the fun no more. Geoff, if you don't wear a wig and dress because it's fun, what's the fucking point? Motherfuckers have called me full of shit for years, but it's how I cope, and what's more, it's a blast. And on top of that, you shouldn't have a problem with looking at Melissa's big, pretty legs. Yo, now, who's gonna break out some sniff?"

Candace rolled over, sat up, looked at Bones, and said, "Damn, a self-aware Bones. This is rare. At least you ain't *pretending* to be about nothin'."

Bones lowered his eyes, swung his head from side to side, and said in a Cajun drawl, "Shucks now, honey, don't you make nothing out of what I done said."

Geoff stood up and kicked several pillows aside so he was able to plant his feet firmly on the carpet underneath. He looked down at Bones and said to him, "I've thought about what you said, and it makes sense. But people with boring, stupid, fucked-up lives love a freak show. There is a great mass of unfulfilled and fucked-up people in this world who just want to see that there's people more fucked up than them, and they are willing to pay handsomely for it too. It just so happens that a significant percentage of them happen to be patrons of the arts—they're my bread and butter, man! So if my adulterous yuppie, lecherous gangster, body-pierced and bush-shaven lesbian, or tattooed faggot clients need to think that Gee-off is a manic-polar, schizo-chotic, cross-dressing, wig-wearing, pillow biter in order to buy art from me, then so be it, Bonesy, my boy, so be it. And *what,* may I ask, in your chemical distraction-wracked and feeble mind, is the difference between what I'm doing and your being on some bullshit all the time? What do you do with your bullshit all day? At least I'm providing a service, no matter how decadently I do it."

Bones, never one to cotton too highly to a direct confrontation, sighed heavily, saying, "How did you turn this shit on me? Let's don't drag this thing out, *Jeffy.* Melissa, you got any more blow? Listen, Geoff, I'm on the survival tip. I don't steal shit from nobody. I've been known to misdirect some people, but that's who the hell I am, and maybe I don't do shit because I don't need to. I've never claimed to be here on any mission to save the earth. I was just offering you a suggestion, is all. I would say I won't do it again, but it's more like I couldn't. Don't try to compare us; compare what you're doing, to who you say you are and who you think you should be. If they match, there ain't shit anybody can say that's gonna mean a rat's ass."

Melissa rubbed Crow's chest and asked, "Did you guys bring any of that shit back with you?" Then she lifted his head up off her thighs and said, "I better get us a blow before this gets too much deeper."

Before she left the room, Crow called out in jest, "Wine, woman! Bring back strong drink!"

Geoff sat back down. Candy said to Bones, "I think this is the first time I've ever heard you talk seriously about anything."

Bones told her, "It pops up every once in a while. My father and his friends were always telling me about the nature of this, the understanding of that, and ways to look at this, that, and a bunch of other shit. It bored the hell out of me at the time, but it seems some of that shit stuck."

Geoff said to Bones, "I'd always heard what a great man your father was."

"Yeah, man, I've heard that all my life, but he blew it. There must have been a flaw in whatever he thought he'd found out, because he decided to leave this motherfucker. He should have known that all anyone can do with the truth is struggle."

No one said anything.

Melissa came back with a bottle of champagne in one hand and half a bottle of brandy in the other. She set both bottles on a stack of books, pulled a plastic bag from the pocket of her robe, and tossed it to Bones. The bag arced across the room and hit Bones in the head and fell between two stacks of books. He found it and saw that inside the bag was a rock of cocaine the size of a golf ball.

"What am I supposed to do with this?" Bones wanted to know. Melissa suggested he put it between two books and stomp down on it.

"That sounds like it might work," Crow agreed, and proceeded to select two hefty titles he thought could endure both his weight and the job.

Candy lay back down and buried her face in the pillows.

Bones took the two weighty hardcover books Crow had chosen. He placed the bag between them, stood up, and slammed his foot down hard. A loud crunch ensued, and tiny chunks of blow shot out of the bag and around the room. Bones retrieved the bag from between the books, looked at the cocaine, now reduced to powder and said, "I done died and went to cocaine heaven."

Geoff cleared his throat, and Melissa passed him the bottle of brandy. Then she popped open the champagne, untied her robe, and sat down, taking a swallow from the bottle. She took another gulp before passing it to Geoff. He sat there holding the bottle of brandy in one hand and the champagne in the other. He felt awkward holding both bottles and trying to avoid staring at Melissa's partially exposed breasts. Crow's attention shifted away from Bones, who was busy looking for small cocaine chunks, to Geoff, who looked as if he might be able to decide which bottle to drink from if he'd do something besides leer at Melissa's fat titties.

"This is getting too involved, and I think it's gonna take someone who's smarter than your average bear to figure it out," Crow announced.

Not sure she quite caught Crow's meaning, Melissa pulled her robe closed over her chest anyway and asked Crow what he meant by that.

Crow didn't get a chance to answer, because Bones found the chunk of blow he'd been looking for under a pillow and rose on two knees, holding it high above his head between his thumb and forefinger, and lapsed back into his slathering madman act, asking, "Has Auggie Doggie Daddy, meanin' *Doggie Daddy,* ever let you down?"

On some kind of a roll, Bones continued. "It should be assumed that Rock Bottom and the Master Cylinder will suffer in the folds of Felix the Cat's bag of tricks; Elmer will blast his *own* brains out with his own gun; Wile E. Coyote will create an avalanche under which he buries himself and then falls off a cliff holding the anvil meant for the R.R.; and it's a given that Daffy—being a *black* duck—will always be made to look like the fool; the fucking rabbit can't never get a single bowl of Trix, period, while that cat gets a whole bag, only to get himself out when it's time to tell all. And I guess I can understand all that shit, but it's beyond me that a motherfucker who's supposed to be some kind a nexus of the art world can't figure out what the fuck to do because he's got titties staring him in the face."

"You're obviously being informed mostly by Saturday-morning television. Explains a lot," Melissa quipped.

Bones sighed, sank into a sitting position, and dropped the rock of cocaine into the open bag. He ran the tips of his fingers along the edges of the books he'd crushed the cocaine between and licked them clean of residue.

"There is just too much bullshit flying around this room for me." Candace muffled her reply from under the pillows. "I guess everybody is just tired and catty, but it's sure getting on my nerves."

"You know it ain't so much bullshit as it is everybody's trying to be clever. Why don't we just kick what's really on our minds?" Crow asked.

Geoff passed the champagne to Bones, then reached for and pulled the cork from the brandy and poured a mouthful, which he immediately regretted. He had gulped the liquor down his throat; when it hit bottom, it rushed quickly back into his mouth, gagging him. After several attempts, he managed to get and keep the entire swallow down. He corked the bottle and moved a pillow aside so he could set it down on the floor.

He wiped away the brandy that had run out of the corners of his mouth and said to Melissa, who had seen the whole thing, "Well, everyone else has taken a turn analyzing my dress-wearing double life. Care to throw your two cents in?"

"Listen, Geoff, all I want to know is if I can let this damn robe loose, or do I have to go upstairs and get dressed?" Melissa said. "Anything else, I figure you'll work out for yourself."

Geoff turned red and stammered, "Wh-what are you talking about?"

Candy pushed the pillow off her head and rolled onto her side so she had everybody in view. She sucked her teeth and said, "This is getting out of fucking hand. Melissa just wants to know if she can sit here and be relaxed without her tits making you nervous. If you feel like looking at her tits, look at 'em." Candy turned over onto her back, opened her shirt, and said, "Shit, if you get tired of her tits, you can fucking look at mine." She grabbed the pillow and pulled it over her face.

Bones looked over at Candace Maria, whistled, and shouted, "Damn!"

Candace snarled from under the pillow, "Just don't fucking touch me, Bones," and snatched her shirt closed.

"I know, I know, it's always the same two rules: Don't touch you, and don't sell drugs to the children," Bones said.

He took another swallow from the bottle and passed it to Crow. "I'd rather some blow, but I'm sure you'll be sending that along soon enough," he said.

"Any minute now," was Bones's reply, as he tried to smash the rock he'd retrieved.

Melissa jumped up and snatched the bag from Bones and exclaimed in frustration, "Why the hell are you fucking with that when we got all this powder already?"

The phone rang, and Melissa dashed out to pick it up on the extension in her bedroom. On the way, she bumped into Geoff. Flustered, Geoff stammered, "Ex-excuse me," his eyes involuntarily focused on her nearly completely exposed breasts. Melissa grabbed his arm and dragged him along with her. Geoff offered a weak and insincere protest but was pulled easily into her room.

He stood quietly while Melissa informed Burt that the car keys would be left in the flower box in front of the house. "Wait here," she told Geoff, as she went to get the keys from Bones. Returning to the bedroom, she asked Geoff to accompany her downstairs to get some more champagne and place the keys in the box at the front door.

Geoff had begun to rummage through the refrigerator when he felt Melissa slip behind him and put her arms around his waist. Startled, he swung around to find Melissa standing there with her robe fully open. His eyes traveled the length of her body, from her firm, full breasts to the down-covered vee between her legs. Geoff stuttered something unintelligible, which made Melissa laugh.

"Come on, don't tell me you're shy. You know you're quite

attractive to me without all that shit you wear," she cooed, and batted her eyes with such extreme exaggeration they both had to laugh. Geoff's tension eased. Backing against the counter, she hopped up and pulled him in between her legs. He began running his tongue up the side of her neck from her collar bone and back down to her breasts. He gently rolled each nipple around in his mouth, and Melissa shuddered, wrapping her legs around him. She lifted his head and gave him a long, deep, sensuous kiss. Geoff pulled away and sank to his knees. Taking the obvious cue, Melissa scooted forward on the counter and lifted her vagina to his open mouth. Quickly, his tongue parted her pinkness, and he licked her feverishly. Melissa threw her head back and closed her eyes. "You do that quite well," she said playfully, but when he slowly flicked the tip of her clit several times, she emitted a deep moan and repeated the phrase in a completely different tone. Melissa's legs flew up in the air as she pushed herself harder against his face. Geoff pulled his head away, gulped some air, and dove back in. He reached up and grabbed her breasts as she began to feel the pressure build between her legs. Geoff's face and mouth were drenched with her juices. Melissa screamed loudly as the first wave of orgasmic rushes hit her. Her legs flailed wildly as she was taken over again by wave after wave of mounting pleasure. When the orgasm reached its crescendo, Melissa dug her nails into Geoff's shoulder, which caused him to cry out in pain and pull away. But it didn't matter; she had already come, quickly and violently. She slumped over and let him go. Geoff sat on the floor smiling and looking up at her.

Finally, Melissa opened her eyes and asked him, "Just how loud was I? You think they heard?"

Geoff responded, "Who gives a fuck?"

"I do!" Melissa said. "But let me tell you again, you sure do that well."

Geoff picked himself up off the floor and went to the refrigerator. He pulled out a bottle of wine and took a swig before saying,

"Right now, my dick is so hard I'd rather fuck than discuss what they did or didn't hear. You started this shit, and now, if I don't get some, I'm gonna die."

Melissa laughed, took the bottle of wine from him, and said, "There will be plenty of time for that later. This was just a prelim, but hold on to the thought, and we'll *come* back to it, OK? The pussy ain't going nowheres. Shit, it's been here at least as long as we've known each other," she said with another chuckle.

Geoff sucked his teeth. "Shit," he said, and went over to the sink to wash his face off.

Melissa slid down from the counter, tied her robe, and handed him a roll of paper towels. She rinsed and toweled herself off and selected another bottle of wine to take back upstairs. Grabbing it, she said, "Let's get back upstairs. We don't want to be rude. And please don't sulk like you always do when you can't get what you want!"

Following Melissa back up the stairs, he said, "Words of wisdom from the wise old sage."

Melissa said, "Exactly, but what I want to know is, what good is sarcasm doing you?"

Before he could think of something else to say, they were back in the pillow room and into the coke still being passed around. She stopped in the doorway, took a toot, and handed it off to Geoff.

Geoff sat down. After he got comfortable, he took a hit of the cocaine and passed it off to Bones, who said, "Now, that's what I'm talking about."

"That's what you're always talking about," Crow said.

The coke went around the room in silence; the only sounds were of sniffing and sniffling. Crow crawled over and slipped his head under Candy's pillow. He whispered something, and she sat up and said, "Yeah, I guess you're right."

Bones leaned back and knocked over part of the stack of books. He rolled over, looked at the books, looked at Candace and Geoff, and then looked at Crow, to whom he finally said, "What the fuck did you say, man?"

Thinking better of the question and the tone in his voice when he asked it, Bones said he was "just joking" before Candy's eyes could completely focus on him.

Candace looked at Bones and smiled. Rubbing her right eye with the heel of her hand, she said, "I don't feel like getting high anymore," but snatched up the decanter of brandy as she left the room anyway, brushing past Melissa without looking at her.

Bones began picking up the fallen books and placing them back on the stack. He watched Candace Maria's ass move past him and out of the room. He looked at Geoff and asked, "What did I do?"

"I think we are all just tired of the drugs and more drugs. It's got to stop somewhere. Do you people ever sleep?" Crow asked.

Bones kept stacking books. And as he picked up the last few that had fallen behind a large blue pillow, he said, "Fuck you, Crow."

Geoff said, "I know some knock-knock jokes."

"I hate those fucking jokes!" Melissa screamed. "Every time someone opens a door, a chicken runs across the road and gets hit by a goddamn tractor-trailer. It's fucking depressing."

Crow waved his arm, beckoning her to come on into the room. As she moved to sit down, he said, "Seriously. Do you do this all the time? This much shit would kill most people."

Melissa scratched her head. "I guess this one is a little extra. Maybe we *should* cool out some," she said.

Geoff tried to pass her the coke, but she didn't want any. Crow didn't want any more, either. Bones took a blow but put it down, saying, "I guess I don't want to be different," but then he picked it back up and took a hit up the other nostril.

Candy came back to the room and stood in the doorway, looking impatiently at Crow, who knew that he'd seen that expression of exasperation before on the faces of many women.

Crow said, "I think we've all played this scene to the bitter end. It's time I break camp for Brooklyn."

"This party ain't over yet!" Melissa said. "It's too late and too early to stop for the day. Let me get some shit on my naked ass, and then let's go get something to eat. Brooklyn will be there in the morning."

"Just when is the party over around here?" Bones asked.

No one answered. The room was silent until Candace Maria said, "Just because I'm tired of *this* shit don't mean it's time for you to go back to Brooklyn!"

Crow rolled over a few times and ended up lying in front of Candace Maria and Bones's feet. First, he bit her calf through the denim and then pulled himself to a sitting position. He sat cross-legged in front of her for a few seconds before saying, "Give me a suggestion."

She thought for a second and said, "Maybe we should take a shower. It could clear our heads, and then we could think better about what we need to do next."

"Good idea," Crow said, having a good feeling about what she might have meant by the "we" suggestion. He rose and followed Candy down the hall back into the bedroom they had shared the night before.

Holding his hand, Candy looked at Crow and said, "I'm really getting tired of all this confusion and bullshit—*too much* bullshit going on *all* the time!"

"I heard you the first three or four times. What do you want me to do about it, Candace?" Crow asked.

"Well, I don't know, but . . . maybe I'm talking to myself as much as I'm talking to you. Maybe I need to see what I'm doing through the eyes of someone else."

"Well, then," Crow said, "what I see is that there's a whole lotta game and shit going on here with no reason to it. It's like we're all actually bored with this artificial excitement we're creating in the lives we're *not* living, and we got to keep the drama going to know we're alive, just to keep fucking breathing. See, this whole thing is almost exactly like what I *thought* I wanted—you know, fine women, shooting the shit with people who wouldn't even be seen talking to a nigger like me, and nonstop drugs I didn't have to pay for. But now that I've had it, it was fun for the first few *days,* but give me Brooklyn *any*time."

Candace closed her eyes for a second. She opened them, reached up, and ran her hand through his beard. "Let's hop in the shower. The water will give all this shit a new perspective," she said.

They shimmied out of their clothes and dashed across the hall to the bathroom. Crow was smiling as he watched Candy's cheeks jiggle. Closing the door behind them and turning on the light, Crow looked at her breasts reflected in the mirror, her proud and dark nipples at attention. As the steam from the hot water began to fill the room, he pulled her to him and slid his tongue down her throat. Eagerly, she returned his kiss with equal fervor.

He broke it off, looked into her eyes, and said, "Of all the things to come out of this little adventure, meeting you was the best shit that could have happened to me. I don't know if I've ever been this attracted to a woman and don't remember when I've felt this good."

The words flowed like melting butter off his tongue. Candy wasn't sure if Crow had just shifted into Mack mode, but the words sure sounded damn good. "Talk that shit," she whispered in his ear, traversing the taut muscles of his back. Candy pulled Crow into the black marble shower and closed the glass door, the steam misting the glass. She began soaping him, running her hands down his back and over his ass, lathering the backs of his thighs, one hand cupping his balls as she soaped the crack of his ass with the other.

Crow moaned. "You sure know how to make a man feel good."

"Turn around," she said, and kissed him again. His hands found their way to the firm globes of her behind. He squeezed and kneaded her ass as if he'd never had one in his hands before, and then his mouth found its way to her breasts. Candace worked up a frothy lather and reached down to grab his manhood, only to find it nonresponsive, limp. A sad situation. The cocaine had finally done the thing coke snuffers dread most of all. It's spoken about in whispers at the after-hours spots, lied about by the hustlers and players, shit-talked about between the hookers and hoes, but it happens to every cokehead who exceeds his limit. For the first time at such a crucial juncture, Crow came face to face with his own *worst* nightmare: when the wood won't! And there wasn't a damn thing he or Candy's fine ass could do about it.

Crow tried to deny it, to explain it away. "Shit, baby," he said. "This ain't never happened to me before." Then he cursed his dick. That didn't help, either. Neither prayer, nor hoodoo, nor the resurrection itself could have gotten the dead to rise again on that day. His embarrassment intensified exponentially with each of Candace's well-intentioned and sincere reassurances that it didn't matter. Every time she said something meant to be comforting, his johnson retreated deeper, leaving him with just the tiny head peeking out from his den of pubic hair. He wanted to cry, protest, testify about how surprised he was, but in the end, all he could say was, "Sorry." He punctuated it with, "Fuckin' cocaine!"

They rinsed themselves off and got out of the shower in silence. Candy tried to dry Crow's back, but he let out a grumble from so deep within his belly that it made her know she'd better tend to her own business. They dashed back across the hall into Candy's room and dressed quickly.

"Don't tell nobody, will ya?" Crow asked.

He kissed her, and they headed back down the hall to the pillow room.

Melissa walked into the room wearing a white lace teddy, her nipples pressed provocatively against the sheer fabric, and violet-blue leather jeans. She was carrying white snakeskin boots in one hand and a makeup case in the other.

"Shit!" Crow and Bones yelled out. Geoff's dick got heavy again.

Melissa played the compliments off with a smirk and plopped herself down on a pillow that looked like a big lily pad. Leaning back against a wall, she first pulled the legs of the butter-soft pants up in bunches to her knees. Next, she unzipped the boots one at a time and slipped her feet inside them. Her calves were thick, and it looked as though she was going to have trouble getting the zippers closed over them. But the boots were so supple that the leather conformed snugly to the shape of her legs. She stood and with equal ease was able to slide the legs of her pants back down over them.

"Why don't you wear the pants inside the boots?" Candy asked.

"Boots with zippers always looked kinda tired to me," Melissa said as she looked at her feet and flexed her toes.

"Either way looks damn good to me," Bones said.

Melissa redistributed her breasts with her left hand and pulled the top up with her right.

Candace Maria sucked her teeth. "Boots is boots, zipper or not. I always liked pants worn on the inside, real military and very sexy."

Melissa started across the floor, trying to step between the pillows.

"My damn nose is starting to clog up. I'm going to get a damn tissue," Crow announced. He brushed past Melissa and pinched her arm as he walked out of the room.

Melissa began searching through the books on the top shelf at the end of the bookcase. She bent down to look on the second shelf. When she didn't find what she was looking for there, she got down on her knees and searched the bottom shelf. As she read over the titles, Bones dragged his ass across several pillows and planted a wet kiss on her violet-leather-clad butt cheek. Before she could say anything, Bones said, as he was sliding away, "I couldn't resist that big ol' blue moon staring me in the face. I ain't mean no disrespec' or nothin'." He laughed.

Melissa responded without looking up from her task. "Oh, no harm done, but touch me again, and your skinny pale ass is going to suffer."

Geoff laughed and asked Candace to pass him the cocaine. She looked around, picked it up, and passed it, whispering, "She had to know hoisting her big ass up in the air like that would be provocative. Who's she trying to entice? Bones or you?"

Geoff didn't answer but instead took a big blow.

As Candace Maria talked to Geoff, Melissa put the book she held back in place on the shelf and waddled on her knees over to Bones to gently smack him on the forehead. "That was real flattering, but you and I both know that it was totally inappropriate."

Melissa found the book she was looking for. Bones grabbed the bottle he wanted, took a drink, and then arranged himself in a lotus position on a big, fluffy white shag pillow. He began chanting a mantra composed of different segments from Crosby, Stills, and Nash songs between sips.

Melissa snapped, "Are you being purposely obtuse, or is all you can ever think to do is make fun of somebody's beliefs?"

Crow came back and said, "Looks to me like Bones is praying for more wine."

Geoff laughed and spilled half the blow on his lap. He said, "You people are fucking ridiculous."

Candace lay back and sucked her teeth in exasperation. "Are we going to lapse back into the petty backbiting?"

Bones began chanting more loudly, and Geoff brushed the powder off his lap.

Melissa shoved the open book into Crow's hand and said, "Here. Sit down and read this," indicating a page and section.

Crow sat and looked at the cover of the book, holding the page Melissa had opened for him with his index finger. It was *Thirty-seven Poems by Someone Passing.* On the bottom of the cover, it said, "By Transient." He reopened the book to the page Melissa had selected for him and read the title: "Transient #17." He asked her why she wanted him to read it, but when she just sat down next to Candace and said nothing, he shrugged his shoulders and began to read:

Of all things I became one of those
who was witness to him on the road.
  Are you more weary
  than my silent
  companions. The woman
  is eager to collect
  memories and
  remains more than proud of her
  swollen and
  callused feet.

Night is camp and low fire, she
sits alone and wonders aloud to
every man why he's been chosen
For accusation.
  I can remain
  uneasy. I've chosen
  to find fuel to
  build the flame.
  I am uneasy
  so I stay close
  To the others.
  His is plight
  Mine is less.

The woman becomes rage. Or
Panic and adds to uneasy as she
rushes to struggle with the night.
Each time she eludes my vision she
screams, defense adds to his

conviction. We can bear no
Children this season.
She is mad.
He's been
duly hung
and the
wolves seem
always
closer.

A pale man slit his wrists and
jumped into the fire. I left
to walk into the night.

Transient 4/16

Crow reread the poem and decided that it should be shared with everyone. He read it aloud without announcement. He finished and wasn't sure if it had been heard. Nothing around him seemed to change, but the silence felt thicker. He looked back at the page and then up again, trying to read everyone's face. They were all blank, but he found Melissa smiling. He didn't smile back and said only, "OK, let's get the fuck gone."

Melissa agreed but asked them to give her a few seconds to put on her makeup.

Geoff said, "You don't need any makeup. With skin like that, you should be happy not to wear it. I would be."

"How could you say such a thing, Geoff?" Bones wanted to know, in his usual attempt to make a joke out of shit that wasn't funny.

Candy brightened up, looked over to Geoff, and said, "Well?"

When he didn't say anything, Crow said another sarcastic "Well?" at him.

Finally, Geoff said, "Well, hell, it's easy enough to see that she's naturally attractive and doesn't need to wear any makeup. Just what do you think I'd look like walking around in spike heels and a formal without my blush and highlighter? I'd look like a damn fool, now, wouldn't I?"

Crow closed the book and placed it at his feet. He shook his head, raised his arms above his head, stretched, and said, "The man's right. Only a fool would walk around in a dress and high heels without makeup. Shit, picture me strolling down Nostrand Avenue swinging my purse with my nails undone. I would never live it down."

"I see your point, man," Bones added. "Only the week before last, a woman refused to give me her telephone number. Now that I think about it, it was probably because my slip had been hanging and my lipstick was smudged."

Geoff laughed. Candace interrupted, saying, "Shit, I wasn't wearing none when I met Crow." She then flipped onto her back and snatched the book of poems out of Crow's hands. Grabbing Crow by his ankles, she looked up at him and asked coquettishly, "Do you think I need to wear makeup?"

Crow gripped her arms and bent over to rub his face into her hair and said, "How the hell would I know? I ain't never seen you wearing none. But I know for a fact Bones and Geoff should never leave home without *theirs!*" He kissed her forehead.

Melissa capped the tube of bright red wet-look lip gloss and tossed it back into the case.

Geoff looked at Melissa and declared, "Shit, who am I trying to kid? I will never look like *that*. I look like *hell* in that shit I wear. Who needs it? I'm swearing off the whole drag thing, right here and now, in front of all you witnesses. You'll see, damn it! I'll be wearin' slacks and a sport coat at the next function. Just you wait and see."

Candace leaned back, looked at Melissa, and said, "Bullshit."

Geoff mimicked her teeth sucking and picked the blow up from the pillow where he had left it. Before he took his hit, he suggested that everybody should take a sniff to perk up before they hit the street.

His suggestion was met with approval, and when it was passed to Melissa, she rubbed a fingertip full around the inside of her mouth, took two tiny hits, stood, and placed the package in her pants pocket. She shook her hips from side to side several times and said, "You know, I *do* look fabulous, you all."

Crow said to Candy out of the side of his mouth, "Ain't this a bitch? *Now* she's looking to be stroked."

Candace testified, saying, "A little *stroking* feels good every once in a while." She winked at Crow. "Even if it's only the kind you do with compliments."

Crow averted his eyes, thinking back to his wounded wood.

Bones took the cue and chimed in, saying rapidly, "Each time you get dressed, Melissa, it seems like you present something a little better than the last time you went out. I think it's just another one of your natural talents. Now, can we *move on?* Next!"

"Each time you move, it's like new art. Alton should photograph you every day for a month. You're a whole exhibit," Geoff told her.

Crow stood up to add, "I guess we can go as soon as you stop purring and preening."

"If that's all you have to add, then I guess I'm done now," Melissa responded.

Bones got up and said, "I'm ready, too."

Candace got up, grabbed the manuscript, tucked it under her arm, and said to Crow, "We better not leave this here."

They all waited for Melissa at the front door as she ran to turn off a few lights. They all stood outside, looking in different directions as she turned the key. Locking the front door, she whispered to Candy, "I think it might be time to become transient again."

Candace looked into and then turned away from Melissa's emerald eyes. Bones and Geoff stood on the sidewalk, talking to each other about nothing. Crow leaned against a dirty blue car with his arms folded over his chest. Melissa and Candace Maria took the steps that led from the door to the sidewalk, which would carry them into the night.

Candace walked over and leaned herself fully against Crow. He looked up, wrapped an arm around her waist, and smiled. He rested the side of his face against her hair and pulled her closer. He felt Melissa's eyes on him and looked to find them sad.

Melissa looked away and patted Bones lightly on the ass, saying, "Let's go." She began the walk into the East Village, and they followed.

Melissa passed under the yellow light from the leaning post. Crow's eyes caught the reflection on her face. She smiled and looked back at Crow and wondered if he knew that she had figured out the lie. She stopped at the light and asked, "Where the hell are we going to eat?"

Bones answered, "That depends on who's buying."

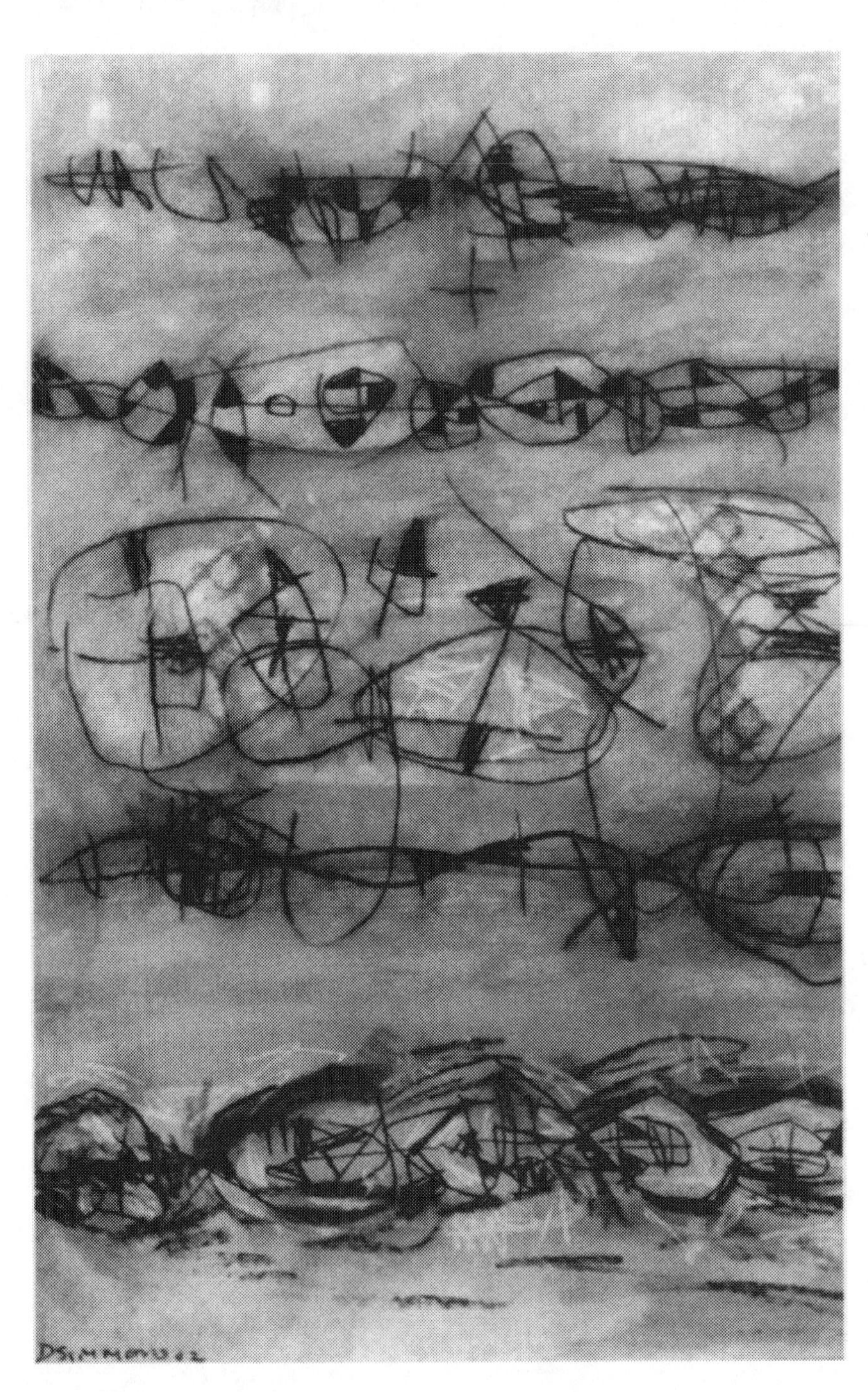

Spell to Lighten One's Load (2002)

14

Shutting This Bad Boy Down

CANDACE MARIA SAT ON THE TOILET and cursed in Spanish because she had to wipe dry with a rough brown paper towel. She was momentarily startled when the guy in the next stall grunted loudly, and she laughed. "I hear that! It's tough trying to clean your ass with this shit."

She pulled up her pants and flushed, but the paper spun around and floated back to the top as the water rose. Candy made it her business to stop at the washbasin, soaping her hands almost up to the elbow. If there was one thing she couldn't stand, it was all the nasty bitches she had seen over the years in public bathrooms just saunter out without so much as a sideways glance at the soap and water, leaving God knows what on everything they touched after that. Just thinking about it pissed her off.

Before she left the bathroom, she said, "Man, I don't mean to get too personal, but you should try eating some kinda fiber in the near future."

On the door, someone had written, "I came, I farted, I left satisfied."

When Candy returned to the table, Crow was arguing the merits of a $6.25 cheeseburger with Geoff, Melissa picked at a salad, and Bones stood across the room, leaning with both hands on the jukebox, playing Bob Dylan's "Highway 61."

"God said to Abraham, 'Kill me a son.' "

Candace slid down in the chair and took another bite of her tuna melt. She grabbed a fry and pushed the plate away. "Shit," she said. "I bet he didn't kill his son on Highway 61 or no damn place else. God could ask me to do all kinds of shit, but I ain't gonna kill my own kid."

Crow said, "Good Lord, woman, it's just a damn song."

Candace sucked her teeth for the millionth time and said, "Well, not according to the Bible . . ."

The combination of cocaine and exhaustion had taken its toll on their appetites, and even though they hadn't eaten anything but each other for days, nobody was very hungry, except for Bones, who finished his chili in a few gulps. Wiping his mouth, he asked, "What's next?"

Out on the street in front of the diner, they stood around for a few minutes talking shit. Everyone was aware that the party was over, but no one wanted to be the first to say it.

"So what the fuck do we do now?" Bones asked again.

"It's too early to go to the club. Maybe we should shoot by the gallery and kill some time," Geoff said.

Candy looked up into the night sky and, seeing no stars, said, "Look, guys, I'm fucking exhausted. It's probably best I went home and got some sleep, y'know? Man does not live by coke alone, and shit like that."

Crow felt a wave of sadness engulf him; the three-day party was coming to an end. He sucked his teeth and said, "Yeah, my father used to say, 'Fun is fun, but you can't laugh all night.' "

They stood for what seemed like a long time, not saying anything. Then Melissa broke the silence. "Maybe I ought to head back to the house. Reading my old poetry has kinda inspired me. I'd like to try and write me a little something," she said. "Geoff, you wanna *come* give me a hand . . . or two?" She winked in his direction.

Bones looked at Melissa as if she were crazy. "What the fuck are you talking about? Write something? What the hell's going on here? You losing your edge? So what if this party's breaking up? There's always another. Me, after what I went through tonight, I'm gonna dance until they put my weary ass out. Crow, what are you gonna do?"

"Man, I don't know how you can keep this shit up, but I'm going the hell home—I feel like I just fought a war."

Bones answered under his breath, "It's easy to keep it up when you don't wanna spend no time with yourself."

After hugs and assurances, Geoff and Melissa left together. Their leaving made Crow anxious. He didn't like the feeling. It didn't jibe with his self-ascribed "tough guy from Brooklyn" image.

As he watched Melissa's swaying ass fade from view, he called out, "Still a fine ol' biddy, ain't you, Melissa?" She didn't reply. But Crow thought he heard a soft laugh.

Candy said, "I guess I ought to be getting home to deal with Tío Manny, get some rest, and start looking for my ass someplace else to live."

Crow stuffed his hands into his pockets and looked down at his feet. He didn't remember ever feeling this uncomfortable before. He fingered the roll of money in his pocket and smiled. "Candace, want me to walk you home?"

"It will just make things more complicated. Besides, you got to go the other way to catch the train."

"I don't mind, really. I've gotten sorta used to you, I mean." Crow swallowed and continued, "I mean, I like you a lot, although I might need some help learning how to express it."

"I like you too, Crow, that's why I don't want you to walk me. I might start crying. I don't want that to happen. Listen, you know how to find me if you want to."

Bones cut in, saying, "Ain't this shit romantic? Just kiss her, and let's get the fuck out of here before I lose the little fucking food I managed to get down."

Candace muttered under her breath, "Where is the night luster, past my trials?"

Crow shook his head and said, "Huh?"

"Nothing, Crow. Just some song a woman wrote when she was sad. Anyway, I better give you this book back. I'd like to get a chance to read it when you finish it."

Crow took the manuscript; a loose page fell out and floated to the ground. Bones picked it up and handed it to Crow. He stuffed it randomly into the folder. When Crow didn't say anything, Bones blurted out, "Thank you too, motherfucker."

Crow and Candy laughed. Crow hugged her tightly and kissed her lightly on the lips and whispered, "Thank you, thank you for everything."

Candace buried her head in Crow's chest, fighting back tears. When she released him, she saw one tear rolling down his cheek, glistening, catching the rays of light from the street lamp. She turned quickly and walked away. Crow wiped his perpetually recurring tear from his cheek and watched her until she turned the corner. He wanted to run after her like in the movies, but he resisted and said to Bones, "That's one fine bitch."

Bones chuckled and said, "Still frontin', huh? You can take the brother out of Brooklyn, but . . . ah, fuck it, let's just get the hell out of here."

"Bones, yo, what you talkin' about with this 'let's' shit? I'm going back to Brooklyn! I don't where the fuck you're going, but it ain't with me!"

Not at all fazed by Crow's rejection, Bones said, "Yo, man, this shit is like *Star Trek* or some shit, the adventure continues. You know: 'Drugs, sex and alcohol, what's the call, belly-up to the bar boys, drugs, sex and alcohol."

Crow laughed and said, "You're one crazy cracker, Bones, you know that? You'll probably get killed in Bed-Stuy, but what the fuck. I ain't my brother's keeper or some shit like that, so I guess if we're going, we better roll."

They started to walk to the West Side to catch the A train. Crow's thoughts about going back to the 'hood were interrupted by Bones saying, "Make sure you call me Bones and not Marvin! Being a white boy in Bed-Stuy is bad enough, but being a white boy named Marvin is a bit much."

"Man, if you're a sucker, you're a sucker. It doesn't matter what you're called, but I'd call you Bojangles if you wanted," Crow replied.

Bones laughed and slapped Crow on the shoulder. "That's mighty white of you, Crow, mighty fucking white of you."

They walked up St. Mark's Place past all the bridge-and-tunnel kids ducking in and out of shops trying to find the right accessories to complement whatever new wave, punk rock image they were going for. Crow shook his head and chuckled as they passed the cube on Astor Place. The cube, where he first became an artist.

A woman, just finishing a harmonica solo, bowed to the applause, but very few spectators dropped coins into her top hat. Crow thought how few people really paid for their entertainment. He fished into his pocket and dropped a few dollars into the hat. As the weariness began to set in from the constant drinking and drugging of the last three days, he wondered how he would pay the cover charge for his pleasures.

Crow and Bones walked up Eighth Street, not saying a word to each other, both lost in thought. Crow was thinking about Candace Maria and wondering when he would see her again. The last three days seemed like some chaotic dream or drug fantasy. Whom could he tell back in Brooklyn about this shit? Would anyone even care? Most of the people he knew were too caught up in the day-to-day bullshit of just living to really give a damn about some strange-ass white-boy adventure. Shit, and absolutely no one would believe the amount of blow he sniffed. He didn't really believe it himself. He fingered the envelope in his pocket and looked at Bones just to make sure it had all really happened.

Bones was walking along, twisting his neck to check out women's asses as they went by. He used a rating system based on the width of the hips and the roundness of the buns. A short sister with long locks and a little mulatto-looking kid in tow rated a seven. *Nice, but too big for her height, and she probably has cellulite,* he thought.

Bones played this game to keep his mind off important things. He was afraid and lonely even in Crow's company, and the effects of the coke were wearing off. He had to keep moving, because if he didn't, he'd have to face himself, and he couldn't allow that. Instead, he'd watch the asses go by and go with Crow to Bed-Stuy, anything to stay one step ahead of himself and out of his own head.

All thoughts came to an abrupt halt when they reached Eighth and Broadway. Police barricades had the street blocked off. Dozens of police cars and ambulances were midway up the block with their cherry tops flashing. Bones and Crow's first reaction was to go in another direction.

But Crow's curiosity drew him toward the cop in front of the barricade. Bones grabbed Crow by the shoulder and asked, "Yo, Crow, what the fuck are you doing?"

"Be cool, Bones. They ain't got nothing on us. I just want to find out what happened."

Bones gave Crow a bewildered look as he said, "What the fuck for? This shit ain't got a damn thing to do with us. Let's just get the fuck out of here. Ain't no need to look for trouble."

Crow seemed transfixed, staring up the block. Eventually, he said, "Stop being paranoid. I'm just curious, OK?"

Reluctantly, Bones followed behind, muttering under his breath, "Curious, yeah, you and the fucking dead cat."

As they approached the barricade, the officer held up his hand as if it possessed some magic powers to halt them in their tracks. Apparently, the gesture had power over some people and not others.

Bones came to a stop immediately, but Crow continued, walking until he stopped two or three feet away from the cop. The officer looked young, younger than Crow. He was blond, very pale, and wore a crisp, new blue uniform. "I thought I told you to stop," he said to Crow.

"I ain't hear you say nothing. What's going on here?"

"A smart-ass, huh? Well, there's nothing to see here. Just keep moving."

Bones rushed over to Crow and said in a low voice, "Come on, man, ain't no need to invite trouble. We got places to go, things to do, man. This shit ain't none of our business, the man is right."

Crow strained to look past the officer's shoulder, paying neither him nor Bones any mind.

There, among the confusion of cops and ambulance attendants scurrying around, Crow could see Dave seated on the hood of his car with his head hanging down. Overhead on the roof of the car, the red police light turned, reflecting a crimson glow on the shards of shattered glass covering the street. Crow began screaming, "Yo, Dave!" repeatedly. The cop just behind the barricade told Crow to shut up, but Crow kept calling until Dave raised his head and motioned for them to come over.

Crow tried to slip past the barrier, but the cop pushed him back. "What the fuck do you think you're doing?" Crow screamed, spit flying in the cop's face.

"*Boy,* I told you to get the fuck out of here. Now I'm going to have to make you," said the cop, simultaneously reaching for his club and wiping the spit from his face.

Bones grabbed Crow and yanked him out of the range of the club. Crow spun around angrily to Bones, yelling, "What the fuck do you think you're doing? I'm trying to see what's up with Dave!"

"Yeah, but what you gonna do is get your ass kicked. I don't give a flying fuck what's going on with that pig. Yo, I ain't about getting beat down and slammed in jail. I'm cutting out, with or without you."

"Listen, man, that black cop over there heard me calling him," Crow said to the red and enraged officer, pointing.

"Who do you think he is, your goddamn uncle Ben or something?" the cop said, as he lunged for Crow but grabbed air instead.

Crow jumped back and shouted, "Yeah, that's right, he's my fucking uncle."

Bones looked at Crow with a puzzled look and said, "What's this bullshit? You been swearing up and down for three days that you ain't know this pig motherfucker! What the fuck is wrong with you, claiming a pig for an uncle?"

Crow exhaled deeply and said, "Yeah, you're right. Let's get the hell out of here. This ain't my business."

Just then, a female officer wearing sergeant stripes, had to be six feet tall, stepped around the barricade and the officer in front of it, pushing down his upraised arm as she did. With only a sideways glance at the officer, she addressed Crow and Bones calmly. "I guess I don't really have to ask which one of you is Crow, and I guess that means you must be Bones," she said, looking at one and then the other. "Dave wants to see you two." Turning bright red, the other officer quietly slipped the billy club back into his holster, facing away as Bones and Crow crossed the barricade, following the female officer up the street.

Dave was sitting on the hood of his car, a half-pint of lemon gin held loosely in his hand. A few feet away, Dave's partner lay dead, blood and brain oozing onto the ground. Dave looked up at Crow and Bones and said, "We were just coming on duty, and we stopped to get my half-pint, and then this . . ." He looked at his partner, tears streaming down his face.

Bones looked over to the nearby liquor store, where two adolescent males lay, both also dead. One was on the sidewalk, and the other had fallen through the plate-glass window, a large piece of glass protruding from the side of his head. Both sported green Mohawks. The one on the sidewalk had a T-shirt that read, "Heroin, heroin, we all scream for heroin, pass that needle to me."

In bright colors, smeared by blood, was a cartoon of a bunch of guys sitting around shooting up.

Bones's shoulders sagged as he said, "Crow, I know that guy, he hangs out at the club sometimes." Crow remained silent looking at the death and confusion around him.

Dave continued, "Those two fucks were running out of the store with guns in hand. As we pulled up, I heard two shots. They saw us and opened fire." He paused and took a deep swallow from the bottle. "Bones, did you say that you knew one of those pricks?"

Bones panicked; he could see himself being questioned in some tiny room with hot lights on him. He answered in a hurry, "Not really, Dave. I've seen one of them in the clubs. I think he plays in a band that lives in a squat on D and Sixth Street; the band's name is Copping and Nodding, but that's all I know, I swear."

"Relax, Bones. We don't want you as a material witness or nothin'." Dave sighed. Bones looked relieved.

Dave looked up from the ground at Crow and asked him, "Where are you and Bones headed, or did I just ask you that?"

Crow said, in a moment of extreme lucidity, "This Village thing has been a good run, but I gotta get back to Brooklyn. I got a bunch of thinking to do. Something happened to me since I been here, and I'm not sure exactly what, you know? Everything happened so fast that I haven't had time to catch up with myself."

Dave, who had been staring at the blood-soaked body that had once held his partner the whole time Crow spoke, just muttered back, "Yeah, that's nice, Brooklyn."

Realizing that Dave hadn't been listening, Crow offered a weak condolence, with Bones piping in that he was sorry too.

Crow and Bones weaved their way through police rushing back and forth. Halfway up the block, as the people thinned out, Crow turned to Bones and said, "That shit is fucked up."

Bones asked, a little bewildered, "What shit?"

"All of it."

"Yeah, but they know the risks going in. They never know

which shift is going to be their last. Shit. Fuck it." Bones tried to sound nonchalant about it. After a few seconds, he said, "Yo, Crow, now I'm ready for Brooklyn."

Crow looked at Bones and sucked his teeth and said, "Don't make a fool of yourself when we get there, man, just be chill, and everything will be all right."

Bones said, "Shit, Crow, I know how to act. Did you make a fool of yourself over here?"

Crow clutched the manuscript tightly under his arm as they headed up the block and toward the subway. He was tired and his thinking slow. He knew somehow he had to return the manuscript to its owner. *What did I think I was going to do with it, anyway?* he thought. It was stupid to have taken it in the first place. Now all he wanted was for Bones to hurry up so they could get on the train to Brooklyn.

Bones came out of the store smiling. He popped the tab of the sixteen-ounce beer and stuck a straw in it. Crow started walking toward the train. As soon as he finished his beer, Bones fell into a deep sleep in his seat on the train. He dreamed of round-butted teenage black girls in Bed-Stuy. As the train rumbled its way into Brooklyn, Crow looked up to see himself in the blackened subway car window and wondered about what had happened to him over the past three days. He composed a poem in his head:

caught in seething
impatience and restless
discontent forever burdens
Borne strong back
Negro and shuckin'
and jivin' my deeper
blues hunger.

My witless blank face
Mask

And all the questions
that loom like so many
cawing crows eyeing justice
Of car-squashed cats.
The fading legacy of my chaos violence and
threats of pillage and frenzy gone to
shallow graves and dripping paint.
My camp surrounded by hysterical beggars

unleashed rabid dogs and quaint survivors.
Crippled by moral conviction I await
smothering siege and the raising of my
altar.

The words flowed through Crow's mind, and when he finished, he shook his head and said out loud to himself, "What the fuck was that about?"

Crow looked back into the blackened window and was able to see the first trickle of blood ooze out of a nostril, over his lips, and hit the cover of the manuscript with a splash.

Spell to Dance on the Graves of Your Enemies (2002)

15

Meanwhile, Back in the 'Hood . . .

Crow wiped his nose on the sleeve of his jacket and got up. He stood at the front window in the first car of the downtown A train. His eyes watched the rails as he fingered the roll of bills in his pocket. *Shit, I got six grand in my pocket. This art shit ain't too bad.*

The entire ride from West Fourth Street was a blur. He hadn't focused on any of the other passengers as he usually did. It was as if he were slowly unfolding the layers of a three-day dream, and as he got closer to home, bits of reality came seeping back in.

The train erupted from the tunnel into the Brooklyn Bridge station, and suddenly Crow began to get nervous. His stomach began to turn. The wheels of the train grinding to a halt unnerved him, so he sat down in the first seat directly across from the motorman's cab. Crow looked through the partially open door at the female operator and thought, *I guess people's roles are changing all over. I ain't gotta stay in the same box I've been in, either.* He looked over to see Bones still dead asleep, snoring, with a thick stream of drool leaking from the corner of his mouth.

He thought of Danny, the stolen paintings and manuscript, and his stomach began to churn again. The train came to a stop at Brooklyn Bridge, and the doors opened. Only a homeless woman got on. She pulled a shopping cart full of old rags and tattered straw hats on behind her, just getting them in before the doors closed. The car was relatively empty, but the woman started her spiel about being hungry. Usually, Crow would have just shut her out, but with all the money in his pocket, he thought it couldn't hurt to share some of his good fortune.

"Hey, old lady," he called down the car to her. She and the four or five other people in the car looked in Crow's direction.

"I don't want no trouble," the woman shouted back.

"Ain't no trouble. I just got a little something for you," Crow said.

The other heads in the car went back to whatever their thoughts had been before Crow's interruption. The woman warily wheeled her cart to the front of the train where Crow sat.

"Listen, sonny, times is tough enough without some young wise-ass making fun of my situation," she barked before reaching Crow.

Crow looked at her for a second and then dug into his pocket and pulled out his roll of bills. Seeing the thick wad of money made both their eyes widen. Crow peeled past the hundred-dollar bills until he got to a twenty and handed it to her. She just stood there looking at him in disbelief, as if at any moment he was going to pull the bill back.

"You want my arm to fall off? Go on, take it, it's real," Crow finally said.

She quickly snatched the bill and stuffed it into a filthy coat pocket. She looked at Crow for a long moment and said, "Boy, what you doing with all that money on this train? Fool, you ain't got no sense, pulling all that money out like that. Somebody gonna take that money if you ain't careful. What you do, rob somebody?" She looked around the car and started walking away, muttering. "Damn fool better be careful, train's full of people who ain't so nice," was the last thing Crow heard as she walked by the other passengers with her cup extended.

Crow sat looking at her as she crossed to the other car. As the door shut, he thought, *Ain't that a bitch! I gives her twenty balls and can't even get a simple fucking thank-you out her ol' ass.*

Her words had rung a little too true, however: "What you do, rob somebody?"

The train rumbled and lurched from station to station. Sitting down next to Bones, Crow shook him as they got closer to their destination. Bones stirred but didn't wake up. For all Crow's pushing and shaking, Bones only snored harder.

"Yo, Bones, man. Wake the fuck up," Crow said. "I'm gonna leave your ass on this train." But Bones snored on. Two stations before his stop, Crow decided to leave Bones a note. He found a blank page in the folder and fished out a pen from his jacket pocket and began writing:

Bones,

I tried to wake your drooling, loud-snoring ass up, but to no avail. Pushed you, pulled you, did everything but smack your ass up, but you still sitting here, sleep like a motherfucker. And I ain't going to ride this train with you till you wake up. Listen, man, thanks for everything. It's been an experience, to say the least. Even though you ain't gonna get to hang with me in the 'hood this time don't mean we ain't gonna see each other. I gotta come back to the gallery to get the rest of the paintings and some more loot from Geoff. I'll catch up with you then. Yo, man, I generally don't make friends that easily and certainly not with crazy-ass crackers like yourself, but I do consider you a friend, we got some more hanging to do. So I catch you soon, be careful, and give yourself a break. You ain't as fucked up as you think. Anyway, it's my stop, and I'm out.

Crow

Crow folded the note and placed it under Bones's arms. The train grinded to a halt at Utica Avenue, and as the doors opened, Crow felt relieved that he didn't have to drag no crazy-talking white boy around the 'hood with him. But as the doors closed behind him and he looked a last time at the knocked-out Bones, a momentary sadness welled up in him. He pushed it down and said, "Fuck it," and bounded up the steps.

When Crow emerged from the subway at Utica Avenue and Fulton Street in Bedford-Stuyvesant, he was exhausted and agitated. He looked at the manuscript and thought, *How the fuck am I going to deal with Danny? Shit, I stole his paintings and book. More than half this money is rightfully his.* He did a quick calculation in his head and thought, *Two grand from one of the paintings I did, and I should get something from the others. Damn, who am I kidding? I wouldn't have dick if I ain't steal his shit in the first place. I gotta give him his.*

Crow walked through Fulton Park and stopped and sat on a bench. *Shit, I am tired! All that cocaine beat the shit out of me. I need a blast.* But Crow's nose was sore and running, and his body ached. He stood up, counted out four hundred dollars, and stuck the rest of the money down in his underwear. *I'll be damned if I am going into the Palm Coast after-hours spot, pulling out some six g's. I may be crazy, but I ain't that stupid.*

Crow walked through the door of the Palm Coast Bar, an after-hours club. All eyes focused on him, then returned to whatever they were doing before he entered. Pete, the owner, called over to him and said, "You ain't going downstairs unless you pay me the sixty bucks you owe me from last week when you slicked out of here without paying."

"Yo, Pete, that shit ain't called for, man. When I left here, you know I was so high I just forgot to pay you. You see I ain't trying to duck a brother, I got your loot right here."

Crow reached into his pocket and pulled out the four hundred. He counted out three twenties and laid them on the bar. "Here's your sixty, and send a fifty of rocks downstairs," he said, pulling another fifty out. "And don't send no cut 'caine, just straight-up rock."

Crow walked toward the back of the bar, where the door that led to the after-hours club was guarded by a huge, bald-headed, country nigga in a black suit, with a mouthful of gold. J.C. looked at Crow with a big gold-toothed grin and asked, "What you do, nigga, fall in a bucket of rainbow?"

Crow looked down at his black jeans covered in paint and realized how crazy he must look coming into the Palm Coast looking like a painter's palette. Crow looked at J.C. and sighed. "Just open the fucking door."

Crow descended the stairs into the dimly lit basement room. At the bottom to the left was a platform stage, partially lit but without performers. Along the right wall were rows of booths holding customers who were huddled tightly together. In the center of the room were several round glass-top tables, four seats to a table. With room for sixty or more, the place was about half full. As Crow made his way to an empty back table, several people looked up and acknowledged him. Crow brushed past Sherman, a tall, thin, balding black man in his late fifties. Sherman was the club's small-time, full-time, resident drug dealer.

"Hey, Crow, what's up?"

"Ain't nothin', Sherm," Crow replied.

"Got a fresh package, fat dimes, almost all rock," Sherman offered.

"Maybe later. I got something coming from upstairs," Crow told him as he continued toward the empty table.

Sherman had been a big-time pimp back in the '70s—white mink coat, jazzed-up Caddy, jewelry, the whole nine. He told the story over and over, but for as long as Crow could remember, he'd been down on his luck. He lived in a small room at the back of the basement and rarely left the bar. The only times Crow had ever seen Sherman outside were when he was going or coming from buying the small amount of cocaine that he cut and sold in ten-dollar packages.

Crow adjusted the roll of bills in his shorts before sliding into the booth. He quickly scanned the room to see who was there. Don, the numbers man, was in a booth with two young girls sniffing cocaine and drinking Moët. Spencer, a retired postal worker who lived around the corner, sat with his son, who also worked for the post office. They were busy stuffing cocaine into cigarettes. A couple of guys Crow didn't know, wearing a lot of jewelry and expensive clothes, were running some blow through a strainer in order to reduce it to sniffing powder.

Derrick, a cop on suspension awaiting trial for robbing drug dealers, and a host of other criminals or addicts all sat looking intent on ingesting as much substance as they could hold. A thick cloud of smoke holding the pungent aroma of chunky black marijuana hung in the air, and Run-DMC's latest single, "Tougher Than Leather," was playing on the jukebox.

Crow began to yawn, and his body felt very heavy; serious cocaine fatigue was setting in. It had been hours since his last blast, and he was getting fidgety. His thoughts drifted back to Danny, knowing that soon he would have to deal with him to make things right. He looked at the manuscript he had laid on the table in front of him and sighed, trying to put the whole thing out of his mind for just a little while longer, thinking, *I'll deal with it when the time comes.*

Just then, Vivian, the hostess of the club, came over and squeezed in beside him. Vivian was a stunning black Latina in her mid-forties. She was an ambulance emergency medical technician during the day and the hostess of the after-hours until she went to work in the morning. Vivian had a huge cocaine habit. Crow had never seen her without blow, and he wondered if she ever slept.

"Hey, Crow, ain't seen you around here in a week or two. Where you been?" she asked.

Crow replied, "Viv, you wouldn't believe me if I told you. Anyway, you got the hit?"

Vivian reached into her purse and pulled out a plastic baggie filled with small foil packets of cocaine. She looked at it and said, "Oops, wrong bag." Stuffing that bag back in her purse, she pulled out another one, this one with slightly larger packets jammed inside.

"Those were twenties, these are the fifties," she said as she gave one to Crow. "By the way, Crow, that artist guy was looking for you either yesterday or the day before. I saw him on my way to work," she said with a deep, throaty sniffle.

Crow looked up from opening the packet and asked, "What did he say?"

"Nothing, really, he just asked if I saw you."

"Damn!" Crown exclaimed out loud, then thought to himself, *I really gotta figure out what I'm going to say to Danny.*

As he poured the contents of the foil into a crisp twenty-dollar bill and crushed the rocks into powder, Vivian passed Crow a straw. He sucked a portion of the cocaine up his nose. Involuntarily, his body shuddered, and his breathing quickened. He offered Vivian some, but she refused, saying she had her own.

"Vivian," Crow asked as the cocaine glow washed over him. "How the hell do you go to work from here high as a fucking kite and drive an ambulance all day?"

Vivian smiled and said, "Easy. I just make sure I got enough coke to get me through the day. Shit, dealing with all the shootings, car accidents, and shit, you gotta be high as a motherfucker just to get through it all."

"Yeah, I hear that. It seems like lately I gotta be high just to get through a damn day without any of that shit," Crow said.

Vivian motioned to the roving barmaid, Valerie, a tall, sickly-looking, slim, gray-haired woman. "Bring us two double Remys, and tell Pete to put them on my tab," Vivian said.

Crow thanked her and took another blow. They sat in silence until Crow said, "You know, I'm starting to get tired of this shit. Over the last few days, I've done more different kinds of things than I've done in my whole fucking life. There's got to be more to life than sitting around and getting more and more high, you know what I mean?"

"Crow," Vivian said, "I think about that shit myself every day, and every day I end up in this bar or some joint just like it. I've tried to clean up two, three times before, but it all comes down to trying to fill this empty hole I got inside. It never quite gets full. Getting high is the closest I've come to not feeling totally empty."

They lapsed back into silence, and Crow thought about what she'd said. Finally he said, "You know, Vivian, a couple of days ago, I painted some pictures, and for a while that empty feeling in me was gone. I didn't know it then, but thinking about it now, it felt pretty good." Crow laughed to himself and said under his breath, "Yeah, but I guess I was high then, too!"

Valerie came back with the drinks, but before Vivian could take a sip, one of the guys in the jewelry and expensive clothes called her over.

"Business calls. I'll be right back," she said, picking up her purse and heading across the room.

Crow poured a small amount of cocaine into the cognac and absently stirred it with his index finger. He called across the room to Don, who was busy trying to entertain his two cocaine-hungry women at the same time. "Yo, Don, you want a blow?" Crow asked. Don either didn't hear him or was too preoccupied to answer. Before Crow could call out again, he heard from across the room, "Put your hands on the table, you are under arrest!"

The basement became dead silent for all of a split second as everybody looked in Vivian's direction. One of the guys was standing up, waving a badge and a gun in Vivian's face, while the other screamed, "Police, don't anybody move!" Which is exactly what everybody, including Crow, did. Between throwing drugs and weapons on the floor and running for the door, the club had turned into a madhouse.

Uniformed and plainclothes officers came rushing down the stairs, and everyone was trapped in the basement. A heavy-set black sergeant in uniform came down the stairs, yelling, "Everyone grab some wall, and don't make me say it again!"

As people stood spread-eagled against the dingy white-painted brick walls, the sergeant and two other uniforms patted for weapons.

"Cuff 'em all. We'll sort this bullshit out at the station house!" he bellowed.

Suddenly, the lights came on in the basement, and Crow saw the floor was littered with drugs and weapons. Vivian was led upstairs first, her head hanging low. Crow's head was swimming. His thoughts jumped from the money stuffed into his shorts to going to jail, to Danny's manuscript, and to his unfinished drink on the coke-laden table. He kept shaking his head from side to side, muttering to himself as a white female officer patted him down.

She called out to the sergeant as she handcuffed Crow, "This one's clean," having missed the money tucked securely under his balls.

Crow, in shock, was led by the officer to the stairs. Just as they reached them, he looked up, and the sergeant caught a glimpse of him.

"Officer Levin, bring that young man over her," called the sergeant. Crow was led to the sergeant, who looked at him and shook his head. "Officer, please wait over there with the suspect."

Crow was taken to the side while everyone else was led upstairs. As Don went past, he looked at Crow with suspicion. Finally, the only people left in the club were the sergeant, Officer Levin, and

Crow. Standing in front of Crow, the balding black man in the sergeant's uniform said, "Levin, I'll take care of this one." She went upstairs.

Crow stared at his feet until the cop said, "Look at me," in a stern voice. Crow continued to stare at his feet. The cop said, "Damn it, I said look at me." Slowly, Crow looked up, finally meeting the cop's gaze. "I *knew* it was you!" the cop said. "It's a fucking shame! Your father must be turning over in his damn grave to see you turn out like this. You don't even fucking remember me, do you?"

Crow stared into the face of a man of whom he had no recollection. "I'm sorry, officer, I really don't remember you," Crow said in a cracked low voice.

"Don't you fucking remember coming out to Hempstead every fucking Fourth of July for ten years with your father to my barbecues with my kids?" the sergeant asked. "Don't you remember my son, Mike, or do these fucking drugs have you so fucked up you can't remember the good shit you had in your life?"

Crow's mouth went dry. "Mr. Dobson. Oh, my God, I am sorry, sir. I am sorry." And he broke down and cried.

The sergeant watched him cry for a minute before he said, "Turn around." He uncuffed Crow and sat him down at one of the tables. Crow sat with his hands pressed to his face, turning off the flow of tears.

"I haven't seen you since your father's funeral," Sergeant Dobson said. "I guess I don't need to ask how you been, now, do I? Anyway, Mikey's dead. We buried him six months ago. We tried to get in touch with you, but your mother didn't know how to contact you. She said she hadn't seen you since the funeral, either. Crow, your father died more than three years ago."

Crow looked up in disbelief. "Mikey's dead?" he asked.

"Yeah, Mikey's dead. He died of a heroin overdose in an abandoned building in Brownsville. He was in his senior year at NYU."

All Crow could say was, "Damn, I'm sorry."

"Crow, what the hell are you doing in this fucking joint? Don't nobody but dealers, criminals, and addicts hang out in here. Which one are you?"

"I guess if I get to choose, I'll have to say addict. I damn sure ain't no dealer or crook." He choked, knowing that in truth, he was a thief, the worst kind. He'd stole something valuable from a friend.

Sergeant Dobson said, "This sure is a hell of a way to honor your father. The man put twenty-three years on the force fighting shit like this, and I end up taking his son in for sucking down dope. Listen, you little shithead, I'm gonna trust you. I'm gonna give you a walk on this, just this once. You call me first thing tomorrow, and I'll work on gettin' you into some kind of treatment."

Crow looked at the sergeant in disbelief for only a split second before answering, "Sure, I'll do anything. I don't want to go to jail . . ."

"Yeah, I know you don't want to go to jail, none of these assholes do, but do you wanna get clean? Are you ready to leave this life behind you? That's the real question, not do you want to go to jail."

Crow sighed and shook his head from side to side. "I guess so. I'm so sick of this shit, I just don't know how to stop." Then he thought of something his father used to say. "You know, Dad used to say, 'Fun is fun, but you can't laugh all night.' I guess my party is over."

Sergeant Dobson gave Crow his number, and he took down Crow's address, since Crow didn't have a telephone. Crow gathered the manuscript and tucked it under his arm. The sergeant asked what it was, and Crow replied, "Just somebody's book I'm reading."

The sergeant took Crow upstairs in handcuffs and drove him into Crown Heights before letting him go. He didn't want Crow tagged as an informant, so he had to make it appear Crow had been arrested.

Three Days as the Crow Flies

As Crow got out of the car, Dobson said, "If you don't call me tomorrow, I'm coming after you. I'll be goddamned if you're gonna end up like Mikey. I owe at least that much to your old man."

"Yeah, I guess I owe him a lot more than this shit, too," Crow said. "I appreciate you cutting me some slack. Not for nothing, Mikey was my main man when we was kids. I'm real, real sorry, Uncle Paulie. I'll call you tomorrow. You ain't gotta worry. Thanks."

Dobson said, "The wife will be glad to hear it. We couldn't save Mikey. Call your mother. We'll keep what happened between us."

As the sergeant rolled up his window and began to pull off, Crow called out, trying to thank him one more time. As he walked down Bedford Avenue, he felt washed over with a sense of relief and release. He thought about how Candy, Melissa, and the rest of them made the drug scene look so glamorous. But this was the real side of drug life for him. His father's phrase kept running through his mind. He sighed and said out loud, "Can't laugh all night." He decided, despite the late hour, he'd head over to Danny's and deal with that situation. He fished the money out of his shorts and stuffed it into his pants pocket and started the blocks-long walk to Danny's brownstone.

As he turned the corner onto Macon Street, he could see a light burning in the first-floor window. Danny was up and probably painting. That's how Crow had met him. One night at two in the morning, Danny had taken a break from painting and was sitting on his steps getting some air. Danny spoke first, and they started a conversation that led to Danny inviting Crow into the house to see his work. After that, they had developed a casual friendship, with Crow dropping by, usually early in the morning, to shoot the breeze. Eventually, Crow offered Danny some coke, but Danny had refused, saying, "I used to get high, but now I am in recovery, attending Narcotics Anonymous and AA to help me stay clean."

Crow thought maybe that would be a good way to square things with Danny. Tell him about the last three days and then ask for his help in getting clean. As he climbed the stairs, he brandished a sly smile and thought to himself, *Yeah, that's the best way to go. Honesty is the way to play it.* Crow hesitated for just a second before he rang Danny's bell.

About the Author

Danny Simmons is an acclaimed painter of abstract-expressionist oil works and produced all of the paintings featured in this, his debut novel. All of the photography was done by Mark Blackshear.

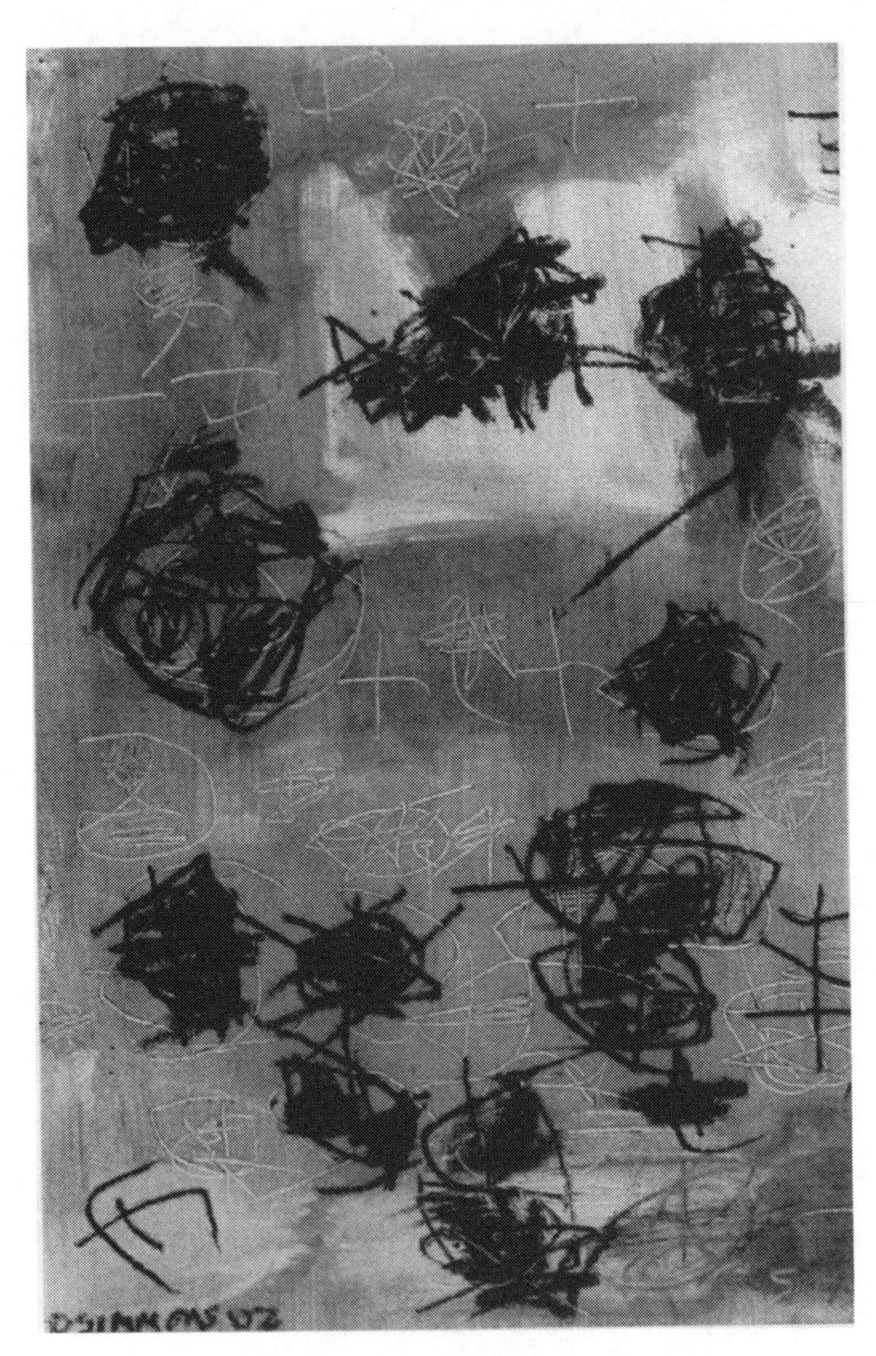

Spell to Calm Anxieties (2002)

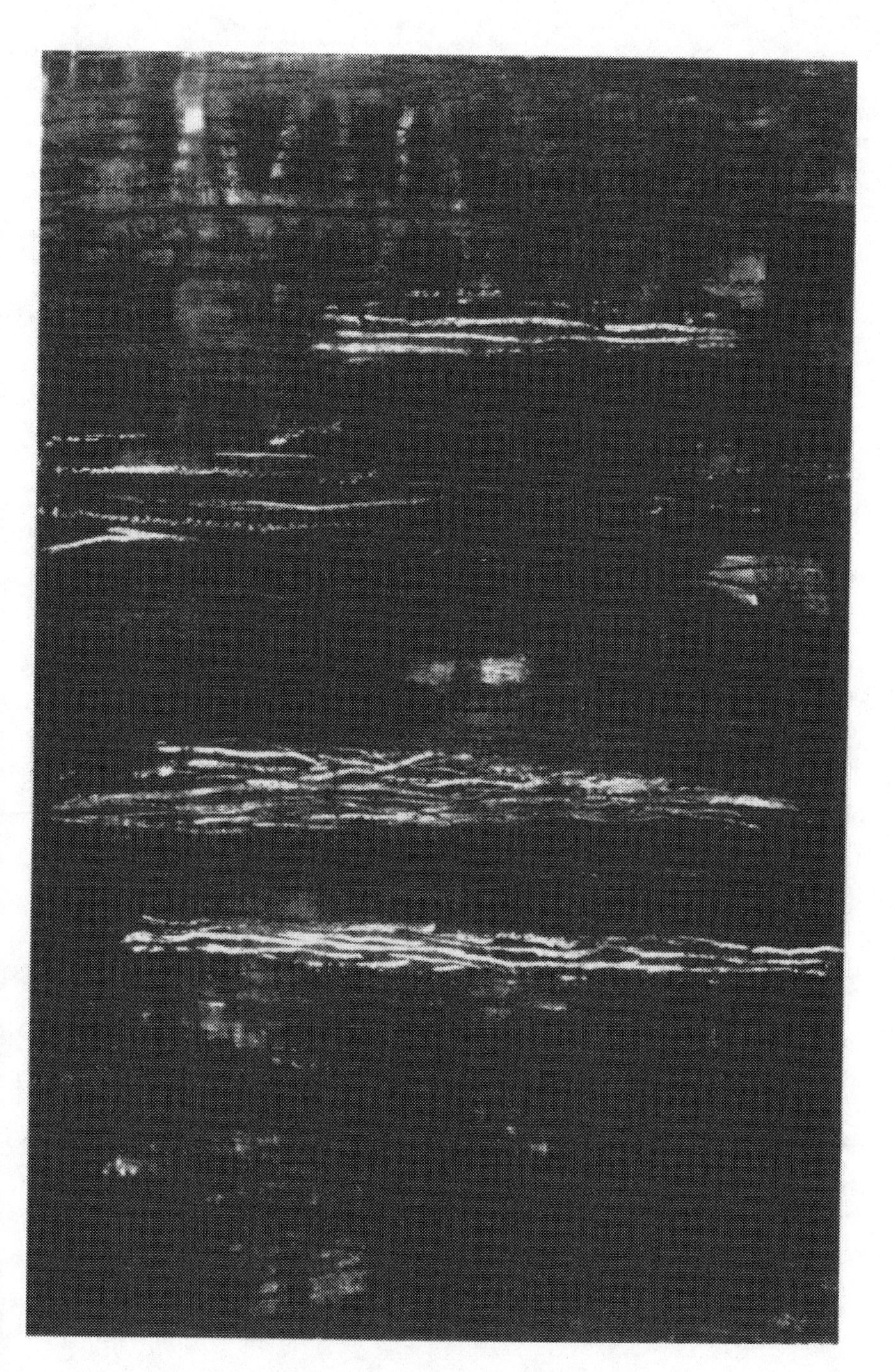

Spell to Wake the Dead (2002)

9 780743 466417